VALERIOS
ROAD TO MASTERY
5

aethonbooks.com

ROAD TO MASTERY 5
©2024 Valerios

ALSO IN SERIES

———

Want to discuss our books with other readers and even the authors?

JOIN THE AETHON DISCORD!

CHAPTER ONE

FAMILIAR FACES

THE RUSTLING OF LEAVES WAS QUIET. THE WIND WAS WEAK. A BIRD'S cry hung in the distance as a small, wheat-colored hand parted the branches, spying on its prey from above. The prey stepped closer, pebbles cracking underfoot. It was unaware. The hunter smiled—then leaped.

A little girl was revealed. She had skin the color of wheat, eyes of amber, and a long, dark ponytail fluttering behind her. Her clothes were simple yet elegant, green robes which merged as one with the foliage. She was five years old—and her face was covered by a wide, bright smile.

"Got you!" she shouted, falling from the branches onto the passing gymonkey below. The monkey yelped, backpedaling, while the girl landed awkwardly on the bumpy soil. "Ow," she concluded. "No fair! You saw me coming!"

The gymonkey was confused. Then, it shrugged and mimed something.

"No way you just reacted on time!" Ebele Eragorn Rust protested with a pout. She rose to her feet and dusted herself off, completely unhurt—though young, she had a slightly tempered body. "You can't be better than me. I am fast!"

The gymonkey mimed something again.

"You know what? Okay. You are faster, but only because you're older! Just let me grow a couple of years, and then— kapow! I will get you!"

The gymonkey laughed. She patted Ebele's head, then held out a bananarm, which the girl grabbed with a glimmer in her eye. The monkey then mimed something else.

"Really!" Ebele cried out, glancing at the sun. "You're right! I'm late! See you, aunt monkey!"

She broke into a sprint. The bananarm dangled by her hand as her feet flew over the dirt paths of the Forest of the Strong, crossing trees and streams to reach an open clearing riddled with gym equipment. A massive brorilla was already waiting.

Like every time she saw him, Ebele had to suppress a shiver of fear. This was a hulking behemoth. His massive body stood almost thrice as tall as her, covered in gleaming dark fur with spots of silver. This silver also appeared around his temples— but she knew it was an indication of stress, not old age, because his body was ripe with power. His arms were wide like tree trunks, his legs like barrels, and all corded with thick, iron muscles. Moreover, like all brorillas, just his resting face held a deadly stare.

"Uncle Harambe!" Ebele shouted out, rushing to a stop before him. "Sorry I'm late!"

Harambe snorted. "Where brother?"

Unlike his son, Brock, Harambe had a somewhat limited affinity to language, even five years into living with the Bare Fist Brotherhood.

"I don't know," Ebele replied truthfully.

Harambe frowned. He closed his eyes and released a rudimentary form of Dao perception to cover the nearby forest area. Suddenly, he sprang into motion, grabbing a nearby bananarm and flinging it out like a boomerang.

Seeing that, Ebele remembered to eat her own bananarm.

Harambe's projectile flew between the trees, spinning crazily around itself and producing a shrill "eee" sound. The bananarm left Ebele's sight, but the sound persisted, growing weaker with time before abruptly changing its mind. The "eee" rose in volume, coming from somewhere above, and it gradually took on the aspects of a little boy's voice. Finally, the bananarm returned, carrying with it a pale-skinned, delicate-looking, blond boy around whose leg it had gotten entangled.

"Heeelp!" Eric Eragorn Rust shouted, flying in, until both he and the bananarm came to a stop in Harambe's palm. Harambe frowned at the boy.

"Why you running?" he asked.

"I, uh..." Eric hesitated, his eyes growing wider from being stared at by a brorilla at such a close range. Finally, his mouth flew open. "I don't want to exercise!"

Harambe sighed. He gently laid Eric on the ground, dusting him off as he spoke, "It only an hour. Good for health. You play after."

Eric sniffed. "You promise?"

"Yes."

"Okay. Then I can exercise... I guess."

Ebele sighed at that. While she loved to exercise and temper herself, her brother was different—he preferred playing or exploring the forest.

Then again, she could understand. Uncle Harambe's practice sessions could be a little... intense.

"Let start with light running," Harambe said, rising to his feet. "Small warm-up, ten laps around forest. That wake us up. Then, true exercise begin."

Ebele and Eric groaned as one, but there was nothing they could do. They set to running. Their little feet tapped against the dirt, following Harambe through snaking paths and forest trails. Their route circled around a part of the Forest of the Strong and totaled half a mile in length. Ten laps meant five miles—a decent warm-up when done at seventy percent maximum speed. Despite the body tempering baths both children had received, Harambe's exhausting regime always left them panting, though never too much—Harambe said that, at this age, cultivating good habits was the important part, and overexerting regularly would only create a dislike for working out.

Ebele had to admit she enjoyed this part of training. Running was freeing, simple, a way to release the pent-up energy inside her and get stronger, like her father! Plus, the route was nice. It took them between streams and the living places of various animals, as well as a treehouse standing proudly on top of an old oak.

Eric's eyes brightened every time they came past this spot, and so did Ebele's. This was the treetop Eric and their father had once built—both children enjoyed sitting in it, making up stories about their father and what he might be doing. He hadn't returned in three years. Mother said he was busy fighting to keep them safe—and, though Ebele missed him greatly, she understood. She admired him. One day, she would grow so strong she could join her father, so that she wouldn't need to stay here and wait until he returned. They could spend all their time together!

As she was thinking that, she wasn't paying attention to what was in front of her and ended up smacking her face into a tree. "Ow," she said, holding her nose while Harambe gave her an odd look. Eric stopped running to laugh out loud. His laughter was like the sound of a clear stream—and Ebele, though still in pain, couldn't help smiling.

"If body here and mind there, you get nowhere," Harambe said, but Ebele didn't mind.

"Let's go!" she yelled, jumping and punching the air, then laughed as she kept running. "Time to get strong!"

———

Jack, Brock, and Min Ling had emerged from the hidden realm into an empty patch of space in the fringes of Heaven's Egg Galaxy. Thankfully, Jack still possessed a high-end starship called the *Bromobile*, so they could easily cross the void to reach civilization.

Only five days later, they arrived at a medium-sized planet called Vengalo. They had chosen this place because it possessed a teleportation hub, just like the Belarian Outpost that Jack had visited in the past. Of course, they were wanted criminals of the System, so they had to take precautions.

Min Ling was well-equipped. She carried several high-level disguise pills. Their facial features were jumbled up and the screens that appeared when they were Inspected had changed. The red System warning about them being wanted criminals was no longer visible. As long as they didn't encounter B-Grades, they would be safe.

Of course, even in an advanced galaxy like Heaven's Egg, B-Grades held far too high a status. They weren't easily found outside the headquarters of major factions.

As the three of them walked into a bar of the teleportation hub, they were surrounded by E-Grades alongside the rare D-Grade. They were completely safe. After all, Jack's real stats were far, far, far above a D-Grade's.

ERROR: PLEASE REPORT TO THE NEAREST AUTHORITIES IMMEDIATELY OR FACE EXTERMINATION.

Name: Jack Rust

Species: Human, Earth-387
Faction: Bare Fist Brotherhood (C)
Grade: C
Class: Gladiator Titan (King)
Level: 301

Strength: 6000 (+)
Dexterity: 6000 (+)
Constitution: 6000 (+)
Mental: 1000
Will: 1000
Free sub-points: 2

Dao Skills: Meteor Punch IV, Iron Fist Style III, Brutalizing Aura III, Neutron Star Body III, Supernova III, Space Mastery III, Fist of Mortality III, Death Mastery II, Titan Taunt I
Dao Roots: Indomitable Will, Life, Power, Weakness
Dao Fruits: Fist, Space, Life, Death, Battle
Titles: Planetary Frontrunner (10), Planetary Torchbearer (1), Ninth Ring Conqueror, Planetary Overlord (1), Grade Defier

Unexpectedly, a man stopped them by the entrance. His cultivation was at the early D-Grade—a small fry to people like Jack, but a titan to the ordinary populace. Him serving as a doorman seemed far too luxurious.

The doorman took a good look at all three of them, inspecting them but finding nothing out of the ordinary. To him, they appeared as factionless peak E-Grades. "Names?" he asked in a bass voice.

"Crock," Brock said.

"Esmeralda Archenstain," Min Ling replied, borrowing the first name of her friend on the Cathedral.

"Rack," Jack said. The doorman gave him a second glance.

"Rack what?"

"Just Rack."

Min Ling rolled her eyes. The doorman grumbled something under his breath, then noted down their information and let them pass.

"That was weird," Min Ling said. "Is something going on here?"

"Let's find out," Jack replied, grabbing a random customer with a polite but firm hand on the shoulder. "Excuse me, friend. Can we buy you a beer for a quick chat?"

The guy under Jack's hand froze. He then looked up. Hard eyes met Jack's—this guy and his entire group looked like hardened veterans, but their bravado melted under a wisp of Jack's aura.

"Don't worry," he pacified them. "We just want information, then you're free to go."

The man glanced at his friends, then nodded. He stood up. "I don't know what beer is, but I have a drink," he said, raising a tankard filled with some blue liquid. "What do you want to know?"

"Does this place always have a D-Grade doorman?"

The man raised a brow. "You don't know?"

"You're testing my patience, friend."

"Sorry. It's just that everyone knows about it. We're at war. Only a few months ago—"

The man kept talking, but Jack was no longer listening. His head had swiveled to the side. Just now, two people with familiar auras entered the bar. At the same time he noticed them, they found him as well, seeing the disbelief in each other's eyes.

"Well, I'll be damned," Jack said, a bright smile blossoming on his lips. "Gan Salin! Nauja! What the hell are you guys doing here?"

Gan Salin laughed, his canines sticking outside his lips. "Incredible! I guess war criminals do come together!"

Meanwhile, the random guy grabbed by Jack noticed he was no longer needed. He sat back down, muttering under his breath, "Weirdo."

CHAPTER TWO

REUNION

Jack took a deep gulp, downing the blue ale he'd been served. The locals called it Verneditch—similar to beer, except far stronger. Slamming his tankard on the table, Jack exclaimed, "So, what the hell are you guys doing here?"

"Hehe. Wouldn't you like to know?" Gan Salin responded with a big smile. "As a matter of fact, the princess of this place and I got into an entanglement. You know, the physical sort. I mean sex."

"There is no princess," Nauja cut in, rolling her eyes. "We arrived at this galaxy to explore, then ended up hunted by some factions."

"It was their fault, too," Salin added. "They shouldn't leave their starships unattended."

"Starships are expensive," Brock agreed.

Min Ling gave Jack an exasperated stare. "Are they really your friends?"

"Not just friends—these are some of my best friends in the universe!" Jack replied with a smile as wide as Salin's.

The canine was exactly as Jack remembered him. Aloof,

relaxed, with a penchant for randomness and an insane glint in his eyes. His short dark hair and white skin made him resemble a friendly human youth, if not for the long canines in his mouth.

As for Nauja, she had exchanged her fur clothes for more civilized attire—a set of brown leather armor which revealed her paper-white but highly muscular thighs and arms. Despite this change in clothing, she maintained a brutish, carefree aura, like an untamed wild animal brought to the city.

The two were like peas in a pod. And, in the five years since Jack had last seen them, they'd reached the late D-Grade.

Jack leaned in. "So, you stole a starship and are being chased down. Are you at least enjoying it?"

"Oh, for sure!" Nauja replied. "We've been to so many places. Tribes, metropolises, wilderness, settlements between stars... Do you know there is a whale space monster so large it contains its own civilization? The people there are called Devons, and they are extremely pleasant. There was even a tornado spiraling from star to star. Tell him, Salin!"

"It was impressive." Salin nodded in agreement. "I have to admit, these five years have been much crazier than I expected. What have you guys been up to?"

Jack didn't know whether to laugh or cry. "Far less than you, apparently," he replied, then retold his adventures since they liberated Earth. He spoke about the Cathedral, the many opponents he faced there, and his meteoric rise to power. He then explained about the hidden realm, only withholding the Archon's inheritance—not because he didn't trust them, but just in case anyone searched their mind in the future.

"Now we're on our way back to Earth—discreetly, of course," he finished. "As soon as we reach any base of the Church, we can go to the Cathedral, and it's a straight line from there."

Salin and Nauja looked at each other. "Which Cathedral?" Salin asked. "Surely not the one that was just conquered."

"Excuse me?"

"Oh, man. This is going to suck for you guys. The Hand of God launched an all-out war against the Black Hole Church just a year ago. They started off by discovering the Cathedral and completely conquering it, then embarking on a witch hunt across the universe. They had spies, apparently—dozens of Church bases have been routed, with millions of cultivators killed."

"Are you serious!" Min Ling cried out. Her eyes were almost popping out of her head. Though she rarely lost her composure, this was one such case. Her voice was filled with worry. "If you're lying, I will pierce my spear through your heart."

"There are better ways to claim my heart," he responded calmly, drawing an eye roll from Nauja. "But, I'm not lying. That is why there's a D-Grade cultivator scanning everyone here. All seventy-three galaxies of the System are in all-out war, with various major factions clashing against each other. It's not just the bases of the Church—many factions allied to them have been discovered and forced into hiding. The Hand is executing a massive purge, with wanted lists containing tens of thousands of powerful individuals. It's a huuuge mess," he finished, leaning back and spreading his arms wide.

Min Ling had paled. "What about the Far Isles? Have you heard about them?"

"Doesn't ring a bell. If it's in another galaxy, I wouldn't know—we've been in a grand total of two and a half."

"We must hurry," she said, standing up. "My people are in danger. I have to get to them."

"Don't panic," Jack said calmly. "It's been a year already—a few minutes now will make no difference. It's better to gather all the information we can first."

Min Ling was, in the end, a genius of frightening caliber. Even facing the possible extermination of her people, she forcefully calmed herself down. Jack turned to Salin. His face serious. "You mentioned seventy-three galaxies," he said. "Does that include our Milky Way?"

"Unfortunately. Your old friend, Artus Emberheart, is in charge of the Purging there—and the Exploding Sun was the first faction to be impacted. I hear that a B-Grade of the Hand appeared in their faction and slaughtered all their B-Grade powerhouses. The faction dropped a Grade overnight, and they have since disbanded, their members scattered across the galaxy and forced to live as fugitives."

Jack's brows fell. The Exploding Sun... His sworn brother and former master, Shol, was there. So was another of his former masters, Huali. He'd once spent a few months at the Exploding Sun, received their grace on multiple occasions, and enjoyed their resources. He owed them.

Artus Emberheart... he thought, his gaze darkening. The name brought back memories. Artus had been the Warden of Hell when Jack rampaged through the planet. The hatred between the two of them was irreconcilable. Jack had killed Artus's son—Rufus Emberheart—back during the Integration Tournament of Earth. During his time on Hell, he had repeatedly ridiculed and humiliated Artus, eventually killing his best disciple before the eyes of the entire galaxy and then leaving unharmed.

Afterwards, Jack found out that Artus had been removed from his position as Warden and exiled from his faction. He never expected to see him return and at an even greater position... but that was how the world turned.

The one enemy I let go returns to haunt me... Will my bad luck ever end? Jack wondered, his expression stormy.

"What about Earth?" he asked. "Artus Emberheart hates me to the bone. If he can get to Earth, I have no doubt he will destroy it."

"I wouldn't know," Salin replied, shrugging helplessly. "But I don't think he's found it. The Hand publishes their greatest military achievements to boost morale, and Earth is quite the beacon of hope for the Milky Way."

Jack nodded with relief. Thanks to the Church, Earth had been moved outside System space but still inside the Milky Way Galaxy. That was a large area. Finding it in such a short time-frame was nearly impossible no matter how many resources Artus Emberheart commanded.

But Jack still worried, because the conquered Cathedral contained a teleporter which connected directly to Earth. Thankfully, it seemed that teleporter had been destroyed in the battle—or somehow rendered unusable.

It could also be destroyed from the Earth side, but nobody would do it because they had no way of knowing about the fall of the Cathedral. Jack and Brock were the only ones with a reason to visit Earth—for all intents and purposes, it was completely cut off from the rest of the universe.

"We must return," he decided.

"That was our idea," Nauja agreed. "But entering the Milky Way is even more difficult than leaving it. It's not fully Integrated, after all. Until it develops its first A-Grade, all teleportations to and from the galaxy are strictly monitored so as to let it develop naturally."

"Forget about the monitoring. I'll handle it. Do you know any teleporters connected to the Milky Way?"

"There is one—the B-Grade faction controlling this place holds such a teleporter, but it's smack dab in their headquarters. If you're thinking of infiltrating, forget it—they will have swarms of D-Grades protecting that place, along with many C-Grade Protectors. If we try to forcefully activate the teleporter, even B-Grade Elders might appear, and then we won't even have time to cry."

Jack and Brock exchanged a calculating glance. "How strong is that faction, exactly?" he asked.

"They're a peak B-Grade influence. Their strongest individuals are at the peak B-Grade, and their Elders are all at the B-Grade. However, most have joined the war—only the early B-Grade Elders have remained to hold the fort," Nauja said.

"You seem to know a lot about them."

"We also wanted to return, so we researched them. Unfortunately, there is nothing we can do. We can't infiltrate a place guarded by B-Grades. Even with the three of you, it remains impossible."

Jack grinned. "Have you forgotten who I am?"

"...Jack?"

"Exactly. But also, the Jack far stronger than his level would indicate. Leave the B-Grades to us—if you can activate the teleporter, we're out of here."

Intergalactic teleporters weren't simple to use. Due to the distance, all sorts of tuning was needed.

"Activate the teleporter?" Salin exclaimed. "The large ones are complex! I can say please, but I don't know if it will work."

"I can," Nauja cut in. "I met a magic formation expert on Dulupedam. He taught me some tricks—as long as the teleporter doesn't have security measures against ill use, I can activate it just fine."

"Perfect. Then we're good to go."

"But..."

"Are you concerned about our strength?" Jack asked, giving her a confident grin. "Don't worry. We can handle a B-Grade or two."

"I won't be joining you," Min Ling said. "My faction is in the Far Side Galaxy. I must get there as soon as possible."

"Can you do it?" Jack asked.

"It will be much easier than your side. My galaxy is fully Integrated. Even in wartime, I should make it without a problem."

"Okay. I believe in you."

"And so do I. Jack..." Her eyes softened for a moment. "Don't die."

He laughed. "I wasn't planning to! Now that I'm back and stronger than ever, I would like to see just who can stop me!"

"Many people. Don't get arrogant."

He smiled softly. "I'll be fine. Thanks for worrying."

"Mm." She nodded. "You too, Brock. Promise me you'll be careful—and don't let your brother do anything too stupid."

"Don't worry," Brock replied, thumping his chest. "Nothing too stupid for big bro."

"...Yeah. I don't know what I expected." She turned her gaze toward Gan Salin and Nauja. "Can I at least count on you two to keep them from doing anything crazy?"

Salin gave her the widest grin his face could accommodate. "Girl, you have no idea who you're talking to."

———

Their goodbye was short and sweet. After spending years together in a cave, the three of them had developed a deep friendship. But duty called. Min Ling hugged everyone and bade them goodbye, leaving behind enough disguise pills and other supplies to last—she was filthy rich, apparently.

She then departed in her own starship, crossing space to disappear between the stars. Jack watched her go. Then, turning around, he summoned his starship—the *Bromobile*.

Seeing it, Salin and Nauja were filled with memories. Its dark hull and glass walls were nostalgic.

"All aboard," Jack declared. "This ship is going to the Milky Way!"

CHAPTER THREE

STORMING THE GATES

THE *BROMOBILE* SHUTTLED THROUGH SPACE, TELEPORTING OVER AND over as they neared their destination.

Jack had discarded his robes and reverted to wearing only pants, as he used to do in the Milky Way Galaxy. Right now, he was lounging on the deck, his perfect muscles revealed by his lack of shirt. "Tell me more about this faction," he said.

"They're called Falling Star," Salin explained. "They mostly use physical power or illusions to fight, and they're also pieces of shit."

"Aren't they all?"

His gaze cut into the distance. Soon, the flickering stars gave way to a massive celestial body hanging in the void.

The Falling Star faction headquarters were built on a large meteor shooting through space. There was no tail behind it, making it appear still, while several smaller meteors circled it like satellites. Despite the lack of nearby stars, the meteor exuded faint luminescence through means unknown to Jack.

"Pretty," Brock said. "Shame it's occupied by enemies."

"Won't be for long." Jack's eyes were hard. "Salin, take us to land."

"In the open?"

"In the open."

It was impossible to arrive sneakily, anyway. The *Bromobile* slowed down, approaching the meteor and flying in parallel to it. People walked all over it like ants—this place was at least the size of Earth's moon.

One area had many starships resting on the ground, so Salin led them there. Conveniently, the teleporter was nearby—the Falling Star faction having arranged all newcomers close to each other. Before they even landed, a procession of a dozen E-Grade servants led by a hard-faced, peak D-Grade man approached.

The starship's door slid open, and Jack walked out first.

"Welcome to Falling Star," the hard-faced man said. "I believe your arrival was unannounced?"

"Correct," Jack replied.

"That is not how we usually do things. Your names, please."

Jack opened his mouth, then paused as Salin whispered something in his ear. He smiled. "My first name is Your," he said.

"Your. Okay. And your last name?"

"Mother."

The official frowned, then his aura began to leak out. "On the Falling Star, troublemakers are—"

Jack sent him flying before he could even finish his words. The people in the surrounding starships were dumbfounded. The E-Grade servants froze—they were so fragile that just the aftermath of an attack could easily kill them. Thankfully, Jack had been careful.

Waving a hand, he shrank the *Bromobile* and stashed it into his space ring. "To the teleporter!" he said, taking to the air, followed by Brock, Gan Salin, and Nauja.

"Can you really do this?" Nauja asked, worriedly looking around.

Meanwhile, Salin was cackling madly. "Oh, I missed you so much!"

Alarms went off in every direction. Dozens of people took to the air, mostly D-Grades led by a few C-Grades. "Halt!" a middle C-Grade enforcer flew in their way. "Who are you? What do you want from my faction?"

"None of your business," Brock replied.

"Hmph! Then die!"

The man pushed out a palm, galvanizing the surrounding Dao for miles. Starlight appeared in the void. The motes gathered, forming a large palm that pressed down on the four of them, trying to restrict them. The surrounding people gasped—many fled at full speed. The power of a middle C-Grade was unfathomable!

Facing the man's attack, Brock stepped forth. He did not panic, nor did he summon any great phenomena. Instead, he opened his mouth to say three words: "Not cool, bro."

It was like the decree of God. The moment Brock's words rang out, the man's palm collapsed. All starlight was extinguished, and the world itself lost color as these words echoed over and over, dominating existence, rewriting reality. The enforcer shook, then vomited blood, flying backward as if struck by a giant hammer.

The surrounding crowd gaped. A middle C-Grade cultivator, an unrivaled existence in their minds, had been defeated by just a few words. The disparity wasn't small at all!

Just who were these guys?

After the hidden realm adventure, Brock's strength had also risen tremendously. Not only had his cultivation reached maturity of the fourth fruit—the middle C-Grade—but his Dao comprehension had advanced by leaps and bounds. Compared to before, he was simply a different beast.

Though he couldn't reach Jack's power, defeating an eight-fruit cultivator of the Cathedral wouldn't be a problem, let alone this four-fruit who wasn't even an elite.

Seeing the enforcer fly away, the crowd realized these four weren't playing around—they were powerful entities here to cause trouble. The brorilla who just attacked didn't even seem like the leader! Several starships instantly shot into the air, trying to escape the aftermath of the coming battle, while the cultivators of Falling Star streamed in from all directions. Dozens of C-Grades covered the air around Jack's group, followed by hundreds of D-Grades.

"Stop right there!" a peak C-Grade shouted. "Why are you acting against us?"

No matter how this person wracked her brain, she couldn't remember making enemies with a group like this. She had never seen them before!

Facing this encirclement, Jack frowned. They couldn't waste too much time here. He stepped forward, a deep and foreboding aura spreading out of his body and into the surrounding space. "All of you..." he said, his voice menacing. "Fuck off!"

Brutalizing Aura erupted. The void was colored black. Every D-Grade cried out and fell from the sky, while the C-Grades went deathly pale. A few even died on the spot.

Level up! You have reached Level 302.

Seeing the notification, Jack's eyes shone. Just now, he had shown mercy to the D-Grades but not to the C-Grades, striking them with the full might of his aura. However, he had forgotten that since this was System space, he could earn levels by killing people!

The moment this fact was revealed, his expression changed. He'd planned to just break through this encirclement, but now, he might as well stay. These people were enemies. The only reason they'd been polite so far was because they feared him— if they knew who he was and were given the chance, they would absolutely slay him to please their Hand of God masters.

Since that was the case, Jack could kill them first.

"I changed my mind," he said. "All C-Grades... You aren't going anywhere!"

His aura erupted. His disguise was ripped apart, revealing his full level, faction, and appearance to anyone watching. The System's blood-red warning was also clear.

The enemies began to panic. "Contact the Elders!" someone said.

Elders? Plural?

Jack acted swiftly. He focused Brutalizing Aura on the nearby teleporter building, knocking everyone inside unconscious. He then warped space around Gan Salin and Nauja, teleporting them over.

"*Prepare the teleporter!*" he told them telepathically. "*Let us know when it's ready!*"

"*You got it, chief!*" Salin replied.

Jack and Brock were left alone in the air, surrounded by a group of terrified C-Grades. They exchanged a glance. Brock summoned the Bro Code, enveloping himself in golden light. Jack cracked his knuckles.

The leader of the enforcers, a peak C-Grade woman wearing blue, gritted her teeth. "Attack together, everyone! They're only C-Grades. They can't stop us!"

Everyone roared and charged. Jack grinned, withdrawing his Brutalizing Aura. He hadn't had a proper fight in three years —he desperately needed to vent.

His fists swam through space. For a time, three different

Daos manifested around Jack. His position blurred, using spacetime to appear simultaneously around four different enemies and smash their chests open. These attacks really did occur at the same moment—through bending time, he could make it appear as if he was in four locations at once.

But spacetime could do much more than that. Three enemies were dragged into a singularity in space, their bodies twisted until they shattered like twigs. Another froze, aging rapidly. Wrinkles formed on his face, his hair turned white, and eventually he released his final breath, turning into dust alongside his clothes.

An eighth person stopped moving. A finger had tapped his chest, using the Dao of Death to directly sever his life. The C-Grade fell from the sky, dead without any injury.

On the other side, Brock was going berserk. A massive golden brorilla had appeared in the space around him, swinging a golden staff. Brock himself sat in a cross-legged position inside the brorilla, chanting from his book—though he still didn't know how to read. His Staff of Stone had been broken by Baron Longform in the hidden realm, but he didn't need it for such weaklings. After all, these people were much weaker than the elites of the Cathedral. The golden brorilla eliminated enemies by the swathe, felling them as one would knife-wielding toddlers.

In the blink of an eye, over a dozen C-Grades died!

"Stop!" a loud cry echoed in the distance. A white-robed old man was rapidly flying over, his expression dripping blood. C-Grades were almost the highest echelon of a B-Grade faction, and raising each of them took a tremendous amount of resources. Losing a dozen in the blink of an eye was an extremely deep loss.

Seeing this man approach, Jack revealed an excited smirk. "So an Elder finally shows up... Great!"

"How long?" he asked Nauja.

"*Almost ready!*"

"*Good.*"

"Handle these guys, Brock," Jack said. "I'll get the Elder."

"You got it, big bro."

Jack escaped the encirclement, flying directly into the sky. As for Brock, he faced the remaining C-Grades by himself. He fell into a disadvantageous position—they possessed multiple peak C-Grades, and while they couldn't be compared to the elites of the Cathedral, they were still powerful. The battle devolved from a one-sided massacre into a brutal melee, but that was precisely Brock's intention. He'd accumulated too many insights—he needed long battles to fully digest them.

As for Jack, he was shooting directly toward the B-Grade Elder. Seeing a mere C-Grade charge at him, the Elder grew enraged. "Insolence!" he shouted. The might of an inner world erupted. Infinite energy filled the sky, dying the entire void white as a falling star descended right onto Jack's head.

Seeing that, he grinned. "A falling star is just a meteor!" he exclaimed, laughing. "Let's see who can do it better!"

He pulled back his hand, diving straight into the torrent of white energy. He cut through it like an arrow. The power he could muster was far less than his opponent's, but his body was incomparably sturdy, and the Dao he used was much deeper. After studying the inheritance of an Archon, how could a B-Grade who'd barely reached that rank compare with Jack?

The Elder's only advantage was the large amount of energy he could wield. An inner world was huge—compared to the small amount of ambient Dao Jack could wield, it was like comparing a firefly to a raging wildfire.

Jack still shot forth. Mid-flight, his body grew taller and sprouted two extra arms. His power peaked. A purple vortex appeared around his fist, drawing in the surrounding light and sound, space and time. Even some of the white energy released by the Elder was sucked into Jack's punch, enhancing its power.

Feeling the weight in his fist, Jack couldn't stop grinning. "Meteor Punch!" he shouted, releasing it all in a straight line. A second falling star appeared in the sky, shooting upward. Jack's was far smaller.

"You want to meet my attack?" the Elder shouted, his voice filled with angry disbelief. "You are courting death!"

The two meteors clashed. The sky was washed away. Space-time ripped, and the shockwave was so intense that it razed the ground beneath their feet, carving a mile-deep crater into the Falling Star's headquarters. The starship dock was destroyed in entirety, and rocks of all sizes flew into the distance, covering the entire celestial object in a cloud of dust.

And this was just a bit of the aftermath. Most of the attacks' energies were used against each other.

In the frightening collision, Jack had been the one to lose, though barely. He flew several miles backward before he could steady himself. He was uninjured and grinning.

In truth, this Elder was the weakest of B-Grades. Jack could beat him. The only reason he'd lost just now was that he used Meteor Punch instead of Supernova, wanting to pit his own meteor against the old man's, just to see if he could gain any insights.

After the attack, the Elder did not attack again. He was too busy being shell-shocked. He'd won the exchange, but only barely—and his opponent was a five-fruit C-Grade! The difference between them couldn't even be described as a river against the ocean—it should have been absolutely impossible for their strengths to be anywhere near each other.

This was... unbelievable!

The Elder's mind raged. Such a talent would not appear from nowhere. He couldn't be unknown. His thoughts churned, going through every possible candidate, but he had to admit that even the most glorious young cultivators of his galaxy were far inferior to Jack.

Suddenly, a person from years ago came into his mind. He contrasted it with the face he saw and the fact that his opponent used the Dao of the Fist. A name appeared.

"You are..." he muttered shakily, raising a finger to point at Jack. "You're Jack Rust!"

Jack grinned.

"Ready!" a voice rang in his mind before he could reply. "Come quick!"

Jack took another glance at the Elder. He wanted to stay here and fight, but that would be unwise. Already, he could feel multiple powerful auras rushing in from the distance, and he wouldn't be able to take them all.

He tore through space without a word, appearing beside Brock. Grabbing the brorilla's shoulder, he teleported again, arriving next to Gan Salin and Nauja inside the teleporter. Purple light already swam around them, barely held back from activating.

"Go!" he shouted, and Nauja pressed a button. They were violently torn through reality, breaking into the gap between space and rushing forth at mind-boggling speed. The Falling Star headquarters disappeared behind them, and they barely caught a glimpse of the B-Grade Elder demolishing the entire teleporter building in an attempt to stop them. But he was too late.

They were headed for the Milky Way.

CHAPTER FOUR

RETURNING TO THE MILKY WAY

BOBBY DICKINSON WAS A HUMAN OF EARTH-179, MEMBER OF THE Wide Swirls faction. After centuries of cultivation, he had finally reached the D-Grade, which qualified him to stay around the intergalactic teleporter and be a guard.

Honor aside, this was a boring job. The teleporter was very rarely used, if ever, and at those times he was actually escorted away for higher-ranking guards to take over. Of course, every arrival of intergalactic personnel was communicated well ahead of time.

That was why, when the teleporter began to ripple during Bobby's shift, he grew suspicious. "Hmm? That's not supposed to happen."

Something crashed. The teleporter shook alongside the ground, and a powerful shockwave threw Bobby away even as a blinding flash of light seared his eyelids. "Ah!" he exclaimed in pain.

He wasn't the only guard. Everyone mobilized, but it was too late—as soon as the teleporter stabilized, whatever was inside it tore through the void and flew away, disappearing in the blink of an eye. Bobby was frozen, left watching the ruins of the large teleporter.

Which had been utterly destroyed during his shift.

"Nooo!" he yelled to the skies.

———

The *Bromobile* tore through space at tremendous velocity. The void trembled beneath its hull, ripping apart every now and then to reveal absolute darkness. Jack had taken the helm. Using his deep understanding into Space, he could push this ship far beyond any speed it had displayed in the past.

Of course, the quality of the ship itself also played a part— an inferior starship would have already crumbled, but the *Bromobile* could easily take this pressure.

This starship had been gifted to Jack by Old Man Spirit, the overseer of Trial Planet. He hadn't known back then, but it was actually an incredible vehicle.

"We should be far enough," Jack finally said after several minutes of all-out flying.

"I don't know, man." Salin shook his head. "It's only a measly billion miles. What if someone stumbles into us?"

"Very funny. Just so you know, B-Grades could still follow our trail and locate us."

"So why is this far enough?"

"Not far enough to be safe. Far enough to activate a warp."

Every high-quality starship possessed the ability to space-warp. Moreover, when executed through a starship's mobile teleporter, this space-warping was far superior to a cultivator's. This was the reason why even B-Grades rarely flew through space by themselves.

Jack's insight into the Dao of Space was astoundingly deep,

but compared to a high-quality starship's formation, it was like comparing a strongman to a mechanical crane.

Energy gathered wildly. The surrounding miles of space were completely sucked dry, while the front of the *Bromobile*'s hull shone with an amber light. Finally, with a tearing sound, space split open, and the *Bromobile* shot through its fabric. Stars zoomed past them—a multicolored spectrum majestic to the eyes.

When they were spat back out into normal space, the astral scenery around them was slightly different.

"Ten light years," Jack said, nodding. "We're finally safe."

"Yep. You're fast where it matters."

Jack raised a brow at Gan Salin. Brock laughed. Nauja coughed. "Where do we go now?" she asked. "As far as I remember, Earth is hidden."

"Right." Jack nodded. "Earth is outside System space. Even I don't know its exact location—and, even if I did, it's part of a new solar system, so it constantly moves across the galaxy. Finding it without using a teleporter is impossible."

"Always the optimist," Gan Salin said.

"If you keep interrupting me, I'll optimize your ass," Jack gave a joking warning. "We need to find someone who can connect us to Earth's teleporter—and there aren't many candidates."

Back when Earth had been moved, Shol was on it as well. He desired to go back. Therefore, the people of Earth worked together with the Black Hole Church to temporarily connect their teleporter to another near the Exploding Sun head-quarters.

Jack hadn't known exactly how teleporters worked back then, nor did he care much. Now, however, he had some idea. A teleporter acted as a beacon. It radiated spatial ripples of a very specific frequency across a wide area. If someone knew a teleporter's frequency, they could latch on to it, detect the ripples, discover their source, and so connect their own teleporter to the target one.

In other words, as long as you knew a teleporter's frequency and its very general location, you could connect to it.

For that reason, teleporter frequencies were considered top secret information. If an enemy had them, they could just appear in your headquarters. The only people who knew the frequency of Earth's teleporter were the Sage, the professor... and Shol! This last person was meant to act as a failsafe in case anything went wrong.

Even Jack himself didn't know the frequency, just in case he was ever captured and mind-searched. He never imagined the Cathedral would be taken over.

Now, his former caution had come to bite him in the ass.

"The professor is on Earth, presumably, and I have no idea where the Sage is or whether he's still alive," Jack explained. "Therefore, our best chance of reaching Earth is Shol."

Salin perked up. "Bald head, monk robes, explosive temper?"

"That's the one."

"And he's in the Exploding Sun, right? Wasn't that the faction exterminated by the Hand of God?"

"Yes..." Jack's face darkened. Salin had already given him this information before, but this didn't make the pill any less bitter. Master Huali could have passed away, and maybe even Shol...

Jack shook his head. "Let's head there first. In finding Shol, his faction is our only clue. Even destroyed, we might discover something."

"Whatever you say, boss. But how?" Salin asked. "From the insignias on the teleporter we just came through, we must be in the Wide Swirls constellation, near the center of the galaxy. The Exploding Sun is far away."

"Not if we're smart about it. There is a network of teleporters spanning System space—if we disguise ourselves, we could use them until we're close enough to the Exploding Sun to fly with the *Bromobile*."

Salin perked up. "Excuse me—the what?" The name of their starship hadn't come up before—Jack had saved it for shock value.

"The *Bromobile*," he replied, remaining calm and confident. "The name of this starship."

"*Bromobile*? You're sure?"

"One hundred percent."

"And they call me the crazy one... Listen, Jack, if you're here to steal my job you better reconsider."

Jack chuckled. "It's a great name and it stays. Right, Brock?"

Brock raised a brow at Gan Salin. "*Bromobile* is great name. Why? You have a problem?"

"I, uh... Not at all, big bro."

"Good. I was thinking the *Bromobile* was one Gan Salin too heavy, but it's okay."

Brock was obviously joking, but it was hard to tell with his hard face and piercing eyes.

Gan Salin gulped. "Well, what are we waiting for? We have a galaxy to explore!"

"That's the spirit!" Jack laughed, stepping away from the starship helm. "Nauja, will you do us the honor?"

"With pleasure," she replied, grabbing the helm. Her mind connected to the formation operating the starship, and her hands jumped over the buttons, turning them in a certain direction and shooting forth.

"How do you know where to go?" Brock asked curiously.

"The spatial ripples of teleporters are easily detectable if you're close enough. All ships have the appropriate devices—teleporters are partly meant to serve as beacons in empty space, guiding us to safe ports amidst the endlessness."

"Oh," Brock replied, nodding. "Smart."

"I know, right?" She flashed him a bright grin. "It's so cool! Only marginally worse than riding triceratopses back at the tribe."

"I can imagine."

"Don't take us to the closest planet with a teleporter," Jack spoke up. "If anyone is after us, they might go there and lay in wait. Choose the farthest planet."

"Alright." She frowned as she consulted the starship devices. "I found it. It's less than a week away—I'll handle the piloting, so you can just relax and enjoy the ride."

"I think I'll read a bit," Gan Salin said, retrieving a rolled-up magazine from his pocket. It was titled *Architectural Boss*, and displayed everyday buildings filled with advertisements. Jack had absolutely no idea what a D-Grade cultivator was doing with such a thing, but he wasn't ready to open that can of worms.

"I'll cultivate," he said.

"Then I will read as well," Brock added, conjuring his Bro Code—a golden book filled with images.

"Oh!" Salin exclaimed, putting his magazine away. "What's that?"

"The Bro Code."

"It has images? Can I see?"

Brock didn't move at first, then made way for Gan Salin to read alongside him. The canine released all sorts of exclamations—though probably not understanding anything. He also made suggestions on how the book could improve. Brock looked ready to smack him.

Jack chuckled as he walked away, heading to a separate

room to cultivate in peace. This journey would be fraught with danger—yet, how come it felt refreshing?

———

In a distant place within the Milky Way stood a massive silver temple. Statues of robots decorated it—and, if one counted them, they would find exactly ninety-nine.

A door opened in the depths of the temple, and Artus Emberheart entered. Compared to the last time Jack had seen him, his aura was more chaotic, as his Dao had cracked—yet, the obsession in his eyes was hard to hide.

"You asked me to see me, Commander?" he said respectfully.

A woman clad in white sat behind a desk. Her hair was also white, not by age, but by purity. This was Eva Solvig, the late B-Grade commander of the Hand of God who had once been tasked with finding Jack Rust and retrieving the Life Artifact on his body. After the war began, she was assigned to purging this galaxy—both because she was familiar with it and as punishment for her previous failure.

"I have received a report from the Heaven's Egg Galaxy," she said slowly. "There is a chance... Jack Rust has returned."

A fierce fire lit up in Artus's eyes. His aged face warped in hatred. "He's here?"

"It is still unclear. Someone matching his cultivation, Dao, and description appeared in Heaven's Egg. He also possessed the power to jump multiple tiers to fight and was accompanied by a brorilla. He even used a similar Life Artifact to enhance his power. It is either Jack Rust or an elaborate trap... but I don't see why anyone would go to such lengths to deceive us."

"It is him," Artus replied with obsession-fueled certainty.

"Commander, I beg you to let me go after him. I must destroy him!"

"You are not his match," Eva replied, shaking her head. "At the mid C-Grade, he could almost match an early B-Grade cultivator."

Artus shook. Such talent... Such power... It was mind-boggling—but it didn't reduce his hatred in the slightest.

"Then..." he said slowly.

"Jack Rust is a high-priority target. He must not be allowed to grow." Eva tidied up the papers on her desk, then stood. "I will personally lead this operation. You follow me. I have also notified every agent in the Milky Way to be on the lookout. That man has escaped us once, but if he really dares to return to this galaxy..." Her eyes sharpened. "He will die."

CHAPTER FIVE
CHOOSING ONE'S PATH

THE TRIP TO REACH THE FORMER EXPLODING SUN HEADQUARTERS would take two months.

Jack's group traveled from teleporter to teleporter, using fake names and disguise pills to keep their identities hidden. They stayed near other people as little as possible, always moving with caution.

They were like fugitives.

In the process, they witnessed the aftermath of the war. Even in the Milky Way, which was isolated from the rest of the galaxies, news had spread. Every ambitious D-Grade had packed up and headed for the Hand of God to enlist, not quite understanding the scale of this war.

"I can't believe they turned me down," an early D-Grade cultivator slammed her cup on the table, her powerful voice dominating the bar. "They said that even C-Grades could only serve as soldiers. To them, it's like D-Grades are trash!"

Her voice contained a mix of anger and humiliation. The only reason she'd mention this out loud was due to her intoxication.

"They must be blind!" agreed another cultivator—an E-

Grade. "C-Grades don't grow on trees. If they only accept those people, they will barely make a few squads, let alone an army!"

Shouts of agreement rose from everywhere. In a corner, Jack, Nauja, and Gan Salin calmly sipped their drinks. Brock was too recognizable, so he hadn't come to gather information. "Is that really the case, Jack?" Nauja asked. "Are C-Grades so common in the universe?"

Jack smiled slightly. "They are not common, no... but the universe is wide. There are dozens of A-Grades, thousands of B-Grades, perhaps millions of C-Grades. In a war of such caliber, anyone below that is useless. It's just that this is a little bar in a tiny outpost in the fringes of a recently Integrated galaxy. How could these people know the vastness of the world?"

Gan Salin and Nauja fell silent. The path of cultivation was full of thorns and pitfalls. From every Grade to the next, only one in a hundred or one in a thousand cultivators made it. With six Grades stacked on top of each other, this tiny success rate diminished to almost zero.

The universe was just too large. There were seventy-three galaxies in System space, each holding millions of habitable planets with millions of people each. In such a wide base of people, there were some who miraculously made it to the top echelons of the cultivation world.

C-Grades were people who could move the winds and rains. To common mortals, they were Gods. Yet, in a conflict of this scale, they could only serve as foot soldiers...

"Did you hear the Heaven Immortal's declaration?" a man said, changing the subject. "The Church is almost routed!"

"I heard as well," another person added. "They lost two Elders and are running away like mice—forced to retreat outside System space again."

"Let's hope they stay there!"

Everyone laughed together. The people of the universe were

all in the sphere of influence of the Immortals, so they received their propaganda. They were naturally biased toward the Hand of God.

Jack did not begrudge them. They were ants to him. How could he blame them for going with the flow?

"I heard something else!" a woman shouted, eager to participate. "The Arch Priestess of the Cathedral activated a tremendous weapon during a battle. They still lost, but they annihilated an entire solar system with millions of people!"

"What monsters!" the other patrons exclaimed. "They're terrorists alright—what did you expect?"

"They should all burn in hell!"

"They should be crippled and fed to space monsters!"

The bile of propaganda flowed endlessly from their mouths, so much that even Jack grew uncomfortable. "Let's go," he said. He swiped his credit card over the special screen installed in their table, and the three of them departed the bar.

"Would the Church really destroy an entire solar system?" Nauja asked as they walked away.

Jack shook his head. "I don't know. What I'm certain of is that there is no right or wrong in war. If anything, the Immortals are even more callous than the Church because they're robots; they don't possess emotions like we do. At least, for the Church, I can hope they weigh mortal lives in their decisions..."

"The world is a harsh place," Salin said, his voice not carrying its usual madness. "People die all the time. The weak are just foil for the strong. Between superpowers, there is no good option, only the least of two evils..."

It was a sobering thought. The Church had its ideals, but they were not fighting for the world right now. They were fighting for their survival. Only if they won would they reveal their true face to the public. And, as for what that face was, Jack could only hope it was a kind one.

At the very least, they were better than the Hand of God.

They continued traveling. From their arrival point at the Milky Way, the former Exploding Sun headquarters were very far away. The trip would take months.

In that time, they could observe the current state of the galaxy. Church cultivators had infiltrated everywhere before the war—now, the galaxy was riddled with desolate planets, broken moons, endless bloated corpses floating through the cosmos. These sights were not too common, but to Jack's group, who covered a lot of ground at high speed and visited many planets, there were many opportunities to witness the brutality of war.

Black snakes coiled around Jack's heart. Every time he saw a ruined continent, he pictured America in its place. The mountains of corpses could be humans and brorillas—his wife, children, mother... If he returned to Earth only to witness such a sight, he would lose himself.

I need to become stronger, he vowed, clenching his fist. *Strong enough that nobody will touch me and my people... Strong enough to protect them.*

Throughout their trip, everyone cultivated with fervor. Jack spent a few hours at every ruined location they passed through, using the cruelty and brutality of war to enhance his comprehension of life and death. Whenever they teleported, he meditated on the spacetime fluctuations, deepening his understandings.

After all, he had only grasped a small part of the Archon's inheritance. The seeds remained inside him, but they needed his meditation to bloom. On the bright side, he advanced at speeds incomparable to other cultivators.

As for his understandings into life and death, those had temporarily fallen behind spacetime. He was now spending most of his time aboard the *Bromobile* holding onto the death cube granted to him by Elder Boatman, slowly delving into its mysteries. Day by day, his comprehension expanded.

The death cube also contained an enigma. Elder Boatman had said he'd placed a wisp of his soul inside it so he could always track Jack's position. Since they emerged from the hidden realm, Jack expected Boatman to look for him, but that hadn't happened yet...

Had Elder Boatman perished? Was he too busy with the war? Or had the soul mark vanished after so many years in a separate dimension?

Jack had no way to know. Even if he did, there was nothing he could do to change the situation. Therefore, he focused on himself.

He'd been cultivating for six years already. He was nowhere near the end of the road, but he felt that finally, his direction was close to finalized.

Life and Death. Space and Time. These two pairs of Daos would be the path he followed to the peak—all through the lenses of the Fist.

From an upstart young cultivator experimenting with anything that fell into his hands, he had grown into a veteran consciously making his way forward. He had matured.

But maturity came at a cost. The path before him used to be infinite. Now, it was clearly defined, allowing him to walk it more efficiently but also having an end. And that end... wasn't necessarily the peak of cultivation.

Every cultivator had a limit. Now, Jack was beginning to see his in the far distance. It scared him—yet he trudged on, determined to advance as far as possible. Limits could be illusions— by being exemplary, he would break through the constraints of the world, carving his own path.

That was the meaning of cultivation.

Besides meditating on the Dao, Jack did not cultivate at all.

Not because he wasn't ready—in fact, for the first time since he embarked on this road, his Dao understandings had surpassed his cultivation level. After consolidating his foundation for three years, he was ready to rush forward and advance to the peak of the C-Grade in one fell swoop.

The issue was, cultivating took time—decades, if not centuries, and that was time Jack didn't have available. Since this was a period of war, he would employ the same method he used during the D-Grade and slaughter his way through the levels. Given that his Dao understandings were solid enough, that was a much faster way than peaceful cultivation.

Therefore, cultivating a little bit now was meaningless. Jack would rather spend that time meditating on the Dao—a process which couldn't be accelerated.

Time trudged on. Throughout the trip, the *Bromobile* ran into many dangers ranging from mid-level space monsters to pirates. None were a problem. They smashed right through, smoothly continuing on.

Two months after their arrival in the Milky Way, four people stepped out of a teleporter. The terrain was familiar—out of all the planets in the galaxy, this was one they'd visited before.

Derion, the poison planet.

Jack had passed through here the previous time he was headed for the Exploding Sun headquarters. He'd just reached the D-Grade back then and was heading over to train. During his brief stop at this planet, he'd discovered and attacked a group of Animal Kingdom cultivators transporting prisoners, one of which had been Vanderdecken, the Earth cultivator who used the Dao of Metal. He'd also been attacked by a bounty hunter. That was the first time Jack killed a D-Grade.

"Oh! I probably still have a bounty," he told his friends. "I wonder if anyone will try to get it this time."

Derion hadn't changed much since their last visit. It was a barren planet almost empty of natural lifeforms, where low-level cultivators could only survive for a limited time due to the poisonous atmosphere. And the cultivators themselves, had changed.

They were far fewer. The once-sprawling camp of people waiting their turn to teleport had diminished to only a few star-ships parked in the open, while the guards were more and stronger. There were even people bearing the Hand of God insignia—the picture of a humanoid with a square screen for a face, its open palm facing the viewer.

It was natural. Derion was the largest teleportation hub of the Exploding Sun constellation. In these troubled times, the security measures would be waterproof.

Jack and the others hadn't chosen Derion to teleport, and also not because it was directly connected to Field Nebula, the former Exploding Sun headquarters. They chose it because it was located nearby. They could use the *Bromobile* to just fly over.

According to the information they'd gathered, the Hand of God had turned the headquarters of the Exploding Sun into an outpost after clearing out its previous occupants. Given Jack's identity, flying there was much safer than openly teleporting.

They didn't stay long on Derion. After discreetly asking around for a few hours, they boarded the *Bromobile* and set off into deep space. A week later... they approached Field Nebula.

CHAPTER SIX
RIDDLE

CLOUDS OF VARIOUS GASSES HUNG IN THE VOID LIKE PREGNANT TITANS. They were brown, yellow, purple, green... All colors in existence covered the cosmos, bloating it with the essence of creation just waiting to happen.

"Pretty," Nauja said.

Jack raised a brow. "Just that? I thought seeing a nebula up close would be a little more exciting."

"Oh, I've been around. It's not my first nebula."

"She's right," Salin commented. "You should have seen that whale swimming through a nebula. That, my friend, was a sight to behold."

Nearby, Brock snickered. Jack rolled his eyes. "Well, like it or not, this is the best I have."

"And I'm sure it's great, buddy," Salin replied, patting Jack's shoulders. "So—the Exploding Sun is in there?"

"Somewhere. We just have to find it."

Reaching the headquarters of the Exploding Sun wasn't too difficult. Jack already knew it was inside the Bow Nebula, a cloud of multi-colored gasses and dust so colossal, it dwarfed most other nebulae. Even in the vast galaxy, such a place was visible from extremely far away.

On the downside, finding a few planets nested somewhere inside a massive nebula was like looking for a needle in the haystack. Thankfully, they had the *Bromobile*.

"I'm getting a faint reading," Nauja said, looking at the starship's various instruments. "There *is* a teleporter in the nebula, but it's far away—closer to the other side."

Jack nodded. Back when Master Huali had taken him outside the nebula to watch a supernova, reaching there had only taken a short while. Field Nebula—the Exploding Sun headquarters—should be near the edge.

"What are we waiting for?" Brock spoke up. "Let's go! For the bros!"

"For the bros!" the other three replied, and the *Bromobile* dove straight into the nebula. Suddenly, the star-riddled darkness was replaced by colorful gasses of all kinds. It was like flying through a rainbow. Even Nauja and Gan Salin, who had been indifferent so far, showed a rare, stunned expression.

Jack stuck out his chest. "Your whale had no windows, did it?"

Suddenly, the gasses parted. A comet emerged, shooting straight for them and narrowly missing their ship.

"There's no visibility and we're going too fast!" Nauja explained, rushing for the helm. "Do something!"

"I got it," Jack replied. His form flickered—suddenly, he was outside the *Bromobile*, standing stably on its prow. Waves of Fist Dao emanated from his body. The *Bromobile* adopted a new momentum, suddenly not sailing through the nebula but punching through. A faint purple aura surrounded them, shaped as a fist, and the occasional comet was smashed away.

What was once a starship had become a fist punching through the cosmos, unstoppably tearing through all in its way.

Standing on the prow, Jack couldn't help grinning. Infinite colors swam around him—and it was only thanks to his personal power that he could experience such beauty.

Salin's voice echoed in his mind. *"That's very impressive, don't get me wrong, but don't you think we're a little too eye-catching?"*

They were supposed to approach Field Nebula stealthily. However, Jack's grin remained unbothered. *"I'm dispersing the energy fluctuations into the dozens of miles of space surrounding us,"* he replied. *"Unless someone draws close enough to be detected, we should resemble nothing but a slightly larger meteor."*

"Oh. Okay. You do you, chief."

They tore through the nebula. Teleporting at this time would create ripples that even Jack couldn't suppress, so they chose the far slower method of flying. A distance that would normally take moments would now last weeks. But, this close to potential enemy territory, it was better to be safe than sorry.

Jack still used his powers to shrink space under them, vastly accelerating their ship. Otherwise, even years wouldn't be enough to cross the nebula.

Using Fist and Space Dao to simultaneously protect, hide, and accelerate their ship took a toll on Jack. He wouldn't run low on energy by such limited consumption, but he also couldn't spare the attention to meditate. Therefore, he had to settle for easier matters.

Salin took out a deck of cards and taught them a game called Crazy Guy Goes to Town.

"That's obviously made-up," Jack said.

"All games are," Salin replied. "Now, pay attention."

Surprisingly, the game was fun. Whether Salin had made it himself or was just using a pre-existing game under a more amusing—for him—name, Jack had to admit it was well-designed. Cultivators of their level had extreme mental faculties, able to calculate thousands of variations on the fly. Yet, Crazy Guy Goes to Town had just the right proportion of luck and strategy for the possible variations to increase exponentially, ensuring the game remained challenging.

It was similar to chess, with the added randomness of cards.

Since none of the four focused on the Mental stat, they were equally matched, with Jack emerging as the superior player thanks to his relatively absurd stats. Still, it remained a fun pastime.

The days flowed on and they approached their destination —the starship slowed down to be less easily detectable, while all other activity was reduced to a minimum.

"We should be getting close," Nauja said. "Be ready."

"How close?" Salin whispered. "A minute or a day?"

"Why are you guys whispering?" Jack asked in a normal voice.

"Don't be boring," Salin whispered. "We're approaching stealthily—it's good manners to speak in whispers."

"Good manners to whom?"

"To the people we're about to ambush! Have I taught you nothing all these years, Jack?"

Jack shook his head. As he was about to reply, the gasses grew thinner around them, and Nauja hurriedly brought the starship to a stop. Pale lights could be seen through the dust— manmade ones.

The four cultivators glanced at each other, nodded, then stepped outside the starship. Jack shrank it—a function of the *Bromobile*—and stashed it in his space ring.

"Be careful. Let's go," he instinctively whispered.

Salin's eyes brightened. "Ah-hah! You're doing it!"

"Shut up. It's good manners."

They flew closer. Finally, the gasses disappeared completely, revealing a pocket of emptiness inside the nebula with three planets suspended in the center. Jack's mind was filled with memories—this was Field Nebula, where he once lived and trained for several months. The headquarters of the Exploding Sun faction.

Except, it was no longer their headquarters.

One of the three planets was cracked and deserted. Beside it, the Inner and Outer Planets remained whole, but parts of their surfaces were ruined, turned into desolate expanses of unnaturally pure white sand. The once lively planets had been reduced to boulders. The apocalypse had washed over this place—an apocalypse going by the name of Eva Solvig.

Jack clenched his fists. The Exploding Sun had been kind to him—to see their headquarters reduced to such a state brought him sadness. He wasn't the only one, either—the other three had spent even longer here, taking the Outer Planet as their home for almost a year. Now, white deserts were reflected in their eyes, places where once-glorious metropolises used to span.

"That bitch," Salin said, his eyes oozing hatred. "I'll fucking slaughter her."

"Don't lose heart," Brock encouraged them. His eyes were dark but clear. "A true bro must remain composed at all times. Anger is a tool, not a reaction."

"Sorry, man. You make sense, but I'm insane."

"Brock is right," Jack said. "Let's calm ourselves before approaching. If there are enemies here, a single mistake could get us killed."

"There are," Nauja replied. "Look over there. I can see their flags."

The rest followed her finger with their eyes, settling on the center of Field Nebula. It wasn't just three planets—a small moon was stable between them, formerly acting as a teleportation hub. Now, that moon had been transformed into an outpost for the Hand of God, if the flags flying above it were any indication.

In a display of unhinged imperialism, a massive pole had been stabbed into the Center Moon, rising ten miles above the ground and at least as much below. A large flag lay motionless on its top, held in place by iron chains—there was no wind at such altitude.

In fact, there was no wind at all, as the Center Moon had no atmosphere. The smaller flags waved due to some magic.

Seeing the massive pole which destabilized the entire moon for the sole purpose of flying a flag, bitterness rose in Jack's throat. He suppressed it. "Let's focus on getting information," he said darkly. "Even if we destroy this place, it will alert the Hand's B-Grades. Let's not take such a risk without reason."

The other three agreed. They were not here to reclaim Field Nebula or punish the Hand cultivators. Their goal was to find Shol or information pertaining to him—after all, Shol was one of the very few people who knew the frequency of Earth's tele-porter. As tempting as it might be to rip that pole out of the ground and stab it into the backside of the Hand outpost leader, that was a sentiment better saved for later.

"I know where Shol's house was," Jack said. "Follow me."

Space curved and hugged them like a blanket. Light passed around, not touching them—they were invisible. Like this, they flew toward the inner planet, the place where the D and C-Grade cultivators once lived. Much of the planet was now a life-less white expanse, and there were no occupants to be seen. Still, Jack could make out that the area he once inhabited—Master Huali's estate—remained standing.

Of course, it had collapsed due to the many earthquakes caused by the battling C-Grades. Blood even littered the once peaceful paths and corridors—a reminder of how brutality ruins beauty.

The estate was completely empty. Jack brought his friends to Shol's little wooden cabin and stepped before the entrance. "Here it is," he said. After scanning the house with his perception, he pushed the door open, revealing a place only partially dusted by the passage of a few months.

The furniture and items were thrown all across the room. Jack sighed deeply. With a wave of his hand, everything floated back to its original position, and the cabin looked as if a day hadn't gone by.

"I've come here twice," Jack said. "Two times Shol poured me tea, and neither time was I able to finish it. Today, again, I will not taste tea..."

"Do you think there was any clues that you just moved back into place?" Salin asked.

Jack stared at him. Salin stared back. "Shit!"

Forgetting sentimentalism, they began searching the house. If Shol had fled, he might have left behind some hint for Jack— otherwise, meeting again would be far too difficult.

"I got something!" Nauja exclaimed. She pushed away a stack of papers on the table to reveal a single parchment—it looked more recent than the others, and also written in haste. On it, Jack could make out Shol's handwriting.

"*Endless stars and fire flight, gather where we won the fight...*"

Salin groaned. "I should have known. Shol is a monk; of course he speaks in riddles."

"This could indicate his hiding place," Jack said. "Or... it could be completely unrelated. But there's nothing else here."

"There is an easier way to find him. If he's been captured and held prisoner in the Center Moon, we can just rescue him."

"That would be ideal." Jack nodded. They kept searching, coming up with nothing. "Well, no time like the present. Guess we got to beat them up."

"Actually, big bro," Brock said, placing a firm hand on Jack's shoulder, "let us handle it."

"Us?"

"Me, dog bro, girl bro. Us three. We got this—you just search for monk bro."

Jack raised a brow. He glanced at the other two, both of whom were excited. "That's right! We're not useless!" Salin exclaimed. "We can do this! And, if it gets too hard, you can always join later."

"That's... I don't know, guys. It could be dangerous. We're pressed for time."

"We don't lose time," Brock said. "We keep them busy, you search in secret. If you fight, you have to fight and then search. Takes more time."

"Besides," Nauja said, stepping forward, "don't forget where we are—this is Field Nebula, the birthplace of the bro army. If the three of us, the original bro squad, don't take revenge for what happened here, how will we face our other bros in the future?"

Jack laughed. "Fine. I trust you guys. Let's do it this way."

"Awesome!" Salin exclaimed, punching the air. "Bro squad... assemble!"

CHAPTER SEVEN

BRO SQUAD, ASSEMBLE!

THREE FIGURES HOVERED IN SPACE, TEN THOUSAND MILES AWAY FROM the Center Moon. They were Brock, Gan Salin, and Nauja. These three bros, who had once bonded on the outer planet of Field Nebula, were preparing to assault an outpost of the Hand of God.

"Girl Bro," Brock said. "What do you see?"

"A thousand people. Most are D-Grades—only a handful are C-Grades, with the strongest among them at the late C-Grade."

Nauja was an archer, and her vision, incredibly sharp—even from ten thousand miles away, she could distinguish the cultivators wandering through the outpost and even inspect the auras left behind by their powerhouses.

"You can make them out," Salin noted, "but can you make out with them?"

His comment was ignored. "I am ready," Brock said. "Are you ready?"

"I was born ready."

"Do I have a moment to pee?"

"Let's go!"

Their restrained auras erupted. Two late D-Grades and a middle C-Grade may not have been much in Jack and Brock's recent escapades, but they were almost apex existences in the Milky Way Galaxy. The moment their auras appeared, the outpost below went on full alert.

"To what do we owe this pleasure?" came a sonorous voice. Space warped as a long-haired man stepped into the void, his aura firmly but politely resisting theirs. He was not the late C-Grade cultivator Nauja had mentioned, but a middle C-Grade. "The Hand of God welcomes guests!" he exclaimed with a smile that didn't reach his eyes. "Could the three fellow cultivators please announce their names?"

"How about I announce your mother?" came Salin's reply. The man's smile froze—then, his eyes darkened.

"Who are you?" he demanded, dropping all pretense.

"We are the bros," Brock replied, stepping forward, "and we are here for war."

His aura shone golden. A book appeared in his hand, illuminating the void for a hundred miles, while the golden phantom of a brorilla manifested around his body, cladding him in the spirit of brohood. Then, without any more words, Brock charged forth.

"Hmph! The bros? What idiot name is that? If you think the Hand of God can be bullied, you are sorely mistaken!"

Facing Brock's charge, the long-haired man's aura didn't weaken in the slightest. They were both middle C-Grades. Neither had reason to fear the other—or so the man thought. A slim sword appeared in his hands, thrusting forward and penetrating space to reach Brock's golden book.

For a moment, the world came to a standstill. Their auras were similar in intensity. The raw power they commanded was around the same level. Yet, their Daos and experiences were incredibly far apart. Brock didn't even pause. Raising his book, he shattered the other man's sword light, charging straight through.

The man paled. He withdrew his energy and conjured a hasty defense, but how could that compare to Brock's attack? A golden cannonball smashed into his chest. His sword bent and flew out of his hand while his body folded and shot backward at tremendous speed. Blood shot out like red flowers.

"What!"

This wasn't the only enemy present. Many people were watching from Center Moon. Seeing one of their strongest protectors destroyed after a single blow, they couldn't believe their eyes. "Quick, summon reinforcements!" a man shouted.

"The bros are here! The bros are here!" a woman cried out, not recognizing the name but hoping someone else would. In the next moment, space beside her parted to reveal an aloof young man whose face radiated insanity.

"You can also call us the three brosquetters," he said calmly even as his palm pierced through her chest to grab her heart. "Whoops. Guess I should have let you live to tell the tale. Don't worry though, I've got many more catchphrases to use—I've been coming up with them for a month!"

Seeing Gan Salin appear in their midst like an angel of death, the cultivators stirred into panic. It wasn't that he alone could kill them all—it was just that, since these people dared attack, they must have confidence in their victory. In this situation, the surprised and ambushed Hand of God had already lost half the battle.

"Get into formation!" a steady voice echoed over Center Moon. Another C-Grade appeared in the void, and she was even stronger than the last one at the late C-Grade! Moreover, even amongst people of her level, she was considered an elite. She was also bald and wearing monk robes.

Salin's eyes widened. "Shol!" he shouted, even though this

person clearly had nothing to do with Shol. "Is that you? You became a woman!"

"A worthy opponent," Brock said, turning to face her. "Come. Our battle will be legendary!"

A steel staff appeared in the woman's hands, and she rushed to battle. The other C-Grade had also recovered slightly and returned to join her. For a time, the three C-Grades waged war deep in space, the shockwaves of their clashes spreading for dozens of miles. Yet, a steady golden aura was slowly but steadily taking the lead—Brock was facing two people by himself and winning.

Meanwhile, Salin was brawling against a crowd of D-Grades. He wasn't weak. After experiencing so many things and reaching the late D-Grade, he was even more powerful than most peak D-Grades—and a core part of that were his Trial Planet titles.

Against a crowd of mostly middle D-Grades, he was like a wolf against a group of armed toddlers.

"Formation!" a man shouted, stepping ahead of the other D-Grades. They formed into three groups of nine—and some stragglers—with each group combining their powers to form an assault greater than the addition of its parts.

"Oh boy!" Salin exclaimed. "I was never good at math. Riddle me this: If there are three groups of nine, which is the same as nine groups of three, does that mean each of you corresponds to one third of a person?"

His question made zero sense. As it echoed, strings of insanity were woven into the air, entrapping the minds of the enemy cultivators and hindering their movements. The weakest ones were even swayed into his nonsense. "It's four sixteenths, actually," a man responded, only to be slapped at the back of the head by the person standing next to him.

"Focus! Don't fall for his tricks!"

"Crap! Thanks, you saved me!"

Salin was embroiled into heavy battle. He might be strong, but his opponents weren't weak either—as soon as they managed to organize, facing twenty-seven of them was difficult, let alone when they used formations.

Suddenly, a sun illuminated the sky. "Sun?" Gan Salin cried out. "But it's night!"

There was no day or night in Field Nebula. Before the enemies could recover from his words, a tremendous explosion resounded in their midst, demolishing several miles of land. Injured cultivators cried out in pain. Yet another sun appeared in the sky, then another, as a hail of arrows descended toward Center Moon.

Ten thousand miles away, Nauja was pulling her bow and shooting ceaselessly. Golden arrows appeared every time she drew back the bowstring, then shot out as she released it. Strangely, their power did not diminish as they traveled, but rather increased, as if the arrows were made of magnets which gathered the world energy into a mantle around them.

"Sun Piercing Arrows!" Nauja shouted, speeding up as she got into a rhythm. This was the skill she'd inherited from Trial Planet. Though she was nowhere near piercing a sun yet, bombarding a moon was easily done, especially when gravity was working in her favor.

Arrows rained like divine hellfire, submerging a third of Center Moon in flames and smoke. Screams cut through the air. Gan Salin sat on a rock, chewing on a wooden pipe as he began recounting, "It was 1945. Their bombs covered the sky, our children cried as..."

"Make him stop, I'm begging you!" an enemy cultivator shouted, clutching his head both due to the explosions and Salin's words. But it was useless. He was already sucked into

Salin's World of Insanity—the special ability he'd developed after reaching the D-Grade.

This cultivator's world transformed into an illusion of Second World War London, and the person himself had become a powerless mortal facing endless bombardment. "I don't even know what this place is!" he shouted in despair. "What am I even wearing!" A bomb landed on him, extinguishing his mind and soul. The cultivator's intact body slumped to the ground, his life severed.

"*Salin!*" Nauja's words echoed harshly into his mind. "*How many times have I told you not to imitate real tragedies in your attacks?*"

"*Thirty-nine!*" he replied.

The two of them had fought together many times. They moved in sync. When Nauja's bombardment was combined with Salin's World of Insanity, the two skills overlapped and cut away all paths of retreat for the enemy. Even the twenty-seven D-Grades facing them could do nothing but try their hardest to survive. Their only hope was the C-Grades arriving to save them... Unfortunately, they were too preoccupied.

A golden brorilla hovered in the void. His one hand held a book—the other, an open palm ready to swat the enemies. A staff and a sword besieged him on either side, but the brorilla was unperturbed, calmly defending and waiting for his chance to strike.

"You are not true bros," Brock's words resounded through the void like heavenly judgment. "You occupy the territory of fallen innocents. You support authoritative butchers. In the name of all bros in the universe, I will end you."

The more he made his case, the stronger he became—and the enemies could not refute him in the slightest. "What bull-shit are you spouting?" the bald woman yelled. "What *bros?*

What *butchers*? The only thing that matters in this world is power!"

"You are not wrong," Brock replied calmly, "but you are not right, either. Power is the foundation of the world. Brohood is its essence—a different kind of power. To deny brohood is to swim against the current, to try and roll uphill; it is not impossible with enough power, but you are far from reaching that boundary. As for me, while I do not claim to be strong, I represent the world's heavenly will—the brohood of the bros. How could you hope to stand against me?"

His words made a stark contrast against Salin's because they sounded equally nonsensical, but they actually weren't. As Brock spoke, the bald woman sensed the grip of the universe tighten around her, she sensed her powers weakening while his grew stronger. Soon, she was completely unable to resist—just a firefly diving into the sun.

"You have been out-bro'd," a voice echoed from above, sealing her fate, and the woman screamed as the golden sun enveloped her, turning her into dust. The man beside her lasted only a second longer before he, too, disintegrated.

Brock withdrew his powers. He was panting but nowhere close to his limits—as for the two enemies, they had been washed away by the powerful flow of brohood. "Good warm-up," he said. He stretched out a hand—the woman's steel staff appeared in his palm, but after a deep glance, he discarded it and shook his head.

He sought a replacement for his broken Staff of Stone, but unfortunately, that steel weapon was far from meeting his standards.

He looked down. The Center Moon was already flattened, with the Hand of God outpost completely eradicated. Not a single enemy cultivator remained alive. This place had been thoroughly recaptured.

Only one eyesore remained—the massive flagpole stabbed deep into the earth. Brock wouldn't let that stand. A massive golden hand appeared, grabbing the pole and ripping it out of the ground. He then threw the pole into the nebula and tore off the Hand of God flag, turning it into a dozen pieces of cloth which he set in orbit around Center Moon.

In war, the flag of an army was their insignia, the heart of their soldiers, and the cornerpiece of their morale. To attack one's flag was a grave insult. What Brock had done, ripping the flag apart and scattering its pieces around the conquered outpost, was equal to spitting in the face of the Hand of God.

But they were already at war. Why would he care about the enemies' hatred?

Brock then looked toward his two bros, one of whom was wounded but both were beaming. "I am proud of you," he said. "We restored justice. We took revenge."

"Couldn't have done it without you, big bro," Salin replied with a toothy smile, and Brock's usually stern face morphed into a bright smile.

"We are all bros," he said. "After so many years... it is nice to see we have all grown."

"Damn right!" Nauja shouted, still excited. "Hey, Jack! What are you doing? Come here and celebrate!"

Space warped beside them. A bare-chested man appeared, his every muscle perfectly defined as if sculpted from marble. Jack had never been too handsome a guy, but after cultivating for so long, his current appearance would be enough to have most women swooning.

In contrast to the three bros' victory, however, his face was dark. "I looked through the entire Center Moon and all three planets," he said. "I didn't find Shol. Not a trace."

"That sucks," Salin said. "I hope he's okay."

"Me too."

A moment of silence went by. "So," Brock said, "what do we do now, big bro?"

"What can we do?" Jack replied. "We try to decipher the hint he left behind and hope it really points somewhere. If that fails, we'll have to bear the risk and go after more Hand of God cultivators for information. I can only pray that the worst hasn't occurred."

There was a reason he was dark-faced. If Shol was missing, there was a chance he had been captured by the Hand of God elsewhere and forced to reveal the frequency of Earth's teleporter. Jack didn't believe Shol would break even under the cruelest of tortures, but if they had a way to read his mind...

If they reached Earth before him...

"We're going," he said. "The longer we stay, the higher the chances of reinforcements arriving."

Just as he said that, he frowned. Then, his face paled. "I can sense fluctuations from the teleporter. Someone's coming. Hurry!"

He waved his hand, taking all three of them to the teleporter. It was already shining—someone would arrive any second. "Nauja!" he shouted, but she was on it, pouring her energy into the teleporter, forcing it to activate faster than usual. Purple light enveloped them.

"Take us anywhere!" Jack shouted.

Two streams of energy collided. One outgoing, one incoming. For a moment, it felt like the teleporter was about to break. Then, Jack used his Space Dao to twist the two streams around each other, forcefully activating the teleporter at the cost of its structural integrity. They were sucked into space with an explosion—and, almost at the same time, two new people appeared next to the now-destroyed teleporter.

One was a hate-filled leonine—Artus Emberheart—and the

other was the late B-Grade tasked with purging the Milky Way Galaxy—Eva Solvig.

"Damn it all!" Artus shouted after looking around. "They escaped!" He clenched a small sack hanging by his side, causing whatever was inside it to release a small scream.

Eva did not respond immediately. Her gaze landed on the ruined flag, the flattened outpost, the corpses of her soldiers. Hatred was born inside her heart. "It doesn't matter if they escaped," she responded icily. "We know they're here. In our territory. Jack Rust... Let's see how long you can keep running."

CHAPTER EIGHT

RETURNING TO HELL

"Hey," Salin said. "That was nice. We escaped."

"Narrowly," Jack replied, frowning. "Did you sense their aura? That was a B-Grade—and not a weak one. They're here for us."

"We're here for them, too. So what?"

"Come on, Salin. We fought for, what, a minute? And they arrived. Not only were they waiting just next to a teleporter, but they even supercharged it to move at extremely high speed. They were looking for us specifically. They know we're here, and they're making it their priority to hunt us down."

"Oh, come on. Not to underestimate myself, but we're not that important."

"I hate to say this," Nauja stepped in, "but I agree with Salin. You may be thinking too much into this. Besides our teleportation into the galaxy, we haven't shown up anywhere for months. I don't think they expected we'd come to Field Nebula and had a B-Grade lie in wait next to a teleporter to catch us. It's much more probable they were just on standby so they could respond to Church attacks anywhere in the galaxy."

Jack opened his mouth, then closed it again. "That makes

sense. But, in any case, they know where we are now. And Artus Emberheart hates me more than anything in the world. I wouldn't be surprised if they devote a B-Grade or two to tracking us down."

"That, they could do." Salin nodded. "But what do we say to the God of Death?"

Jack gave a defeated sigh. "Not today?"

"That's exactly right! Not today! We just won, godsdammit, let's enjoy it a bit!"

"Dog bro right." Brock nodded as well. "Victory demands celebration."

Nauja gave Jack an expectant gaze. He sighed. "Fine," he said. "You're right. We did win; and they can't track us down immediately, anyway. Let's celebrate our victory!"

"That's more like it!" Salin shouted, drawing a bottle from his little pocket.

"That doesn't even fit," Jack replied weakly, but Salin was already stuffing him full of alcohol. Everyone else, too. The *Bromobile* shuttled through the vast cosmos accompanied by the sound of laughter and joy.

They had won—and, before considering how to run for their lives, a good night's celebration was necessary.

It was only a day later that they finally recovered. Brock paced through the *Bromobile*'s living room, thanking the Big Bro Above for their blessed lives, while Jack rested on an armchair. A piece of paper was in his hands—his gaze pierced into it intently as if trying to telepathically set it aflame.

"No progress?" Brock asked, reclining to watch the stars.

"None," Jack replied, shaking his head. "Endless stars and fire flight, gather where we won the fight... This doesn't make much sense. Do you think Shol was just trying to write a poem?"

"Hope not. But he seems like a bro who writes poems."

"That's what I fear as well." Jack leaned back, massaging his temples. "I just can't see anything. What is endless stars and fire flight? If it's a hint, that part makes no sense. And, gather where we won the fight... That could mean many places."

"Are you sure?"

"I guess? There was the Integration Tournament, where I won under his tutelage. The Exploding Sun, where I earned many victories in the sparring arena. Hell, where we beat a bunch of people; or Earth again, where we defeated the planetary overseer. But none of those places check out. Earth is obviously useless as a gathering point, since we can't go without him, and the Exploding Sun was already destroyed. Even if it wasn't, the sparring arena doesn't fit the endless stars or fire flight—and, to be honest, I didn't win any important victories there. As for Hell, it's right in the middle of enemy territory. Only a suicidal man would go there."

"Hmm. Perhaps you're right. It was just a poem."

Brock returned his gaze to the stars, soon followed by Jack. A few hours passed, while the *Bromobile* toured the universe aimlessly. Suddenly, Jack cupped his chin. "You know..." he said slowly, "I could be called suicidal. Shol, too. And you."

"Pretty much everyone we know," Brock agreed.

"And, fire flight... Hell contains fire. As for endless stars, that could be space. The space around Hell."

"Which leaves only the flight part."

"Yes... Perhaps it refers to when the Church took us away from Hell, helping us escape the pursuit of both Animal Kingdom and Hand of God. They'd built a portal on a meteor. Do we need to find that meteor?"

"Meteors are fleeting things."

"True. I have no idea how we could locate it now. Unless the Kingdom took it in to scavenge the teleporter materials, but still, I have no idea where or how they would do that."

"Wisdom comes at its time."

"You're right. Maybe we'll figure it out when we get there. I mean, since there's a chance, we might as well go."

"You're so bright today, big bro."

"Thanks, Brock. I try my best."

———

Once upon a time, traveling across the galaxy had been a major hurdle for Jack. He'd needed to disguise himself and board a roaming starship—the *Trampling Ram*—as a sailor while watching out for enemies at every step.

Now, though the enemies he faced had gotten much stronger, the journey was smoother. He had his own starship. What were they going to do, locate him in quadrillions of miles of empty space?

Therefore, for the second time in his life, Jack traveled from Field Nebula toward Hell.

Since they had been almost caught, they avoided all teleporters as much as possible. When a stop was unavoidable, they used the disguise pills Min Ling had left them. Another month passed.

The galaxy remained broken. Several factions had been uprooted, including the Exploding Sun. That had created a power vacuum which smaller factions were eager to fill, recklessly warring against each other. And, given the general uproar in the universe, nobody had the energy to stop them.

It wasn't just one war—not just the Crusade. Changes rippled, and slowly but surely, the entire universe was submerged in the flames of war.

The *Bromobile* crew appeared on another planet Jack had visited in the past—the Eternal Gate. Once upon a time, a merchant had snuck him and Shol from here into Hell. Now, they couldn't have that liberty. They would just fly.

As soon as they appeared, multiple Dao perceptions scanned over them. Jack remained cool. His disguise couldn't be seen through unless he used his Dao, or a B-Grade personally arrived—and he doubted the Animal Kingdom could afford using B-Grades as guards.

He was accompanied by a tanned woman with long legs wrapped in a cloak and what seemed like the love child of an 80s gangster with a cyberpunk playboy. Both wore sunglasses. These were Nauja and Gan Salin, impeccably disguised. Behind them was Brock, in the form of a hard-faced dwarf with a beard which reached his ankles and a pointy pink hat.

Gan Salin had insisted that hiding in plain sight would work—and that being chased was no excuse for dullness. Even Jack had been convinced to wear a mustache and beret.

"Can the circus come to the side, please?" a D-Grade guard motioned them over. They complied. "This is standard procedure," continued the guard. "I'll just ask you some questions. Failure to give a complete and true reply will result in up to a hundred years of imprisonment. Is that okay?"

"Shoot, loverboy," replied Salin, much to Jack's chagrin.

"Place of origin?"

"Belarian Outpost."

"Reason for arrival?"

"We're visiting some friends in Escadril." Escadril was a planet near Eternal Gate.

"Can I have the names of your friends?"

"Of course. They are Bobidi Doo and Plipiti Yap." Seeing the guard's raised brow, Salin added, "Djinns. You know what they're like."

"I'll note it down. Keep in mind that this information will be cross-checked before you are allowed to teleport out of Eternal Gate. And your names?"

Salin blurted out four slightly more coherent names, and the guard finally let them go.

"It's much stricter than I remember," Jack muttered.

"They're at war," Nauja replied, shaking her head. "No wonder they treat everyone like a potential criminal."

"Yeah..."

The information Salin gave out would soon be cross-checked and proven false. Which didn't matter, because they weren't planning to teleport out of this planet. After flying a thousand miles away, they simply took out the *Bromobile* and launched themselves deep into space.

"Hell is a week away," Nauja explained after consulting her star chart. "I recommend taking a detour around the Animal Abyss. We can spare the extra day."

"Animal Abyss? What's that?" Jack asked.

Both Nauja and Gan Salin gave him an odd look. "You never did any research on the Animal Kingdom?"

"I was busy killing them."

Salin sighed. "Oh, Jack, Jack, Jack. The Animal Abyss is an important location of the Animal Kingdom. It's a small black hole, basically, but with the caveat that it occasionally spits out treasures."

Jack frowned. "Black holes do that?"

"No. But this one does. Nobody really knows why, but then again, nobody knows much about black holes."

"Okay. So it's a black hole which conveniently spits out treasures?"

"That's the idea! It's also surrounded by a spatial field which is hard to detect and even harder to escape, so the working theory is that various cultivators have passed by this place in the last few billions of years, accidentally getting sucked inside. Then, after being forced to orbit the hole for incredibly long periods of time, their bodies dissolve but their treasures don't, and they are somehow spat out in random intervals."

"That makes no sense."

"What can I say? Even the Kingdom's B-Grades are helpless before the abyss. As long as it keeps spitting out treasures, they're happy."

"Hmm." Jack cupped his chin. "What kind of treasures are we talking about?"

"All sorts of things. This Animal Abyss is actually a corner-stone of the Animal Kingdom. Various precious items have been discovered, including the cultivation manuals of the Ember-heart and Lonihor families—the origin of their special battle forms."

"I thought those came from their bloodlines."

"Of course not. That's just propaganda. Did you also think Santa was real?"

Jack remembered those battle forms very clearly. The Emberheart family could clad their body in electricity, vastly increasing their speed and power. As for the Lonihor family, they could give themselves wings and summon spectral soldiers from the skies to fight for them.

He'd always chucked it up to magic, but actually, having such power contained in one's bloodline was pretty impossible.

"I see," he said, his eyes sparkling. "So there is a black hole which conveniently spits out extremely high-quality treasures."

"Right. It's part of the reason why the four ancestors of the Animal Kingdom could reach the B-Grade and rule over a constellation."

"And why should we take a detour around it?"

From the side, Nauja smirked. "Are you interested?"

"Who wouldn't be?"

A black hole was the endpoint of space and time. Jack had long wanted to study one, but he never had the chance—though the Cathedral orbited one, he hadn't been strong enough at the time to approach it. Now was as good an opportunity as any. Plus, the special properties of this Animal Abyss intrigued him. Based on what he knew, both from Earth physics and from the Dao of Spacetime, a black hole which regularly spat out things wasn't normal. There had to be a secret behind it.

And just because the B-Grades of the Animal Kingdom couldn't unravel such a secret didn't mean Jack couldn't either. He had inherited the legacy of an Archon. He was confident that his understanding of spacetime was solidly in the B-Grade by now, and his reference material was far superior to what the random B-Grades of a newly-developed galaxy had access to.

"I'm just interested," he replied. "Even if there's only a tiny chance I can get anything out of it, it's worth a look."

"As long as you don't get your hopes up," Salin said. "But... the reason Nauja suggests a detour is that there's always a B-Grade stationed there. A few years ago—and I don't know if that has changed—it was the High Elder of the Emberheart family. He was responsible for looking after the abyss and gathering any treasure it happened to spit out. Plus, there are all sorts of space formations surrounding the abyss. If we fly too close, there's a chance we'll be discovered."

"Hmm."

Jack considered it. He really was interested in that Animal Abyss—even the chance of getting more insights into spacetime was something he was unwilling to pass on. However, it could ruin them all. Was it worth the risk?

Brock suddenly spoke up after being silent all this time, "A good cultivator must adventure, and a good bro must walk the tightrope. Let's seek balance. We can pass some distance away, take a look, and escape if things get dangerous. Big Bro can discover space formations before they activate."

"You're right, I can. Unless they've been laid down by a peak B-Grade excelling in spacetime, I can at least detect them ahead of time."

"The Kingdom has never had a peak B-Grade," Salin informed them. "Alright then! Let's go!"

CHAPTER NINE

ANIMAL ABYSS

THE UNIVERSE REMAINED DARK. ENDLESS STARS GLITTERED IN ALL directions.

How horrifying this could be, Jack imagined, leaning against the glass window. *To be isolated here without a starship or the ability to fly... This is a prison of another kind, an inescapable loneliness. No matter how you float around, the closest salvation lies many light years away...*

"We're getting close!" Nauja shouted from the helm. "We're in the territory of the Animal Abyss. No more teleporting. Jack, keep an eye out!"

His irrelevant thoughts disappeared. He sharpened his mind, becoming like a different person as he spread out his aura to its maximum range and constantly scanned space. Brock and Gan Salin joined them on the bridge.

"Stop!" he yelled after a half hour. Nauja brought the *Bromobile* to an instant halt.

Jack had sensed something different just now—as if space was slightly wrinkled ahead of them, its nature almost imperceptibly different from everywhere else. Slowly, he focused his perception there, attempting to investigate without alerting whatever that thing was.

His perception pressed against the wrinkles, seeping through them like water soaking through paper. It was like a second layer of folded space hidden behind the normal one. In it, Jack could sense a bubble-like layer covering an incredibly vast area. It was so large, in fact, that he could only barely sense its curvature—if he didn't suspect it encapsulated the abyss, he might have perceived this as a wall instead.

"What is it?" Nauja asked.

"A formation..." Jack replied, furrowing his brows in concentration. "It's not meant to stop us, but to alert someone to our presence. It surrounds the entire Abyss at a radius of a million miles."

"*Really?*" Salin raised both brows. "That's big!"

"Yeah. Even for a B-Grade proficient in spacetime, creating such a large formation must have taken millennia—and I doubt it's the only one."

"Can you break it?" Nauja asked.

"Not without alerting whoever controls it. However, if it's just getting past... I think I can do that."

The four of them exited the *Bromobile*, which Jack shrank and received into his pocket. Then, he wrapped the four of them in a space bubble and approached the formation. He spent three hours examining it. Then, when he was sure he could succeed, he very slowly pushed their bubble forward.

While he had called this a wall, it wasn't really one. Instead, it was a collection of energy streams circulating at extreme speed. They all passed by a central node at the core of the formation, so if any energy stream was slowed down, whoever controlled the formation would be able to detect it. These streams even sank into the underlying levels of space, making it so nobody could teleport past them.

Bypassing this formation was the equivalent of crossing a river without touching the water.

In Jack's understanding, there were two ways to achieve this. The first was to sink deeper into space than the streams could reach—space was separated into layers, with one's speed increasing exponentially the deeper they went. This was also the principle behind teleportation.

Whoever made this formation wasn't an amateur. The streams reached deeper than Jack could go. To bypass them, he would need to teleport with the efficiency of a high-level tele-porter—which was impossible for the current him, as well as almost everyone in the B-Grade.

The second solution was to divert the streams, making them pass around his bubble without touching it. He would also need to use the Dao of Time to accelerate them just enough that they covered the extra distance in precisely the same amount of time as if he wasn't there. Since there were multiple streams superimposed over each other and moving at different speeds, this was more difficult than it sounded. Even with Jack's current understanding, he didn't have a hundred percent certainty of success.

But he believed he could do it.

The bubble pushed against the formation at a snail's pace and passed through it. Jack was fully focused. His perception covered the surrounding space, catching all streams and diverting them into a precise trajectory at an exact speed. With every inch the bubble moved forward, he carefully released the streams behind them and took control of the ones they'd just entered. His control wasn't perfect, but he was confident it was good enough to not alert the formation. After all, miniscule discrepancies were expected in such a large area.

They advanced one inch at a time. Jack didn't dare hurry at

all, devoting all of his attention into manipulating the streams of space energy. This process required all of his expertise.

Finally, they made it through. Jack released the last energy stream and groaned, his body going soft. His eyes swerved from exhaustion.

"Did we do it?" Salin asked.

"Yes..." Jack replied, his voice weak. He took out the *Bromobile* and flew into it, slumping into a couch. "Just... give me some time. Let me restore myself before going deeper."

"Absolutely! Good job!"

Jack smiled, then entered meditation. His tense mind gradually recovered, regathering its energy and re-entering its apex state. A few hours later, Jack stretched. "I'm good. Let's go."

The *Bromobile* kept advancing. Nauja guided it at a measured speed, so Jack could scan ahead of them. Though it was only a million miles, which would normally take them less than an hour to cross even without teleportation, they covered the distance in two days.

They could still see nothing in the distance. The Animal Abyss was a black hole, so detecting it with their eyes was impossible. From this close, though, they could make out the distortion in light surrounding it—the stars seemed warped around a section of space as light curved around the black hole.

When they reached within ten thousand miles, Jack stopped them again. "There's another formation. Let me check."

He flew out, already frowning. This formation was far more intricate than the last one. It followed the same principles but with ten times the energy streams, and it also contained something like a spatial barrier—without vibrating at a specific frequency, it would be impossible to pass, and discovering this frequency couldn't be done in a short amount of time. If anyone tried to enter without discovering this barrier, they would be stuck here for several minutes, enough time to let the B-Grade guarding the abyss arrive.

Of course, the formation could also be broken through with force, but that required far more power than Jack could currently wield.

He spent ten hours inspecting this formation. He tried all sorts of discreet experiments and ran various scenarios through his head. In the end, he was forced to admit he was outclassed. He could not cross this formation without alerting it.

"It's no use," he muttered as he re-entered the *Bromobile*. "I found the frequency to bypass the barrier, but I cannot control the streams well enough. If we so much as touch it, whoever controls the formation will know."

"Well, you did your best. It was worth a shot," Salin tried to comfort him. "Our goal was just to take a look, anyway. See there? That area of warped light? That's the periphery of the black hole. It's an area of warped space which renders one's perception useless. B-Grades can enter it to look for treasures, and so can C-Grades who understand the Dao of Space, but there is always the chance of running into a space anomaly and getting sucked into the abyss without a chance to resist. Many of the Animal Kingdom's Elders have died in such a fashion. However, that area is precisely where the treasures appear, so they still send people every now and then."

Jack frowned. The more he heard about this black hole, the more abnormal he realized it was.

Archon Green Dragon's inheritance contained a lot of insights into the Dao of Spacetime. That included knowledge about black holes, which were the natural end of all spacetime. After studying that inheritance for three years, Jack could be considered half an expert—and he knew with certainty that the spacetime surrounding a black hole was highly warped but also completely smooth. The area of irregular space that Salin described was impossible, because the black hole's gravitational pull would straighten out any and all spacetime disturbances.

Could it be something else? he wondered.

There were more celestial bodies with intense gravitational fields. For example, neutron stars. Those could be surrounded by a field of irregular space, but they wouldn't possess the light-swallowing capabilities of a black hole. As Jack considered the issue, he concluded that if this wasn't a black hole, he had no idea what it was.

Could it be a mutated black hole? he wondered. *Perhaps existing in a spacetime anomaly itself, or maybe surrounded by another spacetime phenomenon which is responsible for the irregular space field? But it still doesn't make sense. Could it be some extremely rare but previously-undiscovered celestial body?*

The more he learned about this place, the more curious he became. He wanted to check it out. Unfortunately, since he couldn't bypass the formation, it simply wasn't worth the risk.

Not to mention that, if he did check it out, he would likely come out with nothing. The Animal Kingdom had many B-Grades and a million years—if this enigma was easy to unravel, they would have done it already, and they wouldn't have to sacrifice people to look for treasures.

When I get stronger... After I destroy the Animal Kingdom... I should return to have a look, he told himself, sparing a final glance at the mysterious black hole. Then, Nauja turned the starship around and they flew back out, penetrating the previous formation again to reach the outside space.

"Let's go," Jack said. "We still have to find Shol and Earth. Everything else can wait."

They broke through space, teleporting a trillion miles in an instant, and just like that, they were gone.

CHAPTER TEN
SEARCHING THE COMET

JACK SAT CROSS-LEGGED IN HIS ROOM. SIMPLE WALLS SURROUNDED him, fitted with a wide window which overlooked the vastness of space. Endless stars twinkled. They gathered in rivers, stamping their presence into the cosmos as the arms of Jack's home galaxy—the Milky Way.

Despite the beauty, Jack's eyes were closed. He wasn't looking out, but in.

Life and Death.

Space and Time.

These were the Daos on which he focused. Life was represented by the Fist, and still remained the core of his Dao. Death was the antithesis to life, a necessary component to comprehending it, and Jack's understanding into this concept had benefited greatly thanks to Master Boatman. As for space and time, while they had begun as supplementary Daos, they had taken up more of his attention after acquiring Archon Green Dragon's inheritance.

Most people focused on one Dao. If they were particularly ambitious, they might choose a set of interconnected concepts, such as space and time. Very few would have the courage to cultivate two sets of Daos, because reaching mastery in even one was a herculean task—why would they further split their attention? At the same time, a second set of Daos was considered unnecessary, as a single one was enough to reach very deep into the cultivation road.

For these reasons, very few people chose to do what Jack did. Even extreme individuals like Elder Boatman or Archon Green Dragon chose one point of focus.

Jack, on the other hand, had a striking difference compared to everyone else; he wasn't born in the System world. He hadn't grown up studying the possible paths of progression and what his predecessors did. In a normal B-Grade or A-Grade influence, the young cultivators were discouraged from biting off more than they could chew because it was a road extremely unlikely to work. In ten thousand extreme talents, perhaps not even one would succeed. Any faction would rather cultivate a group of decently powerful individuals than stake its entire existence on a tiny chance of overwhelming success.

Jack had never been conditioned like that. Since the start of his journey, he had carved a path of perfection with his own two hands, and staking everything on himself was the natural decision. Even if his path was difficult, he would still choose to pursue perfection, because that was who he was.

After cultivating for several years to his present power, he could sense that a single Dao was not enough to reach perfection. Life and Death were not all-encompassing. They mostly pertained to the soul, but their ability to influence the physical world was limited. Therefore, spacetime was perfectly suited for him—it provided him with much-needed utility and also rounded out his Dao. In the future, if he pushed all his Daos to perfection, he would be able to create a system of understanding that contained the entire world.

Of course, such perfection was astoundingly difficult to

achieve, or others would have done it already. While Jack was brave, he certainly wasn't reckless. He had chosen this difficult road because he truly possessed the capital.

His soul and Dao of the Fist had been tempered through the endless difficulties he'd experienced. His willpower was unyielding. He had the Life Drop for the Dao of Life, the death cube alongside Boatman's guidance for the Dao of Death, and the inheritance of an Archon for spacetime. Any single one of those would be enough to produce at least a peak B-Grade— when combined together, and added onto Jack's own prowess, gave him the courage to reach for the sky.

These four high-level Daos, combined with his highly tempered body, were the reasons for his overwhelming strength.

Today, he sat with the death cube in his hands. He no longer needed to look at it—the lines were mostly memorized, and just brushing them with his perception was enough to bring anything to the fore.

This death cube was an item Master Boatman had given him, and on which he placed tremendous importance. Jack still had no idea what exactly it was or how it had been produced— but what he did know was that the death cube was a highly mystical existence.

Even after all this time, it remained filled with insights. The 999 lines each represented a life and a death—when one learned how to read them, each line hid a wealth of knowledge, as they were the patterns which defined the cycle. The greatest benefit of this cube weren't the many insights it contained though, but the ingeniousness with which these insights had been arranged.

There was always something to find out. Meditating on a line gave insights—and, if he increased his understandings and returned to the same line, he would find more hidden insights. Just as he mastered one insight, a new one would appear on the cube, and the progression was so linear that Jack's understanding into death advanced at a terrific pace. Let alone him, even if someone more average took ahold of this death cube, they would still be able to advance tremendously.

No wonder Master Boatman seemed so reluctant to part with it and had even left a wisp of his soul inside. This thing was like a step-by-step guide to the Dao of Death.

My Dao of Death has almost caught up with Life. Soon, I will need to focus back on the Fist... Jack thought. His eyes slowly opened, while his lips curled. *Perfect.*

He enjoyed cultivating. But it was only the Fist, the core of his being, which truly fulfilled him. Everything else was secondary.

Just as he was about to return to meditation, a voice reached his mind. "Jack," said Nauja. "We're approaching. Are you coming?"

"*I'll be right there.*"

With a thought, the death cube sank into his space ring, and he effortlessly stepped through space to appear at the *Bromobile*'s deck. "Is that it?" he asked, looking through the glass window.

"You tell me," Nauja replied. "I've never been here before."

A lone meteor floated through space. It was a large rock, unassuming if not for the half-destroyed teleporter on its back. The mountain of energy stones under it had long been taken by the Animal Kingdom, but the teleporter itself was not made of precious materials so they let it be. Now, after several years of unuse, its remains were filled with cracks.

But no matter how useless or broken, it remained a tele-porter. The *Bromobile*'s sonar had caught its fluctuations as soon as they approached Hell, letting them head directly here.

There were guards around this solar system, of course, but nothing that Jack's space concealment couldn't trick.

"Endless stars and fire flight, gather where we won the fight," Jack muttered. "This place... should be the destination."

"Unless it was just a poem," Salin's voice arrived as the canine entered the room. "I don't see anyone on the meteor."

"Let's land and inspect it. We might find something."

There wasn't much else they could do at this point. The *Bromobile* approached and landed on the meteor. All the while, Jack's heart was flooded with unease—if they really found nothing, this trip would have been made in vain. And, even worse, he would have no other leads to find Earth. He would remain stranded away from his family for who knows how long. His children would grow old without him.

I've already spent three years away. And before that, I only visited a few times. Only their first six months were spent with me, he thought, guilt encroaching upon his heart. He clenched his fist. It wasn't that he regretted his decision, because it was necessary to keep them safe. It was only that... *I miss them so fucking much.*

"As you may know, I'm a detective. Let me handle this," Salin said in stark contrast with Jack's mood. He looked around. "Mhm. This is a meteor." He then picked up a stone, weighed it in his hand—though there was no gravity—observed it from all sides and finally licked it. "Rock. As expected."

"Are you done?" Nauja asked, rolling her eyes. She spread out her perception to easily cover this mile-wide comet. "I can't find anything... Maybe it's hidden inside."

"Let me," Brock said. He squatted down, placing a hand on the meteor's surface. "Hey, space stone bro. Anything to share?" After a moment of waiting, he shook his head. "Nothing inside."

"Are you sure?"

"Of course. Space stone bro wouldn't lie to me."

"So we found nothing," Jack said, his voice heavy. As much as he wanted to, he couldn't share his friends' joking mood.

"Sorry, Jack," Nauja said, placing a hand on his shoulder. "We tried. Maybe... there are more clues somewhere. We'll find them. Don't give up hope."

"Yes. Perhaps in ten years, when my children are fifteen, I will finally be able to see them..." Jack replied, raising his head to gaze at the stars. To celestial bodies, and even to cultivators like him, ten years were nothing. But, to his children, they were a lifetime.

And besides them, there was also the professor. His mother. She was old, and he didn't know if she'd managed to reach the D-Grade and extend her lifespan. If not...

"Is this supposed to be shining?" Salin asked. Everyone turned to find him gazing at the broken teleporter. Looking closely, a tiny spark flickered in its center.

"No," Nauja replied, her eyes widening. "That's... certainly not supposed to happen."

There were many kinds of teleporters. Hastily constructed ones, like the one before them, needed a large amount of energy to operate and couldn't form a stable connection to other teleporters. That was why nobody had bothered to search it before.

Jack jumped forward, instantly arriving to the teleporter. His hopes were rekindled. Could Shol have left a message inside?

"Careful!" Nauja shouted, arriving beside him, but she was too late. Jack had already reached out to touch it. As soon as he made contact, a single spark shot out—and then the entire teleporter exploded in a mass of fiery death. The meteor disintegrated under their feet. Spatial fluctuations flooded their surroundings, while Jack barely had time to form a shield and protect them from the explosion.

A mix of feelings ran through his heart. He wasn't injured,

but the teleporter had exploded. There was no road to Earth here. He was trapped away from his family. It was only after he went through the sadness that he realized the explosion had been far too large—far too artificial. Somebody had flooded this teleporter with energy and kept it right at the edge of exploding.

They were close to Hell. Though they had avoided all guards before, such an explosion would be easily noticed.

This was a trap!

Everyone glanced at each other, arriving at the same conclusion. "Quick!" Jack said, taking out the *Bromobile*. They entered it instantly, but teleporting away took time. Moreover, the explosion had contained spatial ripples specifically designed to disturb space and delay the process.

They needed time. Time they wouldn't have. Jack could already sense light tremors in space as powerful cultivators were approaching at high speed.

"I'll delay them!" he shouted, shooting out of the *Bromobile*. "Charge up the teleportation!"

Space parted before he even finished his words. Animal people emerged. Some were leonines, some canines, some sharkens, eaglers, or elefs—all five noble families of the Animal Kingdom were present. Moreover, these weren't young elites— they were aged, their eyes filled with dignity and their bodies exuding immense power.

As Jack swept his perception over them, his heart chilled. These people were all at the middle C-Grade and above—they were Elders of the Animal Kingdom.

This wiped away all doubts about the exploding teleporter being an accident. There was no way the Animal Kingdom had so many Elders on standby. This was a trap—a trap specifically meant for him. And, in his single moment of weakness in several years, he walked right into it.

Jack gritted his teeth. Such was the cultivation world. It didn't matter how fierce you were, how carefully you'd handled everything in the past, or if you were filled with grief and at your most vulnerable moment. Triumph and defeat were separated by a single line—one mistake could kill.

Amongst the many Elders surrounding Jack, a leonine with flowing red hair stepped forward. His cultivation was at the peak C-Grade, and he wasn't weak for his level either. This was the Animal Kingdom's Grand Elder—an existence just below the B-Grade Ancestors.

"Jack Rust..." he said, his eyes sparking hatred. "Give up. You are already dead."

Jack snorted. At this point, holding back was pointless. An ocean of power erupted from his body, flooding the surrounding space and even washing away the auras of all the Elders present. His body grew taller and two extra arms protruded from under his armpits.

These Elders were incredibly powerful people... but Jack was not the weak D-Grade he'd once been. Now, he was strong as well—strong enough to match a B-Grade, let alone these people.

"Do you really think you can kill me?" he asked.

The Grand Elder's smile grew wider. "No. But we can delay you. It doesn't matter how powerful you are. This is our territory, and stronger people are already on the way. If you want to escape before they arrive..." His eyes flared. "That is impossible!"

CHAPTER ELEVEN
MATCHING A B-GRADE

JACK'S MIND WENT COLD.

On the outside, he showed no difference. His aura flared, his back shielding both his friends and the *Bromobile*. Until they were ready to teleport, he wouldn't let anyone touch them.

"Come at me," he challenged. At the same time, he sent a telepathic message to Brock, telling him to stay with the others and serve as the last line of defense.

His message was heard. Bro chants filled the void, and a golden shield appeared around the starship. A massive golden brorilla sat cross-legged on its top. Under Brock's protection, the *Bromobile* could defend against any stray attacks.

"Useless!" the Grand Elder spat out. He laughed. "This is already over, Jack Rust. Just give up and die!"

"Make me."

A punch shot out, cracking the endless voided sky. Jack couldn't just sit back and be reactive—he had to take the initiative!

Facing his attack, the seven Elders did not meet it head-on. They scattered. Everyone flew in a different direction, surrounding both Jack and the starship, while the elef Elder drew back and readied her healing powers. At the same time, the Grand Elder and the other five waved their hands, unleashing a barrage of attacks headed directly for the *Bromobile*.

Jack's form flickered. He appeared next to the starship, and a hail of punches tore their attacks like paper. Only fireworks remained of the continent-crushing powers. Yet, the Elders only laughed, unleashing even more attacks. Jack gritted his teeth. His fists swept out again, easily defending against everything. He tore through space to approach a sharken Elder, but the moment he did, every other Elder ignored him to attack the starship.

Jack's eyes widened. He shot a hasty Meteor Punch into the Elder, severely injuring him, then rushed back to defend. He didn't make it in time. Five of the six attacks, he blocked—the sixth smashed into the *Bromobile*, shaking Brock's golden shield. It had persisted, but it wouldn't forever. Jack needed to defend.

"Damn!" he shouted, anger seeping into his voice. The Elders laughed again.

Jack was more powerful than all of them combined. He could use his Dao of Space to wildly teleport around and eliminate them one by one. Except, if he did that, the rest would pummel the *Bromobile* until Brock's shield shattered and their ship was impacted, stopping its teleportation. That would delay them massively.

On the other hand, if Jack only defended, he would be forced into a passive position. Defending wasn't his forte—a few attacks would inevitably seep through. And, even if Brock's shield did manage to defend, all the shockwaves would still delay their teleportation.

Jack could already sense a powerful presence heading his way, far more mighty than these Elders. Attacking would not work, and neither would defending. He had the strength, but it was useless if he only punched empty air.

He felt checkmated.

"Dammit!" he shouted again, releasing his aura wildly. It buffeted the Elders, but they simply used their Daos to defend. They laughed again, a cacophony of arrogance.

"It's useless, Jack Rust! Just bow down and accept your fate!"

Jack's eyes sharpened. *Even if it's risky... I will kill at least a few of them!*

Killing intent erupted. His body flashed, appearing behind the same Elder as before. He no longer held back. A massive meteor tore through space, exploding right on the Elder's back —and though he tried to escape, Jack locked space around him, rendering him unable to move. The Elder could only defend. With a tremendous explosion, he was sent flying away, spitting blood and severely injured.

Unfortunately, he wasn't dead yet. Jack would have liked to use Supernova, but it took a longer time to charge—as it was, he only barely had time to return, defending against four of the attacks of the other Elders and letting two impact Brock's shield. Cracks appeared. The golden brorilla sitting atop the shield shook, its color dimming a little.

Meanwhile, the far-off elef shone with green energy. The Elder that Jack had injured was enveloped in her power, his wounds regenerating at a rate visible to the naked eye. He laughed and charged back into battle.

The powerful presence from afar kept drawing closer.

Jack gritted his teeth, his eyes falling to sub-zero temperatures. The Brutalizing Aura rolling out of his body rose in intensity, assaulting the Elders with visions of being wildly mutilated, but they were powerful enough to resist. Their attacks kept coming—a ceaseless onslaught.

Jack teleported again. The Elder he'd attacked before had been the weakest one, but it was clear that half-measures would get him nowhere. He had to kill someone instantly. He had to use Supernova, even if it took longer to charge. And, since he was using Supernova, he might as well target the strongest Elder he was sure to eliminate.

The one he'd targeted was a leonine, the second strongest after the Grand Elder.

As he saw Jack appear behind him, this Elder's eyes flashed with terror. He hurriedly withdrew his power and smashed it all toward Jack, his body flashing with electricity—he was part of the Emberheart lineage. A large palm violently shot through space.

But how could it compare to a supernova? A part of the universe was sucked into Jack's fist. Space, time, light, matter, even the Dao itself, everything was sucked inside and compressed on the tip of Jack's middle knuckle. The energy density reached a terrifying degree. The world came to a standstill.

And then, as the energy grew too dense for Jack to control, it erupted in a massive explosion pointed forward.

You have to hold, Brock!

Flames seared the world. Chaotic energies ran wild. The void shattered, and the stars lost their luster. The leonine's palm simply disintegrated, and his body cracked apart as it bore the brunt of Supernova. All his organs shattered instantly. He was dead before he knew what hit him.

Jack had no time to rejoice. He hurriedly withdrew, even letting the energy shockwaves strike him to arrive faster, but he couldn't be quick enough. The only attack he managed to stop was the Grand Elder's. The other four shot past him and into Brock's golden shield, rocking it with far greater intensity than before. The golden brorilla roared—the shield's light flared for a moment, withstanding the attacks, but it paled greatly afterward. Brock had consumed a massive amount of energy just now. He couldn't necessarily do it again.

There were still five Elders remaining, plus the healer. Jack had no way to handle this. For a moment, he didn't attack again.

If Brock's shield shattered, it wouldn't be as simple as the *Bromobile*'s teleportation getting interrupted. Maybe even the entire starship would blow up. Nauja and Gan Salin, both of whom were D-Grades, would die in the aftermath. He couldn't afford that risk.

And the teleportation was still a far way from completion.

"I can take one more," Brock's weak voice resounded in Jack's mind.

"*Save your energy,*" he replied decisively. "*Stop the teleportation. We cannot make it in time. Prepare to run.*"

The powerful presence approaching was almost here. It was probably a B-Grade, and Jack had no illusions of defending the *Bromobile* against five powerful C-Grades and a B-Grade. As for fighting them, though he could maybe do it, that would mean giving up on the *Bromobile* and letting Brock, Nauja, and Gan Salin die.

The only choice was to capitalize on his Space Dao and run away as fast as possible. But there was a reason he hadn't done that before. A prolonged chase would give other people the opportunity to catch up, including the Hand of God's late B-Grade.

Unfortunately, he was out of options.

Jack's aura boiled over. The golden shield flared temporarily, and the starship's gathered energy dispersed, aborting the teleportation. Instead, it prepared to dash away.

Jack and Brock's souls were connected. In that moment, they didn't need to speak. They knew what needed to be done.

With their hearts feeling incomparably heavy, they dashed away... in opposite directions!

Escaping together was useless. Jack could not fight while protecting them, and they would slow him down. At the same time, the *Bromobile* was fast even without Jack's assistance— even if the Grand Elder chased them down, there was no guarantee he could catch them. However, if Jack tried to travel with the *Bromobile*, the approaching B-Grade would soon catch up, so he had to fly separately. He was much faster alone.

At the end of the day, he was their target, not the *Bromobile*. And, right now, he was left alone in space, without a starship. Long-range teleportation was impossible. He was a turtle in a jar.

Inside the starship, everyone was silent. Even the usually jovial Gan Salin could only feel despair. Nauja's knuckles were hard around the starship's helm, and as for Brock, he hated himself for being weak. As much as he wanted to fight and die alongside his big bro, he would only drag Jack down. He wasn't fast enough. Staying here would surely doom Jack to death, robbing him of his tiny chance to survive.

He could only escape. He had to protect dog bro and girl bro. That was his role—but he had never felt as useless as at this present moment. He roared out, letting his animalistic instincts take over and pouring the entirety of his feelings into the bro shield he'd conjured. The golden brorilla atop the starship mirrored him, screaming into the void—and the shield's speed shot up, reaching a peak in exchange for all of Brock's energy.

The *Bromobile* shot into the weakest Elder like a missile, smashing him away with ease and escaping the encirclement, then shooting into the distance. The Elder spat blood but did not give chase.

It was as Jack and Brock expected. Chasing the *Bromobile*

wasn't worth the risk—they would rather invest all their energy into killing Jack.

As for Jack himself, his grief and anger exploded. With nobody to protect, he couldn't be stopped. A Supernova erupted, shaking the world and flinging the Elders away. He dashed out of the encirclement, wanting to escape—and space split before him, revealing a wide-chested, golden-haired leonine. His eyes were like stars, and his aura was immeasurably deep.

This was a B-Grade, one of three Ancestor-level characters of the Animal Kingdom. He was also the one who once joined Eva Solvig to chase Jack to Earth, but had been intimidated into inaction by Sovereign Heavenly Spoon. Now, seeing Jack again after so many years, he laughed wildly.

"I finally caught you, Jack Rust!" he shouted in the void. "With nobody here to stop me, let me see just how you can escape!"

Jack did not reply. His aura erupted. A tremendous amount of energy gathered into his fist, overshadowing the auras of everyone present, and he charged straight into the B-Grade, not changing his course even a little.

The Ancestor's gaze flickered with surprise. "Do you really think you can match me?" The starlight around him intensified —endless white clouds appeared in the sky above, and his body was covered in awe-inspiring, world-shattering might. Glowing white armor covered his skin, a heavenly lance appeared in his hand, and eight wings proudly unfurled behind him.

The Ancestor laughed out loud, his voice carrying the majesty of a God. "An ant before a king! Laughable!" he exclaimed, drawing back his lance. Intense energy gathered, cracking the void through its sheer weight.

To Jack's surprise, this leonine was not a simple character. His level had reached the peak of the early B-Grade, and his talent was nothing to scoff at. Just in terms of battle power, he wasn't that much weaker than Spacewind or Uruselam. Jack had no idea whether he could win or not.

But it also didn't matter. If he stopped now and let himself be surrounded, his chances would be even lower. He had to break through.

"Supernova!" he roared, punching forward.

"Lance of God!" the Ancestor cried out, driving out his lance. Divine might shrouded the void. Cracks spread for endless miles. The fragments of the previously-shattered asteroid disintegrated completely, and even the Elders were pushed back by the shockwave of this collision.

Purple clashed against white. The world was washed away. And, when the shockwave dispersed, the Ancestor hadn't been pushed back, but neither had Jack!

"What!" the Ancestor exclaimed, his eyes growing wide with disbelief. "How... How can you resist me?"

As he was surprised, so were the Elders watching. To match a B-Grade from the mid C-Grade... this was an unprecedented level of power!

Jack did not bother with them. He overdrew on his Dao to keep pushing forward, rushing past the leonine and shooting into deep space. He was confident that his speed was superior —with any luck, he would be able to escape before anyone else caught up, then hide himself in the endlessness of space. Flying to another planet would take some time, but it was doable.

Just then, a faint ripple passed through the void, originating from the nearby planet of Hell. This ripple birthed despair in Jack's heart.

A late B-Grade had just teleported in—and they would be here in moments.

CHAPTER TWELVE
I AM SPEED

JACK DID NOT PAUSE. HE SHOT FORWARD, THOUGH IT DID LITTLE TO inhibit his latest pursuer. The void shimmered behind him, parting to reveal a white-haired, young-looking woman.

The moment she appeared, the universe seemed to have found a new master. Starlight danced around her, and the void curved as if wanting to bow. Her aura naturally billowed out, commanding the respect of reality.

Jack's movements slowed even as his mind fell into disarray. This... was a late B-Grade!

Though they'd never met, both knew of the other's name. Eva Solvig had once chased Jack through the Milky Way Galaxy, and he'd used all kinds of tricks to slip out of her grasp. Back then, Eva had been at the middle B-Grade—it was only in the last few years that she made another breakthrough, stepping into the late B-Grade.

In other words, she was not one of the strongest at her level... but so what? She and Jack were separated by a Grade and a half. No matter how talented or heaven-defying he was, there was no way he could fight her. Even middle B-Grades were too much for the current him.

"Jack Rust," she said. Her voice was colorless, tasteless, almost sterilized. "I have chased after you for years. Who knew you'd be dumb enough to fall for such a trap?"

Jack gritted his teeth, pausing his escape. It was clear they would chase after him—but, if they wanted to chat and let him catch his breath first, he wouldn't say no. He'd run the moment they did. It wasn't like anyone stronger could arrive.

This also saved time for the *Bromobile* to escape farther and farther away. Nobody cared about it—everyone's gaze was glued on Jack.

"Eva Solvig," he replied coldly. "We've been acquainted for a number of years, but this is actually the first time we meet. Can't say I'm pleased."

"I am," she replied. "Killing you will make the purging of this galaxy much simpler."

"Are you related to Purity of the Hand of God?" Jack asked. Elder Purity was the late A-Grade Elder he'd met at the banquet just before entering the hidden realm. That Elder's hair was also white, like Eva's, and the two women cultivated very similar Daos. Maybe it was even the exact same.

Eva Solvig frowned. "Elder Purity is my mother and master," she said. "You may not address her by name. You must use the honorific of Elder."

"Mother?" Jack asked, raising a brow. "I guess, no matter how pure one tries to be, we are all still human."

A chilling wind spread from Eva's body. Her white robes fluttered, while the surrounding void lost its luster, all tiny particles purified and extinguished. "Why do you taunt me?" she asked. "You are worsening your position."

"Can it get any worse?"

She thought for a moment—then, smiled. "No."

It was then that space parted behind her. Another person showed up. Jack's first reaction was to gauge their strength, then sigh in relief when it was only a late C-Grade. The only peculiarity was a large sack hanging from their waist.

Right afterward, he recognized that cultivator. It was Artus Emberheart—the man who hated Jack the most in the entire universe. As Artus appeared, his dark robes fluttering and his leonine eyes warped with obsession, he opened his mouth and laughed out loud. "Jack Rust!" he shouted. "You took everything from me! Today is the day you die!"

"Why did you bring the clown?" Jack asked Eva. She did not reply—Artus did.

"Your tongue is as sharp as ever, but you no longer have a place to hide. There is no one to protect you. I will ruin you, Jack Rust, and before I do, I will make sure you suffer the same pain I did!"

Artus laughed again, the sound shaking the surrounding void. Jack, however, only shook his head. "Just the whining of a defeated dog," he replied. "The reason you lost everything, Artus, was your own weakness. You are incompetent and talentless. You may hate me, but from the very start, I never cared about you. You were always doomed to be my stepping-stone, just another character I would surpass on my way to the peak. Even if I die today, it won't be your achievement—you're just a clown jumping on the sidelines while greater people than you try to hunt me down."

Artus's gloating gaze froze on his face. His visage warped into deep, blue hatred. He seemed as if he would attack. Then, surprisingly, he calmed down. There was even a hint of dark longing in his voice. "I hope you remember these words, Jack Rust. Soon, you will regret them."

"I look forward to it," Jack replied, unwilling to bother with Artus any longer. He turned to Eva. "Is there any way I can convince you to let me go? Since you haven't attacked me yet, I suppose you have something to say."

She smiled weakly. "The Hand of God appreciates your talent. We are welcome to let you live on the condition that you open up your soul and let us turn you into a slave."

Jack laughed. "I would rather die!"

"I know."

She attacked. The purified space around her expanded at tremendous speed, overtaking Jack. His eyes narrowed as all particles in his vicinity evaporated. This was a Dao Domain, one so refined it had turned into a battle skill. He instantly released his own. A purple meteor appeared in the middle of purity, billowing like a caged god of flame. Fist particles flooded the empty space, constantly eroded by purity and equally regenerating.

Dao Domains were mostly the weapons of D-Grades. After that, many lost their usefulness, which was why Jack rarely used his Dao Domain in battle lately. Eva Solvig, however, was different. Her domain was one of her greatest weapons. Since she was stronger than Jack to begin with, his domain of the Fist was immediately suppressed, barely able to make any waves at all.

The most he could do was maintain control of the area a few dozen feet around him, and that was only because of the great distance between them.

Eva charged, but Jack did not wait for her to arrive. In a head-on clash, he would be annihilated. He had to run.

With a shout, energy erupted out of him. The Fist took control of the surrounding space and he shot out, forcefully piercing through the domain of purity. His skin was burning—a strange energy was prevalent in the void, one which sought to wipe him clean, but he resisted. An explosion resounded behind him. Jack coughed out blood as he was shot out of the purity field, only for it to come crashing down again an instant later.

"You cannot escape," Eva Solvig calmly stated as she flew

forward. Her hands were covered in a white glow—and, staring at them, Jack could feel an instinctive fear deep in his soul, as if this white light was the nemesis of all life.

"Hahaha!" the Animal Kingdom Ancestor laughed out loud. "The Hand of God is well worth its reputation!" The Elders present followed behind Eva, ready to participate in Jack's execution, while Artus himself was just a step behind her, his eyes filled with dark satisfaction and a hand patting the sack he carried.

Jack gritted his teeth. He could not win this battle. Even if he somehow ran away, what then?

Elder Boatman, if you're going to appear at the last moment, this is it!

Yet, nothing happened. Nobody arrived to save him. Jack had sent away his friends and was now alone, trapped in the vastness of space with enemies far stronger than he was. The only one who could save him was himself... but he had no idea how.

It was only now that the severity of this danger sank in. If nothing changed, it was very probable that today he would die.

He gritted his teeth. *If I'm going to die... I won't go quietly!*

Purple light flared on his fists. Seeing that, Eva Solvig dropped her slow walking and teleported before him. She wasn't going to give him a chance.

"Goodbye," she said, pushing out her palms.

"SUPERNOVA!" Jack shouted. His fists shot forth—space exploded, the void erupted, purity was washed away. Jack's two hands bore the brunt of the collision, broken into bloody bone stumps. He was sent flying away. As for Eva, she'd barely slowed down—even his strongest attack was not enough to harm her.

But he'd used the momentum to escape her domain.

Her brows creased slightly. She did not expect him to

survive a direct attack, but in the end, surprise was just surprise—he could not escape. Her domain expanded again, seeking to encircle him. Jack smashed his stump of a wrist into the void, shattering it in the instant before she reached him and teleporting away. He reappeared a dozen miles into the distance, pale and shivering—escaping like that had taken a toll on him.

Eva Solvig scoffed in annoyance. "You're just wasting your time," she said, teleporting after him. "You cannot escape!"

Jack agreed, actually. Even if he survived for a few moments more and used his expertise in space to run away, so what? He would grow exhausted eventually and die all the same. It wasn't like he could outrun a late B-Grade.

But he couldn't just give up.

Space warped below him. Time stretched behind him and shrunk in front, letting him shoot through space like a fish in water. Distance became meaningless as he rushed forward at hundreds of miles per second.

"After him!" Eva commanded. Her Dao could directly disintegrate space—even without relevant insights, she used brute force to surpass Jack's speed, leaving a line of emptiness wherever she passed.

Jack glanced backward, and his brows fell further. Eva Solvig was steadily behind him, calmly riding a wave of purity. As expected; even at full speed, even using all his insights into space, Jack couldn't outrun her—the gap steadily shrunk, and he suspected she wasn't even going all-out. He would grow exhausted long before she did.

Battle was hopeless. Escape was impossible. Was he really doomed to die here? Was his only option to keep running away in the hopes that someone else would save him?

Since when was he, Jack Rust, so helplessly weak?

He roared into the void as he shot forward. His weakness

pained him, drove a stake through his heart. Even after working so hard and achieving so much, he had to depend on others.

"Damn it all!" he shouted, piercing deep into the void in his attempts to escape. It was useless—Eva Solvig remained close behind him, even if everyone else had faded far away.

Jack was fast. After mastering spacetime to such a degree, he was possibly the fastest C-Grade in the universe, but all tricks were meaningless before the suppression of absolute power.

Two lines cut through the void—one purple, one white. Eva kept closing the gap. Every time she drew near, she would unleash an attack which severely injured Jack. He coughed out blood and kept going, using the shockwave to open up the distance a little, but she just closed it again.

Eva couldn't catch up directly, but she could use this method to whittle Jack's energy. His rate of consumption was far higher than hers, and he also had to suffer heavy injuries. Moreover, his Dao usage was more delicate than hers, demanding more mental resources.

Thankfully, he could use the endless energy of the Life Drop to regenerate his wounds, greatly easing his load, but he still couldn't keep doing it forever.

CHAPTER THIRTEEN
THE ABYSS STARES BACK

The two meteors streaked through space. Jack was bound to be caught eventually. All he could do was delay—and spend that time despising his own weakness.

This was not a new experience. He'd been through the same thing many times in the past. It was just that, during the three years he'd spent training and the easy battles that came afterward, he'd forgotten just how imperative his quest for strength was.

Without sufficient power, he could not control his fate. He was just a leaf doomed to blow with the wind. His life or death were not in his hands, and his ability to affect the world was miniscule at best. If he wanted to protect himself and his loved ones, the only option was to have power, more power than anyone else. To have a large fist. Only then could one be safe and free.

Another attack fell against his back. Jack screamed as the skin was boiled away, devolving to nothing. He used his powerful body to survive. The momentum shot him forward, deeper into the endless darkness.

"You are prolonging the inevitable," Eva Solvig shouted

behind him, her voice cold. "Do you think someone will arrive to save you? That will not happen! Boatman is occupied else-where. So is Heavenly Spoon. Every powerful individual you've met is being closely monitored in other galaxies. Nobody will come for you, Jack Rust—just give up and save yourself some pain."

"Fuck you!" Jack shouted, not slowing down in the slight-est. The despair rising in him was suppressed—he had to find the one sliver of hope, any chance to survive. Even if the odds were stacked against him, there had to be something he could try, some desperate gamble with the tinniest of chances for success. There always was.

But nothing came to mind. He was lost in endless space—there was literally nothing around him.

No—there is! he realized. *The Animal Abyss!*

The Animal Abyss was an odd black hole situated near Hell, and surrounded by a complex gravitational field where one's perception was useless. Jack had already visited it once. Perhaps, if he dove in there, he might have a chance.

It was almost suicidal. There was another B-Grade guarding the Animal Abyss, as well as several magic formations around it. Even if he managed to make it inside, the gravitational field around the Animal Abyss was a land where even B-Grades regu-larly perished. Any spatial anomaly he ran into could suck him into the dark hole—if that happened, he would die instantly. Eva Solvig wouldn't even need to act.

Even if he wasn't sucked into a spatial anomaly and somehow managed to hide in there, so what? They'd just surround the Abyss. It wasn't too large. Eva's perception could easily cover all the surrounding space and wait for him to exit.

Maybe I can hide until reinforcements arrive?

Jack disliked this path, but what choice did he have? When

every other option meant certain death, the almost-certain death sounded ideal.

As for returning to Hell to try and escape through a teleporter, that was impossible for several reasons, the greatest of which being that Eva was between him and that planet.

He angled his flight, shooting sideways into the void. That allowed Eva to momentarily catch up. "Where do you think you're going?" she shouted, pushing out a palm. They were still separated by ten miles, but that distance was nothing to a B-Grade. Her palm crashed down, locking space around Jack and forcing him to face it. He turned, shouted, and smashed out a Supernova. The void shattered. His barely-regenerated hand was broken again, and he was sent spinning away while losing massive quantities of blood.

Ignoring the pain, he regained control of his flight and used the momentum to soar deeper into space, directly toward the Animal Abyss.

"Useless!" Eva shouted, easily deducing his destination but not caring.

Jack cradled his hand as he shot through the void. His eyes were narrowed, and his teeth gnashed. The Animal Abyss was close to Hell, but that was only at an astronomical scale. In truth, the two were millions of miles apart. Even for Jack, flying such a distance without a starship would take a long time, let alone with someone chasing him at top speed.

He braced himself for an extended chase. He slowed down a little, adopting a more manageable pace. This would allow Eva to attack him more frequently, but he could use the Life Drop's energy to regenerate his wounds. He couldn't use it to keep flying.

"You cannot escape, Jack Rust," Eva felt the need to remind him.

The chase continued. Endless millions of miles passed

around them, vanishing in the tracts of time. They flew for hours. Clashed hundreds of times. Yet, in the deep darkness of the universe, it felt like they were staying still—the surroundings remained exactly the same.

Jack was beyond exhausted. He was already running on fumes, gasping for breath. His Dao Tree felt caught in draught, its roots desperately trying to absorb energy from his barren soul. He didn't even know how far the Animal Abyss was—it wasn't like he could see it. In the depths of his soul, he was afraid he'd miss it. Even the outermost formation around it was only a million miles wide, just a grain of sand in all this empty space. Jack's only compass was his sense of direction—if he miscalculated, he would be lost in endless void.

A new attack crashed into his back. His defenses had waned over time. He was sent tumbling forward, no longer able to smoothly utilize the momentum as his back was ripped open. White bones showed, and scarlet blood spilled out.

As he tumbled forward, he finally noticed something: a faint layer of trembling space up ahead, stretching for as far as his perception could go. Hope surged into his limbs. This was the magic formation a million miles away from the Animal Abyss, the one he'd slowly unraveled before to avoid being detected.

There was no time to do that now. He shot right through, the ripples of his Dao spreading across the formation and announcing his presence like a trumpet in a sealed room. The B-Grade guarding this place would soon move against him.

Eva followed right behind, similarly disregarding the formation. She drew close again. Even after all this time, she didn't seem to have lost much energy, and her attacks came stronger and more frequently than before.

Jack was bruised and battered, bones showing in several parts as the pace of his regeneration fell off, but he still had some life left in him. The Animal Abyss was only a few thousand miles away. He hoped he could reach it.

"What is going on!?" an aggressive voice rang through the void as a leonine appeared in the distance. He wore a pale yellow robe, and his eyes shone like lightning, hands clasped behind his back. Most importantly, he was positioned right between Jack and the Animal Abyss.

And he was a middle B-Grade.

Shit!

"In the name of the Hand of God, capture this man!" Eva shouted, but the Ancestor didn't need a reminder. He had watched a recording of Jack's Grand Duel on Hell five years ago and clearly recognized him.

"You're Jack Rust!" he exclaimed, already assuming a battle stance. "We lost a good man because of you. I don't know what you're doing here, but since you came, you can forget about leaving!"

Jack didn't know whether to laugh or cry. He really didn't have the energy to deal with this old man. He simply barreled forward, directly at the Ancestor, investing half his remaining energy into a powerful Supernova.

The Ancestor sneered. "Hmph!"

"Don't underestimate him!" Eva shouted from behind, exploding in a burst of speed to reach Jack and attack him. The Ancestor shot out a punch that could cover the void—faint traces of electricity swam around it, and its colossal power was visible for all to see.

Tracts of space shattered. Jack was trapped between two massive attacks, each stronger than what he could achieve in his peak state. In that razor-sharp moment, he couldn't afford to hesitate. Supernova shot forth, colliding directly with the Ancestor's punch. At the same time, he released a burst of Fist Dao behind him, weakening the impact of Eva's attack.

His strike collided with the Ancestor's. For a moment, it was like a new sun was born. Both attacks wrapped around each other in a vast eruption of power, eventually dispersing. "*What?*" the Ancestor exclaimed. He hadn't gone all-out just now, but someone an entire Grade lower had matched his attack?

Even with Eva's warning, he'd thought that attacking earnestly was already being far too careful and even a little humiliating. Yet, this man could *resist it?*

As the two attacks met and were mutually neutralized, so was the majority of Jack's momentum, as he'd relied on it to make his attack somewhat stronger. His hand had evaporated from the elbow down, sending streams of burning pain into his brain. It was right then, before he could regather himself, that Eva's attack arrived. It was like a waterfall of white acid, raining onto his back and attempting to purify him to death. He screamed again. He used almost all of his power to resist, but white waves still spread over him, burning him deeply and sending him flying. His entire body was smoking, while white patches of lifelessness had appeared all over his skin, slowly drilling in.

In that moment, he focused completely. He ignored the pain and used some of his energy to block the invasive Dao of Purity. At the same time, he turned and smashed another Supernova into the void behind him, utilizing the momentum of Eva's attack to shoot forward at tremendous speed. He even warped space around him to go even faster.

He was like a missile. The Ancestor was in his way, already activating his electricity-based battle form, but there was no time. Jack was just too fast. All the Ancestor could do was stick out his claws and rake them down on Jack, carving three deep red lines into his already mangled chest.

Jack felt his life almost whisked away. Those claws had shattered his ribcage and passed a finger away from his heart.

But he'd made it past.

He was shooting into the distance at extreme speed. The Ancestor laughed. "Fool! There's a formation there! You're trapped!"

There was a second formation surrounding the Animal Abyss, this one at only ten thousand miles away. It also had an isolating effect. If one wanted to pass, they needed to vibrate their bodies at a specific frequency, and finding that frequency couldn't be done in a short amount of time. In the Ancestor's eyes, and even in Eva's, Jack was trapped.

It was to their surprise, then, that he passed through the barrier like it was nothing.

"What!" the Ancestor exclaimed. "How?"

How could they know that Jack had already been to this place? He hadn't gone past the formation because he couldn't bypass its detection mechanisms, but he'd already discovered the frequency.

"After him!" Eva shouted. She reached the barrier and used pure force to tear it open, passing through and letting it regenerate behind her. At her level, she could just barely achieve it. As for the Animal Kingdom Ancestor, he naturally knew the frequency.

Except the barrier was only ten thousand miles away from the Animal Abyss. Such a distance was short at their level. Jack was already halfway there. At some point, his perception ran into a strange field in front of him, dispersing in all directions and becoming useless. This was the abyss's treacherous spatial field, filled with endless dangers and surrounding one of the deadliest objects in the universe.

"Stop!" Eva shouted, unleashing another attack. So did the Ancestor.

Before their attacks could reach Jack, he gritted his teeth and shot straight into the abyss!

CHAPTER FOURTEEN

HIGHEST STAKES

THE ANIMAL ABYSS—THE PERIPHERY OF THIS BLACK HOLE—WAS A mysterious place where even B-Grades regularly perished. One's perception was useless, while spacetime was so chaotically warped that finding one's way through here was basically impossible. Even the Animal Kingdom, with its million years of history, had not managed to solve this enigma.

Additionally, Jack was a lamp without oil. His already lacking strength was deeply exhausted, he was injured all over, and generally in terrible shape. Wanting to survive this place would be difficult—let alone escape Eva Solvig afterward.

The boundary between normal space and the abyss was invisible. Black within, black without. The only indication it existed was a thin sheet of chaotic space far less orderly and far more powerful than the formations the Animal Kingdom had established.

Before anyone could stop him, Jack had dived into the Animal Abyss.

His world was toppled. Everything swam. Light no longer moved in straight lines, making his vision unreliable, while space was so deeply scrabbled that no matter how deep into its layers he searched, any sense of direction was missing. From the moment he entered, he was blind and deaf, oblivious to the wider world. All his mighty perception could illuminate was the space ten feet around him. That was nothing. He was basically face-to-face with the darkness.

Jack had instantly come to a halt. Running around here was a surefire way to die. He didn't even know whether his pursuers would follow, but he hoped they wouldn't, because he still didn't dare to move quickly.

Even if they did want to chase him, it wouldn't be easy. The chaotic spacetime made it so that even if they entered from the same location, they wouldn't necessarily arrive at the same place. They'd just be lost somewhere else in the abyss.

Jack waited and didn't sense anyone following him. That didn't mean he could relax, however—this area was completely submerged in chaotic turbulences of spacetime. Ever-changing distortions barraged him from all sides, and resisting them took a toll on his already spent energy. He was forced to conjure a barrier of the Dao around him. If he let up, his body would be teleported to a dozen locations at once and he would die.

Jack gritted his teeth. He couldn't do this forever. This was crisis after crisis, out of the frying pan and into the fire. He quickly calmed himself and investigated the spacetime around him, seeking patterns. He found some—altering his barrier in accordance, he dropped his energy expenditure to a level which could last him around an hour.

This was already great. A normal C-Grade would be torn apart as soon as they entered this space storm, and an early B-Grade could have used brute force to persist for around an hour as well. To achieve the same while severely spent and wounded was a testament to Jack's deep understanding of spacetime.

It was also useless. While he stayed here, Eva Solvig could freely restore her power outside. She would pursue him as soon as he exited, and the disparity between them would only grow larger the longer he stayed inside.

"Damn!" Jack shouted, clenching his only remaining fist. The other arm had disintegrated from the shoulder down and was very slowly regenerating—at no lack of pain. He'd been through this before, and calmed his mind, shutting away the pain to think.

What can I do? he considered. *Damn it all, what can I do?*

At least two powerful B-Grades were waiting outside. Chaotic space storms existed inside—soon to tear him to shreds. Nobody was coming to help him.

Am I doomed?

The thought was bitter. If Jack was being honest with himself, he never expected to die here. He'd been through countless desperate situations before—he always found a way to turn the tables, turning certain death into an opportunity. Yet, no matter how he wrung his brain, there was no hope to be found this time. He couldn't even imagine a scenario in which he lived.

His only possible salvation was the black hole at the center of the Animal Abyss. He suspected it was not an ordinary one, and as for what it was, he had no idea. The chances of it helping him escape were astronomically low, so low it could only serve as a suicidal final resort.

However, the abyss itself sometimes contained powerful treasures—perhaps he could discover a high-grade starship, or a treasure which could erupt with enough power to vanquish his pursuers.

Yet... how could such powerful treasures be found just because he needed them?

I need to search, Jack concluded.

Suddenly, a black whirlpool entered his perception range, only ten feet away. Jack sensed a powerful suction force. It was unbelievably intense—as if he'd ran into the actual maw of the black hole. His mind cried out in panic, and he pushed away from it with every bit of power he could command. His only saving grace was that the whirlpool was pulled along by the space currents at an extremely slow speed, like a stone thrown by a mortal. He just barely managed to escape its trajectory and avoid getting sucked inside. Cold sweat covered his body.

If he entered that thing, he would absolutely die.

What the hell was that? he wondered, batting his eyelids to push away the sweat. *The black hole? Or... a spatial tunnel into it?*

Unfortunately, the information he had about this place was very basic. He could only assume the black whirlpool was a spatial tunnel sucking things into the black hole—nothing else could possess such suction force in this place. His understandings into spacetime soon helped him arrive to a hypothesis.

The event horizon of this black hole has shattered! It's turned into countless small whirlpools roaming around in here. That's why the abyss is such a chaotic and dangerous place—but how could an event horizon break?

A black hole's event horizon was the boundary after which nothing could escape, not even light. It was the true edge of a black hole. However, it was nothing but a line in space—there was no reason for it to break into pieces.

Something was very, very wrong with this black hole.

Jack gulped. He could vaguely sense that the chaotic storms grew more intense the deeper he went—would these whirlpools become more common? If they traveled just a little bit faster, he couldn't necessarily avoid them.

Going deeper was dangerous. But not going meant certain death, and he was also rapidly running out of time. Jack grimaced, then resolved to search along the edges of the Animal Abyss. He had no idea what he expected to find, but he couldn't just sit here. On the bright side, he had an hour to consider it—

if Eva Solvig braved the risk to enter this space, he might find a way to one-up her.

In these chaotic space flows, finding one's direction was challenging. Most people in Jack's position might have headed deeper inside while thinking they were going out, or end up walking in circles and never escaping. Jack could use his understandings of spacetime to just barely navigate—he shifted himself to the very edge of the abyss, only a few feet away from normal space. He then turned his perception range into a needle and stuck it out, using it as a feeler to grasp the situation outside. He wanted to see what Eva Solvig and the other enemies had decided to do.

Of course, perceiving things like this was difficult. The image he got was blurry and vague. He could, however, see some things—and, as soon as he did, his blood turned cold. His eyes widened. For the first time since the Integration, or perhaps since he was born, he felt genuine, bone-deep horror.

No!

———

Artus Emberheart had been left behind. He couldn't keep up with Eva Solvig or Jack Rust. He sped forth regardless, following them with just his eyes. They were in empty space, after all, and the clashes of those two were colorful.

Hmm? The Animal Abyss? he thought, watching them turn. His lips curved into a grin. Too bad, Jack Rust. You can never escape. He patted the sack hanging off his waist, still speeding after them. He was slower, but not by too much—their constant fighting slowed them down.

After Jack entered the Animal Abyss, it only took Artus a few minutes to catch up. The Elders of the Animal Kingdom were behind him—from start to now, he hadn't spared them a single glance, and they hadn't spoken to him either. They'd been like brothers and sisters once—but after his exile, they had nothing to talk about.

Artus bowed as soon as he arrived. "Ancestor Red Lion. Ancestor Heaven Lance," he greeted the two B-Grades—the one who'd participated in the original trap had arrived here before him.

The two Ancestors did not reply. Only Red Lion, the patriarch of his Emberheart family, spared him a glance—this was the same person who'd exiled him once upon a time, but their statuses were similar now. How the world turns.

"Jack Rust entered the Animal Abyss," Eva Solvig said, addressing Artus. "I've already been briefed on this place. The Animal Kingdom has understated its importance to the Hand of God—a matter we will certainly investigate later."

"Just a misunderstanding," said Ancestor Red Lion, taking the lead as the strongest person from the Animal Kingdom side. "What do you suggest we do, Envoy? With Jack Rust's skills in the Space Dao, he can only remain in there for some minutes. I believe we should not pursue. If he doesn't exit soon, he will perish inside."

This Ancestor was afraid to chase Jack into the abyss. That was why he said what he said. However, how could Eva Solvig not see through him?

"I have no time to waste," she replied calmly. "If Jack Rust does not exit soon, the two of you will go in to look for him. Since you safeguard the information around this Animal Abyss so intensely, surely you will be more familiar with it than him."

The Ancestors bowed, both cursing inwardly.

Eva Solvig was not done speaking, "Fortunately for you, that might not be necessary. Artus?"

Artus Emberheart had been waiting five years for this moment. His lips spread so wide they almost cracked. A manic glint seeped into his gaze, and he roughly dug a hand into his pouch to retrieve an object.

On closer inspection, it wasn't an object, but a person. A small one. And Jack, who was watching from inside the abyss, knew exactly who it was. Even after a few years of not meeting each other, even though the other person had grown a lot, Jack could never mistake this aura.

This was Eric. His five-year-old son—alive, gagged, and shaking in fear.

"I know you're watching, Jack Rust!" Artus shouted at the abyss. "An eye for an eye, blood for blood. You once killed my son; I will now kill yours before your very eyes! Hahahaha!"

CHAPTER FIFTEEN

AN UNFORTUNATE LETTER
TWO MONTHS AGO...

ARTUS EMBERHEART WAS IN A TERRIBLE MOOD. HIS MORTAL ENEMY was back in town but kept evading capture. It made Artus feel useless. Like he was fumbling his only chance.

He was currently resting inside the Hand of God starship he commanded. Endless stars stretched outside the window, yet he couldn't care less.

A knock came on his door.

"What?" he barked out.

A trembling voice responded, "Sir... There is a message for you, sir."

"I'm busy! Fuck off!"

"Sir, it's... It's an important message from the New Cathedral, sir... The coordinates of Earth-387 have been discovered."

Artus had been about to lash out at this useless underling, but he paused. "Earth-387? The planet of Jack Rust?"

"Yes, sir! You had asked to be notified immediately if that happened! I rushed here to let you know!"

Artus remained frozen. This was like a dream come true.

When the Hand of God occupied the Cathedral, they naturally took control of the Cathedral's teleporter as well. That teleporter connected to all Church outposts across the universe, but there were obviously fail-safes. The locations and frequencies were all encoded—moreover, even activating the teleporter safely required certain secret procedures, so it couldn't be used.

The only ones who knew those codes were the Arch Priestess of the Church—its highest leader—and Elder Shield, who'd managed the teleporter but had died in the battle for the Cathedral.

Since then, the Hand of God had assigned experts to decode the information, though they never expected anything. It was just too complex a task, and every teleporter entry was encoded in a unique manner. Even decoding one destination every thousand years would have been a good result.

But those experts had already decoded a destination? And it was the very Earth-387 Artus was desperately searching for? This was almost too good to be true!

However, if he received this report, it had to be.

"Hahaha!" Artus laughed out loud. "Luck has finally abandoned you, Jack Rust!"

He flashed outside his cabin, grabbing the underling by the shoulder with a strong grip. "Tell me more," he commanded, madness glinting in his eyes. "Has anybody visited that planet?"

"Not yet, sir..." the underling replied, fear clouding his face. "The matter was reported to Envoy Solvig, who respectfully asks you to use the frequency and occupy the planet in the name of the Hand of God."

As the man spoke, he handed over a sheet of paper containing complex teleporter frequencies. The name "Earth-387" was written underneath.

Artus laughed again. He snatched the piece of paper and, without giving the underling another glance, teleported away. He barely even watched where he went—his mind too preoccupied imagining Jack Rust's face when he found out his planet had been destroyed.

Eva Solvig had commanded Artus to occupy the planet, but he wasn't planning to obey. Jack was his mortal enemy. He would just destroy the planet and claim they'd put up resistance. That was reasonable.

Plus, by assigning this task to him, Eva had tacitly accepted such an outcome.

After a series of short-range teleportations, he reached a large-scale teleporter only half an hour later. He used his authority to cut the line and input the frequencies directly. Light flashed, and he was gone.

Space warped around him, in much the same way his soul did. Artus couldn't contain himself. He spent the teleportation period laughing. The tables had finally turned in his favor. He was heading to Earth!

He landed in a cloud of dust. His perception howled out, covering a large landmass. He was in a small forest—green trees rose out of the ground, while several weak cultivators patrolled the surrounding area.

A brorilla stood right in front of the teleporter, shocked by Artus's sudden arrival. It raised a hand to stop him—Artus simply pierced through its heart, killing it instantly. The brorilla toppled to the ground. Alarms blared. The land came alive, but Artus didn't care. He was a late C-Grade—even with his Dao cracked, there was nobody on this planet who could stop him. He shot into the air.

"Hahahaha! People of Jack Rust, prepare to suffer!"

He gathered a large amount of power, intending to decimate the land for many miles around—keeping the teleporter intact so he could leave later. Just as he punched toward the ground, however, sharp whistling filled his ears. His attack was sliced to pieces, only breaking a few large trees. A young man holding twin daggers faced Artus in midair—this was Dorman Whistles, the boy who'd fought in the Integration Tournament once upon a time before joining the Black Hole Church.

Jack had met Dorman at the Cathedral. At that time, Dorman had been bloated and overweight due to consuming a far too powerful treasure. However, before leaving for the hidden realm, Jack had used his understandings into life energy to suck all the extra power out of Dorman, restoring him to his original fit condition. He'd also given the young man more than enough Dao stones to break through.

Three years later, Dorman had reached the middle C-Grade. He'd returned to Earth when the Cathedral was invaded and remained ever since, acting as the planet's protector.

Today, he was finally needed.

Artus laughed again. "I don't know who you are and nor do I care! You're only a four-fruit cultivator! Do you really think you can stop me?"

"Yes," Dorman replied simply. He kept his daggers at the ready—his eyes were cold.

A new arrival shot toward them from the other side of the planet. Artus hesitated—the aura of the incoming person was much stronger than his own. When they arrived, his eyes widened.

"You!" he said.

"Me," Elder Huali replied, her smile not reaching her eyes. She had received the frequency of Earth's teleporter from Shol and retreated here when the Exploding Sun was annihilated. Not many people knew of her existence—she lived in isolation, still grieving the loss of her faction and many of her fellow cultivators.

It seemed like a joke that she'd been made Grand Elder just a few years ago.

Of course, Huali knew about the ongoing war and the

Cathedral being occupied. However, Dorman came from the Cathedral, and he was aware of how extensively encoded its teleporter was. The Hand finding their frequencies had been basically impossible—that was the only reason why there were no countermeasures in place and why they'd let the teleporter stand. They needed it so Shol, who was searching for Jack in System space, could teleport back when he found him.

Artus paled. He was a seven-fruit C-Grade with a broken Dao—his combat efficiency had never been lower. Facing him was a talented four-fruit and a powerful nine-fruit cultivator. No matter how much he wanted to destroy this planet, it was impossible. He needed Eva Solvig. She should have come along —but how could they have imagined that a peak C-Grade was hiding in this tiny planet?

It was too late for regrets.

Artus turned into a ray of light, shooting toward the teleporter. Dorman and Huali dove after him, but they didn't intend to fight. They were too powerful. If they really battled here, though they would certainly win, the continent below them would not come out unscathed.

Their intention was to ensure Artus left the planet while keeping casualties to a minimum. To them, this was already a terrible situation. If he went berserk, they couldn't stop him before he eradicated tens of thousands of lives, including Jack's family which was nearby. They just hoped he wasn't too crazy.

As for Artus himself, he was filled with bile. He had finally discovered Jack Rust's planet, and not only could he do nothing about it, he also had to willingly walk away. After he left, they would certainly destroy the teleporter. He couldn't return. This was his only opportunity.

Yet, he feared that if he attacked, they would ignore all casualties to kill him. However great his hatred for Jack Rust was, his wish for self-preservation was stronger.

Once again, he had been one-upped.

He began activating the teleporter from afar, roaring out in impotent fury. These two C-Grades had robbed him of his best chance for revenge. He hated this. He hated everything.

Although, he could still attack once. They couldn't stop him without using excessive force. He gathered power, intending to smash into the ground next to the teleporter as he passed by and at least destroy part of the forest.

Then, just before attacking, he paused. His spread-out perception caught something. A child was sitting in a treehouse very close to the teleporter. A small young boy, barely five years old, watching with a mouth he had forgotten to close.

Artus had met Jack Rust before—he would never forget that man's aura, and he could tell that this boy carried a hint of that same aura. It was Jack Rust's son.

Artus's eyes widened, and a laugh bubbled to the surface. "What a great gift you gave me, Jack Rust!"

Artus abandoned his attack. The gathered energy caused a backlash inside him that he ignored—instead, he directed the entirety of his power toward that boy, no longer caring about enraging the other two C-Grades. Before he even reached the teleporter, Artus made a grasping motion, and the boy flew toward him as if pulled by gravity. He yelped.

"NO!" came two voices from above, accompanied by a shrill scream from deeper inside the forest. A D-Grade, dark-skinned woman flew toward the boy like she'd gone mad. A large brorilla followed her. Yet, these two were weak. As for Dorman and Huali, they could not attack in earnest, otherwise they'd blow up the entire forest and kill everyone. And, without using real power, they couldn't stop him.

Streams of power fell toward Artus, attempting to distract him and save the boy. Artus laughed. He let the attacks land, let himself get bloodied all over. He raised a hand to protect his

vitals and let it be cut off from the wrist. This would permanently weaken him, but so what? His Dao had already cracked.
He was never going to advance again. All he cared about was
causing Jack Rust pain, and this little boy was his ticket to
achieving just that.

"NO!" the sky rained shouts yet again, but there was
nobody who could stop Artus. A dazed Eric Rust fell into his
grasp. Artus flew into the teleporter and activated it, whisking
them both away. Screams filled Artus's ears like music.

He was heavily injured, and he would need to spend even
more power to ensure this mortal boy arrived safely at the other
side of the teleportation... but it was all worth it.

Jack Rust had taken everything from him. Now, he
would pay.

———

Jack was frozen from the soul up. The chaotic space storms
around him disappeared, as did the powerful enemies pursuing
him, leaving only Artus Emberheart and Eric Rust.

His own son had been taken hostage. This was... unbelievable.

"Hahaha!" Artus laughed madly. "How does it feel, Jack?
Your own son being at the mercy of another. You, powerless to
stop me. This is perfect!" He tore the tape covering Eric's
mouth, letting him release a terrified scream.

"Dad!"

Eric wore tattered blue robes. His hair was dirty, his cheeks
marred by tears, and his eyes sunken as if he'd been like this a
while. He hadn't started cultivating yet—the only reason he
survived in the vacuum of space was a Dao shield conjured by
Artus. The moment it went down, Eric would die instantly.

It was also Artus who'd used his powers to spread Eric's voice through the void, letting it reach Jack's ears.

Hearing it, Jack was completely and utterly stupefied. His panic subsided, turning into cold terror matched with calmness, and a powerful instinct surfaced from deep within his soul. He had to save Eric—no matter what.

How did this happen? he wondered as his mind turned somber. *Have they conquered Earth? Do they have my family? Or just Eric?*

One part of his mind said that if they had everyone, there was no reason to bring out only Eric. Another part couldn't shake off the fear.

"I know you can hear me, Jack!" Artus shouted from outside the Animal Abyss. "Come out or I'll kill your boy!"

Eric could hear this as well. His little eyes widened as he just realized what was truly going on, and his fists balled up. He stubbornly shut his mouth—even with things having reached this point, he didn't want to endanger his father.

But it no longer mattered.

Going out there was suicide for Jack. He knew that, even if he did surrender himself, the chances of saving Eric were nearly nonexistent. But he still had to do it, because if he ignored the death of his own son, he wouldn't be human. He wouldn't be a Fist.

With steady steps, he exited the Animal Abyss. He now hovered in the void. Darkness was behind him, and invincible enemies at the front. Yet, Jack stood brave and tall, not cowering in the slightest. His many wounds were badges of honor.

"Release my son," he commanded. "You can have me."

CHAPTER SIXTEEN

THE RESPONSIBILITY OF A FATHER

JACK AND ERIC HADN'T SEEN EACH OTHER IN OVER THREE YEARS. IN Jack's memory, Eric was just a little boy with whom he'd toured the world and built a little treehouse in the forest. Besides a few vacation weeks, he'd only been consistently present for the first six months after his children were born; he watched them grow, watched them develop their personalities and become aware of themselves. He'd heard them call him daddy.

Now, facing the five-year-old boy that was Eric, though the form was slightly unfamiliar, he could never mistake him for anyone else. Fatherly love filled Jack's heart, a hard but gentle thing, and he could feel it deep in his soul that there was nothing more important in his life than protecting his son. This was his job. This was the reason he'd adventured and trained for so long, the reason he'd been mostly absent from his children's lives. Even if it meant sacrificing himself, he wouldn't bat an eye.

This was the responsibility of a father.

As for Eric, his eyes were hazy. New tears pooled, though he thought he'd run out. This was his father, the sky of his skies, the king of his planet. He'd heard stories about this man his entire life. This was Eric's hero. And, coupled with the gentle love they'd shared when Jack was back home, Eric both loved and deeply looked up to his father.

In these past three years, Eric had grown, but Jack hadn't changed in the slightest. Only, Eric now got to see the other side of Jack—the warrior, the hero, the legend. He was filled with joy at his father still being alive—he hadn't shown up for three years, after all—but even deeper, something in Jack's heroism stirred Eric's heart. He was a burden. Because of him, his hard-working father was in trouble. That was why Eric bit his lips and refused to scream and cry—even if it killed him, he wouldn't burden his father anymore.

Father and son exchanged a glance, and Jack knew everything. His heart grew heavier.

"Release him?" Artus laughed. "Where, into the vacuum of space? Do you really want me to?"

"You know what I mean," Jack replied calmly. "It's me you hate. Don't take out your anger on children."

Artus laughed again. "And who's going to stop me?" The hand that was holding Eric from the nape tightened, causing him to twitch, though he did not scream. "You did not show mercy when you killed my son. Now, you're begging me to spare yours. Just how pitiful can you be?"

Jack didn't reply. His only priority was saving Eric. Nothing else mattered.

The two Animal Kingdom Ancestors remained silent at the sidelines.

"I will approach and apprehend you," Eva Solvig stated. "Do not resist."

"Can you guarantee my son's safety if I surrender?"

"No."

The word hung heavy in the void, and Jack had no grounds to argue. He let his aura drop, indicating his surrender. Eva

Solvig flew closer, caging him in a field of purity—he could no longer escape. "We want your death," she admitted, "but the secrets on your body are tempting. My orders were to capture you alive if possible. Don't force me to kill you."

"Have you captured Earth?" Jack couldn't help but ask.

"No. We found a way in but were pushed back and the teleporter destroyed. This boy is the only one we got—the rest of your family is safe."

He glanced at her. Eva Solvig was his enemy, but there was no great hatred between them. At this stage, since Jack had already surrendered, she'd let her heart soften a bit and given him some information. The situation he was in was something that any cultivator would dread.

And, perhaps, she felt a twinge of guilt. The cultivation world had no greater taboo than going after someone's mortal family.

"Thank you," he said. "Please promise to protect my son. I have surrendered. You don't need him anymore. Drop him off at a mortal planet and let him fend for himself—he will be fine."

She smiled coldly. "Sending the wolf back to the mountain?"

"He can swear to never rise against the Hand of God and never seek revenge. I'm begging you."

Jack had never spoken such words before. Yet, he didn't feel the least bit hurt—this was the highest purpose of his existence, and all concessions were within reason.

However, Eva Solvig shook her head. "I was not the one who captured him, nor do I care about either of you. Your son's life belongs to Artus. Convince him."

Jack raised his head to stare at Artus. He gritted his teeth. His eyes were shaking. "Please," he said.

Artus met his stare with madness—then laughed. "What an idiot you are, Jack Rust! What a complete imbecile! Cultivators live for thousands of years—what do you care about a son? You could have hundreds of them, thousands. One boy is nothing! He's not even particularly talented in cultivation. You could be an A-Grade, a king of the world, you could have all the women and wealth you desired, all the authority, all the power, and you threw it all away for a single F-Grade boy! Truly, you are the most idiotic genius I have ever encountered, a complete waste of talent! I pity you, Jack Rust! *I pity you!*"

Jack let all these words wash over him. He did not care. All he wanted was Eric's safety. However, his heart was beginning to seize, because even now, Artus's grip had not eased on Eric's throat.

"You once told me that I was nothing, just an insignificant character for you to surpass! Just a stepping-stone on your road to mastery. Tell me now, Jack Rust, am I still insignificant? When I hold your son's life in the palm of my hand, am I worthless? When I made you surrender, am I useless? Hahaha!"

Artus raved crazily, seeming as if he'd forgotten about the presence of everyone else. Jack's heart had frozen over—his eyes were wide, his breath short. Time slowed down, and it felt like he was watching everything from the bottom of a well, desperately far away from reality. Despair was crawling up his spine. He was beginning to sense that Artus wasn't planning to let go.

"You killed *my* son, Jack Rust!" Artus shouted. "You *humiliated* me, had me exiled, and ruined my life. You are the person I hate most in the world. I want to tear out your spine, flay your skin, and suck the marrow from your bones. I want to destroy your planet and rape your wife, kill your sons and enslave your daughters. Everyone you know will die at my hand. And this... This is just the first!"

"NO!" Jack roared. His aura erupted. The cosmos around him was suppressed as he tried to drill through the domain of purity, but Eva Solvig flashed before him and slapped out. He was thrown backward, powerless to resist. Her eyes were cold.

"NO!" Jack roared again, shaking the world, but it was too late. There was nothing he could do. In a fit of mad laughter, Artus squeezed, snapping Eric's throat. The boy died instantly. Only a shocked look remained in his open eyes, since he'd realized what was going to happen at the last moment.

Eric was dead.

"Hahahaha!" Artus laughed still. "How does it taste, Jack Rust? The despair you made me feel, I will repay a hundredfold! This is fate, this is justice! Hahaha!"

Jack was no longer listening. His gaze was glued on Eric's listless eyes. His own son, gone. Dead. Because of him.

There were no words to describe what Jack felt. He couldn't believe this. His soul was whisked away. The despair, horror, grief, and regret mixed into a dark cocktail of epic proportions, completely blocking out his sanity. He lost himself.

With a loud sound, a crack appeared on his Dao Tree, splitting it down the middle. The Fist had given way. The Fist had failed. Everything that he was, everything that he did, had been for nothing.

It was over.

A primal roar emerged from Jack's lungs, tearing his throat. The void shivered like a beast was born. A dark storm raged inside him. The pain was indescribable. The rage, complete. It was like dark winds blew from behind and propped him up, throwing him forward in a fit of rage which could only be expressed with a single word:

REVENGE!

He would kill Artus Emberheart.

He would kill everyone.

The domain of purity came down to suppress him, and he refused. Every Dao Root and Dao Fruit he possessed burned with blinding brilliance, venting all their power in a single instant. His Daos of Life, Death, Space, and Time bloomed at the same time, giving him unprecedented power. He smashed a fist into the domain of purity, shaking but not breaking it.

He reached even deeper. He invaded his own soul and grabbed the Life Drop, no longer caring about his safety. He crazily siphoned its power. His body grew taller. Another two arms appeared, and he kept pulling, damn the consequences. More energy than ever flooded his body. His blood vessels groaned and cracked. His muscles tore. His hair fell off. His body turned stronger and stronger, far surpassing its previous limits in a single moment of brilliance traded for everything. A primal titan stepped into the void. His fists could shatter stars, his stomps could crack the earth.

The tremendous stream of power scraped his Dao Tree from the inside, drying it up, but he still kept pulling until he was a bomb, a devil whose only purpose was to kill Artus Emberheart.

Jack roared again. He shot forward, and this time, the domain of purity shattered like glass. Eva raised her brows and flashed away. Jack had never been more powerful—but what did it matter? No matter how strong he was, he couldn't bring his son back from the dead.

His grief intensified. His rage rose, the only form of protection he possessed against his mind breaking. He hurtled forward like a meteor, channeling all of his power into his right arm, intending to explode it in Artus's face.

The leonine laughed as he drew back. "Savor the despair, Jack! Savor it! You caused this!"

Eva Solvig flashed in Jack's path. She no longer held back. A tremendous wall of white came crashing down, filling the universe, and clashed head-on against Jack's attack. Shockwaves spread everywhere. Spacetime was sundered. The world shook. Eva had to retreat, a line of blood flowing down her lips, but Jack was far more injured. His right arm had completely disintegrated to produce this explosion—his entire body was a wreck, every cell teetering on the verge of collapse. He could barely fly through the void, let alone fight. All of his power had been burnt for that one strike.

As for Eva, she remained on guard, her eyes calm.

"Hahahahaha!" Jack laughed, mad with grief and pain. "I couldn't save my son, and I cannot take revenge... How unfair the world is! *How ugly*! I did everything right, and I still lost everything! I am useless! Useless!"

"That's right, Jack Rust!" Artus shouted. "You deserve this! You made this happen! You and your weakness!"

Weakness...

The word struck Jack's fragmented mind like the deep sound of a gong. *That's right. I am weak. I couldn't save Eric, and I couldn't get revenge... All because I am weak. It is my fault.*

I couldn't save Eric... I have already failed. I must get revenge— no matter what.

A hint of reason appeared in Jack's bloodshot eyes. "Artus Emberheart!" he shouted, his voice shaking with darkness. "I swear that I will make you regret this day! I will make you wish you were dead! I will kill your children and disciples, I will slay your family, everyone you've ever loved. I will wash the universe with their blood. When I'm done with you, the name Emberheart will no longer exist in this galaxy! I, Jack Rust, swear this on my son's life!"

Artus laughed from afar. "I look forward to it, Jack Rust! But what a pity—you will die today, right here, right now!"

Jack did not reply. His mind was on the verge of breaking— all he could focus on was revenge, the only way to distract himself from the endless pain. But there, in the deepest recesses of his mind, a hint of the true Jack Rust remained. The hero, the warrior. He needed to get revenge—and, as liberating as it would be to charge again and die right here, that would not achieve anything. It was the easy way out. He wouldn't die here. He would survive, and grow stronger, and return to make Artus Emberheart and everyone else involved weep bloody tears for this day. The debt would be paid back—a hundredfold.

Eva had expected him to attack and was ready to match him. Instead, he flew into the Animal Abyss before anyone could stop him. He no longer feared the space storms—his perception was spread out, looking for one of the black whirlpools.

He needed to survive. Staying here, either inside or outside the Animal Abyss, meant certain death. Nobody was coming to save him. This black hole was abnormal—since treasures could be spat out whole, it meant there was a separate space inside, or perhaps it led to some other place, like a wormhole.

That was his only chance of survival.

Of course, there was an overwhelming possibility of instant death. He would never have made this choice in normal circumstances—but now, there was nothing else.

He did not believe the world would abandon him yet again. If it did, he might as well die. At least they would never have the satisfaction of finding his body.

Jack located a black whirlpool, sucking everything in with promises of death. He unhesitatingly flew over—and was sucked inside.

CHAPTER SEVENTEEN

RIPPLES ACROSS THE UNIVERSE

INSIDE A STARSHIP SAILING AT FULL SPEED, A BRORILLA SUDDENLY opened his eyes. "No..." he muttered. For the first time since he was born, his voice held pain. "Big bro..."

Their souls were connected. The moment Jack's Dao cracked, Brock felt it like a spike of burning pain through his own heart, accompanied by deep, wrathful grief. Then, when Jack flew into the black hole, Brock's connection to him was abruptly... severed!

In Brock's understanding, this severing could only mean one thing.

A mournful wail filled the *Bromobile*. The lights dimmed, and the entire vessel shook. Gan Salin and Nauja covered their ears with tears in their eyes. Brock's grief rippled out—across the universe, every bro wept.

"*BIG BRO!*"

———

Jack's disappearance into the black hole affected even the world outside System space. On an asteroid shuttling through the void, a man sat alone. He was dressed in rags, while his teeth were yellowed from years of poor hygiene. Despite his rough exterior, his aura was dignified.

Everywhere the asteroid passed, large groups of Dao particles were absorbed, sent into this man's body, letting him cultivate at prodigious speed.

Suddenly, his meditation was interrupted. "Hmm?" His eyes snapped open, gazing in the direction of System space. He remained puzzled for a moment. His hands moved, piercing through reality to grasp at an invisible tether, a net encompassing the entire universe in which every change was clearly written.

He stared at the tether for a long time. "I see... Is this the end? Or a new beginning?"

He looked toward System space again. His gaze crossed trillions of miles, landing on a small, isolated planet filled with energy and brotherhood. He saw a dark-skinned woman, diligently cultivating, and a girl enduring an icy pond with a stubborn pout. His gaze pierced further, coming to rest on a wailing brorilla who seemed to have lost his mind. Finally, it settled on a black hole wrapped in an odd spatial field. No life came from inside it.

"I'm sorry, Jack," the Sage finally whispered. "I wish it didn't have to be like this..."

———

After the Purging began a year ago, the Elders of the Black Hole Church had not stayed put. There were dozens of them—as they received the summons of the Arch Priestess, almost all of them left seclusion, brimming with the intent to fight.

The Church was weaker than the Hand, but they could still fight back.

Tons of battles had erupted since then. A year was nothing to these organizations, but the war was kicking off. Each side possessed hundreds of B-Grades, tens of thousands of C-Grades. Planets and solar systems collapsed everywhere they fought. The rivers of stars inside and outside System space were disrupted.

The Church had once hidden many of their forces in inhabited planets. The Hand did not care—great battles erupted, vanquishing planets and ruining billions of innocent lives. And this was just the beginning.

The Church had been slowly pushed outside System space, forced to hide in distant galaxies. The powers of the Hand cultivators were limited there, but that didn't mean they wouldn't pursue—cataclysmic battles often washed away the cosmos, and even A-Grades clashed occasionally.

Finding the hidden Church forces in a vast Systemless galaxy was easier said than done, giving the weaker party opportunities to conduct guerilla warfare. That was the current state of the war, and it had reached a temporary stalemate with each side bleeding out the other.

However, the real powerhouses of each faction—the Archons—had yet to move. The Church had no desire to accelerate things, and as for the Hand, their true opponents were the Old Gods. The Church was only a prelude, thus they wanted to preserve their powers.

To better hide themselves, the Church had divided their forces in several parts, giving command of each of them to a high-level figure and having them hide separately.

In a Systemless galaxy called Great Divide, Elder Boatman commanded a heated battlefield. Though it was called as such, it spanned an area of tens of thousands of cubic light years. The forces he was responsible for were hidden in a dense nebula. Given they were only a few thousand people, finding them in such a large area was like searching for a needle in a haystack.

That didn't mean he would underestimate the Hand Elders. Powerful formations were arranged around their temporary residence, concealing them from divination and other detection magic.

Elder Boatman himself stood on the bridge of a massive starship, surrounded by his peak B-Grade lieutenants. A star map projection hovered before them. Their position was indicated as a blue dot, while the enemy forces they were aware of were shown as red triangles. In the past few months, through using various means, the enemy had pinpointed their location to within a range of a thousand light years. A carpet search was carried out. They couldn't hide forever, nor could the Church's other forces afford to send them back-up.

The situation was dire.

As the lieutenants discussed battle plans, Elder Boatman's ominous figure stood silent. He wore a dark cloak with a hood which covered his face, revealing only two red dots where his eyes should be, while a scythe hung on his back. Just from being there, a powerful aura rippled out, reminding the peak B-Grades not to slack off.

This discussion had already gone on for days, and Elder Boatman had yet to say a single word. Then suddenly, he moved. His head swiveled to the side, his urgency clear. Everyone shut their mouths.

Elder Boatman's heart shook. He'd sensed it when Jack had returned from the hidden realm—it was just that he was trapped here, so he couldn't rush over. Even if he managed it, he would be in great danger once he entered System space. The Immortals could pay a certain price to track him down. It was a high price, of course, but it was worth it for a late A-Grade like himself.

Ever since Jack and the death cube had reappeared, Elder Boatman could only hope for the best, unable to help. Now, however, he sensed the connection severed again. And not just that—unlike when Jack was trapped in a separate dimension, the severing this time was complete. It was highly likely the death cube had been destroyed—and anything that could destroy such an object was enough to kill Jack ten times over.

Elder Boatman had long been sunken in grief and helplessness. Now at his weakest, the news of Jack's death and the death cube's destruction left him hopeless. He shook his head, sighing deeply. "Have the heavens truly abandoned us?" he wondered. "Everything has an end. Death always comes. I thought this might not be the time for us, that we might have some hope left, but it seems our era has indeed come to an end. Without geniuses, we have no future—without future, our present is worthless."

Of course, those words were only spoken to himself. No matter how ugly things got, no matter how discouraged he was by this terrible news, he remained a war commander. He would never bring down the morale of his troops.

Even if fate seemed inescapable, he would still fight. He was Elder Boatman—and, in his long life, he had never once surrendered.

———

Silence reigned outside the Animal Abyss. Eva Solvig, Artus Emberheart, and the two Animal Kingdom Ancestors gazed at the darkness where Jack had just disappeared. Their perceptions couldn't pierce it—they would never have imagined he'd willingly throw himself into the actual black hole.

"That was unfortunate," Eva said, glancing at Artus. "If he loses his composure and stays inside until the space storms kill him, we'll have lost the opportunity to capture him alive. In fact, given his injuries, it's highly likely he's already dead."

She clearly blamed Artus—if he hadn't killed Jack's son and pushed him to the edge, Jack would have surrendered peacefully. However, she couldn't express those things aloud. At the end of the day, she was a Grade and a half above Jack, and she'd let him escape from within her grasp. No matter what desperate means he'd used, this was still a stain on her honor.

Artus Emberheart, however, didn't appear to care. A wide smile hung on his lips, and he was absorbed in his own thoughts.

"Good riddance," he finally replied. "Jack Rust was my life's most hated enemy. I feel better now. I only wish I could kill his son again, just to rub it in."

The two Ancestors glanced at each other. They were glad they'd exiled Artus—he was clearly insane.

If Eva shared the thought, she didn't show it. "We'll stand guard here for two days, then return."

"We can handle it, Envoy," one of the Ancestors stepped forward to say. "If Jack Rust emerges from the Animal Abyss, he'll be extremely weakened. We can easily subdue him."

Eva shook her head. "He has already given us too many surprises. Even if I have other responsibilities, I will not give that man a single chance to recover, no matter how impossible it seems. With his injuries and regenerative powers, I estimate he can last at most an hour inside the Abyss. I will personally stand guard for two days, and you will all join me. No matter what, he must not be allowed the slightest chance of recovering!"

The Ancestors glanced at each other again.

"*What's her problem?*" one of them asked telepathically. "*It's just a C-Grade. No matter how strong he is, there is no way he can last an hour at his current state, let alone two days. He's just gotten into her head."*

"Does it matter?" the other replied. *"I agree she's afraid for no reason, but two days mean nothing. Let's do as she says."*

The two Ancestors bowed, then spread out to surround the Animal Abyss from all directions. Artus and Eva Solvig did the same. Two days passed. As expected, Jack did not emerge.

And yet, Eva couldn't rid herself of the unreasonable feeling that Jack Rust was still alive. He had survived too many impossible situations. Moreover, he was far too talented. If she made the slightest miscalculation here and let him grow just a little bit more, maybe they'd need to mobilize an A-Grade to hunt him down next time, which was just a joke.

This was obviously pointless. Jack Rust was dead beyond the shadow of a doubt. Yet, she couldn't help herself.

"You, keep watching over the Abyss as you were doing," she told the middle B-Grade Ancestor of the Animal Kingdom. "I will summon an Envoy of the Hand specializing in Space and have him personally search the Abyss. Nothing can be allowed to go wrong."

Nobody dared to disagree. Three days later, a middle B-Grade Envoy who cultivated the Dao of Space arrived and spent a week personally scanning the entire Abyss. No trace of Jack was found. He had certainly not exited either because they'd constantly kept watch. After all this time, there was no scenario in which he still survived.

"We still haven't found a body," Eva told the other Envoy. "If he really had died to the spatial storms, shouldn't you have found some clues?"

However, this other Envoy wasn't much lower in rank than her. He possessed the qualifications to argue. "With all due respect, Eva, you're thinking too much into this. Jack Rust has gotten inside your head. I personally scanned the entire Abyss

—even though I found no residue of his life force, that means nothing. It's a black hole—anything would get sucked in eventually. He is dead, dead beyond the shadow of a doubt. I guarantee it."

"Alright," she replied after a moment of thought. "Perhaps I've been affected by the past. You're right. He cannot be alive. Thanks for coming, Sylvan—I will return and meditate to clear my mind of all prejudice."

The other Envoy nodded, and the two of them departed alongside a euphoric Artus Emberheart. It was only Eva who spared a final glance at the Abyss—then, she shook her head and teleported away. One of the Kingdom's Ancestors also left, returning to his duties.

Two weeks after Jack's disappearance, the Abyss finally returned to tranquility. The only one left behind was the middle B-Grade Ancestor who'd guarded this place to begin with.

Three days later, a new war merit of the Hand of God was proclaimed across the universe:

Jack Rust, the troublemaker hero of the Milky Way, had perished.

CHAPTER EIGHTEEN
BLACK HOLE WORLD

JACK AWOKE GROGGILY. HIS ENTIRE BODY WAS IN PAIN. HE COULD NOT move his limbs, nor could he sense them—as if the only thing awake about him was his brain.

A young woman emerged in the mist of his vision. She seemed human—pale skin, blonde hair, blue eyes, soft hands tending to his wounds. She was beautiful, too. As she gazed at him, she smiled. "It's okay," she said. "You don't need to wake up yet. Rest."

Jack wanted to protest, but he could barely remember his own name, let alone speak. Just thinking this far exhausted him. Powerless to resist, he drifted back into sleep.

———

The second time Jack awoke, he did so with full and immediate clarity. Linen beddings, stone walls, unfamiliar yellow robes draped over his body. He was alone in what resembled a bedroom. He jumped upright, ready to tear everything around him to shreds, but it was then that his perception howled outside the room and glimpsed at people.

Mortals.

He restrained himself. If he rampaged now, all those people would die instantly. It was easy to keep his powers in check, but much harder to do the same for his thoughts—the memories of the last few hours were all too clear. He had been chased into a corner, and then Artus Emberheart had killed...

Eric...

Sad emotions warred within Jack. His period of unconsciousness had given them time to recover from the insane state they'd reached before, but it hadn't made his grief any lighter. His son had died—the boy he'd given up everything to protect. He'd failed—both as a father and a cultivator.

Jack would have liked to roar wildly and vent his feelings. As it was, he could not. His anger was hollow. All he could do was bury his face in his palms and weep for the life he had not been able to protect.

"I'm sorry, Eric... Vivi, Ebele, I'm so, so sorry..."

When a man was distraught, the world lost its colors. Jack didn't know how long he spent alone in that room. The weight of his grief was crushing. It was only when he calmed down somewhat that he managed to consider his situation.

Where am I?

The last thing he remembered was that he'd been sucked into the black hole. He should have been dead. He'd stepped past the event horizon, where nothing or nobody could have rescued him.

Yet, here he was, still alive. In inhabited terrain, no less. Could this be the inside of the black hole, the cause of its irregularity? Or had the black hole acted as a wormhole to a completely different place?

Was he even in the same universe?

Now able to think, Jack sensed the distorted spacetime in this environment. It resembled nothing he knew of. Spacetime was supposed to be an endlessly stretching curtain, but here... it felt more like a taut piece of cloth. Small, yet unbelievably sturdy.

If spacetime was the sea, he was on an island.

Archon Green Dragon's inheritance contained no hint to such a place—not in the part Jack had comprehended, anyway. Therefore, he temporarily suppressed both grief and curiosity to look inward. No matter where he was, his own situation was the most important thing.

It was not good.

His soul felt dry. The Dao density inside him was thin, like the humidity of a desert, and his Dao Tree had almost withered due to the lack of energy. A large crack also ran down the tree's length, from leaves to root. Jack's heart throbbed when he saw it.

Such a crack appeared when a cultivator ran into a situation irreconcilable with their Dao. It basically meant their Dao was incomplete—with such a crack, any further progress was difficult, and even the cultivator's current power level would experience a massive drop.

Jack had long heard about the cracking of one's Dao. He'd even caused it to some people. However, it was only when he experienced it himself that he realized how painful it really was.

While this crack existed, he was crippled.

Let alone reaching the A-Grade—with such a massive crack in his Dao Tree, even developing the next Dao Fruit would be difficult. Unless he found a solution... but that was easier said than done.

And the grief...

Jack sighed. He had temporarily suppressed those feelings, but they remained vivid in his heart. Pain, fury... A seed of darkness had been planted inside him, one which consumed both himself and others. As if he'd swallowed his very own black hole.

And all this had been caused by Artus Emberheart. The one enemy he'd let roam free.

Emberheart... Jack thought, his eyes flashing with darkness. *I will rip out your heart and make you watch as I kill everyone you love. Only then will my hatred be satisfied.*

He opened his status screen.

ERROR: PLEASE REPORT TO THE NEAREST AUTHORITIES IMMEDIATELY OR FACE EXTERMINATION.

Name: Jack Rust
Species: Human, Earth-387
Faction: Bare Fist Brotherhood (C)
Grade: C
Class: Gladiator Titan (King) (cracked)
Level: 303

Strength: 6040 (+)
Dexterity: 6040 (+)
Constitution: 6040 (+)
Mental: 1000
Will: 1000
Free sub-points: 2

Dao Skills: Meteor Punch IV, Iron Fist Style III, Brutalizing Aura III, Neutron Star Body III, Super-nova III, Space Mastery III, Fist of Mortality III, Death Mastery II, Titan Taunt I
Dao Roots: Indomitable Will, Life, Power, Weakness
Dao Fruits: Fist, Space, Life, Death, Battle
Titles: Planetary Frontrunner (10), Planetary Torch-

**bearer (1), Ninth Ring Conqueror, Planetary Over-
lord (1), Grade Defier**

The warning remained loud and obnoxious. He'd gained a
level when he killed that Animal Kingdom Elder at the start of
the battle, but a new word had appeared next to his Class.

*Cracked... Does the System's Class refer to my Dao Tree, then? Or
is that position a coincidence?*

It was only after Jack finished taking stock of himself that he
once again released his perception. It easily bypassed the walls,
finding more and more structures. All were rough and simple,
emphasizing space efficiency over appearance. They were also
brightly colored. Looking farther, these buildings followed a
broad, dark stone floor which curved in the distance like the
surface of a tiny planet.

The ground was made of stone, and so was the sky. As Jack's
perception spread up and down, he could sense that the place
he was in was divided into manmade layers separated by floors
of stone, each layer further crowded with structures. It was like
the inside of a beehive—or like the dwellings of an underground society. There were no streets in the traditional sense.
Jack was in a three-dimensional city, a network of manmade
tunnels interspersed with large rooms which served as houses,
shops, gardens...

His first thought was that he was underground. To his
surprise, there was no dirt or stone surrounding all these rooms
and tunnels. The empty space between them was hollow, as if
this place hadn't been dug out but constructed.

It was almost magical.

Even Jack's downcast mind forgot about its troubles for a
moment to enjoy this otherworldly scenery.

"Where am I?" he couldn't help wondering. He shot his
perception outward, spreading it in all directions, as far as he

could reach. The odd space here hindered him, but even crippled and restrained, Jack could easily scan a radius of several miles.

The place he was in wasn't a city—or, if it was, he couldn't reach its limits. In his perception, the buildings and tunnels stretched endlessly in all directions, whether in this layer or the ones around it.

The layer he was in was neither the bottom nor the topmost one—there were layers above and below him, all occupied by the same people as the ones surrounding his room.

As for those people... The truth was, Jack hadn't paid much attention to them. They were weak—either mortals or low-level cultivators barely reaching the E-Grade. Their clothing was bright and colorful, designed for a good mood, though their features were all kind of similar. In fact, the lack of diversity there was almost alarming—as if Jack had stumbled into a city of clones. At least they seemed joyful.

Nobody had sensed his perception or his awakening. They went on about their menial jobs, occasionally glancing at his nondescript room with a mix of worry and intrigue. The room he was in was just one of many—as it turned out, what he thought of as a bedroom was in fact the entire house.

This place, wherever it was, was certainly overpopulated.

Jack did not disturb these people. The more information he had before he made his move, the better—he was content just watching them go about their everyday lives. It was only an hour later that someone special appeared—a D-Grade cultivator, hunched by age and with a beard almost reaching his ankles, accompanied by a young F-Grade woman.

The moment Jack saw this woman, a new memory flashed into his brain. He'd seen her before. She had been the one tending to his wounds when he briefly woke up before.

Everyone else made respectful way to the woman and old

man as they approached his room. It was only when they arrived within a few hundred feet that the old man's perception passed over Jack. Those old eyes faintly shone. "He's awake!" he exclaimed, not realizing Jack was listening in. "What do you say, Mia? Should we check in?"

"Yes!" she replied, her smile pure and dazzling.

Jack sensed no bad intentions from either of them. He let them approach, and when they knocked on his door, he politely replied, "Come in." The door swung open.

It was only then that he could observe them with his eyes. The old man walking ahead was even more decrepit from up-close—his eyes were misty, as if clouded by the approach of death, while his body leaned almost entirely on an unadorned wooden staff. Though a D-Grade, Jack doubted this man even had the combat efficiency of a normal peak E-Grade.

Despite that, his gaze was pure and excited.

As for the woman, she was like a gentle breeze on a prairie. She must have been in her twenties, but innocence wafted off of her like the fragrance of a flower. Her blue eyes gazed at him without a hint of fear, only excitement, and her posture confirmed she didn't fear him in the slightest.

To Jack's surprise, he could inspect them.

Human (??), Level 161 (D-Grade)
Faction: Black Hole World (B-Grade)
Title: Direct Descendant

Human (??), Level 23 (F-Grade)
Title: Direct Descendant

The fact he could use System inspection proved he was still in System space. *How is that possible?* he wondered. *Was the black hole a wormhole leading me somewhere close-by? But the faction name... Black Hole World. What is going on?*

And that title... It's the same one Nauja's tribe had. Are these people connected to the Ancients?

"Greetings, stranger," said the old man. If he'd inspected Jack and saw the red, strongly-worded System warning, he did not react. "My name is Vermont Crest the 2,376th. Most people call me Elder Vermont—and this Mia."

"Nice to meet you," the girl said, bowing lightly.

Jack nodded in return. "I'm Jack. The pleasure is all mine. If it's not too much of a bother, could you tell me where I am?"

"This is the Black Hole World," Elder Vermont explained, gesturing all around. "A world created by our ancestor, Archon Black Hole, one billion, thirty-seven million, eighty-six thousand and twenty-one years ago. We are the Black Hole people— and you, my good friend, are the first outsider we've met since our ancestor sealed us here."

Jack raised his brows. "A billion years ago? Are you telling me you've been sealed here for a billion years?"

"That's right. To be precise, it was one billion, thirty-seven—"

"A really long time," Mia spoke up, eager to participate. "Our ancestor sealed us here to save us from the Immortal Crusade. We were meant to exit after a million years, but unfortunately, the power of our clansmen declined in isolation. When the million-year deadline came, we had no B-Grade clansmen proficient in the Dao of Spacetime to help us escape. Afterwards, even our C-Grades perished. We have been trapped here for a thousand times longer than intended, and with our clansmen unable to reach high enough levels of powers, escaping by ourselves has become impossible."

A sad smile adorned her face as she finished. Jack took some time to process this information, and soon realized why they were so excited to see him. "I'm sorry," he said. "I cannot help you. I was strong once, but I am now weak. No matter the method to escape this place, I cannot achieve it. Not right now."

Their gazes turned cloudy. "Is there any way we can help?" the old man asked.

Jack shook his head. "I fought my enemies and became crippled. The only one who can help me now is myself."

Mia glanced at the old man, who kept his helpless gaze glued on Jack. A moment later, he said, "It looks like the outside world is not yet safe."

"Never was, never will be."

"Hmm." Elder Vermont released a long sigh. "Let us not rouse your past grievances," he said, trying but failing to hide his immense disappointment. "If you must be stuck here with us for the foreseeable future... should we show you around?"

CHAPTER NINETEEN

A DIFFERENT CIVILIZATION

THE BLACK HOLE WORLD WASN'T TOO VAST, BUT IT SURE SEEMED SO. Layers of city were stacked on top of each other, each stretching endlessly. No matter how high or low Jack's perception spread, all he found was more layers.

At the same time, the city itself seemed like it was built underground. Rectangular tunnels stretched in all directions. Illumination came in the form of large electrical lamps hanging from the thirty-foot-high ceiling, while all walls were painted in bright colors—perhaps to brighten the mood of their sunlight-deprived occupants?

As Jack, Mia, and Elder Vermont walked through the city, people stopped to greet them. Most were smiling; they waved or bowed respectfully to the Elder while shooting curious glances at Jack. They were dressed in simple, colorful clothes, and though they ranged from the F to the rare D-Grade, Jack noticed no obvious difference in their statuses.

According to the buildings and lifestyles he saw, this was a society forced by overpopulation to maximize its space efficiency. The technological level was pretty advanced—similar to Earth.

"There are eighty-three layers to our world," Elder Vermont explained proudly, touring Jack through the present layer. "Each hosts millions or billions of people, and they cover an area from twelve to twenty-one thousand square miles!"

"So at minimum twelve thousand square miles..." Jack muttered, whistling. "That's a lot."

Vermont gave him an odd stare. "Not twelve thousand. Twelve. The smallest layer has a surface area of twelve square miles."

"Excuse me?"

"You heard him," Mia piped in, giggling.

Jack shook his head. "And what's under this entire tower? The black hole?"

"What tower?"

"You have eighty-three layers stacked like a tower."

"Oh, no, no, no. Not a tower. More like... a planet."

Jack raised his brows. A memory popped into his mind— Trial Planet, a hollow planet made up of nine layers. Could this place be similar?

Mia was all too happy to explain, "At the core of our world lies the Vortex—a dark whirlpool through which we are connected to the outer universe. Our world is built in concentric spheres around it, each covering an increasingly large area and each exactly half a mile tall. This is the twenty-first layer—if you go down twenty-one times, you'll reach the Vortex."

Most tunnels were around ten feet tall, but there were many levels of tunnels in each layer. This was really a goliath of a city.

As much as Jack tried to remain sad, the intrigue of this world suppressed it. "And if I rise to the top?" he asked.

"Nothing. The end of our spacetime. The end of the world."

Jack paused to look up. His gaze drilled through a dozen layers, not quite reaching the end. "There can't be nothing," he argued.

Mia shrugged. "You can go check whenever."

"We would like to bring you to our council first," Elder Vermont hurried to add. "You remained in Mia's home so far, since she was the one who found you, but that would be improper now that you've awoken. The other Elders and I eagerly await to hear about the outside world."

He wasn't lying. The passion in his voice, the hope, was impossible to mistake. If what they said before was true, these people had been trapped here for a billion years, millions of generations. The outside world was a dream passed down through their lineage, the fervent hope of them all, the only thing keeping them alive. Now, with him as their first ever visitor from outside, the excitement of the Elders was indescribable.

Perhaps, after a billion years of imprisonment, it would be their generation that would finally escape.

Facing the Elder's invitation, Jack could only shake his head. "Your strongest cultivator is at the peak D-Grade?"

"Late D-Grade, actually. Grand Elder Pasan," Vermont replied proudly.

"Then, I hate to be the bearer of bad news, but you're better off staying here. The universe is no place for the weak. I recently found that out the hard way."

Jack regretted his words the moment he spoke them. Elder Vermont almost physically melted—his wrinkled eyes deepened, wallowing in sadness, and his body seemed more fragile than a pile of dust in the wind.

"Jack!" Mia exclaimed. Her cute eyes turned stormy. "What are you saying?"

Jack did not reply. He regretted putting down the old man's dream like that—his grief had gotten the best of him. However, he also didn't want to lie. A weak group like theirs would be chewed out by the universe in no time at all.

Or, perhaps, this was his terrible mood speaking.

Silence reigned for a few minutes. They crossed alleys, streets, and squares, climbed down some ladders and up some others. Each was lost in their own thoughts.

"I always feared the outside world would be dangerous," Elder Vermont finally said. His aged voice was tired now—it carried the distinct sadness of old people, that bone-deep exhaustion which had experienced all of life's suffering.

"Elder..." Mia began, but Vermont raised a hand to stop her.

"Don't blame Jack. He simply speaks his mind—and the truth, most likely. However, if the opportunity ever arises to leave this place, I believe our people will still decide to go. Even if the future is bleak. Even if we are weak and will probably die or be enslaved. This is a wish we have cradled for a billion years —even if the entire world is against us, we will still go out there and strive for the best, because what is life without hope? We may be weak, but we are no cowards!"

Jack had been occupied with his dark thoughts, but he turned to gaze at Vermont. Those were powerful words—brave ones. Spoken with conviction. This old man would have made a great cultivator of the Fist.

"I respect your determination, Elder," he said. "I will not stop you from doing anything—I will go to your council and speak what I know. However, as for exiting this place, I cannot promise anything..."

Vermont gave Jack a wide smile. "That's fine! As long as you try your best."

Mia nodded, satisfied, and the three of them traveled deeper. They descended one layer through a massive ladder surrounded by glass walls. The rest they descended through an elevator.

Jack and Vermont could have flown, of course, but they didn't. Jack had a lot of things to consider. As for Vermont, he didn't seem in a hurry—perhaps living in a sealed world for so long had eliminated any sense of urgency from their culture.

As they traveled through the Black Hole World, Jack caught glimpses of its people. None were hurried. Many cultivated or busied themselves with menial labor. There were waiters, doctors, gardeners, salesmen... Many were renovation workers, repairing the buildings in worsened states. Since they'd run out of space, this was a job which needed to be regularly done.

An entire society lived inside this black hole, with most of its mundane needs eliminated by the existence of cultivation.

Now, they simply lived. It was peaceful—if dull.

These are kind people, Jack thought. *A billion years with just themselves and their society hasn't devolved to warlords. On Earth, we can barely go a hundred years.*

Was it related to their Ancient ancestry? Though the System called them humans, not all humans in the universe were genetically identical. Maybe Earth's people were particularly warmongering—or these ones were extremely war-averse.

In any case, Jack not only didn't see any problems, but he also used his perception to spy high and low and still didn't discover any signs of hidden trouble. There was nobody controlling things from the shadows—these were just genuinely good people.

Maybe they really should stay here, he thought bitterly. *The outside world... would never allow such beauty.*

"Here we are," Vermont said, approaching a heavy iron door. This was the only area so far which wasn't densely constructed—the Council had some degree of prestige, though not much, given by the rather ordinary appearance of the building they were about to enter. It was like the average town hall.

The inside was as simple as its exterior. Clean corridors made of brightly-colored wood, decorated with long lines of statues. Most were well-preserved—the Black Hole people were masters of preservation.

Jack reached what seemed like a conference room. Five old men and six old women sat on either side of a long table, with yet another old woman at its head. "Grand Elder Pasan," Vermont greeted her, then walked to the empty chair at the men's side of the table.

"Hello," Jack said simply. He was polite but saw no need to be overly respectful. In his eyes, these D-Grades were desperately weak.

He caught himself. *Have I lost my mind? These are people... They could be my mother.*

Before they could respond, he corrected his greeting. "My name is Jack Rust. It's an honor to make your acquaintance."

The leading woman's face brightened. "I am called Pasan, the current leader of the Black Hole people."

The other eleven Elders also introduced themselves.

"Would you like some tea? Or anything to eat, perhaps?" Pasan asked.

"I'm fine, thank you," Jack replied, sitting down on a chair Mia had brought him.

Pasan nodded. "I believe you know our situation. We have been trapped here for a billion years with no way to access the outside world. You are the first visitor we've ever encountered... if you could explain some things, we would be in your debt."

"What would you like to know?"

She smiled. "Everything!"

Jack tried to laugh, but the sound only came out as half-dead panting. He spoke regardless. He hid nothing. Everything he knew about the current state of the universe, every piece of history and insight, he told them, all the way from the Immortal Crusade to the present. Pasan and the other Elders occasionally interrupted to ask questions, but they mostly listened.

While detailing the history of the cosmos, Jack included parts of his own story. Intuitively, he felt safe here. He voiced some of his grievances, framing everything in the current darkness of his mind. Of course, he mentioned nothing about Eric—he was far from ready to discuss that issue.

By the time he was done, two hours had passed. He was startled. Speaking like this hadn't really lightened his mood, but it had made his mind slightly less dark. Apparently, talking to good listeners was therapeutic. Who would have known?

The Elders sat in silence, not hurrying to respond. They digested the information. Finally, it was Pasan who spoke again.

"You sound like you've been through a lot," she said.

"More than I would like," Jack replied honestly.

"Mm. It's fine. You don't have to show your heart to us—just know that this is a safe place."

Jack raised his gaze, meeting her smiling, deep eyes. Had she seen through the darkness in his heart? Then again, he hadn't tried to hide it.

Old people had their ways to judge people.

Unfortunately, his mind remained a mess. Speaking about the world had helped him put his thoughts in order, but he desperately needed to take some time alone and work through his feelings—as much as he dreaded it.

"Thank you," he replied. "I would like some time alone now, if it's not a problem. If there is anything you would like me to clarify, I can do so at our next meeting."

"Of course!" Pasan agreed. "Thank you for everything you told us. We will also take some time to consider things. For now, we have already arranged a house for you to live in. Mia, would you be so kind as to lead Jack over?"

"Sure thing!" Mia responded. "Thank you, Grand Elder."

Jack said his goodbyes and followed Mia out of the room. She led him deeper into this layer—toward a sizable house not too far away from the Elder Council.

"What's your deal?" Jack asked, eyeing Mia. "You're not an Elder, are you?"

"Nope. Just an ordinary girl," she replied with a wink. "Here in the Black Hole world, we all have similar statuses, and there are no barriers between us either. As for why I was allowed in the Elder Council... Well, I've just volunteered to take care of you. I'm nobody special."

Jack would have smiled if he wasn't mourning. The pain bubbled up from inside him, and he urgently needed to be left alone so he could let it all out. "Thank you, Mia. Here is fine. I can travel the rest of the way myself," he said, using his powers to instantly teleport inside his house. Though space was weird here, a short-range teleportation was still within his abilities.

Jack sat on his bed. For the first time in a while, he did not care about the state of the world or any other matters. He did not think.

For a while, he just sat there being sad.

CHAPTER TWENTY

THERE IS ALWAYS HOPE

NIGHTMARES.

The phantom of a large leonine laughing before red skies. Dark rain and booming thunder. Blinding flashes of lightning. Jack running at full speed, yet remaining in the same place, forced to watch as a young boy was shred to pieces by the razor-sharp falling rain.

"Dad!" the boy screamed.

"NOOO!"

His eyes snapped open. With a pained grunt, he grabbed his head. Tears had formed at some point—not of grief, but of frustration. The pain of being helpless.

Jack smashed a fist into a cabinet, tearing it to pieces. "No!" he roared again, his voice cracking the walls.

This was not the first time in Jack's life that he'd experienced grief. His father had died a few years before the Integration. They had been very close—and that man, Eric Rust, was the person Jack's son had been named after.

Yet, the difference between then and now was astounding. It was simply a different world, and not only because of the circumstances. Losing one's father was painful, but also natural; the way things were supposed to be. It was a pain through which a person could grow and mature, a sort of rite of passage to true manhood.

But losing one's son went against the natural order. It wasn't supposed to be experienced. While Jack's heart had supported him last time, now, it could not. It was unprepared. Bursts of agony shot through his brain. Grief and fury warred with guilt and fear, the slithering feeling of weakness numbing his limbs.

It was all a jumbled mess of feelings Jack had to unravel. He would be fine, eventually—he genuinely believed and hoped so. But, until then...

Why does it have to be so hard? he asked the sky he could no longer see.

His mind sought peace. It fell into the familiar routine of meditation, though it achieved little. The grief was insurmountable, at least for now—it was not something that could be overcome in a short period of time. Jack could only turn to bright thoughts. His son was gone, but he still had a daughter. A wife. A mother, a brother, friends, and a planet to protect.

And Eric had lived a good life, minus its last act.

How are they doing? Jack wondered, thinking back to the rest of his family. Eva Solvig had told him they were safe, and he didn't dare doubt those words, but the circumstances of Eric's kidnapping were still unknown to Jack.

Do they know? Do they think I am dead as well? Are they mourning, or are they struggling to become stronger?

Ebele is definitely cultivating. That girl is talented and hardworking—I only hope she doesn't push herself too much. And Vivi... She's a fighter as well. If she knows about my situation, I'm sure she'll take the safety of Earth into her own hands. She'll keep everyone safe until I can return.

Thinking about his family dispelled the darkness in Jack's

mind somewhat, giving him the power to consider other matters.

My Dao is cracked... he thought with sadness. He looked inside himself—the Dao Tree lay barren, its roots misshapen and unable to absorb the surrounding Dao efficiently. A massive crack running down its trunk had even split apart the door of the Life Drop, and the five fruits on its branches were pale and lifeless, no longer glowing as they once had been. Even the Life Drop was unresponsive.

Now, his previously glorious days were but a dream of old, a memory of ages long past.

As Jack investigated his situation, he discovered that his combat prowess had dropped from the early B-Grade to the peak C-Grade. It seemed small, but it was actually a tremendous drop—his current power was just a fraction of what it used to be.

Half of his losses were due to his Dao cracking. The rest was the price he paid when he overdrew himself to escape Eva Solvig's grasp and rushed into the black hole—a temporary, if severe weakening.

Jack sighed and shook his head. He had to admit this was the lowest point of his life. He'd suffered a devastating loss, and even recovering his former power would be difficult. On the bright side, if he did manage to recover, the benefits he would reap from this adventure would be incalculable... but that would be as difficult as climbing the heavens. Cracks in one's Dao tended to be permanent.

And, in any case, no matter how great his potential benefits, he never would have traded his son's life for them.

Jack took a deep breath, then another. The pain of his grief receded to the back of his mind, a dark numbing he endured while focusing on other things. It felt like he'd lost everything, but he actually hadn't. Brock and his other friends, Vivi, Ebele, the professor, all of them were still alive. He had to fight for them.

Most importantly, he had a very clear sense of purpose driving him through these hard times.

Revenge.

Jack's eyes flashed darkly. *Artus Emberheart... and everyone else who participated in the death of my son, I will destroy you. When I'm done, the name Emberheart will no longer exist in this galaxy!*

This was a solemn oath he'd made in the name of his dead son, and one he was determined to see through. However, killing innocent people would only make him the same as Artus. It would rob him of his humanity, turn him into a cultivating monster.

Was that the path he wanted to follow? He wasn't sure. All he knew was that, right now, that dark vengeance was the driving force he needed to ignore his grief and keep pushing forward.

I need to restore my powers, he determined. *As soon as possible.*

After all, time hadn't stopped. Who knew what was happening in the outside world while he was trapped here? He had to hurry—but repairing a cracked Dao was easier said than done.

What failed in my Fist? he asked himself. *The fist is power. The fist is strength. The fist is to straightforwardly break through all obstacles, laughing in the process. Either I succeed or I die—that is the essence of the fist. Even in death, I would laugh.*

But I never thought my son would die. What meaning is there in charging forth when I cannot protect those behind me? How can I face all problems head-on when that endangers my loved ones? Should I bend my back sometimes to keep them safe? But that is not the Fist.

This problem wouldn't exist if my power was high enough, but it

*isn't. How could it be? There are always stronger people in the world.
My Fist was fine with that because it was fine with dying, but failing
to save someone while living myself is not an acceptable result.*

Was my Fist doomed to fail?

Jack could see this now. From the very first moment he'd
embraced the Fist, this was bound to happen. It was just a flaw
he'd never perceived. In the past, he'd coated over it by advo-
cating that his path was set, and that anyone who followed him
had resigned themselves to the consequences of that path. If
one of his followers died as a result of Jack's Fist-guided
actions, then that was fine, because by choosing to follow him
they had become extensions of that Fist. It wouldn't be much
different than Jack himself dying.

In a few words, he owed nothing to anyone. Even if all of
Earth was destroyed, that was their fault for not being strong
enough—Jack had already saved them, so he could not be
faulted for being unable to save them the next time.

That all stopped being true when it came to people he truly
cared about—people who, perhaps, had never had a choice.
Eric had never chosen to follow Jack. Moreover, by being Eric's
father, Jack tacitly accepted the responsibility of protecting
him. It was his job—and failing was a tragedy that his Dao of
the Fist had never taken into account. That was why it had
cracked—it had no way to reconcile its understanding of the
world with the reality before Jack's eyes. His Dao was proven
incomplete, which was exactly what the crack signified.

Repairing that crack now would be a difficult road. First of
all, Jack had to come up with a worldview which fit both reality
and the Fist—resolving the proven flaw in his Dao. The
problem was that his Dao had been set in stone when he broke
into the D-Grade. At that time, he declared his Dao to the world
and gotten it approved by all the other Daos.

Following a Dao was not just a path to power. It was a

commitment. Back then, Jack had committed to a very specific Dao, and that was the foundation upon which he'd built his current strength. He couldn't just go back and alter it. The only way to repair the Dao crack was to find a solution still inside the narrow confines he'd once committed to. In other words, he had to prove that his Dao was correct, and that it was his own understanding at the time which was insufficient.

That was why repairing a Dao crack was such a tremendously unlikely task.

Thinking this far left Jack exhausted. He opened his eyes and released a long sigh—though he saw the road ahead, that didn't mean he could walk it. There was a great chance his Dao could never be repaired. If that was the case, he would be forced to live the rest of his life unable to make another breakthrough, and he would also be trapped inside this dark and stuffy Black Hole World.

Ten thousand years. That was the lifespan of a C-Grade, and that was the time he would remain alive for. Meanwhile, his friends and family would be unprotected in the outside world, forced to fend for themselves against the very powerful enemies that Jack had made them.

"I need some air," he muttered, slowly rising to his feet. He walked to the door and opened it, greeted by the daedalus terrain of the Black Hole World. He was also greeted by Mia.

"Hey!" she said, rising from a chair she'd brought over and pocketing the small book she'd been reading.

Jack raised a brow. "What are you doing outside my door?"

"I've been asked to take care of you, silly. I couldn't just leave you alone."

"But why didn't you wait inside? I have a living room."

"You seemed like you didn't want company."

Jack was forced to nod. His mind had been a mess when he'd just left her and teleported inside. She'd judged correctly.

But how low he'd fallen, that he couldn't even observe basic manners.

"How long was I inside?" he asked.

"Hmm? How long? We don't measure time here. You were in, and now you're out."

"How can you not measure time?"

"It's dangerous. Some of our ancestors were doing that but ended up killing themselves. In this world which never changes, keeping time only brings despair. It's better to just live without a care, becoming one with the world around you, focusing on the present."

Jack was dumbfounded. It was hard to associate such profound words with the innocent girl before him. Then again, this was her reality. A world that never changed, where every generation was as insignificant as the previous, leaving no imprint on the world as if they never existed.

"Then, how do you know it's been a billion years?" he asked.

"Oh, there's always an Elder entrusted with the important task of keeping time and recording history. In our generation, that's Elder Vermont—the one you've already met."

"I see..."

"Well, what are we up to now?" Mia asked. "You're leaving the house. Do you want to go for a walk? Food? Tea? Maybe explore a bit, or see the Vortex, or the endless nothingness outside our world?"

Jack hadn't planned on doing any of that. He just wanted some fresh air. However, since his mood was a bit better, he thought he might as well. "Let's check out that nothingness. It can't be that bad."

CHAPTER TWENTY-ONE

STAR-EYE WONDER

THE NOTHINGNESS WAS IMPRESSIVE. THERE WERE FLICKERS OF LIGHT, multi-colored curtains washing over the void reminiscent of Earth's auroras. They swam and wrapped around each other in the sky, yet they did not exist—nothing but visions the mind invented to protect itself from true nihility.

"What do you think?" Mia asked, puffing up her chest. "Isn't it impressive?"

Jack gave a small smile. He'd seen this before. The so-called nothingness was the interdimensional void, the gap between dimensions in which the Green Dragon Realm was also situated. Perhaps even the whole universe was just an island in this massive sea where space and time held no meaning, where distance and size were irrelevant.

Maybe, much further down the road of cultivation, Jack would have the power to traverse this sea. But he definitely didn't now. If he tried to fly into it, he would just... disappear.

"Have you never tried to explore it?" he asked. He remembered that the Black Hole People used to have A-Grades in their ranks.

"Explore what? The nothingness?" She chuckled. "Don't be silly."

Jack nodded. He'd expected that. Yet, interacting with this interdimensional sea shouldn't be impossible. Archon Green Dragon and the ancestor of these people—Archon Black Hole—had both established their own small world inside this sea. It was a frontier meant for those at the highest peaks.

Jack looked away, choosing not to bother with things so far beyond him. The Black Hole People were right—they called the interdimensional sea "nothingness" and had established lounging spots here, at the top of their eighty-third layer, so people could relax and enjoy the view. Just by looking to the sides, Jack could see many groups of wealthy individuals eating under the aurora.

"I cannot pierce this sea," he said. "There is no point staying here. Let's go."

"Mm." Mia nodded, leading him back to the ladder they'd come from. "Where do you want to go now?" she asked. "Back home?"

"No. Let's visit the Vortex as well."

Mia smiled. The Vortex was the core of their world, the area situated at its very center. It was also the place most closely connected to the wider universe—if Jack was interested in it, he must have decided to look for a way out. That made her happy.

"Are you really going to save us?" she asked through the long journey down. The two of them had entered a large elevator connecting the eighty-three layers. It was usually reserved for the highest occasions, and Jack's existence qualified as such.

"You don't need saving," Jack commented. "You're fine here. Maybe your world isn't infinite, but so what? It's vast enough."

"It's not about size!" Mia protested. "We want to be free! To see the stars, and the moons, and the rivers, and the endless void, and to experience distance! Anything longer than forty-two miles!"

Jack smiled. He'd heard these words before, almost the exact same. This had been Nauja's wish as well, when she was trapped with her tribe in Trial Planet's Barbarian Ring.

The children of the Ancients are like fairy tale princesses, he mused in a rare moment of humor. *Always trapped somewhere, eager to see the outside world, and needing rescue.*

Then again, weren't the Ancients the same? Peaceful, kind, and brave. Trapped in a galaxy-sized prison before Enas gave them the secrets of cultivation. Then, they became explorers.

Jack gazed at Mia with new eyes. For a moment, he thought he saw a vision of the past; an incredibly distant ancestor casting its shadow on this innocent girl with big dreams.

"Is it beautiful?" she suddenly asked, breaking him out of his reverie.

"Is what beautiful?" he replied.

"The universe!"

"...It's dangerous."

"I know that. You've said it, like, a thousand times. But is it also beautiful?"

Jack hesitated. For reasons he couldn't quite decipher, he didn't want to answer this question. It felt too bright, too cheerful, and to indulge would be like abandoning his current state of mourning—letting Eric down one more time.

He kept his mouth shut. Mia didn't push him, but soon, his own stubbornness did. Since when was he afraid of a simple question? Had he become such a coward that he couldn't even state some facts?

Something tiny softened inside his heart.

"It is beautiful," he finally replied. "There are endless rivers of stars washing through the cosmos. I'm talking, humongous. A grain of sand compared to your Black Hole World is about as big as your entire world compared to a single one of those stars, and there are millions. And the distances between them—you cannot even imagine. Forty-two miles is all you've ever known, but just one star to the next can be separated by trillions of miles. And then there's galaxies—each of them houses billions of stars, and they are almost infinitely far apart from each other. The universe is so unbelievably massive that nobody can even fathom it."

Mia was starstruck. The image Jack painted with his words came to reinforce the one she'd built in her mind, and the combined awe left her giggling.

"And are there people on all those stars?" she asked.

"People don't live on stars—those are just giant balls of fire. They live on planets, smaller boulders which orbit the stars. Of course, even the tiniest planet would be far larger than the Black Hole World, but you don't necessarily lose out on living space. Planets are only occupied on the surface."

"Only the surface?" she exclaimed. "That's so wasteful! What about all the empty space inside?"

Jack laughed. "It's not empty. There are rocks, and lava, and tectonic plates on which entire continents are seated. It would be difficult to live there, and there is no need—just the surface is large enough."

"Oh! So every planet has more people than my world?"

"Not exactly. Only a tiny minority of planets can sustain life —most are barren wastelands too hot, cold, or toxic for us. However, even this tiny minority adds up. There are maybe a million inhabitable planets in my home galaxy—if each of them contains just a few million people, that's a terrifying amount."

Mia was like a child eating the first ice-cream of the season. Her eyes drooled with wonder. "Tell me more!" she shouted.

Jack laughed again. "There are many species of people in the universe. Some look like you and me. Others seem half-human and half-animal—though they're actually humanoids evolved from animals other than monkeys—while many are just plain weird. Just in my short travels, I've seen small blue people wearing turbans, large red ones with bushy beards, people made of stone... There was even a species whose people are rectangular and made of glass, like the windows you see in every house. To speak, they vibrate themselves at specific frequencies, the same way we vibrate our vocal cords."

"Wooow!" Mia exclaimed. "How do you know they're people and not windows?"

"They have a head and limbs," Jack explained. "Though I admit, I have no idea how their bodies work. I should look into that when I have the time. Before becoming a cultivator, I was a biologist—a scientist studying the mysteries of life."

"That sounds awesome!"

"It was. But tiring, too. Science is fun, but doing it properly takes a good deal of patience. You wouldn't believe how many edge cases I had to cover just to almost finish my PhD."

"What's that?"

"My scientific research."

"Ohh! What was it on?"

"The evolutionary history of grasshoppers. I wanted to see in what order they developed their telling characteristics."

"And did you?"

"Kind of. I came up with some reasonable hypotheses. All that was left was to write them down and get them peer-reviewed, which can be a bitch. That was when the System arrived to my world. If it had been just a few months later, I would have been Dr. Rust by now."

She gave him an odd glance. "You, a doctor? Yeah... I think you should stick to being a cultivator."

Jack was surprised, then burst into laughter. "Not that kind of doctor! But, just so you know, I am a healer! I studied it as part of my training. I can heal a lot of things!"

Except my own heart.

He was surprised at how that thought popped out by itself —but also at how okay he was with it. At the very least, it didn't stun him with grief. That was a welcome change. It was only then that he realized how swept up he'd gotten in the discussion. He smiled. Not all was lost.

"Thanks," he said in a softer voice. "I needed that."

"Hmm? Needed what?"

"It's okay. Just, thanks."

Mia blinked in surprise. "You're welcome?"

A soft ding came from above. The massive elevator doors opened, revealing a flat patch of ground. Some guards looked at them with questions but swallowed them back down when Mia flashed them a badge.

"This way," she said, leading Jack deeper into the layer. The corridors were empty here and the illumination sparser. It looked more like an administrative space than living quarters. "This is the first layer," Mia explained. "Not many people are allowed here because it's so close to the Vortex, but we get a pass!"

"Shouldn't the Elder Council be situated here?" Jack wondered. "Seems like a great center of authority."

"That's exactly why they're not here. The Council needs to be one with the people, not overlooking them from a distance."

"...That's actually pretty nice."

They reached a spiraling staircase heading downward, painted completely black. There were more guards here, both of them D-Grades—and, this time, they did question them. Jack remained silent—it was Mia who handled everything. They seemed to know her.

Which made perfect sense. Mia had been the one to find

him when he first arrived at this world, and he had to of been spat out by the Vortex. She could only have found him if she worked here as a guard—or something similar, given her weakness relative to these D-Grade guards.

"Come on," she said five minutes later. "Let's go!"

They descended the staircase. Mia, who was leading the way, was not in a hurry. In fact, as they advanced deeper and deeper, Jack could sense her growing scared. She did her best not to show it, but how could she fool Jack's perception?

"Don't worry," he said. "With me here, nothing bad will happen to you."

He cringed at his own promise. How could he say such words after the death of his son? Yet, Mia seemed pacified.

"Thanks," she replied, believing in him.

Her steps quickened, and before long, they'd reached the end. The staircase ended at nothing—just a landing before pitch-black darkness. Jack sent his perception into it, and he easily discovered that what lay ahead of them was a roughly mile-wide sphere of distorted space. There was no gravity, nor was there air—it was similar to the vacuum of space.

"I cannot follow you further," Mia said timidly. "But, uh, I'll be waiting at the top of the staircase, okay?"

Jack shot her a glance. This void was harmless to him, and if he wanted to, he could easily carry her along and protect her. But there was no need.

"I may cultivate here for a bit," he said. "If you grow tired, just return by yourself. I can find the way to my house."

"No way! I'll wait for you!"

"Whatever you prefer. See you later."

With that, he turned and flew into the darkness. He didn't really go yet—he hid himself and waited until he was sure Mia had returned to the first layer. Only then did he actually venture deeper.

Well, as deep as there was to go. The darkness could not hinder his perception. He could see the core of this world directly in front of him—a small black sphere spinning in reverse, emitting a unique form of radiation and unraveling itself little by little. The energy packed inside it was as vast as an ocean, so the process was extremely slow, but Jack could sense that this core, whose existence had supported the entire Black Hole World for over a billion years, was nearing the end of its life.

If nothing happened, this world would collapse in another million years or two. Jack shook his head. Did the Elders know and were keeping it a secret to avoid frightening the populace, or had their cultivation degraded to where they couldn't sense such a thing?

It seemed obvious to Jack, but the rate of decay of this mini black hole could only be perceived by those possessing deep spatial understandings.

"I guess I have to save them," he muttered, sitting cross-legged before the black hole—at a respectable distance, though there wasn't any suction force. This object was an oddity. He could sense that this was the true form of the Animal Abyss, the black hole with the fragmented event horizon. It served not only as the core, but also as its connection to the wider universe. In order to open a passage, Jack would need to fully attune himself to this object.

A normal C-Grade, or even a B-Grade, would be helpless. Jack, however, had already assimilated with the Life Drop, a treasure very similar to this black hole. He had confidence that, given enough time, he would be able to at least let himself out.

But all those were impossible if he did not repair the crack in his Dao. That was his first order of business. And so, with a deep sigh, Jack closed his eyes and sank into meditation.

CHAPTER TWENTY-TWO
VIGILANTE

IN THE UNIVERSE OUTSIDE THE BLACK HOLE WORLD, SOME CHANGES had occurred recently. It had been a month since Jack disappeared—presumed dead. However, before the Animal Kingdom could even finish celebrating, a new menace appeared in their constellation.

A starship floated through the void. Its bridge was occupied by well-dressed, joyful cultivators—its hull was filled with chained-up prisoners, soon to be slaves. They were, without exception, beautiful young women.

"Another success!" a large feshkur shouted, raising a goblet full of wine. "To the captain!"

"To the captain!" everyone echoed. A sharken with a patch over one eye laughed, raising his goblet and sipping it just a bit.

"Are you not going to drink, Captain?" one of the sharken's lieutenants inquired. Their crew had been in this business for decades; it was customary to celebrate after every major victory.

The sharken, however, shook his head. "Not yet," he replied in a harsh voice. "I want to remain sharp. I have... a feeling."

"A feeling, Captain?"

"Yes."

The lieutenant was startled—and intimidated. His captain was very experienced, so his intuition couldn't be ignored. "Should we be afraid? Is the Black Hole Church coming after us?"

In the lieutenant's eyes, besides the major factions, only such a powerful terrorist organization was worth fearing. After all, their crew was not made up of weaklings; they possessed multiple D-Grade fighters, and their captain was even at the early C-Grade. In the Animal Kingdom Constellation, and even in the Milky Way Galaxy, they were a force to be reckoned with.

Even the Animal Kingdom Elders were only C-Grades!

However, the captain laughed. "The Black Hole Church is dead. And even if they aren't, they wouldn't bother with people like us. They have bigger problems."

"Then..." The lieutenant's eyes widened as he reached a stunning possibility. "Could you be thinking about the *Dark Ram*, Captain?"

The captain remained silent, tacitly agreeing.

The lieutenant continued. After being with the captain for so long, he had the right to speak up about certain things. "This is not my place, Captain, but are they really worth fearing? They should only have D-Grades."

"Their rise to fame has been too quick," the captain replied, calmly sipping from his goblet. The crew's rampant celebrations washed over him like the tide over a rock. "I suspect they have more power than they've shown. Given their targets so far, it wouldn't be strange for them to come after us next."

The lieutenant spoke no more, but his hesitation was evident in his silence.

"Do you think I am mistaken, Galaher?" the captain asked.

"I wouldn't dare, Captain... but, if you want my opinion, there is no need to worry about them. The most power they've shown was at the middle D-Grade. Even if they were holding back, their captain is at most at the peak D-Grade. There is no way such a random group would have the power to stand against you."

The captain cupped his chin. "Perhaps you're right. This mission went too smoothly, and my nerves are still taut." He sighed, then raised his voice. "Men! Run to the hold and bring me the two most beautiful women to enjoy!"

The crew cheered. Three men rushed through the doors, heading to the lower level. The captain reclined back and downed his goblet. Before he could swallow, however, their starship shook. Tables and chairs went flying—cultivators crashed against the walls. Their massive starship was sent wildly spinning.

The captain was startled, but he was too experienced to panic. He smashed a hand onto the armrest of his chair, breaking it, then spread out his Dao and forcefully stabilized the ship. "Who dares!" he shouted, his voice spreading through the void.

"I do."

The reply was calm, a statement instead of bravado, yet it carried such resolute darkness that the captain's heart seized for a moment. Without a second's hesitation, he teleported outside. He clicked his lips. "The *Dark Ram*..."

Another starship faced him, having approached within a few miles without being noticed. It was small, yet its walls were made of glass, giving a clear view of the inside. The captain could make out a mace-wielding feshkur, a canine, and a pale human woman. All three looked at him with pity. The captain didn't spare them a second glance.

His gaze was drawn to the two people standing outside the starship. One was a middle D-Grade, hulking minotaur wielding a massive greataxe. He didn't need to introduce himself.

"Bomn the Destroyer," the sharken captain muttered, his voice easily reaching the other's ears. "I have heard of your exploits, but to dare face me? You are tired of living."

Bomn did not respond, nor did he draw his greataxe. The captain's eyes fell to the second figure—a gorilla wearing stretched red shorts and carrying no weapon. He did not emit any aura, causing the captain to have ignored him initially. Yet, as he focused, his heart tightened. This gorilla was not simple. The universe caved around him, as if bowing, and he felt so heavy that even his mere existence pulled people toward him.

As the captain scanned this gorilla, he paled.

Brorilla, Level 301 (King)

A gorilla variant from planet Green. Brorillas usually live with Gymonkeys and train them in the ways of working out. It is due to the Brorillas' unmatched pecks that Gymonkeys use poop to fight—they consider themselves too weak for anything else. Brorillas are usually calm, measured animals. However, if anyone harms their little cousins or invades their territory, they go bananas.
This particular brorilla is a variant that visually resembles a gymonkey. Through cultivation, it has achieved a degree of power at the C-Grade, far surpassing the par for its species. Extermination is advised.

In the C-Grade, the first three fruits were worth ten levels each, bringing the cultivator to Level 280. That was the early C-Grade realm where the sharken captain was stranded. After that, every fruit was worth twenty levels—from 281 to 340 was the middle C-Grade, and from 341 to 399 was the late C-Grade realm.

As the captain read Brock's level, he shivered. Middle C-Grade... How could this be?

It had to be known that a middle C-Grade cultivator at the Milky Way could easily become an Elder of a major faction. How could he just show up at random?

No, wait!

The captain suddenly recalled something. The recently deceased Jack Rust had forged a legend in this galaxy. His stories were told in every bar and village. The captain had naturally heard them as well, and vaguely, he seemed to remember that an animal companion was often mentioned alongside Jack. A brorilla.

Could it be...

Dark snakes wrapped around the captain's heart. He struggled to breathe. All those past targets of the *Dark Ram*, all the Animal Kingdom bases and starships... It had made no sense. Why target such high-profile individuals and taunt a superpower? But now, he understood.

"Wait!" he cried out. "I am not part of the Animal Kingdom! We can talk about this!"

"There is nothing to talk about," the brorilla said. A golden aura radiated from its body, tinged with a hint of black. "We know who you are: Beirut Agretone, former Enforcer of the Animal Kingdom, tasked with supplying them high-quality slaves. Prepare to die."

The moment the captain heard his real name, he had already started running. He couldn't match a middle C-Grade in combat, but he specialized in speed; perhaps he could escape.

He hadn't taken three steps when the void locked around him. He was immobile. The force pushing down on him was beyond anything he could hope to combat. He looked back, and the brorilla was already approaching, a palm poised to strike.

In that final moment, the captain went crazy. "Die!" he shouted, pulling out an axe and slashing it at the brorilla. As their gazes met, the captain only saw darkness—and then his mind was in a different space, inside an enormous ancient temple shaped as a dome. The captain sat in the middle, his knees stuck to the ground, and ninety-nine brorillas stood on balconies around the dome, surrounding him in all directions and piercing him with their stares.

Words constantly left their mouths. A combined chant, a hymn of vengeance, a promise of darkness. Hatred substantialized into a dark-golden plaque which fell from above onto the captain's head. The pressure was impossible to bear. His body shook—his mind crumbled like a tower of cards.

All the while, the captain was in disbelief. He was a veteran cultivator. He'd lived for three thousand years and experienced hundreds of battles. He thought his heart was hardened and iron-clad, one of his most exceptional features. Yet, facing this brorilla's heart attack, he was completely powerless to resist. The difference between them was incalculable—as if his entire life so far had been a joke.

"How..." he managed to mutter, already resigned to his fate. He gritted his teeth to beg for mercy. "I can... offer..."

But his words were lost. The chanting of the brorillas was thunderous, seeping into his very soul and disassembling it, making him feel like a mortal in a landslide. At the same time, Brock's palm slammed into the captain's defenseless body in the real world. That tempered body blew up, smashed into smithereens. He didn't even know how he died.

This felt like it had taken a long time, but only an instant had passed. To the eyes of everyone watching, Brock had just casually reached out with his palm and annihilated the sharken captain.

It had to be known that this wasn't some weakling. It was an early C-Grade cultivator. Even in the Animal Kingdom, these were major characters able to awe the world wherever they appeared. Moreover, every single C-Grade cultivator had a massive amount of resources invested into them. The loss of a single one was a major blow to the Animal Kingdom.

Throughout the battle, Brock's expression hadn't changed once. The slavers watching from the ship were panic-stricken. The three D-Grades scattered in different directions and ran away, but it was useless. A canine, a pale-skinned woman, and a hulking minotaur flashed before them, eliminating them after a swift and fierce battle. Meanwhile, Brock had used his powers to cut away half the slavers' starship, rescuing the slaves and pulling them into the *Trampling Ram*.

"Thank you!" they shouted, but he ignored them. His eyes remained on the starship.

"Please wait!" a panicked voice cried out. This was one of the slaver crew's E-Grades, using a device which could project his voice through the void. "We can offer you anything you want! We can serve you for our entire lives! Show mercy, please —we are nothing but ants to someone as powerful as you."

Brock did not humor them. His words were not directed at them, but at himself.

"I will not show mercy," he replied, "because your Kingdom also didn't when they killed my brother. I failed to assist him; all I can do is take revenge. That is my duty.

"Even if you are weak, you are still guilty. I will pull out every weed that supports the Animal Kingdom, break the fingers they stretch into the galaxy and crush their limbs. I will make sure they are nothing but a flailing mass of power unable to influence others. Then, when I am strong enough, I will storm their gates and kill everyone who deserves it. Because of me, the Animal Kingdom will cease to exist."

The slavers didn't even have time to cry. A golden palm smashed into their starship, breaking it apart and killing them instantly. Only iron beams and panels were left hovering through the void. Brock spared the destroyed starship a final glance, whispered something, then flew back into the *Trampling Ram*, which broke through space and disappeared.

In the endless dark void, only the echo of Brock's voice remained, carved eternally into the Dao of the universe.

"Brohood is not kindness, but righteousness! Indomitable will and honest freedom, dreams can never die. Killing my brother was the greatest mistake the Animal Kingdom ever made—I, Brock, will carry on his will and liberate this constellation!"

CHAPTER TWENTY-THREE
MEDITATION

The area near the Vortex was forbidden to the Black Hole People. They were too weak to stay here for extended periods of time. As a result, it had grown deserted.

In Jack's eyes, it was a great cultivation spot. It could even be called perfect. An artificial black hole hovered right in front of him, letting him perceive it freely, while the darkness and lack of sound calmed his mind.

For a while, he could even forget about Eric, imagining himself in a different world where nothing mattered. He was alone in the darkness. Just him and the Dao—his greatest lover and most noble pursuit. The meaning of his life.

Time flowed like water. Jack isolated himself, resolved to stay there for as long as needed. He had nothing to worry about in the Black Hole World. No responsibilities, no family, no concerns. He was alone—and, though that did not bring happiness, it did bring freedom.

He relaxed. All his troubles merged into the background. He surrendered himself to cultivation, even forgetting about his cracked Dao Tree.

Life and Death. Space and Time.

Though his Dao had cracked, that didn't mean he couldn't keep pondering, only that he couldn't translate his understandings into more power. In truth, he had many things to meditate on.

Spacetime was the most obvious. The Realm Heart inside him and the artificial black hole before him were both holy objects in that respect, a wet dream for even A-Grade cultivators of spacetime. He had two of them—his progress could be maddening.

However, to cultivate was to follow one's heart. Jack temporarily put the Spacetime Dao aside. His heart wanted to focus on its other duality. Specifically, the concept of Death.

Jack's thoughts were tender. He gently reached into the back of his mind and let his emotions resurface, doing his best to keep the grief under control. It wouldn't go away until he comprehended and embraced it; and there was no better place to do so than here, in the darkness, where he was alone with infinite time.

Tears flowed freely. He no longer tried to restrain them.

I'm sorry, Eric...

This was different than the mindless wallowing he'd indulged in when he first lost his son. Some time had passed now. Not nearly enough to recover—but enough to regain his awareness.

Jack was a man of strong will. Moreover, he had never jailed away his emotions before. He recognized that he felt guilt, pain, suffering. At the same time, he knew that, eventually, he would have to move on. No matter how hard the things that happened, no matter how his heart was torn apart by pain, life never stopped. He still had reasons to live—he wasn't ready to throw in the towel.

He would need to move on, and the greatest obstacle to doing that was his own grief.

How can I get over my son's death? he asked himself. *That was my mistake. It is my duty to mourn, the only way I can atone for my sin. If I don't, won't it mean that I don't care?*

These were not the thoughts he hoped for, but the ones which bubbled out of his mind. He let them come, doing his best to perceive them calmly. His guilt was evident—it was the most striking emotion, though not necessarily the greatest. It was the easy first resort.

He had failed to protect his son. It was a massive failure, and the way his brain tried to handle that was to blame himself. He felt that he had to.

Jack sighed. Consciously, he knew that getting over this self-blaming would be the first step, but knowing something and actually doing it were two very, very different concepts. It didn't matter how strong Jack's mind and heart were—such terrible grief wasn't something that could be overcome in a short amount of time. Even working through the edge of his feelings was an exhausting and difficult process.

He'd taken a small step today. He'd realized that self-blaming was the first obstacle to overcome. Only then would he able to genuinely consider his emotions, see things for what they were, and try to repair his Dao crack. However, though he saw that first step, he could sense he wasn't yet ready to take it.

That's okay, he thought, loving himself as he would love another. *This cannot be rushed. I will take my time. When I'm ready, I will know.*

Time was necessary. The best way to handle this was to embrace his feelings as much as possible without losing himself. Gradually, he would become familiar with those feelings, and then he could begin to unravel them.

Death... What is death?

The Dao of Death was one he cultivated. Up to now, he had only had two viewpoints on death—inflicting it, and studying it on the death cube. Both were useful, but he'd always lacked a more personal viewpoint. He'd never actually experienced death—the only time he had, when his father passed away pre-Integration, he hadn't been a cultivator yet.

The current situation was the personal experience he'd been missing. He didn't even have to try—the insights rushed into him, part of the grief he couldn't shake off.

Death was painful—far more so than it seemed from outside. Only now that his son was gone could Jack begin to comprehend how brutal and merciless death was. It had erased a life with the flick of a switch. All the dreams, experiences, friends, lovers, pains, wine under the moon... All of that was instantly gone. Life was an orderly, gradual process. Death was an instant, world-shattering one.

If life was rain, then death was thunder.

And death, like life, extended beyond the individual. Eric's death was over, but the consequences of that event were still rippling out. They would affect Jack, Brock, Vivi, Ebele, the Animal Kingdom... It could be said that the entire future of the world had been altered because of the consequences of one death—the infamous butterfly effect.

If life was a lake and its ecosystem, then death was a boulder thrown inside. It instantly and enormously disrupted a gradual process.

Death was a powerful weapon. If life was a carefully arranged chess game, then a well-placed death was the equivalent of adding an extra piece to the board or flipping the table. It could be said that, while death was available, the calculations of life did not matter.

In that sense, death was too powerful. Maybe that was why the cultivation world had gone to shit. Death was just too common. Maybe the only way for life to thrive was an environment like the advanced societies of pre-Integration Earth, where killing another was an absolutely major deal. Only then could genuine progress be made.

It was... It was...

Jack frowned, losing his train of thought. While meditating on Life and Death, he was constantly snapped out of it by a persistent feeling of wrongness. A voice inside him whispered that he was using the death of his son as a tool to advance further. He knew that was not the case but had no way to force his emotions—it eventually reached the point where he had to stop and address that voice.

I am not using anything, he told himself, trying his hardest to remain rational. *It is the only way forward. I... What else can I do?*

Wallow, came the voice. *Mourn. Resign yourself to suffering because you deserve it.*

Jack found it hard to argue. He disagreed with the voice, but how could he defend himself when he'd sinned that heavily?

He shook his head. Conflict was not the way to go. He opened his mind to the voice, letting it speak. He needed to understand it.

But God, was it painful.

His heart was shaved by knives. Accusatory words flooded his mind. The grief attacking him, hidden behind a shield of guilt he couldn't bear to break. All the while, he endured, picturing himself as a stone in an ice-cold lake. The pain and despair washed over him. He was one entity, and his heart was another—no matter how the latter suffered, he would remain in control.

He struggled to keep making progress.

Hour after hour, Jack grew more aware of his feelings. His understanding sank deeper into the unlit areas of his mind, cataloging and interpreting the angry shouts which dominated that space. He grew closer to himself, moving toward resolution with tiny, tiny steps.

It would be a long process.

In the meanwhile, as Jack worked on his heart, his understandings into Death rapidly grew. Grief was the projection of another's death—he was experiencing a small death for himself, and whether he tried to or not, all the suffering slowly translated into insights.

Over time, his preconceived notions collapsed. He approached the truth—and truth was the core of the Dao.

Jack couldn't utilize that knowledge right now. Since his Dao was cracked, all the understandings in the world could only increase his power by small margins. However, if he ever managed to repair his Dao and return to his former level, he would be a far stronger version of himself—a completely different beast. His cultivation base wouldn't have improved, but his understandings would have skyrocketed.

Disaster and opportunity walked hand-in-hand. This experience had a great chance to doom Jack—but, if he pulled through, he would rise to unprecedented heights of power.

It all came down to the person.

Jack didn't know how long he spent in the Vortex. Time had lost its meaning, and as a high-Grade cultivator, his sense of it was distorted to begin with.

His main task was coming to terms with his feelings. To do that, he meditated on Life and Death, aligning himself with the thoughts of his inner heart as they came. It was a deeply painful experience, but also a profound one. He could feel himself going through a smelting—his level of existence rose, as if being elevated from the mortal coil.

As if grief was the hammer, guilt the wielder, and Jack was a rough piece of metal constantly hammered on.

Throughout that time, he didn't dare meditate on the Fist. It was the source of his problems, where the crack existed. Until his mind was more stable, he wasn't ready to face it.

Whenever he grew too tired of Life and Death, as well as his emotions, he would gently push them to the background and work on spacetime. He already had deep enough understandings, but the artificial black hole held innumerable mysteries. He had to admit it was intriguing.

This black hole was the incomplete inheritance of Archon Black Hole, while the Realm Heart inside Jack—as well as his current understandings—was the inheritance of Archon Green Dragon. Between the two, Jack couldn't tell which was superior, because both were at such a high level that he could only scrape their surface.

However, two was always better than one. Jack could contrast these inheritances, drawing his own conclusions from their disagreements, and emphasize on the things they both agreed on. Even Archons couldn't grasp the entirety of spacetime—by having two separate views on the same thing, Jack could accelerate his progress further.

Especially with the black hole before him. Jack had always been fascinated by the concept of black holes, and it also fit with some of his other skills. Supernova, for example, pulled in the world's essence and compressed it as much as possible before letting it explode.

In the universe, black holes and supernovas were similar. They occurred from the same origin, which was the collapse of a large star and the creation of a gravitational vortex. The only difference was that the supernova erupted, while the gravitational vortex of the black hole grew beyond a certain threshold to the point where it could no longer erupt. The gravity was so strong that nothing could escape.

Essentially, the black hole was the natural evolution of a supernova. If Jack could comprehend some of its principles and apply them to his own attacks, just what would he achieve? Could he make his fist work like a black hole?

As for creating his own artificial black hole, that was too distant a concept. It drove home just how powerful an Archon was. At his current level, Jack couldn't even hope to approach them.

Which, incidentally, put the entire Immortal Crusade into perspective. Green Dragon and Black Hole, two unimaginably powerful Archons sitting at the top of the universe, had both made the same decision to seal their descendants and inheritance in a separate dimension to escape the effects of the Crusade.

Just how powerful were the Immortals and Old Gods? Just how world-shattering was the war between them?

A war which had just been restarted.

Time will not wait for me, Jack realized, strengthening his resolve. *Even if I manage to recover from this, I will still be nothing but an ant before the major powers of the universe—the real players of this world. No matter how great my talent and potential, they are worthless without real power. If I want to protect my people, my strength is far from enough. I must grow stronger, far stronger, so I can be ready when needed.*

Right now, I am not even a chess piece in the grand chess game of the universe. Even if do become a piece, if I reach the A-Grade or even become an Archon, so what? Green Dragon and Black Hole had reached that level and achieved nothing. All they could do in the face of the Crusade was tuck away their descendants somewhere and hope for the best, and how did that help them?

The descendants of Green Dragon ended up becoming beasts. The descendants of Black Hole were stranded for a billion years.

Even as a chess piece in the grand game of the universe, I will have to rely on luck. The only reliable way to protect myself and those I care about is to become a player, then win the game.

But even Archons couldn't do it—what qualifications do I have to try?

I will try regardless. Because that is the essence of my—He hiccupped, thought for a bit, then changed his words.

Because that is what I want.

CHAPTER TWENTY-FOUR

HALL OF WONDERS

CULTIVATION WAS A TIMELESS EXPERIENCE. THE HOURS FLOWED between one's fingers like grains of sand, accumulating at their feet until they were standing on a brilliant sandcastle.

However, it was also tiring. The exhaustion piled up, especially if you were struggling against your emotions at the same time. Though Jack alternated between Death and Spacetime, he also needed periods of rest, and he chose to spend that time exploring the Black Hole World. Others might have preferred to relax alone, but he enjoyed the sense of discovery and observing the culture of these odd people.

Plus, he was a man who liked good company.

"And this is the Hall of Wonders," Mia explained, showing Jack an ivory door filled with intricate carvings.

"How did you get ivory?" Jack asked.

"We have animals here!"

"Do you have elephants?"

"No... Well, when my ancestors entered the Black Hole World, it wasn't with just the clothes on their backs. They brought manuscripts, books, records, cultivation manuals, weapons, armor, materials... All sorts of items, so they could prosper for at least a million years. Many of those have been used up by now or integrated into our world, but some, like cultivation manuals or mementos, remain here."

"Are you saying these items have survived over a billion years?"

"Kind of." Mia pushed open the door, revealing a hundred-foot-long corridor. Inhomogeneous objects littered the shelf-covered walls, while the corridor itself gave off a feeling of endless years, as if every breath of air here was precious. As Mia kept speaking, she instinctively lowered her voice, "Some treasures are made of incorruptible materials. Others deteriorate with time, like history books, but we just copy them over. As for things that deteriorate and cannot be copied, those are long lost."

Jack didn't dare breathe too deeply. A sense of reverence swelled his heart, a deep respect oozing from his very soul. This was a billion years of history. It was unbelievable.

He didn't speak immediately. His feet, which had once crossed dozens of miles with every step, now moved slowly forward. He reached out to touch these objects, then stayed his hand.

There were all sorts of items here. Books filled an entire section of the corridor. There were weapons, armor, and a hundred-some trinkets of indeterminate functionality. There was also a row of transparent jade crystals which seemed to contain... dancing letters?

The first place Jack reached was the books. There had to be dozens of them—was it the accumulated knowledge of a billion years? Or did it start before, at the age of the Ancients? There could be knowledge here which had been lost from everywhere else in the universe.

Jack was a scientist. Not a historian, but he had still learned to appreciate past knowledge. Standing here, at a lost chapter of history, filled him with awe.

"These are just our most important books," Mia said as if reading his thoughts. "We also have a library with millions of them, though most have been added by us through the passage of time."

Jack swiveled around. "This is incalculable wealth!" he exclaimed. "If we ever manage to leave this world, please safe-keep the books. The entire universe will be grateful!"

Mia was surprised, then laughed. "We would never them let be harmed. History is important to us. It's all we have. Focusing on the past and future is the only way to survive a hundred million generations without collapsing. I wonder, what does a world look like when it focuses on the present?"

"If we ever get out of here, I will show you," Jack said, his gaze mellowing a bit. "You've been my guide here. I will recip-rocate in my world."

She chuckled. "I look forward to it."

Next came the jade crystals. They were sharply cut and the size of a man's fist, shining as they reflected the white light of the ever-present lamps. Jack could make out a heap of letters inside them, all jumbled up near the center.

"Try shaking one," Mia said.

Jack hesitated. When she gestured him forward, he grabbed a crystal and gently shook it. The letters inside began to dance like snow in a snow globe, forming innumerable words one after the other before gathering back in the center, slowly turning inert.

"What's that?" Jack asked in surprise, shaking the ball again.

"An ancient cultivation manual," Mia explained, proud to

finally surprise him. "This is a method devised and used by the Ancients. The inside of the ball seems empty, besides the letters, but it's actually carved with very precise lines of the Dao. As you shake the ball, the letters flow along those lines, forming a vast array of texts. It's a way to contain large amounts of information in a small independent storage space, and it also serves as a protection mechanism. The more you understand this ball's contents, the more you familiarize yourself with the patterns governing the revolution of letters and the more knowledge you can perceive."

Jack shook the ball again, watching the letters dance. "Fascinating."

"I know, right?" She gave him a wide smile. "Of course, the precise method to create them has been lost to us. It's a good thing these crystals don't deteriorate with time because we wouldn't be able to recreate them. These are the core cultivation paths our people follow, though as time passes, fewer and fewer people can reach the higher stages."

"Hmm." Jack cupped his chin. "You mentioned that these crystals have ways to regulate the knowledge they disperse, right? That the more one understands, the more they can see, essentially forming a stable path of progression for anyone wanting to cultivate them."

"Exactly!" Mia explained. "You're smart."

Jack didn't reply immediately. In his mind, he was contrasting these crystals with the death cube he possessed. They bore several similarities—both were precise geometrical shapes, both contained cultivation knowledge or insights into the Dao, and both possessed ingenious ways to force the practitioner to cultivate them one step at a time.

Was my death cube created by the Ancients? Jack wondered. *That would explain why it's so mysterious... but, also, where would Elder Boatman have found it?*

In the past, Jack assumed this was a naturally-formed object, but he always had his doubts. Now that he saw something similar produced by the Ancients, he was more inclined to believe that alternative, and that was very important, because it meant the insights contained within the death cube were not perfect.

A natural object would be formed by the purest laws of the world, but a manmade object could only reach the heights of its creator. If the death cube really was created by the Ancients, Jack shouldn't blindly believe everything he discovered. Though the creator was undoubtedly extremely skilled, maybe even an Archon, that didn't make them perfect.

Could Elder Boatman have created the death cube? Jack wondered. It wasn't impossible, but he had no way to know. In any case, whether the creator was Elder Boatman or an ancient Archon, it didn't matter much right now. Those two levels were indistinguishable to him—like a human looking up at two mountain peaks and trying to tell which one was taller.

One thing he could tell, however, was that the death cube was of a higher rank than these crystals. It radiated a greater Dao—this fact was undeniable.

To save Mia some face, Jack didn't bring out the death cube, though he would later. Instead, he asked, "How come these spheres are here? I thought your people were cultivating them."

"We are," she replied. She sounded... embarrassed? "We, uh, aren't too good at cultivation anymore. We can only study the lowest levels of these manuals. Some of our first ancestors, who had achieved a much higher level, had written down these lower levels on paper, which is how we can freely copy and study them. In truth, we have no need for these crystals; we are not qualified to study them."

"I see," Jack replied. "Then, why are some of them missing?"

The shelf before him had nine crystals, each placed on a small pedestal. There were also three empty pedestals.

When Mia didn't reply, Jack turned around only to find her red in the face, as if she was about to speak of something she was ashamed of. "You don't have to tell me if you don't want to," he quickly said, but she shook her head.

"It's fine. We... We have shamed our ancestors. Around a million years ago, we started finding things near the Vortex. Body parts, durable treasures... Little things, but we were overjoyed. It meant there were people in the vicinity of our world. Maybe they could help us out. However, we knew that, from the outside, the entrance to our world seems like a black hole. Nobody in their right mind would enter—no offense."

"None taken," Jack replied, hiding his smirk.

Mia continued, "Well, we were unable to exit, so we had to find a way to let them know we were in here. Our Elder Council at the time decided to send some of our most durable treasures through the Vortex. That would surely tip them off."

"Unless they didn't care."

"It's not that simple. We knew that entering the Vortex came with massive risks; only those with great Dao understanding or extremely durable bodies would survive. Yet, what could we do? We chose some of our least precious and most durable treasures, then sent them into the Vortex at regular intervals. At worst, someone would identify this place as a treasure hunting spot and generate traffic, and then eventually people would know... It's just a shame that, even after a million years, nobody has come to search for us. We even sent three of our cultivation manuals to entice high-Grade cultivators, but to no avail."

She sighed. Jack, however, was connecting the dots. The treasures and body parts that had arrived here must have come from early explorers of the Milky Way soon after this area was

Integrated. Then, when the Black Hole People began sending out treasures, four cultivators discovered it and claimed this place for themselves, eventually using those treasures to increase their powers and found the Animal Kingdom.

The Kingdom was a wretched hive of warmongering arrogance. It was a shame that the assistance of these kind Black Hole People ended up like that.

In fact, Gan Salin had mentioned that the cultivation manuals of both the Emberheart and Lonihor families—the noble leonine families of the Animal Kingdom—had come from the Animal Abyss.

"Tell me," Jack asked, "of these three manuals that are missing, was one of them capable of using lightning to empower the cultivator's body? And the other could give them wings and divine-seeming powers?"

Mia's eyes widened. "Exactly! How did you know?"

"I've had some run-ins with the descendants of the people who found your treasures. They are my mortal enemies, actually, and the ones who pushed me in here."

"Oh." Her voice fell. "I am so, so sorry."

"It's okay. Look at the bright side—I'm here now. Guess your plan worked."

She thought about it for a moment. "Yes, I guess it did."

She still seemed upset, so Jack added, "Don't overthink it. You couldn't have known. You did the best you could."

Her eyes snapped back to the present. "Oh, I wasn't thinking about that, but thanks for worrying about me. I was just considering that, since we know our treasures are used by bad people to harm others, we should stop sending them out altogether."

Jack raised a brow. "That's a terrible idea. Whether good or bad, those people are your only chance of leaving this place."

"So?"

"So, just keep sending them treasures. Entice stronger people to come. If not for you, do it for your descendants. You can't rob them of their chance to escape just to protect strangers like me."

She blinked at him, then laughed. "What are you talking about, you silly? Of course we can. If our children grew up and learned that their parents harmed the world to escape, wouldn't they be ashamed of us? Wouldn't they prefer us to have done the right thing even if it harms them?"

"But you can't make that decision. It's their choice."

Her smile turned melancholic. "My father has said that, sometimes, it's not about making a decision. It's about showing the path. Even if it doesn't always work out, it's the best we can do."

Jack shook his head. He was opposed to this idea, though he couldn't explain why. Maybe his mind was clouded.

In any case, this didn't affect him.

"What about all these?" he asked, gesturing toward the rest of the corridor which was filled with trinkets.

Mia rejoiced again. "Oh, those are treasures! Some of them are magical, some are not, but they're all left behind by the first generation of our people, the ones who'd lived in the outside universe before arriving to the Black Hole World. No matter how much we wanted to contact the outside world, we never sent any of these through the Vortex. They represent the feelings of my people, a reminder that we will one day leave this place. This collection is our most important treasure."

Seeing Jack's hesitation, she laughed.

"It's fine," she said. "You can take a look—just don't break anything."

Jack nodded. He had to admit he was intrigued—he paced deeper into the corridor, running his eyes over every treasure, every trinket, every souvenir. They were all wildly different from each other, and each had their own story to tell. He saw a tiny dolphin carved of pink crystal, a white ceremonial mask, a dagger inlaid with gems, and a bronze telescope with the initials M.N. carved on its ridge.

"May I?" he asked.

To which Mia replied, "Go right ahead."

He reached out to take a small artifact—the statuette of a dark-skinned, female warrior, proudly raising her spear toward the sky even as she cradled a child in her embrace. He caressed its hair. Suddenly, he was emotional. This statuette reminded him of Vivi, whom he dearly missed. It had been over three years since they last saw each other. Was she okay?

Now filled with thoughts of his family, his eyes fell on a bronze artifact which didn't stick out at all. It was a heart broken in four. As he took a second look, he saw that it wasn't broken, just made up of four pieces which could attach or detach from each other.

Each of these treasures carried their own story. Who knows what people had made these and for what reasons? Only now did Jack realize that the corridor's timeless aura came not from the cultivation manuals and history books, not from the magical weapons and armor, but from these seemingly simple artifacts.

They had remained here for a billion years, unaffected by the passage of time, the last keepsake of their previous owners. Something to remember them. Jack was still thinking about his family, and tears threatened to come to his eyes.

These artifacts had waited here a billion years. He and his family had only been apart for three. They could handle it. He could, as well.

But God, how he missed them.

Mia was silent as she watched Jack's face go through a myriad emotions. Her gaze fell on the statuette he was still caressing, and she hesitated over saying something before finally choosing not to.

"Let's go," Jack said, gently placing the statuette back. His voice was emotional, but also resolved. "We have a world to escape."

CHAPTER TWENTY-FIVE

IT'S TIME

THE FOREST OF THE STRONG HAD BEEN A SILENT PLACE LATELY. ERIC had been kidnapped right in front of everyone. The joyful atmosphere had been torn asunder.

Huali and Dorman were distraught. Harambe was inconsolable for having failed to stop this, though he never could have. Edgar sat on the highest tower of his newly-built academy, sipping wine and sighing over the ugliness of the world.

The professor had aged overnight. She had been old before, but it hadn't seemed like it. Now, her age was evident. Messy white hair filled her head, and deep wrinkles had appeared around her eyes. From a combative woman, she'd turned into a despondent grandmother. Even her steady grip over the world's workings had weakened. She was unable to focus. She was forgetting things.

Age took its toll on everyone, and the professor remained stranded at the peak E-Grade, never reaching the D-Grade and extending her life.

Six months after Eric's kidnapping, the professor had retired. She withdrew to a small house near the Forest of the Strong where she passed her days in peace, surrounded by friends and family. In her place, Vivi took over running the Bare Fist Brotherhood, and by extension, Earth.

Vivi had been affected by the loss of her son in a different way. Though she hoped Jack would be able to save him, some maternal instinct spoke against that hope. Deep inside, she could feel that her son was dead—and, after a period of manic grief, she'd regathered herself, resolving to help the cultivators of Earth increase their power so they would never be vulnerable again. So Ebele would be safe.

Unlike Jack, Vivi had ample experience with grief. She'd lived a hard life and even led a bloody revolution when the Integration came. She had mourned many people, both family and friends, including her parents.

Of course, her son was an unimaginably more painful loss. It wasn't something she could get over anytime soon, but prior experience helped her at least gather her bearings and keep operating through the grief.

Under her guidance, the Brotherhood took a more power-oriented turn. She didn't have people kill each other, as the Immortals and the System did, but she imposed stricter training regimes and harder schedules. This was done out of love for her people—when the next enemy came, they had to be ready.

After four years of Jack's absence, though she believed in him, it would be naive not to prepare for all outcomes.

Working hard helped keep her mind off things. Her own cultivation had stabilized at the middle D-Grade—she was now progressing very, very slowly. Maybe she would reach the late D-Grade by the end of her life, if she was lucky. It was how far her talent could take her.

Of course, the late D-Grade realm sounded low compared to Jack and his universe-class standards, but to normal cultivators it was a godlike realm.

On the surface, the one who'd been affected by Eric's loss the least was Ebele. It wasn't that she didn't love him; there were two factors contributing to her stance.

One was her age. When Eric was kidnapped, she had been five years old, and she hadn't watched it happen. She didn't even understand the concept of death. The reality of the situation was only something she'd pieced together from the reactions of everyone around her, so it had been less of a shock to her than, say, her mother.

The other reason was that Ebele's disposition was similar to her father's. Whenever problems arose, her first reaction was to become stronger. When Eric was kidnapped, she didn't change her stance, just dove deeper into it. She worked harder, and with more vigor. She pushed herself more.

Cultivating before adulthood was a risk, because the soul was still changing, and the cultivator may discover they'd accidentally shifted away from their Dao. Ebele, with the guidance of excellent teachers, wouldn't make such a rookie mistake. But she still yearned for power. She looked forward to her twenty-fifth birthday—the age her mother had deemed best to start cultivating.

Until then, she would do everything in her power to grow stronger in other ways. She took full advantage of the many cultivation resources her family possessed—like the Ice Pond. She sharpened her fighting skills. She read books, and studied, and refined and improved herself with every opportunity. She tried to gather as many experiences as possible.

By the age of six, Ebele could speak two languages, draw, and wrestle with children twice her age. She was familiar with most weapons, specializing in the sword, and with several martials arts. Thanks to all the resources she enjoyed, her stats had reached the level of post-System adults despite not cultivating yet. She was hailed as a prodigy across the Forest of the

Strong, with her teachers most praising her attitude—not just her hard work, but also her ability to rest as needed and keep her mind flexible. That was difficult even for adults; to achieve such a mindstate at only six years old was something that didn't come from any resources, but vast quantities of raw talent. It was a concept she understood instinctively.

However, maturity came at a cost. Though Ebele's mind and heart were beyond her age, she lost out on some of the joy of being a toddler.

On this day, she was sitting in the Ice Pond, cultivating at an area near the waterfall. According to her mother, this was where her father had taken his first step into the Dao of the Fist —and Ebele, who was a proud individual by nature, gazed toward that waterfall every time she was about to give up, drawing from it the courage to keep going.

She didn't remember her father much, Though she idolized him. She wanted to be like him, and to do that, she couldn't lose out. If he could endure the Ice Pond, so could she.

Ebele may have been a prodigy, but she remained six years old. Most things in her mind were seen through the lenses of a child.

Mom and Dad will be proud of me, she thought, gritting her teeth as she endured the biting cold spreading over her legs. She was alone in a dark, cold cave, pushing herself to keep going. Her little teeth chittered, but her heart never gave out.

Next time, I will protect Mom. Until Dad comes back, I will make sure she never cries again. I... I will protect her. I must! Because, if I don't do it, no one will!

———

On the path of cultivation, there were times when you could blitz through, advancing at a tremendous pace. There were also times when you had to take things slow, sitting down and waiting for the right time to come.

This was one of the latter periods for Jack.

He stayed in the Black Hole World for around one year. In that period, his power didn't increase in the slightest. If anything, it degraded, as his soul had released the last of his pent-up energy. He was now thoroughly a cripple, with a Dao Tree that could neither gather energy nor utilize it effectively. Despite his incomparably robust foundation, formidable body, and deep Dao, his current battle prowess was no better than the average middle C-Grade.

Jack didn't mind. He took this time to immerse himself in his mortality. With the absence of immediate danger and little sense of time, he could finally relax. Cultivation became a hobby instead of a need. He found pleasure.

For this past year, he would regularly cultivate at the Vortex, deepening his Dao understandings. He let the process be slow and methodical. Simultaneously, he tried to look deep inside himself and come to terms with both his grief and Dao. It wasn't easy, but steps were being made. Through loving himself, he earned the time for the shock of loss to abate, returning all those feelings to more manageable levels.

Between cultivation sessions, Jack had decided to spend time with the Black Hole People. He enjoyed them. In this past year, he concluded there was no secret dictatorship, no control of speech or mind, no mastermind in the shadows. They were just genuinely good people.

They laughed a lot. Though their environment was dull, they did their best to brighten it up, painting everything in bright colors and talking each other up at every opportunity. At day, they would work, and at night, they would relax and enjoy themselves. Bars were aplenty in the Black Hole World, filled with the sound of warm laughter.

The crime rates were low. So was poverty. The only way to survive for a billion years was to form an undeniably great society and educate the next generation to be as kind as the previous. The Black Hole people saw themselves as grains of sand, as members of a larger organism. They were just one in an endless line of generations—by so adjusting their perspective, they could withstand the passage of time and the pointlessness of their existence.

Then again, wasn't all existence pointless?

In spending time with these people, Jack didn't speak much. He didn't tell the populace about the outside universe or the way he thought. He simply listened—absorbing their mindset like a sponge, acclimating himself to calm, peaceful nirvana.

For his entire life as a cultivator, he had been struggling against his fate at every step. The Black Hole People did the exact opposite. They embraced it and laughed.

It was a beautiful way to live.

Over one year, Jack's heart mellowed. He forgot about the violence of his earlier days, letting his mind and soul undergo a subtle transformation. His core solidified, settling down from the craze which had spanned his journey.

His grief represented Death. The Vortex represented Spacetime. And the Black Hole people, with their unique yet alluring lifestyle, represented Life.

This was a cultivation paradise for Jack. All his Daos were clearly expressed. Just by existing, he could draw them in, increasing his understanding every day. Over the course of a year, his Dao soared. He reached heights he could previously only imagine. Through reaching rock bottom and slowly climbing his way back up, he had achieved a complete transformation of himself.

Though his overall power degraded, his Dao had skyrocketed. If he could repair the crack, it wouldn't be as simple as returning to his previous level of power—he would be much, much stronger. All that progress was like a bomb of potential waiting to erupt.

And it hinged on him being able to repair his Dao crack.

One particular day, Jack had been meditating near the Vortex. His eyes slowly opened, revealing the light of deep stars. His lips curved into a thoughtful smile. "I guess..." he whispered in the void, "it's time to give it a go."

CHAPTER TWENTY-SIX

REPAIRING THE CRACK

Jack sank into his soul world, completely isolating the outside world. Even if someone attacked him, he wouldn't know. He needed absolute focus.

Starry light welcomed him from all directions. Purple stars twinkled. In the void, a lone tree stood there, rooted into a floating, multi-colored fist.

This fist was large, around three feet wide. Each of its fingers was a different color—purple, silver, green, red, black—representing the Dao Roots he'd established in the E-Grade, while the fist itself was pointed downward. Where the wrist would be on a normal fist, this one simply ended, with a glowing green gem embedded into its base. This was the Life Drop, a drop of blood from Enas that Jack had acquired in Trial Planet.

On top of that wrist was where Jack's Dao Tree had grown. A sturdy and solid specimen, with roots powerfully drilling into the fist below and branches spreading out uninhibited. With its ten feet of height, it was almost comically large when placed on the three-foot-wide fist, yet its size paled in comparison to the soul world itself.

Atop the tree branches, purple flowers bloomed, twinkling like the stars which decorated Jack's soul space. There were also five fruits—Fist, Space, Life, Death, Battle.

Finally, there was the Realm Heart he'd inherited from Archon Green Dragon; a pulsating mass of crystal inlaid with innumerable spacetime runes, currently orbiting the crown of his tree.

Jack was emotional as he gazed at his Dao. This was all the result of his cultivation. He'd built it up, piece by piece, over many years of effort.

How long has it been since the Integration? he suddenly wondered. *Seven years? Eight? I've lost count... but it doesn't really matter.*

To most C-Grade cultivators, seven years was nothing. Just the blink of an eye. Jack, however, had only lived for twenty-seven before embarking on the path of cultivation. Those seven-odd years were important. Without realizing it, he'd already turned thirty-five.

Happy birthday, he thought. A bittersweet moment.

Unfortunately, a massive crack covered the trunk of his Dao Tree. If he failed to repair it, he would remain stranded in the Black Hole World forever.

It wouldn't be too bad. He could start a new life here, embrace the peaceful happiness of these people, live it out.

Except that wouldn't be him. The bird cannot thrive in a cage—the Fist cannot survive in peace. Jack had to return to the universe, see his family again, discover the secrets of the Immortals and the Old Ones, battle in the Second Crusade, and reach the peak of cultivation. He wanted to fight to his heart's content—make sure the people he cared about were safe.

And get revenge.

The world was waiting for him, and he'd already rested here

for a year. That was more than enough. His mind had stabilized. It was time to go.

Jack cut away all distractions, focusing on the task at hand. He first inspected his soul space, touching on each of the dubious points.

The door on his Dao Tree remained sealed. The crack had split it in half, rendering it unable to open, and the turtle was still asleep. Jack tried knocking, but nothing happened. As for the Life Drop itself, it remained an ocean of green power he could draw on to enhance his body—useless at present. He would have to get through this alone.

The Green Dragon Realm Heart was suspended in the void, orbiting his Dao Tree. It was a powerful object, but one he couldn't use freely. Besides some assistance it offered in comprehending spacetime, its other functions would only come into effect once he reached the B-Grade and formed his inner world.

Finally, Jack flew through the void, approaching a body which rested in a corner of his world. It seemed to be peacefully sleeping—but it looked exactly like Jack.

This was Copy Jack—and Copy Jack had somehow turned into a mystery Jack couldn't unravel. When he first absorbed the Dao Soul after the Integration Tournament, it had evolved into a clone of himself, one with a simple mind. The two of them often sparred in his soul world, and it had helped Jack make progress in various aspects. Copy Jack slowly developed himself, just like a child. He even seemed willing to visit the outside world, and Jack had considered looking for ways to make it happen.

At some point, everything changed. When Jack absorbed the Life Drop, Copy Jack's childlike curiosity drove him to touch it. A tendril of green energy had zapped him, possibly frying something inside him—and changing him in a seemingly permanent way.

Ever since then, Copy Jack's personality shifted. His desire to leave had vanished. He was perfectly content relaxing in Jack's soul world, occasionally interacting with his host but mostly flying around, absorbed in thoughts only he knew. That change saddened Jack, and though he'd asked around, nobody had any idea. There was nothing he could do. Besides, Copy Jack seemed happy.

Now, however, Copy Jack had fallen into a deep slumber. He'd been like this ever since Jack awoke in the Black Hole World—he guessed it was due to overdrawing his Dao to escape Eva Solvig, or maybe the Dao crack had impacted him in an unforeseen way. Regardless, Jack had been unable to wake up Copy Jack no matter what he did, which worried him greatly. Both for Copy Jack's own safety, and also for Jack's—he did not enjoy enigmas buried inside his soul.

Even now, as Jack was about to begin repairing his Dao crack, Copy Jack could not awaken. Jack tried for a while, then shook his head and flew away. At least, he could sense that his copy was stable. He would be better equipped to look into this issue later.

Done with all other variables, Jack reached his Dao Tree again. The crack stared at him like the maw of a hungry beast. Dao constantly flowed out—his Dao—rendering his tree basically incapable of holding any. Due to this crack, the fruits were pale, the flowers were sagging, the trunk was spongy, and the roots were weak. Attempting to muster his Dao was like drawing water with a net—most dispersed, and only an insignificant amount remained.

The only reason Jack had a half-decent level of battle prowess was his formidable body, as well as the trace amounts of energy contained in the tree's roots.

This had to change.

Jack took a deep breath. Slowly, his mind entered its battle state. He hadn't experienced this feeling in a while—he felt rusted, nervous, yet excited, like a former champion returning to the ring of glory.

The crack was daunting. It stared him in the face, taking up his whole world. It was filled with his own darkness—the demons he'd never been able to defeat.

Yet, this time, Jack had come prepared. He'd taken his time. He'd worked out his complex feelings and come to terms with himself. One entire year, he'd spent recovering and preparing for this moment, letting the rest of the world unfold as it will.

He was ready.

His mind blasted outward. The walls and barriers he'd set up shattered. Torrents of darkness flooded toward him as if from a broken dam, and Jack stood tall in their path, accepting them all.

The impact was almost physical. He was shaken, his thoughts growing blurry. Grief and anger filled him in prodigious amounts, submerging his mind completely, and Jack was a drowning man struggling to find the way up. Panic welled up inside his heart—an intense desire to bottle everything up again. He pushed it down. Ignoring these feelings wouldn't repair his Dao crack. He had to face them.

They were fiercer than he remembered. The grief, the pain, the self-blame. How could a man survive this? How could he persist?

"DAD!" Eric screamed, his throat crushed by a laughing leonine. Jack almost lost control. He didn't want to relive that scene, but he didn't have a choice. There was no avoiding it. The only way out was through.

Everything Jack had prepared for came under test. His

temperance, his discipline, his clarity. This was a war against his emotions, a war which his every instinct pushed him to avoid, but a war he faced regardless. He bit his tongue until it bled, using the pain to remain awake. The heartache was insufferable.

"Hahaha!" the leonine laughed. "I killed your son, Jack Rust! What are you going to do about it? What? Come on, you useless *coward*!"

Jack's heart was made of coal. Dark tears rolled down his cheeks, and he was clenching his fists so hard that his nails dug into his palms and drew blood.

This was a heart demon. The emotions he'd felt at the time had been so intense, so unresolved, that they still lurked in a corner of his mind, waiting to assault him at the worst possible moment. Jack knew it, but resisting was so hard. He would rather split his soul in two than be forced to face this.

It wasn't a test meant for humans to endure. But Jack had to.

The laughing leonine was nothing. It was smoke and dust, just a prop to hide the real meaning of this vision. Anger was just an escape—what he really felt was helplessness, defeat. Despair.

"I'm sorry," Jack told the lifeless Eric. "I'm so, so sorry... but I cannot turn back time. I cannot save you."

The words hurt him more than the vision. He'd just taken a wall inside his mind and ripped it apart—but that wall was made of himself, and the pain was staggering.

The vision dispersed. A new one appeared. This time, the leonine was alone, pointing a finger at Jack and raving with rage, "You deserve this! You caused this! It is all your fault!"

Jack wanted to punch out and fight to the death. It took every ounce of willpower he could muster to resist the temptation, the desperate desire to escape. Instead, he saw things for what they really were. Artus Emberheart blurred, and a new form took his place.

It was Jack. Still pointing, still raving, still shouting in anger. This was the guilt and self-blame, the anger he felt at himself for being unable to save Eric. For being the reason this happened in the first place.

Jack forced himself to take a deep breath, his entire body trembling. He did not reply. He let Angry Jack's words wash over him, dying him red in his son's blood. He didn't know how long this went on for. Finally, when Angry Jack ran out of steam, only then did Jack reply.

"I'm sorry," he said, his voice fuzzy from angry tears. "I... am not perfect. I made a mistake. I swear I will be better next time, so please... forgive me."

"NO!" Angry Jack shouted. "NO! NO! NO!"

His words shook the world, his fury so deeply nestled it seemed it would never abate. But Jack and Angry Jack were the same person. He was Angry Jack. He opened his mouth and broke through himself to say, "I forgive you."

Angry Jack tried to disagree, finding he could not. His open mouth released no voice. He dissipated.

By now, Jack felt empty. Like his insides had been removed and he was just a hollow statue of himself. His heart was entirely colored black. He was bleeding from the soul. This was already more than any human should have to bear, and it wasn't over.

Eric's death had caused three knots inside Jack's heart. The first was despair and helplessness. The second was guilt, anger, and self-blame. The third and greatest knot was grief—and this was the most difficult one to untangle, because it did not originate from Jack's heart alone.

A third vision faced Jack. This time, it was not a leonine, not himself, but Eric. The little boy appeared alive and well, just as

Jack had seen him at first, but his eyes were sad and his voice heavy, speaking directly from the world of the dead. Jack remembered the boy with whom he'd built a treehouse, the always smiling boy he'd taken on a tour around Earth and with whom he'd shared his planet's wonders.

"What about me, Dad?" Eric asked. "Should I forgive you?"

Jack would have liked to say yes. He would have liked for that answer to be true. But it wasn't. There was nothing he could do about it.

Eric had lost everything. His life, his future, everything he'd ever be, he'd lost... and it was Jack's fault. That much was undeniable. Even if some of the causal connections were unclear, it couldn't be the fault of anybody else, nor would Jack dare to assume such a thing. He took the blame and placed it squarely on his shoulders, then collapsed under its weight. His knees slammed into the ground. He took his forehead and smashed it down.

"I'M SORRY, ERIC!" he yelled. "I LET YOU DOWN! THIS IS ALL MY FAULT! I'M SORRY! I'M SORRY!"

No matter how Jack apologized, no matter how he cried, this Eric was only a figment of his imagination. He remained unmoved.

"So what if you're sorry?" he asked. "Should I forgive you?"

"I can never deserve your forgiveness," Jack replied. "The things you lost, I can never return to you. But I can be better. For your mother, your sister. I swear I will never fail again. Please, let me protect them!"

Eric smiled coldly. "So I should just disappear?"

A knife was stabbed and twisted into Jack's heart. He lost his words, dropped his train of thought. For a moment, he lost himself—then realized this knot could never be untied. This grief could never be resolved. Maybe it would mellow down in the future, retreat from his conscious thoughts, but it was something he would have to live with forever.

Therefore, Jack did the only thing he could. He transmuted it. His grief was siphoned into a darker feeling. Only like that could he temporarily live past this.

"You should never disappear, and you should never forgive me," he said. "I cannot recover what you have lost. I cannot right this wrong. However, there is one thing I can do for you, and that is to get revenge. I will kill the man who killed you and make him suffer. Everyone involved will die. I will paint this galaxy red with the blood of leonines, and when I'm done, the name Emberheart will no longer exist!"

Eric only watched on. Jack's voice grew weaker by the end.

"I know it's nothing," he said, "but it's the only thing I can do. I hope that... perhaps... it will satisfy you."

Eric stared at Jack for a long time. He did not speak, nor did he express anything. Then, finally, the little boy faded away. His silence was puzzling to Jack, almost like a torture, but he didn't dare continue. He just couldn't. This had already wrung him dry.

The third knot hadn't been resolved. It had only been temporarily bypassed in return for Jack embracing a darkness he would rather not have. That darkness gave him power—and, for now, it was the best he could do. The only way forward.

The three knots were past. Jack opened his eyes in the soul world, facing his cracked Dao Tree again, and for a moment, he could stare at the crack directly. He saw it for what it really was —a gap in his Dao, a flaw in his life's mindset.

Jack had long become one with the Fist. He knew it well, and it knew him. In truth, the way to repairing the crack had become evident after experiencing the three visions. He knew how to fix his Dao.

It was the simplest thing, yet a difficult one.

He smiled sadly. "The Fist can make mistakes," he uttered slowly. "It can miss, it can hit the wrong target, and it can be defeated. It is not perfect, and neither am I. But... that's fine. We make mistakes and live on. We carry ourselves forward. We keep believing, never giving up. That is the way of the Fist. That is me."

The bark around the crack wriggled. New offshoots appeared, wrapping around each other. Jack watched his Dao and soul repair itself. On the inside, some warmth peeked out from underneath the darkness like a rainbow after the rain. He forced himself to feel happy, even for a moment, even as his grief told him he didn't deserve it.

It wasn't over. His path stretched through the darkness. The world would keep rolling, and he would be there, still fighting.

Jack Rust was back.

CHAPTER TWENTY-SEVEN
A TASTE OF HISTORY

THE REPAIRING WAS COMPLETE. JACK'S DAO TREE WAS WHOLE AGAIN. With just a few days of rest, it would recover from exhaustion and return to its former glory. As for Jack himself, he was completely and utterly spent. His mind was in tatters, and his soul was worn out. He was mentally exhausted.

However, the hardest part was behind him. The pain of his son's loss remained, but he'd regained himself and repaired his Dao. He could cultivate again. The only problems remaining now were the grief...

...and revenge.

Jack rested. He gave himself a full day of doing absolutely nothing. For the first time in a while, he actually slept.

When he awoke again, he felt combative, ready to take action. This was the dawn of a new era, and he was full of energy. Even a bit of his lost joviality had returned.

"Let's see where we're standing," he said.

ERROR: PLEASE REPORT TO THE NEAREST AUTHORITIES IMMEDIATELY OR FACE EXTERMINATION.

Name: Jack Rust
Species: Human, Earth-387
Faction: Bare Fist Brotherhood (C)
Grade: C
Class: Gladiator Titan (King)
Level: 303

Strength: 6040 (+)
Dexterity: 6040 (+)
Constitution: 6040 (+)
Mental: 1000
Will: 1000
Free sub-points: 2

Dao Skills: Meteor Punch IV, Iron Fist Style III, Brutalizing Aura III, Neutron Star Body III, Supernova III, Space Mastery III, Fist of Mortality III, Death Mastery III, Titan Taunt I
Dao Roots: Indomitable Will, Life, Power, Weakness
Dao Fruits: Fist, Space, Life, Death, Battle
Titles: Planetary Frontrunner (10), Planetary Torchbearer (1), Ninth Ring Conqueror, Planetary Overlord (1), Grade Defier

The status screen remained the same, except for Death Mastery reaching the third tier. Most importantly, the "cracked" tag had been removed from his Class.

Which did feel a bit odd. If Jack was being honest with himself, he believed his resonance with his current Class was lacking. He had hoped that, somewhere in between everything that happened, it would have changed. It hadn't.

What's the meaning? he wondered. *Gladiator Titan... Well, my*

Classes haven't led me wrong yet. Maybe I should try to embrace it. See what happens.

Thinking about it this way, another question came to him. How can the System work here?

He wasn't talking about his status screen. In the Black Hole World, he was able to use the System to scan people. That indicated he was inside System space. He hadn't given it much thought before, but it suddenly struck him as odd.

First of all, if the Immortals and the System knew about this place, why would they ignore it? Most importantly, how could they know? It was a black hole. System energy could enter but not exit. Whatever maintained System space, its connection to the System itself, should have been cut off a billion years ago.

It could make sense, he thought. *Whatever constitutes System space is sucked into this black hole, but it can never leave. The inside is System space, but the System itself has no idea. Maybe it's some sort of special particle? A Dao of the System?*

That was the most reasonable explanation.

Done taking stock of his situation, Jack turned his gaze to the next step: escaping the Black Hole World.

He'd studied the Vortex for a year. It was an artificial black hole, but it was also much more—similar to a complex machine carved out of Dao patterns. There were unique circulations of energy inside which Jack could decipher, and while far from truly comprehending it, he'd gotten the idea that this Vortex wasn't just the core of the Black Hole World but also its control center.

With proper understanding, he could use it to perform various changes, one of which was the opening of a portal to let everyone escape.

Throughout this year, Jack had developed several theories on how to do that, but he hadn't had the strength to try them out. Now that he did, it should only be a matter of time.

Another month flew by. Finally, Jack opened his eyes and sighed.

"Archon Black Hole... was a damn genius!"

Now that he had the power to experiment, he could confirm or disprove his theories. The Vortex was indeed the control panel of this world, but operating it was more difficult than he imagined. In particular, his current power wasn't enough to open a portal. The most he could do was create a crack for a short amount of time, letting just himself weasel out after enduring a powerful space storm.

The Black Hole People would have to stay here for a little longer... but that was fine. Jack was confident that, given a few more years, he'd acquire the strength to let them out. It was just a matter of time.

He'd also discovered another function of the Vortex. Maybe he couldn't open the Black Hole World... but he could move it!

As it turned out, this entire world was a separate dimension hidden in the folds of spacetime—the interdimensional sea. The black hole at the center of the Animal Abyss was just the end of a spatial tunnel connecting this world and the outside universe. However, distance was meaningless between separate dimensions. The spatial tunnel wasn't anchored to the specific location of the Animal Abyss, but to an artifact which lay hidden at its very center.

Through the Vortex, Jack could alter the state of that artifact, turning it inactive and letting it be moved. He could physically carry the connection point between the universe and the entire Black Hole World.

He shook his head in wonder. This had all been designed and implemented by Archon Black Hole—all Jack did was activate the mechanisms. It would be a while before he reached that level himself. That was okay—cultivation was about the journey, not the destination. He'd get there eventually.

Jack could leave through the Vortex at any time he wished, but that didn't mean he'd just disappear.

He flew backward, slowly ascending through the Black Hole World to reach the Elder Council on the twelfth layer. He called a meeting and waited. Once the Elders convened, he let them know about his situation and everything he'd discovered.

When he mentioned that their escape was only a matter of time, the aged eyes of all the Elders turned misty. Grand Elder Pasan grabbed her chest, her heart fluttering.

"One billion years..." she whispered. "A hundred million generations... And everything will end at ours. Truly, we should be honored."

Jack smiled. "You persisted for a very long time, and you have finally reached the end. Celebrate."

The Elders seemed unable to believe this, too overwhelmed by joy to speak. Mia, however, who was also present, opened her mouth to speak worried words, "What about you? If something happens to you out there, you will be hurt... and we will also be unable to escape."

Jack looked her in the eyes and smiled. "That will not happen."

His confidence stirred something in her heart. Before she could reply, Grand Elder Pasan spoke up, "You have given us great hope, Jack Rust. Simple words cannot express our gratitude. There is something I must show you before you leave. Come."

The other Elders glanced at her with surprise, then nodded. Only Mia was perplexed. Jack gave her a reassuring nod and walked after the Grand Elder, who exited the building.

They walked to the nearest elevator and used the Grand Elder's authority to travel directly to the first layer. It was empty as always. The guards saluted and let them pass.

"Where are we going?" Jack finally asked.

"Our ancestors retreated here during the Immortal Crusade," Grand Elder Pasan replied soberly. "When they did, they brought with them all sorts of knowledge. Some of it was conducive to developing our culture, but some was unnecessary to our people, even harmful—therefore, we sealed it away. Generation after generation of Elders have taken care of this secret knowledge, keeping it away from our people so as to not contaminate them. We are the only ones who knew. However, from what you told us, the Crusade has been reignited, and you will be called to fight in it. There are some things you should know."

Jack did not reply. He had the sense he was about to learn some monumental secret.

Pasan led him to a dark corner far away from all important locations. There were no guards here, no warehouses. It was just a place where nobody had a reason to come. The only warning came in the form of a small sign as soon as they reached the door of a small dark building.

"Do not enter," Jack read aloud. "Did this really stop everyone for a billion years?"

"We are peaceful people," Pasan replied. "If this sign couldn't stop us, our civilization would have long crumbled."

She grabbed an old torch by the entrance and lit it. Flames were born, and shadows danced on the stone walls around them. Just like the Hall of Wonders, this place felt old—far, far too old.

A sacred silence littered the air. Neither Jack nor Pasan spoke, descending through flights of stairs. By the time they reached the bottom, Jack estimated they were at the edge of the first layer, just a layer of stone away from the Vortex.

"We are here," Pasan said. She swiped her torch. The power of her Dao carried the flame, lighting up a dozen more torches on the walls around them, and Jack found himself facing a block of stone carved in ancient times.

The weight of history pressed down on him. For a moment, he forgot to breathe.

"This is a warning tablet," Grand Elder Pasan spoke from beside him, her voice echoing in the sealed chamber. "It speaks of our past… and also our future."

The stone tablet was ten feet wide and five tall. Smooth carvings covered its surface—far more detailed than carvings had any right to be.

One side of the tablet was occupied by an army of cultivators, flying through the void toward the other side. Leading them was a host of robots—exactly ninety-nine of them. At the very helm was a robot larger than the others, with a featureless face shaped as a rectangle.

The other side held twelve beings, grand and majestic. They were arranged in three groups, though not of equal numbers—two groups were made of five beings each, while the last was only made of two. Despite this imbalance, the three groups stood side by side as equals.

As soon as he saw this tablet, Jack had a sense of deja-vu. Back in Trial Planet, he, Brock, and Nauja had run into a cave to escape their pursuers. After a chase of many miles, they'd ended up in unplumbed depths, facing a dusty iron door with carvings similar to this one.

Yet, there were stark differences. The carvings on that door had seemed mostly ornamental—this tablet was not only much larger in size, allowing for more details, but it also appeared to be designed to convey information.

"A portrayal of the Immortal Crusade," Grand Elder Pasan explained, confirming Jack's thoughts.

"What exactly is it showing?" Jack asked. He had a feeling

that many secrets were about to be revealed—that he would suddenly see some missing pieces of the puzzle.

"These are the Immortals and their army," Pasan explained, motioning to the side of the robots. "The army you see is made up of A-Grades—eighty-three of them went to war alongside the Immortals, including eleven Archons. Our world was built in eighty-three layers to commemorate their sacrifice."

"They *all* died?" Jack asked.

"Not all of them. But, they did fight alongside the Immortals—that is sacrifice enough." Pasan's face darkened as she spoke about the robots. "There used to be ninety-nine Immortals—all at the A-Grade. Of them, thirty-three were at the middle A-Grade, eleven at the late A-Grade, and three at the peak A-Grade. There was one Immortal, their leader, at the Archon realm of power. That was the Heaven Immortal—the main creator and wielder of the System. By using it as a weapon, the Heaven Immortal was able to increase its power and reach the level of the leading Old Gods. Unfortunately, that Immortal survived the Crusade."

"But the others didn't?" Jack asked.

"Not all of them. It was a brutal war. Of the ninety-nine Immortals, only thirty-three survived, at various levels of power. None of the Old Gods perished, but most were greatly weakened. As for the cultivators fighting alongside the Immortals, they were pushed to the front line by the compulsion of the System. Most perished. Between them and the many factions crushed by the Old Gods, the cultivation world received a big hit. Most of our inheritances were lost—according to the speculations of our ancestor, hundreds of millions of years would be needed for the cultivation world to recover its previous glory. The Immortals had sacrificed everything for a single flare of power."

She raised a finger to point at a single person following the

Immortals. On closer inspection, that person was painted with more detail than the ones around him—it was a man of dark hair, dark eyes, and dark robes which covered his body.

"That is our ancestor," Pasan explained with pride. "Archon Black Hole. One of the most powerful Ancients."

"Wait," Jack said. "I thought the Ancients were destroyed by the Immortals long before the Crusade."

"Not all of them. The Immortals desired to exterminate our species, but they desired power even more. They offered deals to the strongest Ancients, and some, like our ancestor, accepted. In return for joining and fighting for them, they would let his descendants survive."

"An Archon worked with the people who genocided his species?" Jack asked, his eyes widening.

"He had no choice. If he refused, he would die, and so would all his descendants and disciples. Even back then, we were millions. He couldn't bear to sacrifice us, so he sacrificed himself—at least for a while."

A suspicion emerged in Jack's mind. "Then, he placed you in here to hide?"

"Correct," Pasan replied sadly. "Throughout the Crusade and the years preceding it, our ancestor worked hard to create this world for us. He wanted us to live free, far from the tyranny of the Immortals. Unfortunately, this task was harder than he expected; it was only near the end of the Crusade that he managed to succeed. He created this world, sealed us all inside with instructions to not leave for a million years, and hid us in this far-off place of the universe. We don't know what happened afterward, but his plan was to betray the Immortals and foster a revolution inside System space. He hoped that would create a large enough opening for the Old Gods to strike back."

A connection was made in Jack's mind. Archon Black Hole

tried to create a rebellious organization inside System space. Could that be... The Black Hole Church?

What if their name didn't just refer to Enas, whom they worshiped, but also to their founder?

If so, the Black Hole People would be very important to the Church. This was interesting. Jack wouldn't endanger them, but when they left this world for the outer universe, maybe they could take refuge with the Church.

His gaze scanned the ninety-nine Immortals and their army of eighty-three cultivators. A hundred and eighty-two A-Grades, including eleven Archons and the Old God-level Heaven Immortal, as well as a large number of B-Grade soldiers who didn't even appear in this carving. Yet, all that power had only been able to repel the Old Gods, not killing a single one.

What am I getting myself into...

CHAPTER TWENTY-EIGHT

GIFT SHOPPING

"What about the Gods?" Jack asked, looking at the other side.

"There were twelve of them, as you already know," Pasan explained. "By the time we hid in here, the Crusade was almost over. None of them had died, so it's likely they're all still alive."

"I know a few things about them," Jack said. "However, it's the first time I've seen them arranged in groups."

"That is their battle formation. The twelve Gods are separated into three great domains. Enas and Axelor, the Gods of Life and Entropy, are the strongest of the twelve. Those two by themselves form a single domain—that of the soul. The remaining ten Gods form the other two domains: energy and matter. When the Gods of a domain work together, they can combine their Daos to exhibit power at the very limit of the A-Grade, almost taking that extra step and reaching a new realm entirely. They ripped through the Immortal armies like hot knives through butter. They were nigh unstoppable. In fact, our ancestor believed the only reason the Immortals won the Crusade was that the Gods were not used to working together, as they'd never had to fight before. Otherwise, they could have been invincible."

"I see..." Jack muttered. This made some sense, and it also answered some questions he'd been harboring.

Back when he faced the trial of Green Dragon, he'd had to fight the avatars of the twelve Old Gods. Of course, their power was nothing compared to the real thing, but it shouldn't be random. The first ten Gods had been relatively simple to dismantle, but Axelor and Enas were on a different level entirely. Jack had wondered why. Now, he understood.

If the three domains of matter, energy, and soul were at the same level, then each of the other Old Gods wielded one fifth of a domain. Enas and Axelor wielded half each. How could they not be stronger?

"This is fascinating," Jack said. His eyes ran over the tablet again, taking in all the carvings. With the larger things out of the way, he could focus on the details. He looked at every Archon of the Immortal army—they were many different species, but none was a dragon. Archon Green Dragon must have been born at a later era.

Then, as he was observing the Old Gods, he discovered something. There were little figures surrounding them, so tiny he hadn't noticed them at first.

"Who are they?" he asked, pointing at the figures.

Pasan looked over. "There were some cultivators fighting for the Old Gods," she explained, "but they had almost no influence on the war. They were too weak, that's why they're drawn so small. They're only there for the sake of completion."

"Oh," Jack exclaimed. As he looked at these small cultivators, he was impressed. Whoever made these carvings was so skilled they'd managed to carve them accurately at such a small scale—even their facial expressions were evident, each carving a masterpiece.

Jack was ready to marvel at the skill needed to achieve such a thing, when he paused. His gaze latched onto a seemingly unimportant figure in those small, God-allied cultivators—all of a sudden, his eyes widened like saucers, and his mind was sent into disarray.

There was nothing special about that figure compared to the ones surrounding it, but its face was a familiar.

Wasn't that... *the Sage*!

"Who's that?" Jack exclaimed, pointing at the Sage-like figure.

Pasan frowned. "No idea. Why do you ask?"

"It's just..." Jack shook his head. "Nevermind."

It could be a coincidence. Many people looked similar to each other, and nobody could survive for a billion years. Not to mention the Sage had been a homeless man on the un-Integrated planet of Earth—the connection was almost impossible to make.

Then again, the Sage had always been full of riddles. Last time Jack had asked him, he'd revealed that his soul resonated with Enas himself, which was how he possessed extraordinary insights into Life to begin with. The entire reason the Barren High had divined and revealed Earth's location to the Animal Kingdom was so the Church could recruit the Sage.

But that was a bit far-fetched, wasn't it?

I will ask again, Jack resolved himself. *This time, I will insist. Not because I think he's an old monster who somehow managed to survive a billion years... but because I'm pretty sure he's hiding something. I just don't know what.*

"Is there anything else here?" Jack asked, turning back to Pasan.

"Just the tablet. If you're done, we can leave."

He nodded. He'd seen everything there was to see and gotten significant new information, though he wasn't sure just how it would become useful.

The two of them walked back up the stairs. Grand Elder

Pasan resealed the chamber, and then they paced back to the Elder Council.

"The gratitude and fate of my people rests on your shoulders," Pasan said. "I hate to speak such words, but your survival is critical to us. I believe Mia has taken you to the Hall of Wonders—before you leave, you may take anything you need from there. Armor, weapons, cultivation manuals... We possess a lot of them at a high grade, but we only keep them for sentimental value. They will be much more useful to you."

Jack nodded. He didn't plan to refuse this kindness. There was nothing he needed himself, but the Hall of Wonders contained many things. Maybe he'd find something useful. Even if he didn't, he could always take things to assist the people closest to him.

Brock needed a new staff. Jack could maybe find him one here.

The two of them slightly angled their course and headed for the Hall of Wonders, which was situated nearby the Elder Council. To Jack's surprise, Mia was waiting outside. He raised a brow. The other Elders must have known Pasan would bring him here.

"Hi, Jack!" she said, then bowed. "Greetings, Grand Elder."

Pasan chuckled. "There is no need for ceremony. Accompany Jack inside and let him take anything he wishes."

"Yes!" Mia replied. She was living historic times—how could she not be excited?

Grand Elder Pasan waited outside while Jack and Mia revisited the Hall of Wonders.

"This is amazing," she exclaimed, speaking quickly. "You can leave this place—how awesome is that? Maybe you can bring us out to see the stars, the moons, the rivers, and all those things you talked about!"

"There is no maybe," Jack replied with a smile. "I will definitely take you out."

She swiveled around to look at him. "Promise?"

"I promise."

"Mm." A satisfied smile emerged on her lips, and before long, they were inside the Hall.

Jack surveyed the walls. Last time he came here, it had been for sightseeing—his vision focused on different things now.

He first went over the history books. As much as they interested him, he wasn't willing to bring them out. First of all, he doubted they would have any immediate use, and second, he wasn't a lunatic to just carry precious books around. They were better left here.

He then approached the weapons and armor. Just by taking a look at them, he could tell that every single item here was of extremely high-quality. They hadn't weakened in the slightest after a billion years.

His eyes fell on a simple staff. It was nine feet long and might be constructed of wood, though its presence here indicated it was not that simple.

"That's the Goldenwood Staff," Mia explained, following his eyes. "It was wielded by an early A-Grade cultivator of my people. Unfortunately, she fell during the Crusade, and her weapon was kept by her descendants. You have good eyes—it's one of the best weapons here."

Jack smiled. He'd just chosen it because it was a powerful yet simple staff—he had a feeling Brock would like it.

"I would like to take it," he said. "However, to be honest, it's not for me, but for my little brother. Is that okay?"

Mia chuckled. "What are you talking about, you silly? We owe you our gratitude. Whatever you want, just take it."

"Thank you."

The Goldenwood Staff sent into Jack's space ring. He then

kept observing the weapons and armor, but nothing caught his eye. He himself didn't use a weapon, and as for armor, he actually liked fighting bare-chested or in simple robes. Placing barriers between himself and the battle would only weaken his Dao.

Besides Brock, he could think of no one who needed a weapon, and he wouldn't be greedy enough to take things just because he could. Therefore, he moved on.

The next items were the cultivation manuals. Nine of them, followed by three empty pedestals. Mia obediently explained the properties of each of the manuals present but none attracted Jack's interest. His Daos were already set—for a manual to be useful, it would need to be focused on spacetime or life and death.

"We don't have those," Mia replied sadly after he expressed his preference. "Well, we do possess one manual on spacetime, but it's of relatively low grade. I suspect it won't be too useful to you."

Jack nodded. "There is actually another thing," he said. "You said you keep written records of all these manuals, right? At least for their lower levels."

"Right," Mia replied. "Up to the C-Grade."

"Does that apply for the missing manuals as well?"

Her eyes brightened. "Yes!"

"Good. Then, could I have a copy of the one which uses electricity to augment the physical body?"

He had already considered this before, but amidst all his troubles, there had been no meaning in asking. Now, things were different.

Ever since the Integration Tournament, he'd known that the Emberheart family practiced this skill. Rufus Emberheart had used it to heavily augment his physical body and almost defeated Jack. Now that Jack had grown more experienced, he could recognize it as an auxiliary skill—moreover, a skill which played directly into his strengths. Physicality was one of his greatest weapons.

And, beyond that, there would be a unique flavor to using the Emberhearts' secret technique to beat them to the ground.

Mia's eyes smiled. "Absolutely! We have many copies, you can easily take one! It's just... We no longer have the manual, and I'm afraid our copies only go up to the C-Grade. It won't be too useful for you in the future..."

"Don't worry," Jack replied. "I'll get the original soon enough."

Mia was surprised but didn't say anything. "Very well. Then I'll get you our best copy after we leave here. Anything else?" She gestured around. "Everything you see is for the taking!"

Jack hesitated. There wasn't much he needed, but... there were actually some things he wanted.

"This may be too much," he began, "but is there any way I could have a few of your mementos?"

Mia's eyes flashed with surprise, then with wry understanding. "Do you mean these ones?" she asked. She rushed deeper into the corridor and returned with two objects. One was a statuette of a dark-skinned warrioress aiming her spear at the sky while cradling a baby. The other was a bronze heart made of four separate, interlocking pieces.

Jack was surprised. "How did you know?"

"I saw how you looked at them the other day," she revealed proudly. "They're for your family, aren't they? Take them."

"But... they're important to your people..."

"They're just memories of the past. If they go to you, that's more than worth it."

Jack smiled. He'd long wanted to find good presents for his family, and these two objects fit perfectly. One would go to Vivi and the other to Ebele. Well, Ebele's was more a gift for the entire family, but Jack had a feeling it was exactly what she'd love the most.

"Thank you," he said earnestly, accepting the gifts into his space ring. "There is nothing more I want. I'm ready to return to the universe."

Mia stared at him, as if she wanted to say something. A hint of youthful excitement flashed in her eyes, followed by bashfulness. Finally, she gave a sad smile. "Think about me every once in a while, okay?"

Jack smiled back and gave her a hug. "Absolutely. Thank you for everything, Mia. You're wonderful."

She blushed and whispered, "You're welcome, you silly."

CHAPTER TWENTY-NINE
EMERGING

The strongest Ancestor of the Animal Kingdom was Mure Emberheart—a middle B-Grade leonine. This millennium was his shift of watching over the Animal Abyss.

Generally speaking, such a shift was a highly boring duty. He couldn't leave without reason, so all he did every day was cultivate in isolation. Every hundred years, he would venture into the Abyss to see if he could find anything, and that was the sole break in his routine.

When the chase for Jack Rust ended up on his doorstep a year ago, that had been a pleasant change of pace for Mure, but even that excitement only lasted briefly. Before he knew it, he was alone again, cultivating in darkness.

Mure sighed. If not for the Animal Kingdom founders specifically ordering for B-Grades to guard this place, he would have delegated the duty long ago.

On this day, Mure was cultivating as usual when something changed. An almost imperceptible ripple ran through space. His eyes shot open. What was that? His Dao spread outward, covering a massive range and finding nothing out of the ordinary.

Did it come from inside the Abyss?

The Animal Abyss could not be scanned with one's perception. A Dao ripple there could only indicate the emergence of a supreme treasure—Mure's eyes were instantly filled with lust. He was the only one here. If some great treasure on the level of Thunder Body or Heaven Return appeared, he could just take it. No one would know. Instead of sharing with the other Ancestors, he could cultivate it in secret for a few years and then emerge strong enough to dominate everyone. He could become the King of the Animal Kingdom!

Most factions had a faction master. In the Animal Kingdom, the holder of that position was called King instead, but the throne had been empty for a hundred thousand years. The Lonihor and Emberheart families ran the Kingdom together, so a King appearing from either family would ruin the balance and cause the Kingdom to fracture. That would be unwise. Therefore, the two families had sworn a mutual agreement to keep the position of King empty unless someone appeared who was strong enough to lead the Kingdom into a new era.

Mure Emberheart was already close to the strongest cultivator of the Kingdom. With a supreme treasure in his hands... he would rise!

Such thoughts of grandeur filled Mure's mind. He was no longer paying attention to the Animal Abyss, and why would he? Nothing had changed about it for the past million years. The only exception was the appearance of treasures, which could only be a good thing.

Mure rose and prepared to dive into the Abyss, only to frown. A new ripple escaped the Animal Abyss, stronger than the previous one. Something was wrong.

Astral winds picked up. The void stretched and contorted like an accordion. Stars twinkled in the distance. Mure's robes fluttered wildly, and though his Dao kept him safe, he was not calm at all. This place was the lifeblood of his Kingdom. If something happened...

What is it? he thought frantically. *What could be happening!*

No matter what, this was greater than him. It was not something he could stop.

The vacuum of space compressed around him. The Abyss itself warped. Spatial storms tore free, shooting off in random directions and annihilating the void. Some sank into the fabric of space to reach the interdimensional sea—others, the weakest ones, wrought havoc as they were blasted into deep space.

The Animal Kingdom had set up two formations around the Abyss, at a thousand and a million miles respectively. These formations represented the labor of their Ancestors, thousands of years of effort for multiple B-Grade cultivators. They were the Kingdom's pride.

Now, those formations were pierced through by space storms like sheets of paper. Holes appeared, leaking energy. Space warped around the Abyss, folding in on itself, and the formations cracked and shattered like glass. The formation cores next to Mure exploded one by one, turning into dust.

Millennia of effort, gone in the blink of an eye.

Mure was already breathless. This had occurred too quickly, too suddenly. He had no idea what was going on. The Animal Abyss had remained silent for a million years. Why now? Why on his shift!

The Hand of God! he thought. *Jack Rust! Those people must have done something—it's their fault!*

He roared in impotent fury. There was nothing he could do. He was floating a hundred miles away from the Abyss, and the spatial undulations here were already horrifying. Moreover, he didn't specialize in the Dao of Space—if he went any closer, he could perish.

It's growing stronger! I must escape!

Mure released his Dao and flew away at top speed. Yet, even that was difficult. Space was rugged and volatile. It was spinning around the Animal Abyss as if it was a whirlpool, similar to the water of a bathtub when one unplugged the drain. Such a phenomenon was something that Mure had never experienced in his life—the sheer energy involved was indescribable, the mysteries of space deep beyond belief.

He tried to comprehend what was happening, but it was impossible for him. He had no idea why the world would behave like this—what sort of force was capable of such a thing. The only explanation he could come up with was that the core of the Animal Abyss, that inactive black hole, had finally awoken, and a real black hole was something even A-Grades could only run away from.

Mure Emberheart spared a glance backward. What he saw chilled his heart. The sphere of darkness which was the Animal Abyss had fractured, turning into spirals which wildly spun around its center. Even those spirals were rapidly diminishing. All the energy of space, all the spatial storms remaining were sucked into the core of the Abyss, vanishing without a trace. As tremendous amounts of energy fell into the black hole, the surrounding space began to unexpectedly calm down.

Mure hesitated. His caution told him to run—but his greed whispered about opportunities. If this really was a black hole awakening, space should only be getting rougher, not smoother. Maybe it was just an energy eruption. Such a colossal event would surely be felt all the way to Hell—the other Ancestors might rush over soon, and when that happened, he wouldn't be able to enjoy this opportunity alone.

He flew to a respectable distance away and waited. Astral winds tugged at his robes, and his white leonine mane fluttered, but his eyes were filled with excitement. This was the event of a lifetime. Whatever treasure was being born, it would surely dwarf anything the Abyss had produced before—and it would belong to no one else but him!

Mure watched as the event died down. Endless flows of energy came from deep space and flew by him, diving into the Animal Abyss. He felt like a mortal before a storm, an ant observing a majestic process entire worlds above him. His heart was filled with awe and wonder, surpassed only by his greed.

The darkness receded. Little by little, hints of the situation inside were revealed. Mure saw the stars on the other side of the Abyss.

And then, through the dissipating darkness, he glimpsed other things. Fluttering gray. Bronze skin corded with muscles. Short dark hair, shining eyes, and fists which seemed to contain the world.

Mure was speechless. His previous awe was crushing his heart. The darkness dissipated entirely, and in the emptiness of space, he could make out a man—nay, a titan. He wore only a pair of brown shorts and a fluttering gray cape which hugged his shoulders. His bare chest rose and fell as if he breathed pure power. Every inch of his body was perfect, radiating robustness and making Mure feel like he was staring at a block of divine iron. His back was straight, his head held high. His brown eyes seemed to contain the world—flashing not only with power, but also with depth, like a god reborn.

And his fists... Every tiny movement was reflected in Mure's eyes as if his very instinct commanded him to pay extreme attention to those fists. They seemed larger than space, older than time. They were like divine bells from the ancient past, ready to crash down and annihilate everything below them. If those fists could be cut off and made into weapons, they would be worthy for a god to wield.

That was what Mure saw. Then, as his surprise passed, all

those impressions were dispersed as illusions, letting Mure recognize this person.

"Jack Rust!" he exclaimed, unable to believe what he was seeing. "You... *How?*"

But Mure's surprise was far from over. Jack didn't spare him a glance. The darkness had dissipated, but the spatial storms still went strong, all focused around a point in space right in front of Jack. The energy density around him was horrifying—yet, Jack casually stood there, only his cloak fluttering a little as if these terrifying astral winds were a gentle breeze.

Mure could only watch frozen. All that gathered energy eventually declined to the degree where he could make out what lay at its center. It was a single orb, colored darker than black. Everything that approached would be sucked in—that was the impression Mure got.

Space quietened abruptly. Everything stopped. Mure could only watch from afar as Jack Rust floated next to what could only be the true form of the Animal Abyss, the core of the Animal Kingdom's greatest inheritance.

Without saying a word, Jack grabbed the bead and stashed it in his space ring. Only then did he glance at Mure.

"You!" Mure exclaimed, fuming with rage. "That's... That's our Abyss! Give it back!"

"Spoils to the winner," Jack replied calmly. A faint taunting smile played on his lips. "If you want it, come and take it."

Mure felt like someone had invaded his home, slept with his wife, befriended his dog, then stolen his most precious treasures from right beneath his nose. The range of emotions he'd gone through, from fear to greed to awe to... whatever this was... was indescribable.

"How can you be alive?" he asked, barely restraining himself. "You should have died a year ago. They all said so!"

"And yet, here I am."

Jack began walking through space. His every step was calm, slow, and deliberate, as if taking a stroll through his own backyard. Yet, Mure was surprised to discover that Jack was moving a hundred miles with every step. He had no idea how this was happening—he couldn't see any spatial fluctuations or signs of teleporting. Jack's spatial mastery had already surpassed his scope of understanding.

A hint of fear emerged in Mure's heart. Yet, as he scanned Jack and saw he was still Level 303, he grew enraged. He was a mighty, middle B-Grade leonine, one of the strongest people in his constellation. Trillions of cultivators worshiped him. He'd lived for seventy thousand years, carved his name into the galaxy.

Since when could he be intimidated by a little human who wasn't even fifty years old!

By the time Mure could think this far, Jack had already approached. The leonine snorted coldly. "I don't know who you think you are," he growled in a low voice, "but you made a mistake by appearing before me."

"Oh yeah?" Jack replied. "How about you give me a lesson then?"

"That's exactly what I plan on doing. Call out your backers. Let's see what capital you have to contend with me."

Now that he could think clearly, Mure was not afraid of Jack himself. There was no world in which a middle C-Grade could match a middle B-Grade. If Jack dared to approach, he must have someone guarding him from the shadows. That was the person Mure was really afraid of.

Yet, facing his question, Jack only smiled. "There is no one else. For trash like you, I am more than enough."

"You are courting death!" Mure's eyes widened. He had already been intimidated once—now, Jack's taunting grated against his pride, making him want to attack. He quickly considered things. If someone was here, hidden so well that Mure couldn't detect them, he was probably dead anyway. But why hadn't they acted?

On the other hand, if Jack Rust really was alone...

Mure's eyes flashed. Speed wasn't his strong suit. He had no illusions of catching up to Jack if he decided to run away, but since he was this close, he couldn't possibly react in time. If he could cripple him in one strike, he would win everything. Not just the Animal Abyss which Jack just pocketed, but every other treasure on his body. This was the greatest genius Mure had ever seen. His secrets should be world-shattering—maybe even enough for an old man like him to make another breakthrough!

Mure's breathing turned shallow. He decided to act fast and without warning. Power gathered around him, endless layers of supremacy. The universe bowed to its master. Mure's fist shot out, obliterating space wherever it passed, trying to strike Jack before he could run away. This was the fastest attack Mure could unleash. Surely, it would annihilate this little ant who thought himself a god.

Mure was already grinning, imagining his bright future, when his fist crashed into something impossibly hard. A backlash traveled through his body, making him cough out blood.

"*What?*"

Another fist had risen at some point, clashing squarely against his. Jack had moved in time. He'd grown larger, somehow, and two new arms had appeared on his body, crossed against his chest. He remained relaxed; that taunting smile still on his lips, tinged with a hint of pity.

Mure's mind flashed with panic. How!

"Is this all a middle B-Grade can do?" Jack asked. "How disappointing."

CHAPTER THIRTY

SLAYING

MURE FLEW INTO A RAGE. HOW COULD THIS HAPPEN! HOW COULD someone of such low level match him?

Yet, he was in battle. This was no time to think.

Mure acted hastily before, but this time he listened to his instinct and went completely all-out. Lightning erupted from inside his body—crimson sparks covered him, filling him with power. His strength and speed skyrocketed. His crimson robes disintegrated, revealing the upper chest of a muscular, white-haired leonine. This was an old master at his best—a man who should be able to bulldoze over dozens of youngsters at once.

Jack's gaze only revealed a hint of excitement. His two extra arms unfolded and clenched into fists. "I've never killed a B-Grade before," he said. "You can be the first."

"Insolence!"

Mure charged. He was powerful. Every punch and kick could break planets, every movement carved lines into the void.

This was a middle B-Grade cultivator, and the strongest opponent Jack had ever faced. Yet, he remained calm. His mind was on full alert, even as his heart burned with excitement.

Jack no longer had any idea of how strong he was. He didn't

even know whether he could defeat this man, but even if he couldn't, he certainly had the capacity to run away. Therefore, he might as well go all-out.

Except Jack felt stifled. He hadn't fought for a year. Even before that, his last true battle had been four years ago while inheriting the legacy of Archon Green Dragon. His fighting spirit boiled inside him, overflowing into his limbs, filling him with power.

He wanted to learn how strong he truly was.

Jack roared. The universe roared in return. Purple flames lit within his eyes, and his body was covered in the green aura of life. All five of his fruits flared together, lending him their power —with his Dao Tree repaired, this was the strongest he'd ever been.

Yet, his energy was a drop in the bucket compared to his opponent's. At the end of the day, Jack was an entire Grade lower. He couldn't depend on raw power to win—he had to use skill.

Fist met fist. Jack and Mure Emberheart devolved into a melee in the center of emptiness, every strike echoing out for hundreds of miles. They were like two angry gods. Purple and green mixed with crimson sparks, and roars filled the void.

Jack smashed a fist into Mure's abdomen. A crimson palm slammed into his own temple, knocking him away, while Mure appeared beside him to smash a knee into Jack's ribs. Jack turned and matched the strike. In an instant, he used the Dao of Time to slow down Mure's knee, the Dao of Space to let his own fist arrive in time, then used the Daos of Life and Death to strengthen his strike and weaken his opponent's respectively. The mastery of Dao he exhibited far surpassed Mure's.

However, they were separated by a gulf of actual power. Even after all that, Jack could only achieve an equal clash between his fist and the other's knee.

Fist against knee. Considering the gulf between them, the winner should be obvious. Yet, the moment they clashed, Jack's knuckles remained solid. He was a man of steel, while Mure was made of soft clay. The part of body used did not matter. Jack was just harder.

Mure Emberheart cried out as his knee splintered, bones sticking out of the skin. He spun wildly as he flew away. Jack remained calm.

"How!" Mure shouted. "How can this happen?"

Jack smiled. He'd suffered tremendously to enhance his body. By now, the degree of his physicality was not something Mure could contend with. They were equally apart in Dao understanding—the only reason Mure could still stand was that the volume of power he possessed was far above Jack's, like an adult wrestling a master in the body of a child.

Jack raised his middle finger and beckoned his opponent forward. "Come here, kitty."

Mure threw himself forward. Endless clashes rang in the void. Jack raised his shoulder to block an elbow strike, then swung a fist. He teleported around his opponent, pelting him with strikes. Mure used a full-body combat art—he utilized his elbows, knees, palms, feet, fists. Everything he could throw at Jack, he did, yet the battle remained even.

Their fight turned fiercer. Both were fully invested, but there was a key difference. Jack was feeling so incredibly alive—and Mure was so incredibly terrified.

It should not be like this. A middle C-Grade should not be able to fight a middle B-Grade. What sort of monster was this? Just what enemy had the Animal Kingdom created?

We made a mistake, Mure thought. *If I don't kill this man now, then sooner or later, our entire faction will be destroyed!*

He roared again, overdrawing his own Dao to strike harder. The battle reached its boiling-hot stage. Strikes rained left and right, yet every time Jack was injured, he regenerated. As for Mure, his wounds were shallow, but they built up. Moreover, it didn't seem like Jack was about to run out of energy.

There was no path to victory for Mure.

I must run, he realized. *Not all is lost. The Kingdom may be destroyed, but I will survive! He can't find me if I hide in a distant planet for ten thousand years!*

He turned tail and tried to escape. Before he could take three steps, however, space warped before him, and Jack appeared. He was infinitely faster. Mure's face smashed into a fist, several of his teeth escaping as he was sent flying backward. Jack pointed at him.

"We're not done until I say so," he declared.

Mure's heart sank. Suddenly, he had a vision—the empty space around them turned into a sandy arena, thousands of spectators waiting to watch him die. The crowd was roaring—the excitement was palpable, their cheering thunderous. And not one of them was shouting his name.

"JACK RUST! JACK RUST! JACK RUST!"

There was no exit from this arena. No way out besides winning.

Meanwhile, Jack himself watched him coldly, a gladiator titan, an enemy so overwhelming he shouldn't exist.

"Wanna see something cool?" Jack asked with a fiendish grin.

Mure thought he'd seen it all. How worse could things get? Yet, as he watched Jack's body spark with lightning, as he witnessed the enemy use what could only be the Emberheart family's secret technique, his eyes widened. His heart dropped. The crowd erupted into cheers.

"How!" Mure exclaimed with bitterness. "How can you possess that technique?"

"You don't deserve to know," Jack replied coldly. "I am only showing this to you to test it out. I haven't mastered it yet, but I thought that dying under your own technique—the Thunder Body—would be a fitting end for you. Pathetic all the way to the end."

Mure felt so bitter that he laughed. There was nothing else he could do. "That name, how do you know that name?" he asked, still laughing. "It's the Emberheart Style—always has been, always will be."

Jack's eyes glistened like glaciers. "Then die being stubborn."

Deep exhaustion flooded Mure's heart. He could not escape. Today, no matter what he did, his life would end here.

So he might as well fight.

With a roar, he jumped back into the fray. The crowd thundered. Sand was dyed red. Jack expertly deflected his attacks, meeting him blow for blow. Their fists smashed together. Mure's bones fractured. With Jack having just enhanced himself further, the leonine could barely keep up.

"FIST OF SUPREMACY!" he roared.

"METEOR PUNCH!"

A colossal shockwave engulfed the arena. Crimson and purple warred. The sands flew high. Mure was catapulted backward, his hand entirely broken. Jack teleported behind him, smashing another Meteor Punch into his back, stealing the air from his lungs. Mure heard a terrible crack. His life flashed before his eyes. He gritted his teeth and turned around, swiping in a wild backhand, but how could such a messy strike connect?

Jack ducked under it, then brought his fist in a devastating uppercut. Mure's chin flew up. Before he could recover, a Meteor Punch exploded on his abdomen, ravaging his internal organs and catapulting him backward yet again.

Even now, he was not allowed to escape. A net of Dao

formed behind him, and he was once again floating before Jack, a lamb to the slaughter.

Mure opened his bloodied lips. "No mercy?" he asked, chuckling darkly.

"I have no mercy for your kind," Jack replied. There was no hint of warmth in his eyes, no compassion. He was a cold-blooded killer—a vigilante prowling in deep space.

Mure chuckled yet again. "Then kill me already. I have lived long enough—I don't fear death, let alone you."

Jack only shook his head. "It is not your death that you should fear. You murdered my son. I will kill every member of your family, paint the galaxy red with your blood and that of your children. I will make sure Artus Emberheart regrets the day he was born, and the entire Animal Kingdom will regret it alongside him. So, no, Mure Emberheart. I will not show mercy, and you should fear me, because I will kill every single Ember-heart in this galaxy. You are just the first."

Anger, hatred, and bitterness formed a dark cocktail in Mure's heart. He regretted. At this moment, he regretted every-thing. The despair that filled him was total. All he could do was open his mouth and roar into the empty space, roar so hard that his throat was torn and he could no longer speak.

"Choose," Jack said darkly. "Will you die on your knees? Or standing?"

Mure roared and threw himself forward. He didn't have much to give. The Supremacy he'd cultivated for his entire life had cracked, ground down so completely it had turned into mere specks of what it used to be. A crimson fist flew toward the cold gaze of Jack Rust.

Jack raised his own fist. The world's energy was sucked inside then compacted, again and again, reaching a terrifying density. Just as Mure reached him, that energy erupted.

"Supernova."

The explosion tore apart this area of space. Purple flames clawed at every direction. The void itself was torn asunder, and entire tracts of the world disappeared under Jack's might. The shockwave spread out like a bubble, stretching deep into space.

Mure's body, having lost the protection of his Dao, had disintegrated.

Jack slowly pulled back his fist. His eyes remained cold. Though he'd started on his path of revenge, it brought him no relief—maybe it would, later.

"One down, many to go," he whispered. He raised a hand and summoned a slick new starship—the Black Hole People had gifted it to him when he mentioned he needed one. It was dark, just like his purpose.

Then, Jack walked into his starship and teleported away. He was gone.

The ripples of both the Animal Abyss disappearing and the battle afterward had washed over the nearby planet of Hell, sending the entire Kingdom on high alert. They had no idea what was going on, but they knew it was important.

It was only fifteen minutes later that another Ancestor of the Animal Kingdom arrived. This was the same one who'd fought Jack before—the early B-Grade Ancestor of the Lonihor family.

When he arrived, he was stunned.

"Hmm? What the..."

He checked his spatial coordinates repeatedly. By the fifth time he confirmed his location, his jaw dropped, and he began shivering like a leaf.

"The Animal Abyss... Where the hell is it!" he shouted. "Mure! Mure Emberheart! Show yourself, Mure!"

Yet, it was useless. Both the Animal Abyss and Mure Emberheart, two pillars of the Animal Kingdom, had mysteriously vanished. Today would be the darkest day of their recent history—and they had no idea it was only the beginning.

CHAPTER THIRTY-ONE

COUNTING ONE'S BLESSINGS

"WHAT DO YOU MEAN IT'S GONE?"

"That it's gone! The Animal Abyss is gone!"

"It's a black hole, you idiot. It cannot just disappear."

"Well, it did!"

The Animal Kingdom was shocked. When they sent one of the Ancestors to guard the Abyss, it was so he could keep intruders away, prevent them from stealing an artifact or two. The Abyss itself was a black hole—how could anyone possibly affect it?

Yet, it happened. Not only did they lose the Abyss, one of the cornerstones of their Kingdom, they also lost their strongest Ancestor. Adding all the other catastrophes that the Kingdom had experienced recently, their current status amongst the B-Grade factions was shaky.

However, the mysterious disappearance of the Animal Abyss rippled out farther. All across the galaxy, the major factions were well aware of what such a thing signified. Everyone knew the Abyss was a special black hole. That left three possibilities.

One, Mure Emberheart had accidentally discovered a way to

destroy the Abyss, possibly reaping some great treasure from doing so. Two, an unknown cultivator possessing strength at least at the late B-Grade was the one to discover the Abyss's secrets, somehow destroying it and also killing Mure Emberheart. Three, the Abyss for some reason imploded and the explosion disintegrated Mure.

These were all the possibilities they could come up with. Nobody in their right mind would suspect that someone had physically carried the Animal Abyss away.

As for Jack's connection to the Abyss, not many people knew. Eva had spread the news that they'd killed Jack, not that he'd ran into the Abyss, all to avoid misunderstandings.

As soon as she heard the news, a persistent worry surfaced inside her.

"Don't worry, Commander," Artus Emberheart said. His mood had been excellent for the past year—he was even close to repairing his Dao. "I don't know what happened, but Jack Rust is deader than dead. Even he couldn't survive a black hole."

"A black hole which just up and disappeared one day. That isn't supposed to happen."

"The universe is full of mysteries. If escaping a black hole was so easy, Enas wouldn't have stayed in there for a billion years. This is just an accident."

"An accident?" Eva's eyes flashed. "How can you say that, Artus? This is a time of war and upheaval. A time of change. How could there be such a coincidence that the Animal Abyss, which has remained unchanged for a million years, suddenly disappears one year after Jack Rust goes inside?"

Artus took a respectful step back. "I didn't mean to sound naive, Commander. I understand this is probably not a coincidence. All I'm saying is, the chances of Jack Rust having anything to do with this are miniscule. He died a year ago—

even if he hadn't, he would not possess the power to affect the Animal Abyss in any way. Maybe this is the result of a powerful A-Grade becoming curious about the Abyss, or a last terrorist act of the Church before they abandon this galaxy. In any case, it is not something which should concern us. It does not change the war situation."

Eva mulled over these words. Artus was right, of course. Yet, she couldn't stop worrying. The image of Jack Rust kept gnawing at the back of her mind—defiant to the end, always overcoming impossible odds to survive and grow stronger, turning danger into opportunity.

Maybe I really am affected, she thought.

"I will go into meditation for a few days," Eva said, tacitly agreeing with Artus. "You will be in command of our forces until then. Do not disturb me without reason."

"Yes, Commander," Artus said with the widest smile.

———

From the moment Jack had stepped out of the Black Hole World, he'd sensed something reappear in his soul. A connection which had been severed but never faded. A missing piece.

Brock...

Jack's heart was filled with warmth. Of course, he'd had to put that on hold to fight Mure Emberheart, but after finishing up and flying away on his starship, he had time to consider things again.

How are you doing, Brock? Are you okay? Did you ever believe I was dead?

There was no answer. Jack would know soon. Brock was not like Shol. He didn't need to gather clues and search for him. Their souls were connected; as long as Jack wanted to, he could just travel in Brock's general direction, and they would eventually meet up.

At present, this would happen even quicker. The moment Jack felt the connection reappear, so did Brock. His relief and surprise were keenly sensed by Jack through their soul bond. Doubtlessly, Brock was also hurrying over.

They were two arrows shooting toward each other. Their reunion would come sooner rather than later.

Jack was nervous. It had been a year—this was his longest separation from Brock yet. In fact, the brorilla was someone he greatly worried over while in the Black Hole World—what if Brock, thinking that Jack was dead, did something crazy?

At least he was alive. As to his current condition... that was something Jack could only wait to find out.

The galaxy was a large place. Meeting up was not something which would take a day or two, so Jack had time to relax. He spent that time inspecting his benefits from the previous battle.

He'd possessed the power to fight B-Grades for a while now, but this was his first time killing one. He'd jumped directly to the middle B-Grade, too. Of course, Mure Emberheart was someone who'd reached the end of his potential, far from the talented Envoys of the Hand of God, but he remained a middle B-Grade.

How far I've come... Jack reminisced. *I am one of the strongest cultivators in the Milky Way.*

Mure Emberheart had not possessed a space ring—those things were expensive and all but unknown in this galaxy. It wasn't a huge loss. He was someone so weak the Hand of God hadn't even bothered recruiting him for the war—his "incalculable" wealth would have been nothing but painted stones in Jack's eyes.

No, wealth was not the point.

Killing someone that strong in System space came with all sorts of benefits. The first, and most obvious one, was levels. A large influx of energy had surged into Jack's body the moment he killed Mure—his Dao Tree had groaned under the sheer volume of it, then his fifth Dao Fruit had begun to grow. From its early stages of development, it had rapidly approached maturity.

Jack had earned fifteen levels in the blink of an eye.

Since every level in the C-Grade gave twenty stat points, that left him with three hundred free points which he invested evenly into Physical. The round thousands he had in Mental and Will were too nice to break.

Level: 318

Strength: 6340 (+)
Dexterity: 6340 (+)
Constitution: 6340 (+)
Mental: 1000
Will: 1000
Free sub-points: 2

Even after all this time, three hundred points were a five percent overall increase. Jack felt his body grow more compact, his muscles tighten, his bones harden. His already titanic physicality had taken another step forward.

Although, unlike other times, the change took longer. Even an hour after Jack invested the stat points, the transformation wasn't done. It was clear that, after some point, even the System struggled to fit more energy into him. It was the same barrier he'd run into when body-tempering. This forced density increase was painful, too, but that was something Jack had long grown accustomed to. If anything, he'd learned to enjoy the pain because it brought good things.

When he was finally done, he groaned, stretching his body as his bones made popping noises. He clenched his fist, feeling the strength contained inside. He smiled.

"Nice."

Next came another interesting notification.

Congratulations! Titan Taunt I → Titan Taunt II
Titan Taunt II: A titan's existence is so dominant it constitutes a challenge. Your extreme physicality and domineering stance not only intimidate enemies, but also provoke them. They will either fight you or cower away, losing in both cases.

This was a complete change in the skill. Jack remembered that the previous description was something silly about "channeling his inner punchability" and jokes about his opponent's mother. Now, it swapped to something serious and, if Jack was being honest, kinda cool.

Such a change feels unnatural, he couldn't help thinking. *I'm not opposed, but why? Could it be that the skill adjusts to its user? When I was sparring others on the Cathedral, that silly, crowd-riling version was exactly what I needed. Now that I'm out for blood, this one suits me better.*

Well, it doesn't matter. Thanks.

With all his skills having risen lately, Jack no longer had any skill at the first tier. Even in the second tier, he only had Titan Taunt. Almost everything else was at the third tier.

Dao Skills: Meteor Punch IV, Iron Fist Style III, Brutalizing Aura III, Neutron Star Body III, Supernova III, Space

Mastery III, Fist of Mortality III, Death Mastery III, Titan Taunt II

That third tier, however, seemed like a massive moat. Reaching it wasn't too difficult, but almost all of his skills had been stranded there afterward. The only exception was Meteor Punch, which he'd used since the Forest of the Strong. It was by far his most intimate skill.

Even Space and Death Mastery, where he was confident he easily outclassed almost everyone at his Grade, remained at the third tier.

Why?

Is something missing? Or does the fourth tier require some sort of transformation?

Meteor Punch had reached the fourth tier during his battle with the planetary overseer, when he'd achieved a preliminary fusion between this skill and the power of a supernova, essentially taking it to the next level. Maybe that was the key— reaching the next level.

It made sense, too. Since there were only five tiers, the higher ones had to represent understanding at the A-Grade level. It wasn't weird for him to be unable to advance.

But how? he wondered, coming short of a solution. He eventually put the issue to rest. The System's classifications were nothing but a guideline—as long as he put in the effort and consistently bettered himself, he would achieve greater strength, and the skill tiers would come by themselves.

Which left one thing.

Jack reached into his space ring, fishing out the Animal Abyss—a smooth, fist-sized, dark orb.

In truth, this wasn't the Black Hole World. Shrinking an entire world and carrying it around was impossible even for

Archons—even if it wasn't, there was no way the Black Hole People would be able to survive that.

The Black Hole World was a stable island in the interdimensional sea. As for the black orb Jack was holding, it was nothing but an inactive portal. Similar to how every teleporter had its own frequency and could use it to connect with others, this black orb had internalized the exact coordinates of the Black Hole World and could connect to it. The Vortex in the Black Hole World could also open a wormhole to this orb.

In essence, this was nothing but the connecting point between the universe and the Black Hole World.

It remained an extraordinary device. This little orb, by itself, had acted as the center of a black hole-like field dubbed the Animal Abyss. Given enough energy, it could reach through the folds of space and form a stable connection to a different place in the interdimensional sea. The Dao patterns contained inside it were nothing short of profound.

Unfortunately, it was difficult for Jack to study them. This orb was not meant to serve as a cultivation tool. Its patterns were convoluted, unclear, and all over the place—the kind that would be clear if you already understood its principles and wouldn't help if you didn't.

In that sense, the Vortex was a much more suitable cultivation area, but Jack wouldn't just open a portal to another dimension so he could go study. Not to mention that he already possessed the Realm Heart of Archon Green Dragon—if he wanted to sharpen his understandings of spacetime, he could focus on that.

Besides, spacetime had always been his secondary Dao. His main focus was the Fist, and by extension, the duality of Life and Death. This was exactly what Jack would practice now. His revenge would be the perfect learning ground.

Jack had only been traveling for a few hours, lost in his thoughts, when he felt his connection to Brock grow abruptly stronger. He looked up. Space was torn ahead of him like a reaper emerging from the shadows, and a black starship covered in glass walls flew out. Several figures gazed at him from the windows. Jack's breath caught to his throat. He recognized them all.

And at the very front stood a brorilla shaking with excitement.

"BIG BRO!"

CHAPTER THIRTY-TWO

REUNION

"BIG BRO!" A BRORILLA SHOUTED, SHOOTING INTO SPACE.

"Brock!" Jack exclaimed. Part of his suppressed feelings erupted. Warmth appeared in his heart. With his brother by his side, the world wasn't as dark anymore.

The two men met in the vacuum and hugged tightly. Jack could feel Brock's disbelief, his shock, his excitement. He'd thought Jack dead—how could he not be relieved?

"Brock!" Jack exclaimed again, with pleasant surprise. "You've grown!"

A year ago, Brock had been almost at Jack's height. He'd now grown to seven feet tall, with bulging muscles and dark fur. He'd resembled a gymonkey in childhood, but he'd now become an almost fully grown brorilla.

"How!" Brock asked in a deep, emotional voice. "How are you alive? They said they killed you. I felt the connection severed!"

"I'll tell you all about it, bro. In short, they forced me into the Animal Abyss, which turned out to be another world entirely. That's why the connection was severed. But I meditated, repaired my Dao, and now I'm back."

Brock looked at him with bright eyes. "You are alive!" he repeated, unable to believe this. "Wait. What do you mean you repaired your Dao?"

Jack's eyes darkened. Of course. Using his son as a hostage was a shameful act—nobody would publicize it, and Brock hadn't been there to watch it happen.

"It's a long story," he said. "I'll tell you everything later."

Brock sensed the darkness in Jack's heart. He was confused. This was the same darkness he also contained, but his came from the desire to get revenge over his fallen big brother. What reason could Jack have to feel the same?

He did not speak anymore. He led Jack into the *Trampling Ram*, filled with familiar faces, both old and new.

"You guys..." Jack said, his voice dripping with emotion. "You're all here. Salin, Nauja, Bomn, Vashter... What is this, a reunion?"

"Hehe." Salin chuckled. "We couldn't sit still after they said you were dead. We had to give them a piece of our mind!"

"The *Trampling Ram* answered the call," Bomn said, bringing a fist in front of his heart. "You are part of this crew. Avenging you was our duty."

"You didn't have to worry us so much..." Nauja added, her eyes smiling with relief.

Jack smiled back. Even after everyone thought he was dead, they still remembered him. They genuinely cared. What a unique feeling.

"Thank you," he said. "It's good to be back."

"We missed you," Brock said. His voice was careful. "We are safe here. We are together. Tell us what happened."

Jack shook his head. "How about you go first?"

Brock nodded, then took a deep breath. "After you were gone, I... I was lost for a while. My heart was cracked. You are important to me. I lost my way, but I found it again after meditating on brohood. For us warriors, death is a natural event—the best we can do is keep moving forward, carrying the torch of our fallen brothers."

Jack listened, noticing Brock's speech had reached fluency —even better than most humans he knew. At the same time, he was sad. "I put you through a lot, brother... I'm sorry."

"Don't worry. It's enough that you returned," Brock replied. "After I recovered from the shock, I decided to take on your mantle. I vowed to destroy the Animal Kingdom and protect Earth. Fate led us to the *Trampling Ram*, and the five of us embarked on revenge. In the past year, we have decimated the Animal Kingdom operations and outposts, even killing two C-Grade Enforcers. I know it's not much, but the Hand of God is also after us, so we're forced to move carefully. I'm growing stronger. Soon, I will be able to face their B-Grades."

Jack took another look at Brock. He hadn't noticed it at first, but the aura rising from his body had evolved. In the span of a single year, Brock had developed two additional Dao Fruits, reaching the seven-fruit boundary. He was now a late C-Grade —given his power, dealing with any peak C-Grade of the Animal Kingdom should be a piece of cake.

"You've surpassed me!" Jack exclaimed with pride. "I'm only at five fruits myself!"

"Cultivation is only the foundation." Brock chuckled. "You are stronger than me still."

Jack smiled. "So you guys turned into terrorists?"

"Guerilla warfare," Nauja said. "Like the time you were in Hell. We strike quickly and decisively, then teleport away. The losses we've caused to the Kingdom are steeper than Brock implied—and we couldn't have done it without the crew of the *Trampling Ram*."

"I'm proud of you guys," Jack said. This had been a year of progress for everyone. Brock had reached the late C-Grade,

Salin and Nauja were at the very peak of the D-Grade, and Bomn had also reached the middle D-Grade. Even Vashter, the weakest member of the team, had broken into the D-Grade.

This was a manifestation of the principle that one's environment affected the person. When Jack first met Vashter, that mace-wielding feshkur, he'd been a middle E-Grade with little hope for the future. However, in later years, Vashter had been dragged through one disaster after the other, adventuring with people whose vision reached beyond the Milky Way Galaxy.

Now, that once-mediocre feshkur had become an immortal —the same Grade as Captain Dordok.

Vashter caught Jack's gaze and grinned. "This is all because of you," he said. "Back in the day, I used to despise you after you lied to us and caused Achilles's death and Captain Dordok's capture. Now, I have to admit... my vision was too narrow. You are such a great man that your passage naturally leaves waves for the rest of us to weather. If we can, we emerge greater than before. If we can't, we perish... but I understand now that it is not your fault."

Jack was taken aback. Vashter had turned into a bit of a fanboy, excusing some of Jack's past failures, but that was okay. Everyone could use a role model.

"I guess I have to tell you my side of the story as well," he said, sighing. His mood dropped like a stone in a well. "Ah, but before we start, check this out, Brock. I got you a gift."

He reached into his space ring and grabbed a simple-looking staff, appearing to be made of wood, yet it shimmered slightly as if inlaid with gold. The moment Brock's eyes fell on the staff, he couldn't pull them off.

"This is the Goldenwood Staff," Jack explained, raising it so everyone could take a good look. "It used to be the weapon of an ancient A-Grade. Now, it's yours. You've needed one since Baron Longform broke the Staff of Stone, right?"

Only now did Brock manage to speak. "Good staff," he said. His hand wrapped around the body of the staff as if by itself, twirling the weapon around and getting a feel for it. He nodded again. "Good staff," he repeated. "Thanks, bro. This means a lot. But where did you find it?"

Jack smiled sadly. "You'll see. Let's take a seat first. This will not be pleasant."

The others exchanged worried glances but did as he said. Only Brock, who had sensed Jack's darkness, suspected the nature of what was to come.

Jack told them everything. From the moment they separated near Hell, he spoke about his chase through space until he reached the Animal Abyss. He told them how he broke through again and again, using all sorts of methods to eventually hide inside, hoping for a miracle.

This next part wasn't easy for him, so he narrated it quickly. How Artus Emberheart had revealed Jack's son, forcing him to surrender, then killed Eric regardless. How Jack had gone mad and overdrawn himself to escape. How his Dao had cracked.

By this point, the starship had gone deathly silent. Everyone listened with disbelief. Even Brock was surprised—he knew something bad had happened, but he never expected it to be this tragic.

Nauja had covered her mouth with her hands, shivering. The moment Jack's words stopped ringing, she jumped up and rushed to hug him. "Oh my God, Jack, I'm so sorry! I have no words. I'm so, so sorry..."

Jack wanted to protest. Yet, the moment another person's warmth reached him, he almost cracked. He hadn't realized how badly he needed a hug for the past year. Silently, he hugged back, and Nauja stayed there until he relaxed his embrace. Only then did she slowly back away.

"How are you?" Brock asked.

Jack sighed. "As you can imagine. Terribly... but I have recovered a bit. I can think again. As soon as I have my revenge, I will be fine."

A complex look emerged on Brock's face, but he didn't reply.

"I'm sorry, man," Salin said, placing a hand on Jack's shoulder. "Nobody should have to experience that. Stay strong. Don't lose yourself."

Jack chuckled with surprise. "That's pretty sane for you to say."

"Of course. I'm insane, not an asshole."

"The death of a child is something I have experienced as well," Bomn added with his sonorous voice. "It was the worst period of my life. I was deeply scarred, and even now, I have not fully recovered... I cannot imagine what you're going through. I just hope you eventually find your way out of the darkness. Don't be hard on yourself."

Jack smiled. "Thank you for your kind words. I'm fine."

Nobody responded further, so Jack continued. He spoke about how he entered the black hole as a last resort, partially expecting—and maybe hoping—to die, then unexpectedly emerged in a new world. He described the Black Hole World and its people, their plight and unique perspective on life.

He skimmed over the year he spent there, focusing more on the world than his personal journey of recovery. Finally, he repaired his Dao, furthered his understandings in all his Daos, left the Black Hole World and pocketed it, then killed the middle B-Grade Ancestor before coming over to meet them.

"You killed a middle B-Grade!" Salin exclaimed. "Man, can you be any more awesome? You're like a fairy tale hero at this point!"

"I'm just a man trying his best," Jack replied. "Well, that was everything that happened to me. I know it was a lot to take in, but... Let's try to move on."

"I don't even know where to start," Nauja said, shaking her head. "The Black Hole World, your power... you... It's all so unexpected. It's just... Jack... I know you have a grip on things, but I just hope... Don't fall into the darkness. Please."

"I'm fine," Jack repeated, a little more solidly this time. Talking about this issue made him uncomfortable. Even thinking about it was difficult, let alone discussing it. "I didn't mention all those so we had something to talk about, but so we can be on the same page. I will handle myself. I got this. The way I need you to support me is by helping me get revenge. Are you with me?"

Brock's stare remained steady, not betraying his inner thoughts. The other four exchanged glances. "Of course we are," Salin replied. "Till death do us part. We're all bros here, right?"

"Even me?" Nauja asked, raising a brow.

"Especially you."

"We have been pursuing revenge already," Bomn said. "Be it for us, for you, or for the world, the tyranny of the Animal Kingdom must come to an end. We will not stop until we succeed or die."

"I will never abandon you," Brock said. He had a unique way of speaking candidly without seeming vulnerable. "You are in good hands, big bro. I am here for you. We all are. Let's win this battle."

"That's what I like to hear!" Jack exclaimed. His lips were smiling, but his eyes were dark. "Let's go. We have a Kingdom to destroy."

CHAPTER THIRTY-THREE
SERIAL KILLER

THE *TRAMPLING RAM* WAITED IN POSITION BETWEEN THE STARS. Thanks to its specially designed glass walls, it did not reflect the starlight, lending itself perfectly for an ambush.

Jack stood on the bridge, arms crossed. His chest was bare, while a gray cloak fluttered behind his back. He seemed like a warlord. Next to him, Brock calmly waited, reading from the Bro Code. Golden ripples spread out of him every once in a while, scanning the distance.

"This is fun!" Gan Salin exclaimed. "Just some dirty old friends prowling the galaxy in search of guilty victims. Doesn't get much better!"

"Pace yourself, my canine friend," Vashter said. "Don't be in a rush." He leaned against a wall with his mace in hand, emitting the air of a veteran, eyes glistening.

"Do you want to play some Crazy Man Goes to Town?" Nauja asked, fishing a deck of cards from her pocket.

Salin shrugged. "We could. But I want to be the Crazy Man."

"Nobody is the Crazy Man. It's just the name of the game."

"Hey, I'm a man and I'm pretty crazy."

"They're here," Brock said. Everyone tensed. The deck of

cards in Nauja's hand disappeared, replaced by a longbow, and Salin's canines showed beneath his raised lips. Bomn drew his greataxe, Vashter straightened himself, and Brock took out his new Goldwood Staff—though, probably, none of them would need to fight.

Jack simply waited, staring into the distance. His gaze was inscrutable—his mood, deadly.

A starship entered their view. Red walls surrounded a white interior visible through large windows, and they could clearly make out a pale man bathing in a pool of blood.

"The Blood Baron," Salin said, licking his lips. "I've always wanted to kill this son of a bitch."

Their starship accelerated, matching the other's speed. For now, they hadn't yet been discovered. They were flying almost in parallel—it would be difficult to catch something moving at thousands of miles per minute otherwise.

Jack took a step through space, borrowing the *Ram*'s momentum to approach the other starship. He reached out a hand, then clenched it. Space collapsed around the Blood Baron's starship. It veered off to the side and spun wildly. The pool of blood flew everywhere, revealing a dazed, naked man. The Blood Baron vanished and reappeared outside his starship, already wearing a set of crimson robes which looked macabre against his pale skin.

"Who goes there!" he thundered. He was an early C-Grade Enforcer of the Animal Kingdom out on official business. There was nothing he feared. The only people willing to attack his starship were poor souls too naive to recognize its owner.

His gaze and perception scanned space. Now that he was actively looking, he spotted Jack. His lips trembled. He recognized this man. The Blood Baron had attended Jack's Grand Duel on Hell, and he'd also seen a recording of Jack fighting the planetary overseer. This was a face carved deep into his memory, a dark star he hoped to never meet.

However, Jack Rust had died a year ago. How could he randomly be here?

An illusion! the Blood Baron thought, except no matter how he looked, there was no sign of falsehood. His gaze reached farther, falling onto the dark starship.

A pair of ram horns decorated its front—a recent addition designed by Bomn. The horns weren't only aesthetic; they fulfilled a practical purpose as well, which was to make the starship easily recognizable. It was much easier to spread terror and prestige like this—it was kind of their brand.

Even before Jack appeared, the Kingdom cultivators had learned to fear the starship with ram horns—the *Dark Ram*, they called it. The Blood Baron was one of them. Facing both the *Dark Ram* and a man suspiciously similar to Jack Rust, deep fear rooted within him. The appearance of Jack Rust could be imitated—but the terrifying aura emitted from his body could not.

"Wait!" he said. "I can offer you money!"

Jack snorted. "Just die."

A fist crossed space, exploding on the Blood Baron and his starship both. They were destroyed. The Blood Baron, an almighty Enforcer of the Animal Kingdom, the pride of his home planet, didn't even have time to cry out, let alone defend. An instant after Jack attacked, only broken debris littered this part of space.

Jack shook his head. "Again, no levels..."

Brock flashed by his side. "This is a bit slow..." he agreed.

This was already the third Enforcer he'd taken out, and he hadn't received a single level. He remained stuck at 318.

There were two reasons why he hunted the Animal Kingdom Enforcers. One was to get revenge against the Kingdom, to clip its wings and break off its fingers one by one. The other reason was to level up. He wanted to become strong enough to storm into Animal Planet, the capital of the Animal Kingdom, and massacre anyone who got in his way. He wanted to completely uproot the Kingdom, and to do that, his current power wasn't enough. Eva Solvig would pursue him the moment he appeared publicly.

Targeting Enforcers specifically was a strategic move. The death of each one was a loss to the Kingdom, but each death by itself wasn't enough to truly rouse their suspicions. After all, they had hundreds of Enforcers. Due to the recent uprisings all over the constellation, these Enforcers were often sent on missions, making for easy, isolated targets.

Jack knew that the disappearance of the Animal Abyss would undoubtedly form connections to his name. They wouldn't believe he was still alive just from that, but it was vital that he hid his return for as long as possible to not give them time to prepare. The longer he could hunt from the shadows, the better.

However, this was too slow. He was a middle C-Grade now, and Enforcers were all at the early tier. They just didn't qualify to give him levels. If he wanted to reliably level up, he would need to pursue Elders, who were at the middle C-Grade and above. The problem there was that Elders were important personnel. They held prestigious positions at the center of the public eye. Killing one was easy, but doing so undiscovered was another matter entirely.

Even if he succeeded, the Kingdom wouldn't just sit by once its Elders began disappearing. It would request assistance from the Hand of God. Jack didn't wish to see that happen.

But what choice did he have?

"Never play, never win," he muttered. He turned to Brock. "I think we should start hunting Elders."

The brorilla thought for a bit. "I agree. We must take some risks. However, let's consider our moves properly before we make them. Secrecy is our greatest weapon."

"My fist is our greatest weapon," Jack disagreed. "Secrecy is just a bonus—nice to have, but not something we can't afford to lose."

"You speak wisely. Good. Then, let's search for a target."

"Let's."

They flew into the starship and teleported away. The Blood Baron's disappearance would only be noticed days later, when he never arrived at his destination.

———

"What's going on?" the Animal Kingdom's Grand Elder demanded. "Four Enforcers have gone missing in two weeks, alongside the Animal Abyss, and Ancestor Emberheart. Someone is acting against us!"

"Who would do that?" another Elder replied. They were at an Elder Council hastily convened to discuss the recent disappearances. Thirteen Elders were currently in attendance—the rest hadn't been able to make it in time.

"Someone give me a list of possible culprits," the Grand Elder commanded.

An elef Elder stood up. "Reporting to the Grand Elder," she said calmly. "The two incidents—the Abyss and Enforcers—could be related or unrelated. If they are related, the powers at play are greater than what we can handle, but I don't think that's very probable. Anyone capable of unraveling the mysteries of the Animal Abyss wouldn't bother with mere early C-Grade Enforcers. The two incidents stand at very different levels of power. Unless..." She trailed off.

The Grand Elder raised a brow. "Unless?"

"Unless that man... is somehow alive."

The Grand Elder banged his fist on the table. "Impossible! Stop spreading bullshit. Ancestors Emberheart and Lonihor both confirmed the death of Jack Rust, alongside *two* Hand of God Envoys. Are you saying they were all mistaken? That a middle C-Grade human could somehow escape their perceptions, survive in the Animal Abyss for a year, then find a way to make a black hole disappear? Get serious! I'm busy enough with all the uprisings and disappearances, so save me your stupidity!"

"I misspoke," the elef hurriedly acknowledged.

"The most probable scenario," the Grand Elder thought aloud, calming down, "is that the two incidents are completely unrelated. I have my suspicions for the disappearance of the Animal Abyss and Ancestor Emberheart: The Hand of God was recently made aware of the Abyss's circumstances in the process of chasing Jack Rust. The Envoy must have communicated it to her higher-ups, tempting an Elder of the Hand to secretly arrive and investigate. That person discovered the secrets of the Abyss, whatever those were, shattered it to take all the treasures inside, then killed our Ancestor to silence all witnesses." He clenched his leonine fists. "It is regrettable, but this is the most likely explanation. We can only blame ourselves for being too weak..."

The other Elders glanced at each other, then nodded in agreement. "That man creates trouble for us even in death!" an Elder angrily exclaimed, referring to Jack Rust.

"At least that's a thorn in our side gone," the Grand Elder replied, sighing. "Then, onto the matter of the Enforcers... I see three scenarios. One is that enemy constellations are moving against us. The dissolution of the Exploding Sun left a vacuum that many major factions are eager to fill. It wouldn't be strange for one of them to make power plays in our constellation—especially the Wide Swirls.

"The second scenario is that rogue cultivators of the Church are retaliating against our Kingdom because Artus Emberheart is guiding the purging forces. If this is the case, there's nothing we can do. The Hand will catch them eventually. As for the third scenario... is that the recently-appeared terrorists, the *Dark Ram*, are upping their game.

"Whichever scenario is true, we are facing opponents at the middle or late C-Grade level. How do you all suggest we deal with this?"

The Elders glanced at each other. This time, nobody was in a hurry to speak up—nobody wanted to risk the Grand Elder's wrath. However, the Grand Elder didn't break the silence either.

A sharken Elder finally bit the bullet. "We can temporarily limit the missions of our Enforcers to the minimum and have them move in groups instead of individually," he suggested. "The uprisings can wait—it's more important to secure our Enforcers."

Contrary to what everyone expected, the Grand Elder did not lash out. He gave the sharken Elder a glance of appreciation. "Correct," he said. Those Elders who had the same idea but hadn't dared voice it could only curse their lack of confidence.

The Grand Elder continued, "That was my idea as well. Additionally, we will equip each group of moving Enforcers with escape mechanisms and remotely backed-up recording stones. That way, even if they are attacked, we'll know who did it. That's the important part. If we can find proof against another B-Grade faction, their deaths will have been worth it." He passed his gaze around the room. "Any objections?"

No one spoke.

"Very well. This meeting is adjourned. Enforce my commands at once!"

CHAPTER THIRTY-FOUR

PLANET DESTROYER

EARTHEN GEMINI WAS A DESOLATE, UNINHABITABLE PLANET. IT LOOKED like a red ball covered in fumes, with pillars of smoke occasionally escaping into space. Its atmosphere was low in oxygen and rich in heavy metals, which the nearby sun heated to unhealthy degrees.

Due to these reasons, this planet was unfit for life. Simultaneously, it was rich in precious ores—just the diamonds near the surface were estimated to be millions of tons. The Animal Kingdom wouldn't let such a treasure trove be.

The atmosphere was hot and toxic, though with the proper equipment, even E-Grade cultivators could survive here. Millions of them filled the planet, wearing specialized masks and suits, wielding heavy pickaxes to gather everything they could into leather sacks.

Earthen Gemini was a large source of wealth for the Kingdom. The ores they extracted from here were often traded to other constellations for massive sums of credits. It was their greatest mine operation.

Naturally, such an important place wouldn't be left unguarded. Besides the E-Grade miners, hundreds of D-Grades were stationed at various spots, alongside two early C-Grade Enforcers. Just like Hell, there was also an Elder who supervised, though their status and strength were inferior to the Warden of Hell's.

Even the miners were members of the Animal Kingdom—outer disciples eager to contribute. While the Kingdom leaned heavily into slavery, it wouldn't use outsiders at such an important outpost.

That all goes to say, Earthen Gemini was a critical and very well-guarded location. It had existed for tens of thousands of years and should continue producing ores for many, many more.

But every future is only as good as the next moment.

On this day, Elder Caran was resting in a special room isolated from the fumes outside—though they wouldn't hurt him, they were still unpleasant. Therefore, not only had he sealed them outside his walls, he was also using the planet's heat to warm the waters of his bath, making it similar to a hot spring. It was exactly in this hot spring that he liked to relax while young maids massaged and bathed him.

"More water," he groaned, and a thinly-clad girl slowly poured a bucket over his back. Elder Caran moaned, his canines showing.

Of the Animal Kingdom's five noble species, canines were the weakest and least prestigious. They remained, however, noble. Elder Caran was one of the Elders hailing from the canines, and it was precisely because of his species that he was delegated to such an ugly post. An Elder like him could be a king anywhere on the constellation—being the king of a mine meant little. He couldn't even look outside the window without drowning in noxious fumes.

Of course, the canines were uniquely suited to such posts.

They were all a bit insane, so their tolerance exceeded the others'. They always found a way to make do.

"You," the Elder said, glancing at a maid. "Massage me."

She beamed with joy. These maids were also disciples of the Animal Kingdom—to them, hugging the thigh of an Elder was an excellent opportunity to rise. Just as she was about to begin, she sensed the Elder tense.

"Is everything okay, oh great Elder?" she asked.

Caran growled. "No."

He tore through space and disappeared, leaving behind screaming girls and a vacuum which the hot water was quick to fill.

Elder Caran reappeared over his building, surrounded in all directions by fumes. He teleported five more times in quick succession, escaping the planet's atmosphere to reach the space above. Finally, he could see—endless black surrounded him in all directions, barring the planet below him and the blazing sun to the left.

He frowned.

Just now, he'd sensed something—a sharp sense scanning the planet and locking onto him. It was like being stared at by a wild animal. Cold killing intent washed over him in waves, drenching him in sweat.

Now that he was in space, he couldn't see anything. He was alone. What was going on?

"Show yourself!" he roared into the void. "In the name of the Animal Kingdom, declare your intentions!"

"Hmph!" A cold snort was the only reply. Just this snort alone distorted space for thousands of miles, and Elder Caran felt his organs vibrate. He was instantly filled with fear.

"I apologize, senior!" he shouted. "I didn't recognize your noble aura! Please accept the apologies of me, Elder Caran!"

Though he said that, he could still feel no aura. He just

knew that whoever had released that snort was far, far stronger than himself.

"All you can do is oppress and grovel," a cold voice echoed in response. "I'm sorry, Elder Caran, but some things cannot be fixed with apologies. All you dogs of the Animal Kingdom... should just die."

Elder Caran, for better or for worse, was still an Elder of the Animal Kingdom. When had anyone spoken to him in such a tone? "Senior!" he exclaimed, barely containing his rage, but he didn't have more time to speak.

Space distorted a hundred miles away. A dark starship appeared behind a single man. He wore brown pants and a gray cloak which left his chest exposed. Just by standing there, the aura he exuded was that of a living god, the center of the universe. The laws bowed around him—the starlight curved. His fist contained such power that simply clenching it strained the surrounding space, like an ancient titan born anew.

Elder Caran's legs went cold. He'd met an Ancestor before, but even he hadn't carried such aura. This was the single strongest cultivator he'd ever encountered. He was but a child before him—they weren't even on the same level.

Before Caran could respond, the man drew back his fist and punched. The world lost its colors. The stars disappeared. Endless purple converged from deep space to form a massive fist a hundred miles wide, blotting out the sun and radiating extreme power.

The fist flew toward Caran and the planet behind him.

"No!" he roared. This had been too sudden, too abrupt! He tried to teleport away, abandoning his post in the face of such a terrifying adversary, but he discovered to his horror that space around him had been sealed. Let alone teleport, he couldn't even fly away. There was no avoiding this fist!

Caran shouted in frustration. He was about to die, and he

had no idea why. He should have several more millennia to live
—for his life to end like this was simply a joke.

All that bitterness fed into his insanity, which, at the precipice of life and death, erupted with all its power. "Five Star Warp!" he cried out, pushing a palm forward. Five points glittered in space—the tips of his five sharp fingernails. The strike tore through the spatial lock and shot forward, carrying undeniable momentum.

At the end of the day, Caran was a middle C-Grade. In front of his strike, even a mountain range would have no choice but to collapse.

His palm clashed against the fist. There was barely an impact. Before this massive purple fist, Caran's attack simply shattered like a glass ball thrown against a wall. The fist only slowed down for an instant before resuming its advance, slamming into Caran, breaking all his bones, and effortlessly carrying him backward. He couldn't even scream.

The fist carried on, falling toward Earthen Gemini like a flaming meteor. Before it even arrived, the force of its advance pressed against the planet's atmosphere, forcefully pushing the fumes aside like plumes of smoke against the wind. For the first time in the planet's history, the sky was clear. Thousands of people below looked up in surprise, seeing all the way to space above and to a massive, purple, fist-shaped meteor. The ones with the sharpest gazes saw the broken body of Elder Caran plastered on its middle finger. They screamed.

The fist came down. The world shook. The planet groaned. A massive shockwave erupted, sending large quantities of fumes into space and replacing them with raised dust. A thousand miles around the point of impact was directly annihilated, and the planet itself compacted under the force, cracking. The shockwave traveled around the planet, killing almost everyone. Those who survived perished against the extreme heat and vibrations that followed. Even the two early C-Grade Enforcers, who had the bad luck of being near the crash site, were instantly slain.

The impact was so powerful, it shook the planet's core and forcefully changed its shape. Looking at it from far away in space, Earthen Gemini folded around the point of impact, the land rising to form new rings of mountains which immediately collapsed, and then was compressed toward the planet core. A massive explosion occurred on the other side, sending millions of tons of rocks flying into space and creating a massive crater. Endless ravines opened across the planet, hundreds of miles in depth. Lava shot out.

Soon afterward, Earthen Gemini could no longer take it. The cracks spread past the point of no return. Entire pieces of the planet broke away one by one, and Earthen Gemini fractured into a collection of roughly nine moon-sized pieces which flew off in different directions, escaping their previous orbit around the sun. They would soon become large asteroids aimlessly crossing space, fall into the sun, or be absorbed into another celestial object of this solar system.

Where there used to be a planet, there was now only a humongous cloud of dust.

Jack watched coldly from his vantage point in space. In a single strike, he destroyed a planet. He was not terrified by his powers, nor was he regretful about the many lives he'd taken. None were innocent—all were cultivators of the Animal Kingdom, soldiers of the enemy.

All he felt was fulfillment and dark satisfaction. He looked at his hand, then slowly clenched it into a fist. All this power he possessed... He was glad for it. He needed it to destroy his enemies, avenge his son, and protect his family.

Eight years of cultivation. Eight years of moving from one catastrophe to the next and using them to grow stronger. From struggling to defeat a goblin, Jack had reached the point of punching planets into oblivion. He had slowly but surely stepped into the highest echelons of the universe.

He smirked. An old memory came to mind. A couple years before the Integration, he'd gone to an interview for a job he later refused. They'd asked him where he saw himself in ten years. He didn't remember what he'd answered then, but he certainly hadn't gotten it right.

Planet destroyer, he thought, smiling to himself. *Not quite part of the corporate ladder.*

As for the people in the starship behind him—Brock, Salin, Nauja, Bomn, and Vashter—they were shivering. Not due to the brutality of all this, but because of the power he'd exhibited.

Was this really the power of a cultivator?

All of them were forced to look at themselves and acknowledge that this was a level they could never hope to reach. The only exception was Brock, whose chest ballooned with pride and ambition. Soon, he too would possess such power. The way of the bro would resound across the universe, ushering a brighter, happier era.

Of course, that would all be meaningless if they lost themselves in the process... Brock's face darkened, but he said nothing. Not yet.

Jack looked up. A number of notifications rang in his ears. The System acknowledged his efforts.

Level up! You have reached Level 319.
Level up! You have reached Level 320. Further levels locked until the development of your next Dao Fruit.

He smiled. This was the first time he got so many levels that the System had to withhold a few. It was natural—he'd just killed a great number of cultivators, and while most of them were too low level to give him any experience at all, there were a few at the C-Grade. Elder Caran, specifically, was at a similar level to Jack. The only reason he'd seemed so weak was that Jack's battle power was an entire Grade beyond what his level indicated.

And that wasn't the end of the notifications.

Congratulations! For single-handedly destroying a planet, you are awarded the Title: Planet Destroyer.
Planet Destroyer: A Title awarded to those who have destroyed a planet. Efficacy of all stats +5%.

A rush of power flooded Jack. His body grew denser, his mind sharper, and his heart clearer. No matter how strong he got, a percentage increase was always significant. If anything, it mattered even more to him because of his inflated stats. A five percent increase at this point was more than three hundred points worth of Physical.

Amidst his joy, however, he frowned. This wasn't a hard title to get. Since it didn't specify doing it in one strike, most B-Grades should be able to achieve it given a bit of time. Maybe destroying a planet was a secret initiation ritual for B-Grades at high-level factions. He only hoped they went for uninhabited ones.

Of course, the System wouldn't have done this by accident. It encouraged people to destroy because it wanted to twist them into callous warriors who would stand up to the Old Gods. It was nothing but a war machine.

Whatever the case, Jack had gotten another increase in power. That was always nice. He shook his head and flew back to the *Trampling Ram*.

This was just the beginning.

The Animal Kingdom would pay.

CHAPTER THIRTY-FIVE

SIXTH FRUIT

EVA SOLVIG WAS SILENT. A PROJECTION PLAYED IN FRONT OF HER—A massive purple fist descending from the sky. Then came screaming and an impact. That was all.

She played it over and over. All the while, she remained silent, her brows creased. No one could tell what she was thinking.

The door to her chambers burst open. "*Is it true?*" Artus Emberheart exclaimed, barging in.

She turned to him, and her frown deepened. "You will show respect."

"I'm sorry," he quickly corrected himself, but his agitation was evident. "Is it true? I have to know."

Eva wordlessly played the projection one more time. She watched Artus's face change from doubt, to disbelief, to horror. "No!" he shouted. "No! It can't be! He—He's dead! He died a year ago!"

"Looks like he didn't..." Eva's voice was tired. This issue, this man, had turned from a minor annoyance to a grave worry. Too many times he'd survived the impossible—too many times she thought she had him, only for him to slip out from between her fingers.

For the past year, she'd constantly had a feeling he would one day emerge alive from the Animal Abyss. Everyone told her it was unreasonable, just a manifestation of her heart demon. Yet, it had turned true. She didn't even have the energy to rejoice at being right—grim terror filled her entire being, a premonition of coming death.

Jack Rust was a force of nature. His talent and potential were unprecedented. Soon, he would surpass her in strength, and then he would come to kill her. She had participated in murdering his son—the hatred between them was completely unbridgeable. He wouldn't stop until she died.

Finally, Eva was forced to admit she'd made the wrong enemy... but it was too late to change things.

"How is this possible?" Artus raved from beside her.

"I don't know," she replied tiredly. "It should be impossible, but the truth is before our eyes. When the Animal Abyss disappeared two weeks ago, it was his doing. Not only did he escape, but he even earned some benefits."

"He's a cockroach!" Artus shouted. "He just refuses to die! We must do something, Commander, or he'll come right here and kill us!"

"Do you think I don't know that? Calm yourself, Artus. You may have rendered great services to the Hand, but I will still remove you from your post if you revert to the thoughtless lunatic you used to be."

"Remove me?" Artus laughed. "We're in the same boat now, Commander. We live or die together."

"Perhaps, but I don't need your pestering while I try to solve this problem." She leaned onto the table, deep in thought. "Earthen Gemini was completely destroyed. We can safely deduce that Jack Rust's hatred has reached a genocidal level.

The only reason he's aiming it at the Animal Kingdom is because he doesn't have the power to face me yet—but, if he keeps earning levels so quickly, it won't be long before he does."

"How do we even have this recording?" Artus asked.

"The Kingdom's Grand Elder has commanded all Enforcers to carry projection stones transmitting their recordings to an off-world outpost. That's the only reason we even know of that man's return—we must capitalize on this and catch him before he grows even stronger."

"Even stronger?" Artus said, grasping at straws. "He can't! I killed his son, I broke his Dao. There is no way he can recover!"

"Just because you can't, it doesn't mean he can't either," Eva shot back. Artus grimaced. "We must act on the assumption that he's not only recovered, but also come back stronger. There can be no room for error. We cannot afford to underestimate him. I'm taking over."

Artus clearly battled with wanting to say something but finally held his tongue. "Yes, Commander."

She nodded. "I will exaggerate the situation to headquarters and request back-up. We need high-level Envoys here—we will never succeed if I'm the only person in the galaxy who can catch him. Meanwhile, we need to constrain his growth. Pass down my orders to the Animal Kingdom—every Enforcer, Elder, and Ancestor must immediately return to Animal Planet, where I will personally move to stand guard. They are forbidden from taking a single step outside—otherwise, I fear they will just become fertilizer for Jack Rust's advancement."

"Yes, Commander."

Eva leaned back, her tired eyes filled with resolve. She had not reached this level by being weak of mind. "I will prioritize this issue over the purging of the Church. Jack is worth ten Church Envoys, anyway—there is no point in chasing anyone else. From now on, every resource of the Hand of God will be devoted to forming a net to catch that man. Remember, Artus. No matter what happens, we must kill him before he grows! That is the only way we can survive!"

———

Meanwhile, Jack and the *Trampling Ram* were hovering in space, far away from all inhabited zones. He was sitting cross-legged in his cabin. Powerful undulations were emitted from his body, not harming the starship but filling it with echoes of power.

My sixth fruit... he muttered. *What will it be?*

A few ideas ran through his mind. He pictured them against his current five fruits to find the one which fit best.

Fist, Space, Life, Death, Battle... And then what?

He took a deep breath, then another. He silenced his mind, letting his inner thoughts roam free. Concepts filled him— ideas, emotions, pathways to the future. Yet, one stood above the others.

Jack's eyes slammed shut. He dove into his soul world, finding himself in front of a verdant tree. Dao was sucked in through its roots, then freely traversed the trunk to nourish five fruits and innumerable purple flowers. Unlike the time when Jack had been partially crippled, his tree was now filled with life, as well as power.

He gazed at the fruits. They were purple, blue, green, black, and red respectively. They did not form a complete whole yet, not even close, but they bore the early hints of his future completion.

The next fruit would not be based on furthering such a completion. Jack stared at his tree again, more carefully this time. Hints of darkness hid amidst the purple. They slithered around like tiny black snakes, intertwined into his Dao yet unable to enter his fruits. They could only wander around the trunk, aimlessly moving up and down, wasting their power.

These were the results of Jack's present state of mind. Though he'd mostly recovered from his grief, the darkness remained in his heart. It would stay there until he completed his revenge or, maybe, forever. The transformation he'd experienced was so great it now constituted part of him—that was the only way darkness could seep into his soul.

Jack could choose to ignore this darkness or embrace it. And in his years of cultivation, he'd learned to be true to himself. This didn't mean he would become an amoral vigilante or a man who lost his sense of right or wrong, but that he acknowledged the darker sides of life as well.

Yin and yang. Darkness in the light. Balance.

An eye for an eye. That was also part of the Fist.

Jack spoke resolute words, "My sixth Dao Fruit... will be Revenge!"

All those dark snakes gathered into one stream, recklessly climbing his Dao Tree. They reached the branches and chose one, diving into a single purple flower. The flower turned darker and larger—it transformed. A single fruit began to form, black as the night, crimson like blood. The two colors intertwined, forming a dark crimson fruit as if made of dry blood. It was shaped as a skull.

Jack let the transformation complete and die down, then released a long, long sigh. Power trickled into his limbs, yet his attention was focused on the newly created fruit.

This fruit felt similar to Death, yet they were clearly different. Death was a concept—cold, distant, emotionless, just an understanding of reality. Revenge was hatred, bitterness, rage, a desire to inflict harm on others. One was reality, the other was emotion.

And, perhaps, this wasn't something he wanted to internalize.

Jack shook his head again. He did not know what the future held, but he hoped that, after this was all over, he could return to the light, though the darkness inside him would never leave.

Then again, wasn't that the point of being human? The only people without darkness were the ones who hadn't lived enough.

"What do you think, Copy Jack?" he asked, looking to the side. "Enjoy the colors?"

Copy Jack shrugged. He then gave Jack a thumbs-up, an encouraging smile, and flew away to wander the empty soul world. Jack watched him go.

After he'd left the Black Hole World and returned to the universe, Copy Jack had just... awoken. There was no change in him, as far as Jack could see, and he didn't communicate anything weird. It was just like he'd taken a long and very suspiciously coincidental nap.

Jack wasn't naive. Something made Copy Jack sleep for the duration of Jack's stay in the Black Hole World. Was it related to that world itself, or was it caused by his absence from the universe?

His best explanation was that Copy Jack's slumber was related to Jack's cracked Dao. He was a Dao Soul, after all, and he had been formed around that Dao. Maybe he couldn't exist while it was cracked. That would explain the timing of both his slumber and, roughly, his awakening, but it still wasn't a connection Jack fully grasped. He did not enjoy enigmas inside his soul. He wanted to be in control there.

Maybe the turtle would know once it awakened. Jack gazed at the door on his Dao Tree. It had already been four years since the turtle—Venerable Saint Thousand Shell—saved him and went to sleep... To such an ancient being, that amount of time was nothing. Maybe it would sleep for a hundred or a thousand years. Jack had no way to know unless he awoke it himself.

"So many things to do, and so little time... Let's make the best of it."

He spared another glance at his Dao Tree, whose Dao was now fully absorbed in all the fruits. The newly-created sixth fruit was already growing. Soon, it would reach maturity, and then Jack could work on the next one.

His eyes opened in the real world. Notifications welcomed him.

Level up! You have reached Level 321.
Level up! You have reached Level 322.
...
Level up! You have reached Level 328.

Those were the remaining levels from destroying Earthen Gemini. They were more than he anticipated. D and E-Grades shouldn't give him any experience, so what had?

Could it be the planet itself? Or was it his feat of annihilating multiple C-Grades with a single strike?

In any case, Jack allocated his two hundred extra stat points in Physical, then marveled at his status screen—while ignoring the error message at the very start, which was starting to get repetitive now.

ERROR: PLEASE REPORT TO THE NEAREST AUTHORITIES
IMMEDIATELY OR FACE EXTERMINATION.

Name: Jack Rust
Species: Human, Earth-387
Faction: Bare Fist Brotherhood (C)
Grade: C

Class: Gladiator Titan (King)
Level: 328

Strength: 6540 (+)
Dexterity: 6540 (+)
Constitution: 6540 (+)
Mental: 1000
Will: 1000
Free sub-points: 2

Dao Skills: Meteor Punch IV, Iron Fist Style III,
Brutalizing Aura III, Neutron Star Body III, Super-
nova III, Space Mastery III, Fist of Mortality III,
Death Mastery III, Titan Taunt II
Dao Roots: Indomitable Will, Life, Power, Weakness
Dao Fruits: Fist, Space, Life, Death, Battle, Revenge
Titles: Planetary Frontrunner (10), Planetary Torch-
bearer (1), Ninth Ring Conqueror, Planetary Over-
lord (1), Grade Defier, Planet Destroyer

He was progressing nicely. After exiting the Black Hole World, his Dao understandings had shot through the roof, allowing him to blitz through the levels and reach the B-Grade as soon as possible. Before then, he would pay a visit to the Animal Kingdom and the Hand of God branch in this galaxy. Both should be destroyed with extreme prejudice.

He didn't need to reach the B-Grade to do that. Nine fruits should be enough. Maybe eight.

Jack rose to his feet. "Let's go," he said to himself. "The levels are waiting."

———

In another part of the same starship, a brorilla sat cross-legged. He was neither cultivating nor meditating. All he did was sit there, absorbing the ripples of power released by his big brother's breakthrough, analyzing them.

There was darkness in there—Brock could feel it clearly. More darkness than warranted. Big Bro was beginning to wander in the wrong direction, but Brock was here to set him on the right path again.

That was the duty of a bro.

Wordlessly, Brock stood up and started walking.

CHAPTER THIRTY-SIX
BRO TALK

As much as the Hand of God wanted to hide it, the isolation of the Animal Kingdom was a major event—everyone had questions, and they needed to be answered.

The news of Jack Rust's return spread like wildfire. People celebrated all across the galaxy, and a number of rebellions were ignited or reignited overnight. Jack was a hero. He symbolized resistance, freedom, and most importantly, he'd shown people it was possible to challenge those above you. He showed they could win.

The Animal Kingdom wasn't the only tyrannical faction, but they were one of the most prominent ones. They suppressed the common people to a ridiculous extent, siphoning off massive quantities of resources and dooming entire planets to abject poverty. The only reason such a system of governance could persist was the Kingdom's enormous military power coupled with the fear of the masses.

In their eyes, the Animal Kingdom was made up of gods, and they were only mortals. What meaning was there in fighting back? They'd just get squashed.

Jack Rust proved the opposite. He'd come from humble beginnings and rose meteorically through the cultivation world. He clashed with the Kingdom time and time again, always winning. He'd humbled them—shown they could bleed.

Thanks to a single man, the iron-clad prestige of the Animal Kingdom had shattered overnight. When he became a sensation on Hell, every eye of the constellation had focused on him. The Kingdom had been proven incompetent—and then he'd liberated his planet, defeating the planetary overseer in an epic showdown which was transmitted across the galaxy.

How many young people were there in the constellation? How many had boiling blood, a burning heart, courage, and the determination to die for a worthy cause? When they saw Jack Rust liberate his planet, they wanted to do the same—to save their children, parents, wives, husbands, friends, neighbors, to give them freedom and a good life.

For the last five years, ever since Jack defeated the planetary overseer, the Animal Kingdom constellation had been wrought with civil war. Half the planets had rebelled, either openly or using guerilla tactics. The Kingdom may have been powerful, but they were just too few. How could they simultaneously fight on thousands of inhabitable planets?

The common people were weak, but they were just too many. Moreover, through believing in a purpose and fighting to the death, their strength was rapidly growing. New D-Grade powerhouses appeared everywhere. The constellation was overrun by pirates. The drums of liberation echoed between the stars, and bloody battles occurred often. Casualties were aplenty. The war machine of the Kingdom was beginning to rust.

The rebels hadn't managed to form a stable coalition yet, but this was the first time in Milky Way's history that a major faction was challenged. The Animal Kingdom constellation had never been more tumultuous. That was why the Enforcers of the Kingdom had been rapidly flying around, suppressing rebellions wherever they went.

It was in that state of the constellation that Jack Rust returned. He hadn't been high-profile at the start because he was on a different mission—almost nobody noticed him.

When the Hand of God proclaimed the news of his demise, the flames of rebellion had been half-snuffed. Jack was more than a cultivator by now—he was a symbol in the eyes of all cultivators, a beacon of freedom. He was the one who'd originally set them aflame, the spark which had fallen on their dry wishes and despair. His death had been a hard blow.

If even he failed, how could they succeed?

While Jack was in the Black Hole World, the Kingdom had gone all-out. They slowly pushed back the flames of rebellion and were in the process of reinstating order across their constellation. To ensure this situation was never repeated and replenish their troops, they oppressed the people even harder, sucking them dry of all resources. It wasn't an iron fist anymore, but a steel one.

That was the context in which the *Dark Ram* had emerged as a new symbol of freedom, though weaker than the previous one. Brock and his group had tried their best to fan the flames and generate the greatest impact possible. In truth, even if Jack really was dead, Brock might have been able to turn things around. His Dao of Brohood was perfect for such a situation. He'd already met with several leaders of the revolution and formed bonds of brotherhood. Given enough time, he would rise in power and lead them all against the Animal Kingdom, eventually subjugating it. The brohood was unstoppable.

But there was no need for that.

Jack Rust had returned. The symbol of freedom, the original warrior, the flag bearer of the entire constellation.

It wasn't official yet, but many could connect the dots. Earthen Gemini had disappeared. The Kingdom had recalled every Elder and Enforcer to turtle inside their capital. The smell of their fear reached many noses, and they could only come up with one explanation—that man was back.

Jack Rust was here, and he was strong enough to make the Kingdom cower. A single man commanded the fear of a B-Grade faction, an interstellar empire.

Of course, his name was still a whisper in the wind as nothing was certain. But it didn't matter. The Kingdom had retreated; the rebellions they'd only barely managed to snuff out reignited all at once, spreading wildly with no one to stop them like a wildfire in a dry summer forest. The Kingdom's million-year-old foundation crumbled. They lost control. The constellation was taken over by rebels, each group of planets their own stronghold, all operating in brotherhood.

Nobody was taking their resources anymore. Moreover, the experience of war had furthered their Daos. Even more power-houses appeared, springing up everywhere like weeds. While the main forces of the Kingdom were sealed in its capital, everyone else grew stronger.

It wasn't like the war was over. While the Kingdom retreated, in truth, that was only their C-Grades. D-Grades and below still roamed the constellation, fighting a bitter war against the rebels.

One side had numbers, the other powerhouses. Without the Elders and Enforcers, the two enemy armies were roughly similar in strength, and they duked it out in battlefields of epic proportions.

Jack wouldn't bother with such small fish. D-Grades wouldn't give him any levels, nor would he lower himself to massacring weaklings. Above all, this wasn't his battle to fight. Freedom could only be grasped, not given. Even if he swooped in to annihilate the Kingdom's armies, that would rob the rebels of the opportunity to earn their own freedom.

Everyone needed to fight their own battles. Even if it seemed harsh sometimes, that was the way of the Fist.

Of course, to the common people, Jack was already helping a lot. In their eyes, he had single-handedly occupied the attention of the Animal Kingdom's C-Grades to give them an even battlefield. He was holding off the enemy leaders so they could fight their underlings.

Tears sparked in the eyes of every rebel cultivator. They placed a fist over their heart. "That man... is so heroic!"

"Jack Rust! Jack Rust! Jack Rust!"

"For the Fist!"

It went without saying that pugilists had greatly increased in population recently.

Jack knew all those things but didn't really bother. He belonged to a higher realm now—to him, the Milky Way Galaxy was just a stepping-stone. Meddling too much would be unwise. Let these people carve out their own fates. That was more important than playing hero.

His own war lay in distant space, in the clash of the Church and Hand, of the Old Gods and the Immortals, where A-Grades were only generals and Archons were kings. That was his battlefield.

As for the rebels of the Milky Way, he would help them by destroying the Kingdom's capital. They could dictate their own future afterward.

Jack leaned against a glass wall, sipping on whiskey— they'd found a barrel on an enemy starship they destroyed. He rolled the liquid in his mouth, passing it over and under his tongue, between his cheeks. His gaze was piercing the distance until he finally swallowed.

"So, they're holed up," he said.

"Right," Brock replied, standing beside him. His knuckles rested against the ground, his body weight angled forward as if he'd charge through the glass wall and into space.

"How can we lure them out?" Jack asked.

"I'm not sure. If we make it too obvious, Eva Solvig will arrive. If it's not obvious, nobody will come—the C-Grades have already retreated and will not move without reason."

Jack clicked his tongue. "That's a problem. I need a few more levels."

"Why is that a problem?"

"I need to kill them to get levels. Slowly cultivating by myself will take a very long time."

"I still don't see the problem."

Jack turned around with a puzzled frown. "What are you trying to say, Brock? I can't assault their capital yet, and they will not come out. I have no way to earn more levels. I'm stuck."

"Oh," Brock muttered sagely. "So there are no other C-Grade cultivators to hunt?"

Jack raised a brow. "Other C-Grade cultivators? I wouldn't want to go against innocents, but... Ah! Do you mean the Hand of God?"

Brock smiled. "Excellent idea, bro. You're so smart."

"It's all you, Brock." He cupped his chin, suddenly energetic. "The Hand of God... They're trying to destroy every outpost of the Church in this galaxy, right? If Eva Solvig is leading them, and she's a late C-Grade, everyone else should be weaker. I can take them."

"Right. So we can go after them."

"We can find their outposts. Shouldn't be too hard—they're public, unlike the Church's. And it's two birds with one stone, because not only are they the enemies of the Church, but also our personal enemies. They had a stake in what happened. They must also feel my wrath."

"I wouldn't put it that way, but yes. They deserve to die."

"Well then, who am I to refuse the levels they so kindly offer?" Jack replied, spinning around. "Nauja! Can you check the star map and find the nearest Hand of God outpost?"

"Sure!" she replied from the next room.

Then Salin shouted, "Good idea! We didn't have enough enemies before!"

Jack rolled his eyes, motioning toward the next room. "Shall we?"

Brock shook his head. "No."

"No?"

"I want to talk to you for a moment."

"Okay?"

Jack was confused, yet also suspected what Brock wanted to talk about. Defensiveness and relief alternated in his eyes. Brock stared at him gently, yet deeply.

"How are you, big bro?" he finally asked.

"I'm fine."

"No, you're not."

Jack sighed. "No, I'm not. Nothing is fine. I am exactly as you imagine—bitter, angry, and sad. How else could I possibly be?"

"Yes. I understand."

Jack sighed again. His body relaxed, and from the outside, it seemed as if he'd deflated. Rather than the hard man he always was, he'd become vulnerable—a side he would only show to his closest people.

"This is hard, Brock," he confessed. "I'm struggling. I may have gotten over the shock, but the grief remains, and I don't think it will ever go away. All I can do is lean into the rage.

Am I supposed to live my entire life like this? A sad, angry man?"

Brock placed a hand on Jack's shoulder. They seemed completely mismatched from afar, a human and a brorilla, but they were brothers at heart. "Time heals everything," Brock said softly.

"But that's a lie. Time softens the wounds, that's all it does. Only we can heal ourselves."

"Listen to my words, bro. As long as you keep taking small steps forward, as long as you never give up, then even the deepest wounds will be healed given enough time. That is the meaning of time heals everything."

Jack raised his gaze to meet the brorilla's. "How much time is enough? I do not enjoy this, Brock. I want it to be over quickly."

"As much time as needed. It may be difficult, but you must endure. You must be strong. Guard your heart against the darkness and endure the pain, taking tiny steps forward until it's over. It will happen sooner than you think."

Jack sighed deeply. "You're a good brother, Brock. What would I do without you?"

Brock smiled. "I know it's hard, bro... You are shouldering a lot, and so many things have happened and are happening. What you feel is natural. I just want to let you know I'm here for you. We all are—that is the meaning of brohood. Whatever is happening, we can go through it together. You are not alone."

Jack was touched. "Thanks. I needed that."

"I know. But at the same time, brother, there are some other things I must say. I don't want to, but it's my responsibility as your bro."

Jack raised a brow. He drew back a little. "What?"

"You need to pull yourself together. As hard as this may be, you cannot afford to let it overwhelm you. You wield great power. If you misstep even a little bit, millions of people could die needlessly—on either side."

"There is no needless death at the Animal Kingdom side."

"That's exactly what I'm talking about," Brock replied, his eyes hardening. "You're doing great so far, brother. Your actions are just and measured. You are a hero, but I can see that your mind is clouded. You just developed a dark Dao Fruit. I can sense that you are losing yourself, slowly walking off in the wrong direction. You are giving into the darkness without realizing it. Your resistance is being worn out. That is no good. You must turn yourself around and remember to keep fighting always, because if you don't, then sooner or later there will be a moment when you make the wrong decision, and then you won't be a hero anymore, but a criminal. A deranged murderer."

Jack chuckled angrily. "What do you know, Brock? You cannot understand the pain I'm going through. Do you realize that I had to watch my own son be *murdered*? Just rising to my feet after that is an achievement. The only way I can hope to bring justice to Eric is to avenge him."

"That's fine. I'm just saying, be careful not to go too far, because you're about to."

"How can I not go too far, Brock? My heart is a boat in a sea of darkness, and the only thing keeping me from capsizing is revenge. I cannot, and will not, deliver it calmly. I will strike out wildly and exterminate everyone who ever hurt my son, everyone who assisted in his murder, and everyone related to those people. That was my promise to him: the name Ember-heart would cease to exist. If I go back on it, I will have failed him again, and I cannot stand that."

Brock clenched his jaw. He stared deeply into Jack's eyes, not with anger or challenge, but with sadness. Jack did not look away. Finally, Brock shook his head.

"Your words are wrong. I understand that your burden is

heavy, brother, and I know that anyone else would have collapsed already, but you need to beat this. You need to be strong. Because you are my big bro, and I demand that of you."

Brock turned and walked away. Jack did not speak. His thoughts were hazy, and his anger was still seeking an outlet. Since when am I so irritable? he thought. Is he right? Am I going too far? Or is he just afraid of shadows?

Fuck this.

CHAPTER THIRTY-SEVEN
LIGHTING SOULS ON FIRE

As the true overlord of this galaxy, the Hand of God liked to keep a discreet though solid grip on every major faction. Their outposts were placed in important locations.

Of course, the Hand of God was more than just a supervisor. Every galaxy branch had its own base, resources, disciples, and troops. They could be called a major faction of their own. Even back in Trial Planet, one of Jack's main opponents had been a beast tamer called Minerva—a disciple of the Hand of God.

The Hand of God branch in the Milky Way Galaxy possessed twenty-six cultivators at the B-Grade, either as full or guest members, and its leader was at the peak B-Grade. However, for the purposes of the Second Crusade, most of those people had been withdrawn. The strongest person remaining was Eva Solvig alongside an array of early B-Grade Branch Elders.

Those people were naturally spread across the galaxy. The branch headquarters of the Hand of God were nowhere near the Animal Kingdom constellation. They did, however, possess a few sizable outposts, one of which was the Crown Meteor Outpost.

In the darkness of space, a meteor traveled alone. It was not shaped as a boulder, but roughly as a crown—this was its natural shape, and also the reason it was chosen to hold an outpost. The crown possessed seven tips, each of which housed the personal quarters of a Branch Enforcer. As for the main tip, which was usually reserved for the Head Enforcer, it was presently occupied by an early B-Grade Branch Elder who'd been dispatched here specifically to keep an eye on the widespread rebellion.

While the Hand couldn't spare the resources to help the Animal Kingdom, they wanted to be near the situation.

The Hand of God branch nurtured its own disciples, but even so, they weren't at the level where they could produce a large number of B-Grades. Of the twenty-six they commanded, most were forcefully borrowed from other factions—the Hand demanded that each major faction send a fraction of its B-Grades to serve them as both a tribute and a sign of unity.

The Branch Elder who had been sent to watch over this rebellion was exactly one such case. His name was Edelstein Magnifold, a feshkur cultivator from the Wide Swirls faction. Unlike most of his species, who tended to be barbaric warriors, he was a refined gentleman often seen wearing a suit and a top hat. He was a man of progress—which wasn't always a good thing.

On this particular day, Elder Edelstein leaned over a clean, white bench. He frowned at it, then rotated his monocle in thought. The only object on the bench was a bare human brain suspended in green fluid.

"Hmm," the Elder muttered to himself. "Odd. It's not reacting." He then looked up toward an assistant. "Get me another, will you? I think this one came broken."

"Yes, Elder," the assistant replied obediently. She was a

human at the peak D-Grade, one of Elder Edelstein's most devoted disciples. She grabbed another jar of green liquid and was about to rush to the prisoner quarters when the ground below them shook. The disciple swayed, then caught herself. She flew outside the laboratory, finding that Elder Edelstein had teleported there before her. He was cupping his chin.

"Curious," he said. "I could have sworn this meteor was whole."

The assistant's face paled. Of the Crown Meteor's seven tips, two were missing, crushed into smithereens. A gap had been created in the perfect circle—it no longer resembled a crown but a thorny half-moon.

Even worse, one of those two tips had contained the outpost's teleporter.

"Greetings," Elder Edelstein said. The assistant looked up, glimpsing a tall, rough man floating above them. He wore only a set of brown shorts and a gray cloak which fluttered behind him, revealing a bare and thickly muscled chest. A natural air of savagery radiated from his body. His eyes shone like dark stars, and his fists... Just by standing there, he gave the feeling of an immovable object, an unstoppable force. Gravity itself bent around him.

The man did not return Elder Edelstein's greetings. The Elder didn't appear to mind. He continued, "You must be the infamous Jack Rust."

The assistant gasped. She noticed the many C-Grades who'd risen from around the meteor shrink back, with only a few at the peak C-Grade still daring to stand straight.

"That's right," Jack Rust replied.

"And I suppose you are here to do battle?"

In response, a heavy aura spread from the man's body. It felt almost physical. The assistant recoiled like she'd been submerged in a vat of mercury, and even the surrounding C-Grades hesitated. Elder Edelstein motioned at them. "All of you stand back for now. This is not an opponent you can beat."

His voice was perfectly calm as always. However, the assistant had been with him for many years, and what she found hidden deep beneath that calmness was an emotion she never expected to see in her master—hesitation.

"You can't beat me either," Jack Rust replied. "How about you stretch your neck? I'll make it quick."

The Elder laughed. "There are no grievances between us, Jack Rust. I'm only a guest Elder from the Wide Swirls. If you have something to settle with the Hand of God, I can step aside as long as you don't go too far."

Jack's face warped into a hard smile. "Too far? Well, I'm going to completely destroy this place. Does that count as taking it too far for you?"

The Elder frowned. "That would make things difficult. I have no desire to clash with you, but if I just let you kill all these people and word gets out, that will mean a lot of trouble for me."

"Too bad; that's exactly what I plan on doing."

The Elder remained absolutely calm on the surface while everyone around them was sitting on nails.

A peak C-Grade burst into motion without warning. His form blurred as he shot into deep space. Jack didn't even turn to look. Space warped around the escaping C-Grade, who suddenly found himself running straight toward Jack. A hand easily grabbed his throat. Then, with a simple squeeze, the C-Grade's neck snapped and he perished instantly.

Nobody had the time to react. Even Elder Edelstein could only stare on. He, too, could easily kill a peak C-Grade, but would it be so effortless?

He hadn't been certain about Jack Rust's power before. His middle C-Grade cultivation made him easy to underestimate, but as a Branch Elder of the Hand of God, Edelstein was privy to more information than the common person. He was aware that Jack Rust possessed the power to tussle with an early B-Grade like himself, at least for a bit. The reason he'd been avoiding battle was that he was a cautious individual by nature and saw no reason to risk his life here, even if that risk seemed small.

Now, however, he was forced to reevaluate. Could it be that Jack Rust was stronger than him?

By all accounts that was impossible. He was an early B-Grade, while Jack Rust was only a six-fruit C-Grade. They were separated by several small realms and a large one. Moreover, Elder Edelstein wasn't some weakling. He had decent hopes of reaching the middle B-Grade in his lifetime.

The Elder thought hard. "I favor the young," he finally said. "Let me make you an offer, Jack Rust. There is no need to fight, but I also can't just let you kill my underlings. How about this: If you can withstand a single strike from me, then I will consider this issue as bygones. If you have a personal grudge with someone in this outpost, I will even let you handle it. What do you think?"

In Elder Edelstein's mind, he was being very smart. This offer ensured he didn't have to fight while saving most of his face—if he lost this gamble, as he certainly would, he had an excuse to retreat without seeming like a coward. At the same time, Jack Rust would gain prestige and also conclude his business for coming here, whatever that was. It was a win-win situation.

He believed this a great offer. Which was why he was shocked when Jack Rust only laughed.

"You want me to endure a single strike and *you'll* forget about this? Are you stupid? I'm here to kill all of you!"

Elder Edelstein finally frowned. His monocle fell. He thought this was just a fake declaration Jack made to exude bravery, so why was he insisting so much? It couldn't be that he really wanted to fight him here, right? Not when he had so many C-Grades to support him?

"You're going too far," he said. "I've made you an offer with consideration for both our faces, but don't think I am truly afraid of you. Just accept my gamble. There is no enmity between us—no reason to shed blood."

"No reason to shed blood?" Jack gave a hard smile. "How convenient for you. Just because you come from another faction, you think I will spare you? That you can distance yourself from the Hand of God's wrongdoings? Tell me this, little Elder. If I wasn't standing before you as an equal, but as the weaker party, would you spare me on account of having no previous enmities, or would you capture me and surrender me to the Hand of God?"

The Elder's brows fell even lower. His calm manner of speech finally cracked. "You're pushing it."

"So what if I am? What are you going to do about it?"

Elder Edelstein inwardly considered whether to attack immediately. The only reason he still held back was a sharp instinct inside him insisting that was a terrible, *terrible* idea— that Jack was much stronger than he seemed.

"I will ask you one last time in the name of our neutral relationship," he said. "Leave this place. Otherwise, don't blame me for being rude!"

Jack only laughed. "Oh, Elder, you little Elder. You keep mentioning our lack of enmity like it's something important. Let me tell you something: even if I hadn't come here with the express purpose of killing you, even if I didn't plan to use you to level up, even if you could somehow absolve yourself of the Hand of God's crimes, I still wouldn't spare you. Do you think I can't sense the prisoners you keep in that crown tip over there? Those humans you've laid out on racks, some broken, some dead, with their organs exposed in jars? Just for that, you deserve to die. You're a lunatic."

"Cruelty is nothing in the face of progress," the Elder replied, slowly releasing his aura. A storm of gray filled the world—an endless Cruelty. His eyes sharpened. The monocle swayed by his aura, but the hat remained on his head as if glued to his flesh. "I don't blame someone as young and naive as you for not seeing that... but you will. I will make sure of it. When you join them and are unable to either live or die, only existing to further my experiments, then you will realize how sweet your pain feels. When nothing else remains, my progress will become your inner purpose."

Jack shook his head. "You sicken me. Go die."

Purple and gray collided. The two auras ground against each other, pushing back and forth, but the stronger side was soon revealed. Jack's aura was expanding, continuously pushing back the Elder's. He paled, as did everyone around them. "C-Grades, assist me!" the Elder shouted, redoubling his efforts.

Jack flickered. Nobody saw how he moved, but in the blink of an eye, the eleven C-Grades surrounding him were all dead. Some had their chests punched through, some had their heads shattered. None escaped. Only then did Elder Edelstein's attack arrive—a cold gray light as if born from the depths of a glacier.

Jack turned to look at it. Then, he reached out and directly crushed it with his hand. The Elder gasped. "How!" he shrieked. "That's impossible! That attack could cut through everything— how can you block it?"

He was shocked. He thought he might be weaker, but he never imagined the difference to be this great. Facing his question, Jack only smiled—a smile which brought terror to the heart of every onlooker.

"Simple. It's because I am strong, and you are weak."

The Elder tried to run away, but his surroundings transformed. The crown meteor became a colosseum, the panicking cultivators turned into a screaming crowd. Sand was below his feet, and the cold breeze smelled of blood.

He did not consider this too much. He tried to escape, certain it was just an illusion, only to find himself crashing against the unbreakable walls of the arena. Spatial barriers! he realized in horror. The arena may have been an illusion, but the walls were real, formed of the Dao of Space. He could not break them—not in time. He could not escape.

He found Jack approaching one step at a time. "Goodbye, little Elder," he said. "I hope you're less of an asshole in your next life."

Elder Edelstein screamed, "Don't come any closer! I will detonate my—"

He didn't have time to finish his words. Jack's body flickered with lightning. The energy was done gathering in his fist, an incredibly dense point which erupted right in the Elder's face. The explosion was titanic. In despair, the Elder channeled all of his bitterness into his inner world, exploding it and his body in the greatest strike he could reveal. He was full of hatred—he was surely going to die, so he hoped to at least take Jack with him. His last thoughts were bitter.

However, all that energy achieved was to clash evenly against Jack's Supernova. The shockwave ruptured the spatial barriers and the vision of the arena, as well as the entire Crown Meteor around them, blasting the entire outpost into smithereens. Only a tiny part remained—the prison where Edelstein kept his prisoners. Jack had protected them and would release them later, saving as many as he could.

As for Jack himself, though he was a little battered, the majority of the explosion had spread outward—his Supernova had successfully matched it in a frontal clash.

Level up! You have reached Level 329.
Level up! You have reached Level 330.
...
Level up! You have reached Level 340.
Further levels locked until the development of your next Dao Fruit.

Jack smiled. He was so far ahead of the power curve that getting levels was trivial. The only difficult part was finding suitable opponents.

"Not bad," he muttered, watching his bleeding fist. "My all-out strike can defeat an early B-Grade. Maybe it wouldn't have killed him if he didn't explode himself, but he would be left unable to fight. At this rate, it won't be long before I can fight late B-Grades."

The gap between the different minor realms of the B-Grade was significant. Jack could one-shot most early B-Grades and defeat most middle B-Grades, but that didn't mean he could win against late B-Grades. At most, he could fight them for a while.

However, with a few more fruits...

He shook his head, not allowing himself to fall into thought just yet. This Elder also didn't possess a space ring, just like Mure Emberheart, and every other cultivator here had already died. Though Jack still had some work to do.

The prisoners weren't the only thing he'd protected. He stretched out a hand and a large projection stone flew to him through the rubble. This was an advanced model capable of constellation-wide broadcasting. Of course, any broadcast was useless if no one tuned in to the right frequency, but Jack had planned ahead of time and had Brock notify the rebellion bros.

He activated the stone and set it to the agreed-upon frequency. The projection stone blinked red.

"Hello, everyone. This is Jack Rust speaking." He couldn't see himself, but he imagined that he cut a pretty heroic image with his dusted face and the sea of debris behind him. "I understand news of my death has been spread, but it is false. I am very much alive. In fact, I am standing in the remains of Crown Meteor, a former outpost of the Hand of God. I just killed the early B-Grade cultivator commanding this place, along with every other enemy present, and I have a message I would like you to spread across the galaxy: The Hand of God and the Animal Kingdom took something very important from me, so I will take everything from them. I will destroy them completely. Every single disciple they possess, I will kill; every base they have, I will annihilate. Their Elders will crumble before my fist."

His eyes flashed with dark light. He hoped he was making the right impression. "I don't need assistance in this. I will do it alone. I have the power. So, act for yourselves; if you are currently fighting for freedom, keep doing it. Don't depend on me, but on yourselves. That is the way to grow strong. And, if you are a disciple of the Animal Kingdom or Hand of God listening to this... Then I advise you to leave your faction and start running. Because I am after you, and I will find you. I will slaughter you to the last man. Too long you have made us suffer; now is your time to be destroyed. Your leaders made the wrong enemy, and you will all pay.

"As for you, leaders of the enemy... Just sit tight. Keeping turtling up in that Animal Planet of yours and wait for me patiently. I will kill all of your underlings, all those criminals you abandoned, until my strength is enough. Only then will I show up at your doorstep to kill you all, and there is nothing you can do about it. You will die. Count your days."

He raised a fist. "For freedom. For Eric. For the Fist."

And then he shut down the projection stone, shattering it. He didn't need it anymore. The message had been given. The flame was lit.

And the Animal Kingdom was aflame.

CHAPTER THIRTY-EIGHT

SPOON SQUAD!

THE BARS OF ANIMAL PLANET WERE NOT IN GOOD SHAPE. FIRST OF ALL, the planet was overpopulated by everyone retreating here in a panic, therefore the bars were crowded. Second, an aura of fear hung over everyone's head, pressing them down with unceasing persistence.

"Can you believe it?" a man whispered to his company. "We, the overlords of the constellation, have been reduced to this!" He banged a fist on the table, not hard enough to break it, but enough to make a sound.

"I just pray for our survival," another replied with a heartless laugh.

"Don't say that. The Animal Planet is protected by the Ancestors! Even Ja—"

"Shhh!" everyone shushed him at the same time. These days, anyone who spoke the name of Jack Rust in any bar was immediately escorted outside.

"Sorry," the cultivator continued. "Even *that man* wouldn't dare to come here. We are safe."

"And what do you know?" another argued. "He hunted down immortals on Hell. He defeated our strongest inner disciple, then escaped. He killed an Elder on his first year of cultivating. It's been seven since then—who's to say he can't contend with our Ancestors?"

"You're spouting bullshit."

"Oh yeah? You saw the projection. He killed an Elder of the Hand of God—those people are at the B-Grade, just like our Ancestors! Who knows how many levels he got from that? We are just waiting here to die!"

"Shut up! What are you, a spy sent to demoralize us?"

"Open your eyes, idiot. How much more can we be demoralized?"

Nobody got angry at his words. Their eyes were simply filled with sadness. The Animal Kingdom, the overlords of a constellation, had been reduced to a gathering of scared people at bars gossiping about a man whose name they didn't dare to mention—a man who might soon come to destroy their planet. They might die at any point without knowing what was happening.

And there was nothing they could do about it.

The Elders of the Animal Kingdom were also powerless. They were currently gathered in a grand hall, usually filled with servants and wine. Today, both of those were missing. The Elders sat on hard chairs with equally hard expressions.

"Give us the daily report," the Grand Elder commanded in a tired voice.

Another Elder stood up. "Reporting to the Grand Elder. Today, we lost two planets at the outer side of the constellation —Earth-207 and Djinn Heaven. Our armies stationed there had no survivors. There were also skirmishes in the general space territories of those planets, where neither side won, as well as a major battle near the Orion nebula. We suffered light casualties."

The Elder was ready to provide more details as asked, but

nobody replied. It was understandable. This situation was depressing.

Two planets lost in a single day. It wasn't much compared to the entire Animal Kingdom constellation, which contained tens of thousands of them, but it painted a clear picture of the rebel army advancing while they retreated.

They were in dire straits.

"What about Jack Rust?" the Grand Elder finally asked.

"He has not made a move yet."

The Grand Elder nodded, waving for the Elder to sit back down. It was hard to imagine that this situation, the collapse of an interstellar empire, had come about by a single man.

Jack Rust had repeatedly challenged and humiliated them, shattering their image of dominance and encouraging others to do the same. They thought him killing an Elder was bad enough, but now, he'd returned after several years for more.

He'd somehow destroyed the Animal Abyss and slain Ancestor Mure, the strongest Ancestor of the Kingdom. It didn't matter if he had help or not. Soon afterward, he'd slain several Enforcers and an Elder, then stormed a Hand of God outpost and publicly proclaimed his return and intention to completely destroy the Animal Kingdom. The Hand of God had completely recalled its forces from their constellation in response. Moreover, they'd long forced the Kingdom to also recall everyone, giving the rebel armies ground to expand and solidify. The entire constellation had turned into Jack Rust's playground.

As much as the Grand Elder wanted to oppose that decision, he couldn't. It was the best they could do. Any Elder outside their capital was just a bag of levels waiting to be picked up by Jack Rust. Even the rebel armies were a small threat compared to him.

Everything converged on that man.

The Grand Elder had no hopes of reconciliation. The grudge

between them and Jack Rust was unbridgeable—this battle would be to the death. If he survived long enough, he would eventually come here and challenge their entire planet.

If they managed to kill him before that, then they could send out Elders to route the revolution. It would be hard for a while, but after a few millennia, they would probably be able to recover. All the losses they were suffering now, all the skin that was torn off their Kingdom's body, those could all be recouped as long as they killed Jack Rust—the greatest catastrophe their Kingdom had ever experienced.

The Grand Elder was tired, like he'd grown several millennia older in the span of a few years.

"Honored Grand Elder," said the Elder giving the daily report, "would you not like me to expand on any piece of information?"

"What's the point? If there is no news about Jack Rust, anything else is meaningless," the Grand Elder replied with a heavy sigh. Everyone waited for him to continue, to lead this meeting, but he took time to gather his resolve. His gaze grew heavier.

"I have already convened with the Ancestors," he said. "The reason I called for this council was not to discuss the present circumstances, but to announce something to you all. We... are awakening the Supreme Ancestors."

The Elders gasped. Their eyes widened—though, in their hearts, they'd expected this.

"Are you sure, Grand Elder?" one of the Elders couldn't help but ask.

The Grand Elder gave him a hard stare. "Do I look unsure?"

Supreme Ancestors were the Animal Kingdom's final reserve. In truth, this was a common practice in high-Grade factions. Once a particularly powerful Ancestor approached the end of their life, they would be put into cryogenic stasis to greatly extend their lifespan. If the faction ever experienced a great catastrophe, the Supreme Ancestors would be awoken and asked to help—but, of course, they could only do this once or twice before their bodies naturally expired.

Due to the high cost of maintaining a cultivator's body, the Animal Kingdom only possessed two Supreme Ancestors; one from the Emberheart and one from the Lonihor family. The only time in history they'd been awoken was the final stage of the war between the Animal Kingdom and the Exploding Sun. This would be the second.

The Grand Elder was at a loss. Having to awaken the Supreme Ancestors meant he'd failed in his duties. It was a tremendous expense which would likely end with one of them, or maybe both, dying. Just the resources required to put them back to sleep afterward could bankrupt a C-Grade faction. Thinking about it made his heart bleed.

What else could he do? Even the Supreme Ancestors weren't omnipotent. He feared that, if he waited until Jack Rust brought the fight to them directly, it would be too late to make a difference. He had to awaken them now and ask them to help the Hand of God find Jack Rust. He had to send his own dying ancestors on a wild goose hunt.

What a shameful act. But, for the Animal Kingdom, he would endure. It was his duty.

———

Far away from the Animal Kingdom constellation and its struggles, a much grander war was playing out.

The Hand of God and Black Hole Church were clashing. Their conflict spanned several galaxies both inside and outside System space. Only C-Grades and above qualified to participate in this struggle—B-Grades were elites, and A-Grades were generals. The Second Crusade was a war of unprecedented scale, even surpassing the First Crusade, and this was only the beginning. The Old Gods hadn't made their move yet. Nor had the Heaven Immortal.

Of course, a war of such scale unfolded over a long period of time. The present state of things was that the Black Hole Church had been chased out of many System galaxies, and they had voluntarily retreated from others. After all, any battle inside System space put them at a disadvantage.

However, the Church hadn't completely retreated. Small, elite teams still roamed System space, striking critical locations for the Hand and retreating swiftly.

Sovereign Heavenly Spoon was the leader of one such team. As the Head Envoy, he was one of the most important people in the Church army, just below the Elders, and he also possessed extreme battle power. Over the last few years, he'd reached the late B-Grade. He was said to be invincible within the B-Grade— some even speculated that his strength touched the A-Grade.

In this stage of the war, Sovereign Heavenly Spoon led the most effective and elite team of Envoys. They roamed behind the enemy lines like ghosts, striking swiftly and powerfully. They were the nightmare of every Envoy in the Hand of God.

On this day, the Spoon Squad struck again. A lone starship appeared next to an isolated planet full of magma. The spatial barriers set up around it didn't even ripple—whoever guided this ship possessed an understanding into spacetime which far dwarfed Jack's.

Five people flashed outside the starship. At the head was Sovereign Heavenly Spoon, wearing his aloof smile and carrying a small silver spoon. To his right stood a form clad entirely in a dark hood which rippled as if made of spacetime, and to his left was a man with yellow teeth and ragged robes—the Sage.

Two more people followed. One was a bronze-skinned man

with long hair like rivers of stars, and the other a woman wielding a long spear. This was Min Ling. She had suppressed her cultivation for many years to consolidate her foundation as much as possible, but as the war began, she'd finally broken into the B-Grade. She was now an Envoy of the Church, and a powerful one, too.

Though all of them were below the A-Grade, this was the strongest squad the Church had to offer.

"Let's begin," Sovereign Heavenly Spoon said. "Sage?"

"All safe. We have five minutes."

"Bottomless?"

The form wearing the rippling hood raised its hands. The fabric of spacetime around the planet rippled. Suddenly, the entire planet warped, twisting and turning, ready to shatter. Just before it broke apart, a silver shield appeared over it, forcefully twisting the planet back into shape. As the magma clouds drifted into space by the intensity of the shaking, the atmosphere cleared, and a city-sized facility was revealed. The shield seemed to originate from there.

Sovereign Heavenly Spoon smiled. "Found you."

Swarms of cultivators flew into space to face them. There were hundreds of C-Grades led by eleven B-Grades—this was an important location for the Hand, so its guards were nothing to scoff at.

But they were still not a match for the Spoon Squad.

Without a word, Min Ling and the star-haired man flew into the crowd of guards. They were like wolves among sheep. Blood washed the void, and the ripples of their battle slammed into the planet below, forming craters dozens of miles deep. Only the facility remained intact, protected by a more condensed version of the previous silver shield.

"Hahahaha!" a man laughed—the head of the guards, a peak B-Grade. "Run away while you can, Heavenly Spoon! That shield was personally created by Elder Purity—it is impregnable! Even you can't break it before the Elders arrive!"

He was so sure of himself. The Sovereign only smiled. "Oh no, whatever will I do now?"

He raised his spoon. A massive green shadow of a spoon appeared in space, dwarfing the entire planet. It was positioned right above the facility. It mirrored the movements of the Sovereign's little spoon as it reached down, gently cupping the entire continent the facility was based on—its radius much greater than the shield's.

"No!" the head guard screamed. He tried to interrupt the sovereign, but the rippling form of Bottomless easily stopped him.

Meanwhile, Sovereign Heavenly Spoon raised his spoon, and the giant green phantom effortlessly scooped up the continent. "Thanks for the meal," he said, slipping the little spoon into his mouth. The large green spoon mirrored the movement —and the continent completely disappeared.

He burped, then winked. "Why break it when I can digest it?"

"No!" the head guard shouted again. The form with the rippling cloak—Bottomless—annihilated him, and by that time, Min Ling and the star-haired man were done slaughtering the others. The Spoon Squad was intact. They all flew back into the starship, then Bottomless teleported them away.

"How long did we take?" the sovereign asked.

"Two minutes," the Sage replied. "Not bad at all."

"Yeah. Maybe I should have taken another bite."

"What's the next destination, Head Envoy?" Bottomless asked, their cloak fluttering in an unfelt wind.

The sovereign replied, "I received a message from Elder Boatman some time ago. We're headed to the Milky Way Galaxy, Animal Kingdom constellation."

"The Milky Way Galaxy?" the star-haired man asked with disgust in his voice. "That empty, weak place? Why would we go there?"

"To pick up an old friend."

"They're sending us to *escort* someone?"

"Yes, well, those are the orders. If you disagree, bring it up with the Elders."

The star-haired man fell silent, though his disapproval remained evident on his face. As for Min Ling and the Sage, both seemed excited.

"What's our travel time, Bottomless?" the sovereign asked.

"Two weeks," they replied. "The Milky Way is at the edge of System space. I just hope this isn't a waste of time."

"Hmm?" The sovereign raised a brow. "Even you disagree, Bottomless? I guess it's understandable. You haven't met that man. Hey, Sage—do you also think this is a waste of time?"

The Sage gave everyone a toothy grin. "You have no idea."

CHAPTER THIRTY-NINE
BROTHERHOOD

JACK'S MESSAGE HAD BEEN BROADCASTED THROUGHOUT THE constellation. Various rebelling forces received it, spreading it through their planets. His war declaration to the Animal Kingdom set aflame the hearts of his supporters, and the fact that he'd already killed a B-Grade negated any doubts about his ability.

Fireworks crackled in the sky. Cheers echoed. People ran to the streets and celebrated. Their idol, the source of their courage, the angel of freedom, had returned for them! Their liberation was no longer just a dream—they could do it!

They believed!

In a single week, the scattered rebels across the constellation united in one common front, campaigning in the name of Jack Rust. It didn't matter that he wasn't with them—they knew he was fighting the same war, battling against the same enemy. That was enough.

For the first time, they believed they could win.

Banners and flags flew over starships. The drums of war beat. Elite squads zipped into space, aiming to ambush the Animal Kingdom forces, while armies prepared for war.

And Jack calmly went about his own business, letting them fight their battles.

———

Developing a new Dao Fruit tested three things.

One was the cultivator's comprehension into their Dao. It needed to be deep and multifaceted enough to support more manifestations. The second was the robustness of the cultivator's Dao Tree—the degree to which they identified and respected their Dao. Finally, the third test was the cultivator's ability to withstand the influx of power. In Physical cultivators, this manifested as their bodily intensity.

Needless to say, Jack excelled at all those things. Developing a new fruit was a trial for most, but for him, it was just another day.

Jack sat in meditation. Six fruits hung before him, proud and full, and one question filled his mind: Which would be the seventh?

Again, he had plenty of ideas. Perseverance, Grief, Wrath... Those and more were available, as Jack had already embraced them to a degree. Although this time, he thought he'd do something different.

Brock's words resonated within him. That he was beginning to walk the wrong path. It wasn't that Jack didn't see it himself, but that he struggled to face it. No matter how tenacious his willpower, he was bound to make tiny slips, and they weren't easy to notice. He needed someone to stand by his side and let him know when he misstepped. He needed a brother.

Brock was there for him.

Jack thought back to their previous conversation. It had been a few days, and after his defensive anger subsided, he could see that Brock had... at least half a point. Without him,

Jack would have been lost for longer. Who knows if anyone else could have mustered up the courage to tell him he was wrong.

Therefore, Jack decided to make his seventh fruit about that one critical thing. Not his composure or the correct path forward—the real kicker in this situation was the fact that someone reliable was beside him.

If you want to go fast, go alone. If you want to go far, go together. Nobody could reach the top by themselves. And Jack had Brock.

The seventh fruit was one of Brotherhood.

It grew on the branches of his Dao Tree, resembling a monkey fist. Jack smiled and bumped it with his own. "Thanks, bro," he whispered. "I couldn't have done it without you."

The way forward was cloudy, and his mind remained filled with darkness. He would surely misstep again. Though as long as he had Brock by his side to show him the way and the willpower to see it, he would never be truly lost.

That was the way.

After developing his next Dao Fruit, the remaining levels from destroying that outpost also arrived.

Level up! You have reached Level 341.
Level up! You have reached Level 342.

He, obviously, invested everything in Physical.

Name: Jack Rust
Species: Human, Earth-387
Faction: Bare Fist Brotherhood (C)
Grade: C
Class: Gladiator Titan (King)
Level: 342

Strength: 6820 (+)
Dexterity: 6820 (+)
Constitution: 6820 (+)
Mental: 1000
Will: 1000
Free sub-points: 2

Dao Skills: Meteor Punch IV, Iron Fist Style III, Brutalizing Aura III, Neutron Star Body III, Supernova III, Space Mastery III, Fist of Mortality III, Death Mastery III, Titan Taunt II
Dao Roots: Indomitable Will, Life, Power, Weakness
Dao Fruits: Fist, Space, Life, Death, Battle, Revenge, Brotherhood
Titles: Planetary Frontrunner (10), Planetary Torchbearer (1), Ninth Ring Conqueror, Planetary Overlord (1), Grade Defier, Planet Destroyer

As Jack left meditation, he whistled in joy for the first time in a while. He was already back at the *Dark Ram*.

Brock looked over. "Sup, bro? All good?"

"All good, Brock. My seventh fruit is ready. Say whatever you want for the System, but it's damn good for leveling up."

"Hmm."

"How do you think that works, anyway? How does the System give me levels?"

"Good question."

"I know!" Salin exclaimed from a nearby chair where he lounged. "They told us that when I was studying in the Kingdom. The difference between the ambient energy of the universe and a cultivator's inner energy is that the latter is more condensed and also attuned to the cultivator's Dao. That's why you can't just absorb energy; it needs to go through a purifying process. The caveat is that while you can't recklessly absorb energy from the universe, you can steal the already purified energy in another cultivator's soul."

Jack raised a brow. "You can?"

"Damn right you can! Stealing is always on the table!" Salin laughed. "It's not easy, of course, but the System is good at its job. When you kill an enemy, that causes their soul to implode, harmlessly releasing all their gathered Dao into the atmosphere. The System uses the Dao of Swallowing to absorb part of that energy for you."

"But then how is it attuned to my Dao? If I kill someone with the Dao of Water, do I absorb Water Dao?"

"Not really. The System can't make it into your own Dao, but it can transform it into distilled energy—similar to absorbing a Dao Stone. Then it uses this energy to either enhance various aspects of you, like your body and mind, or feed it to your soul so you can rapidly rise in cultivation. At the C-Grade, it does a bit of both."

"Oh," Jack replied. "I didn't know that."

"You never asked."

"I'm pretty sure I did."

"Then whoops."

Jack rolled his eyes. "And I guess the higher you go, the more energy goes into your soul compared to being used to increase your stats?"

"Yeah!"

"Bullshit. The stat gains per level becomes larger the more I rise in Grade. By what you're saying, they should be lower."

Salin narrowed his eyes. "Oh, you want to play hard. Okay then. The full explanation is that the higher you rise, the smaller the fraction of energy which goes into your stats. However, your opponents are also much stronger, meaning the total volume of stolen energy is larger. That is why the actual stat increases are greater. They're a smaller piece of a larger pie."

Jack cupped his chin. "Yeah. I guess that makes sense."

"See? Never doubt me again, Jacky."

"I've told you not to call me that."

"So what? You think I'm afraid of you just because you destroyed a planet or two?"

Jack raised a brow. Salin coughed in his palm. "Okay, I'm a little afraid. Can you not murder me please?"

Jack stared a moment longer, then burst into laughter. "Just kidding, man. You should have seen your face."

"You should have brought a mirror."

"Never change, Salin. Never change."

"I hear someone left seclusion," a new voice came from the corridor. Nauja emerged, chewing on a piece of hexagonal candy. "Congratulations on your new fruit, Jack. I guess it's time for a strategy meeting?"

"High time," Jack agreed.

Nauja plopped down on a chair, as did he. They were flanked by a large glass window showcasing the colorful emptiness of space. Stars twinkled in the distance, a symphony of innumerable suns, while the branches of the galaxy stretched overhead.

Underneath the starlight, the four of them sat in comfortable chairs, reclining into the pillows and enjoying this moment of peace. It was only after Bomn and Vashter arrived that they resumed.

"The rebellion is proceeding in full," Nauja reported. After learning how to read, she enjoyed it, so she'd become the crew's information gatherer. It paired well with her excellent eyesight. "Since we forced the Kingdom's C-Grades to retreat, there are only D-Grades on the battlefield. It's the equivalent of a D-Grade faction against a constellation. Unless the Hand of God acts, the rebels are going to win. The Animal Kingdom will lose its constellation—that is not a price they can afford. If we just sit back and wait a bit, they will be forced to send out their C-Grades again, at which point we can go around assassinating them."

"That's a good idea," Jack said, "but I don't want to wait. I like how they're all grouped together. I want to storm their capital and take them all out at the same time."

Salin raised a brow. "I appreciate the bloodthirstiness, but how exactly are you going to do that? They have Eva Solvig, a late B-Grade, and who knows what else."

"I need to level up just a little more," Jack said. "If I can reach nine fruits, I'm confident in defeating Eva Solvig. Even if a peak B-Grade shows up, I should be able to escape."

"Strong," Brock said.

"Thanks. I try."

"Speaking of storming their capital and killing everyone," Salin said, "my father is a C-Grade of the Kingdom. We aren't in touch anymore, and he's a little bit cooked in the head, but would you mind sparing him?"

"Absolutely," Jack replied. "You're my friend. I wouldn't kill your father."

"Thanks. You know it's a bit weird that you had to say that."

"Yeah."

"Can we not talk about this like we've already succeeded?" Nauja asked. "The Kingdom is a hard nut to crack! Eva Solvig must be shivering by now—she might call more late B-Grades to assist her, or maybe she'll even summon her mother, that late A-Grade Elder of the Hand of God. We can't afford to take this lightly!"

"Elder Purity is not going to come," Jack replied with certainty. "The war between the Church and Hand must be proceeding in full force. If not, Elder Boatman would have arrived first. Either that or he's dead."

"I hope Grandpa Dead is okay," Brock said. "He was cool."

"Yeah," Jack agreed. "We should find a way to contact him. We need to go over after we're done here."

"Guys. Focus," Nauja said, waving her hands to get their attention. "Animal Kingdom, B-Grades, danger. Stay on subject, please."

"I'm so proud of them," Salin said, wiping a fake tear from his eyes, while Bomn and Vashter glanced at each other and shrugged.

"We can go after more Hand of God outposts," Jack said. "Just one of them gave me sixteen levels. A couple more and I'll reach the nine fruits boundary."

"That couple more will be difficult," Nauja argued. "They know we're after them now. They'll either evacuate everyone important or send late B-Grades to secretly guard the outposts."

Jack sighed. "I know that, but it's the only plan that comes to mind."

"Then we need to think a bit harder."

So, they thought. Five minutes later, Gan Salin said, "Sorry, I fell asleep. Are we done yet?"

"I have nothing," Jack said, slightly annoyed. "We could go to other constellations and try to hunt down random C-Grades, but I don't want to involve innocents. It's not like I have any more enemies right now. Who knew a lack of them would become a problem?"

"True," Brock replied. "That used to be our strong suit. What went wrong?"

"We can always go after Hand of God outposts in other constellations," Nauja said. "They can't evacuate the entire galaxy. Constellations are large though... Traveling there would take a long time if we want to avoid major teleporters, and if we don't, we might fall into a trap. If it's our only option, it's predictable."

"Can you fight a late B-Grade, bro?" Brock asked.

Jack shook his head. "Maybe, maybe not... It would be hard. But I can probably run away."

"Then, we can afford some risk."

"True."

"Only if the ship stays at a safe distance," Bomn said—this was the same trick they'd utilized when Jack assaulted the previous outpost. "That way, if things go wrong, Jack doesn't have to think about protecting us. He can just escape."

"As much as I hate saying so, I'm good at that," Jack said. "But I don't think the Hand would make such a mistake. They know I'm fast. If they predict our next move and prepare a trap, escaping will not be so simple."

"Then, what?" Nauja asked. "We've come full circle, and we still have no ideas."

"There is only one solution," Jack said. "If they find us, we lose... but they can't know what we'll do if we don't know what we'll do. Salin?" He turned to the canine. "You're insane, therefore unpredictable. What do you suggest?"

Salin gave everyone a triumphant smile. "I know just the thing. Let's attack Hell again."

"What?" everyone replied at the same time.

"What? They won't expect it."

"But what's the point?" Nauja asked. "They've already recalled everyone. Hell has no objective for us."

"They say they've recalled everyone," Salin explained, "but I don't believe it. Hell is full of D-Grade disciples. Most remain there even at times of war, and they're too many to evacuate into Animal Planet. I don't think they'd just leave the planet unprotected—if only to defend against sabotage from another major faction. There has to be at least one C-Grade there—probably at a pretty high level, too."

Everyone looked at each other.

"But it's so close to Animal Planet," Nauja said. "Eva Solvig might make it in time."

"Unless she's setting up a trap elsewhere."

"So you want us to assault Hell, risking being found, just in case they've left a late C-Grade to watch over the D-Grades."

"Hey, you're the ones who asked for an insane plan."

"I don't know," Jack said. "I think we can get in and out pretty quickly, but is it even worth it? A late C-Grade will only give me a couple levels."

"You said that destroying Earthen Gemini last time gave you a bunch. You can just destroy Hell. Plus, it will throw them off, and we can more safely assault a high-value target next time," Salin said.

They mulled over it. "I mean, sure," Jack finally said. "Even I feel a bit bad for bullying Hell so much, but what the hell? They deserve it."

"I agree with big bro," Brock said. "This is war. The more they fear us, the more we can harm them, the better."

Everyone else eventually agreed. For the third time in his life, Jack was about to visit Hell—one of the Animal Kingdom's most important locations. Unlike the other two times, he wouldn't sneak around. He would arrive in force.

CHAPTER FORTY
MEETING A LEGEND

JACK WAS ON THE *TRAMPLING RAM*, SHUTTLING THROUGH A FAMILIAR region of space. The first time he was here, he'd engaged in guerilla warfare and managed to earn levels in the D-Grade. The second, he'd fallen into a trap and been chased into a nearby black hole.

This would be the third time he visited Hell, and hopefully the last one.

"We'll be waiting here," Nauja said as the ship slowed to a crawl. "If you need anything, just give the signal. We'll arrive in seconds."

"Don't worry," Jack replied.

This wasn't the first planet he attacked. He was stronger than ever—unless Eva Solvig showed up, he was confident in handling things.

He left the *Ram* and flew forward by himself. Hell was several hundred thousand miles away, so he had time to observe it before he arrived. He saw its many continents separated by lines of sea—its gargantuan size, many times larger than Earth. He couldn't identify the continent on which he'd spent some months once upon a time.

Weirdly enough, he'd never actually seen Hell from space before. He hadn't witnessed its grandeur. Though it came across wild and pure, it emanated a certain majesty, making him realize just why the Kingdom had taken this planet as part of its core.

He arrived before the planet unnoticed and gazed down at it.

The original plan had been to destroy Hell as he had Earthen Gemini. That would give him the most levels. On Brock's insistence, however, they'd dropped that plan.

Like Earthen Gemini, Hell was mostly occupied by D-Grade disciples of the Animal Kingdom—soldiers of the enemy. Unlike the other planet, however, Hell was habitable. It contained forests, plains, oceans, and jungles. It was filled with animals. If Jack destroyed it, he would be reaping trillions of innocent lives, and that's not even including the scattered prisoners of the Kingdom roaming the planet's many continents.

Even for a good cause, he wouldn't do that, so he couldn't destroy the planet. He'd do the next best thing.

Jack flew around Hell, taking care to remain undetected, scanning its surface. The administrative center of Hell was a large prison from which the Warden ruled—it was the greatest building on the planet, the size of a town itself and surrounded by an Animal Kingdom city. Most of the cultivators should be gathered there—destroying it would give half the benefits of destroying the planet.

He soon discovered what he was looking for. A towering fortress, unpainted and undecorated, emanating an aura of brutal cruelty. Flags of the Animal Kingdom flew above its walls, portraying a roaring lion, while a city spread around it. Just by looking at this ugly fortress, Jack could imagine the inhumane conditions inside.

His lip twitching, he zoomed in. The atmosphere heated

him up into a crimson comet. His cloak fluttered. Without slowing in the slightest, he plummeted through the upper layers of the atmosphere and descended toward the prison.

He did not plan to taunt and grandstand. Hell was littered with teleporters. He couldn't destroy them all, so there was always the chance of Eva Solvig arriving if she was nearby. Jack needed to strike swiftly, then depart.

Protective barriers appeared as he fell from the sky, but he broke right through. Glass-like fragments filled the air. Alarms sounded from the prison, but Jack was already in the air above it.

"Die," he muttered, shooting out his fist. He borrowed his fall to increase its momentum—a purple meteor blossomed into existence, parting the air as it crashed at tremendous speed. More barriers appeared—more shattered. A few attacks flew at the meteor from below, but they were like toothpicks thrown at a giant. The meteor smashed into the fortress, breaking through its roof and nailing into the ground. A large shockwave spread from the point of impact—the fortress was demolished, the houses upturned, the cultivators sent flying. A wave of dust rose to submerge the city, and the flags of the Animal Kingdom were ripped apart by the wind, their pieces fluttering wildly.

The entire city was destroyed in the blink of an eye. Most hadn't even realized there was someone attacking. Hundreds of D-Grades were instantly killed.

Jack knew that, while this place looked like a city, it was actually the Kingdom's main training area for D-Grade cultivators. There were barely any innocent people down there, all soldiers of the enemy. The only exceptions were the prisoners held inside the fortress, but Jack had made the conscious decision to strike regardless.

The prisoners here weren't many—most were running

around the planet as animals to be hunted—and, even if he didn't kill them directly, he wouldn't be able to save them in the little time he had. They were doomed to stay here and be tortured by the Animal Kingdom for some time more. Therefore, he believed their sacrifice was worthy—by greatly accelerating his leveling speed, he could save many more of the millions of people dying to the Kingdom every day.

Level up! You have reached Level 343.
Level up! You have reached Level 344.
Level up! You have reached Level 345.
Level up! You have reached Level 346.

Only four levels... he thought, sighing. It was less than he'd hoped for. The average C-Grade would be happy to get four levels in a decade, but to Jack, this speed was far too slow.

There wasn't much he could do about it right now.

It had been less than ten seconds since Jack entered Hell's atmosphere, yet the prison was already destroyed. He didn't have much time left—his job was done. He turned around and flew back into space, teleporting rapidly to escape faster.

No matter how quick their reaction was, even if Eva Solvig was waiting right by a teleporter, there was no way she would arrive within the first minute. However, to ensure success, Jack had resolved to stay here for half a minute—go in, destroy the city in one strike, rush out. Simple and clean.

Jack rushed in the direction of the *Trampling Ram*.

Suddenly, space solidified before him, interrupting his series of teleportations. Jack's danger sense acted up. Without thinking, he flew to the side, barely dodging a spear which appeared in the space he previously occupied.

"Hmm," an elderly voice rang out. "Good reflex."

Jack tensed. He hadn't sensed anyone nearby. A figure

stepped out of the void ahead of him as if stepping through curtains.

It was a leonine Jack hadn't seen before. He reeked of age and death. His fur had fallen off, leaving only white patches, and his skin was so wrinkled it seemed fake. He was small, too, shorter than Jack, as if old age had shrunk this once majestic leonine into the size of a child. Gazing into his eyes, Jack found them pale and muddied—like he could barely see.

This person, whoever he was, gave off the impression that he just barely clung onto life. Yet, despite his appearance, there was nothing weak about him.

Jack's hair stood on end. Something inside him screamed to be careful because this decrepit old leonine was a genuine threat to his life—a feeling he hadn't experienced since he faced Eva Solvig.

"It's just like the young to be overeager," the leonine said. "Attacking Hell... What wonderful recklessness." His voice was weak, yet it easily spread through the vacuum of space. He sounded joyful—and partly bitter.

"Who are you?" Jack asked. He scanned him at the same time.

Leonine, Level ??? (B-Grade)
Faction: -

No faction? Is he not with the Animal Kingdom?

The level wasn't visible, as it never was for people of a higher Grade, but Jack could still use his Dao perception to gauge the old man's strength. It was tremendous—even greater than Eva Solvig's, though shriveled up by old age just like his body. At his peak, he was probably at the peak B-Grade tier. Now, he possessed the strength of a normal late B-Grade cultivator.

But even a late B-Grade wasn't someone Jack could necessarily match.

"I guess you could say I'm nobody," the leonine replied, chuckling. "If my name still existed, I would be Travelus Lonihor, pioneer of the Milky Way and one of the founders of the Animal Kingdom. For an old man like me to return just to deal with a boy like you... It is a bit unsightly."

Jack was dazed. Founder of the Animal Kingdom? As far as he knew, the Kingdom had been founded shortly after the System arrived at the Milky Way, almost a million years ago. Was this old man claiming to have lived that long? B-Grades could only live for a hundred thousand years at most. What was going on?

Wait. He mentioned he has returned from somewhere... Could it be he was revived?

Jack was unfamiliar with the concept of cryogenically-maintained Supreme Ancestors. It wasn't something people tended to share. He naturally arrived at wrong assumptions, but whatever the case, he didn't dwell on it too much.

There was no time to chat. He needed to escape. His mind quickly analyzed the situation. This old man had solidified space to stop his teleportation. Their Daos of Spacetime were at similar heights—or, at least, the old man wasn't too far off. Jack could probably outrun him, but that didn't mean he could escape. He'd already approached the *Trampling Ram*. If the old man discovered that, Jack would be placed in the same conundrum as last time, when he needed to protect the ship or let it leave alone. There would be no time to teleport away.

He needed to defeat this old man, and swiftly.

Jack's aura rose. Waves of purple whipped at the surrounding space. His cloak fluttered wildly, and a condensed aura hugged his body, making him resemble a devil warrior. He didn't know if he could win, but he was ready to go all-out from the very start.

Facing this display of power, the old man was unbothered. "Pretty good for a C-Grade. Let me stretch these old bones."

The void split above him. Divine radiance rained down an amount tremendously vaster than anything Jack had ever witnessed. It hugged the old man, completely hiding his appearance, and the silver light morphed into shiny plate armor. A lance appeared in the old man's hand. His aged face seemed to recover a hint of vigor, while sets of wings unfurled from his back one after the other.

Eight white wings flapped majestically, showering the world in radiance. Even a fifth pair of wings was faintly visible, just a shadow which hadn't yet materialized. Meanwhile, a dozen divine warriors appeared around the old man, each possessing strength at the early B-Grade.

This was the Lonihor family's angel battle form—the same technique every single member of the Lonihor family had used so far. By now, Jack knew this was a cultivation technique originating from the Black Hole World, but this old man had comprehended it to a greater extent than anyone Jack had ever fought before.

Jack had read the description of this technique—whose original name was Art of Divine Providence—at the Black Hole World. The practitioner could manifest two wings at the E-Grade, four at the D-Grade, six at the C-Grade, eight at the B-Grade, and ten at the A-Grade. There was even the theoretical level of twelve wings when one became an Archon.

This old man hadn't reached the A-Grade even in his prime. Yet, he could manifest a shadow of the ten wings. That was a testament to his great talent, unfathomable power, and deep understanding. It drove home how this decrepit old man was one of the greatest talents to ever grace the Milky Way Galaxy, the founder of a B-Grade faction and interstellar empire, a pioneer of cultivation who'd ushered his entire species into a million year-long era of prosperity. This was a hero returned from the dead—and Jack was asked to cross an entire Grade to face him.

Jack was fighting for his life. There were many weights on his shoulders. Yet, despite all that, he found himself fired up at the prospect. This man before him was a legend—he was late-game material. And Jack was about to take him down.

"I have half a minute, old man," he growled. "Bring it on." His aura erupted, and he charged.

CHAPTER FORTY-ONE

LATE B-GRADE

THE UNIVERSE SMELLED OF BLOOD AND POWER. TWO DIFFERENT forces warred between the stars—a Fist and a divine spear of supremacy.

Jack didn't dare hold back. Not only was he facing an extremely powerful opponent, but he was also struggling against time—if this took too long, more enemies would arrive.

His aura flared. Purple flames licked the void, just the after-effects of Jack's Dao, as he'd already entered the Life Drop battle form. Each of his four fists shone a dark purple—each carried the power to annihilate planets.

He smashed out. The old man facing him, Travelus Lonihor, met Jack's fist with the tip of his spear. Neither gave way. From their clash, cracks spread through the void for hundreds of miles as if the universe was a giant glass window shattering under their tremendous power.

The Dao in that area of space had already gone wild. It flickered everywhere, caught in the raging streams of their collision, gathering in massive waves that blasted outward. The planet of Hell wasn't too far away—the shockwaves of each clash crashed into the planet, manifesting as powerful gales. Trees bent, small animals were lifted and thrown around, tornadoes formed. Every living being on Hell bowed their heads and sought shelter against the battle of gods occurring far above their heads.

Of course, Jack and the old man were almost a hundred thousand miles away. If not, the planet itself would be suffering under the shockwaves, not just its surface.

"You're strong!" the old man exclaimed, drawing back. His old eyes shone beneath the helmet—his spear steady despite the shakiness of the hands holding it.

"I could say the same!" Jack replied, laughing out loud. His cloak fluttered in the wild astral winds. "You are about to become the strongest person I have defeated!"

The old man laughed back. He had been a stunning talent in his youth, a battle fanatic obsessed with reaching the peak of martial arts. How could this battle not light his blood on fire? How could he not be excited to fight the single greatest talent this galaxy had ever seen? Leonines worshiped strength above all!

He had awakened one last time to fight Jack Rust. Even if he were to die here, it would be worth it.

"The young will surpass the old! Show me your best, Jack Rust!"

They flew at each other again. Jack drove his fist forward. It contained his desire to reach the peak, his need to protect himself and the people he cared about. Life and Death intertwined. All seven of his fruits pulsed in tandem—seven different streams of Dao merged as one in his soul, blasting outward with the might of a supernova.

The world shattered. The spear shook. The old man flew a few steps backward, but so did Jack. In that collision, they were evenly matched.

A hint of disbelief entered the old man's eyes. Jack was, after all, an entire Grade lower than him. To match him even momentarily was a tremendous feat. It was good that he had awakened—even if he and the other Supreme Ancestor both had to die, killing such an opponent in the crib was worth it!

Jack charged again, but this time, Travelus Lonihor calmly blocked and retreated. He was old, after all. As excited as he was, he was way past the age when he'd let burning blood cloud his vision. Reinforcements would arrive soon; he didn't need to win, just stall for time. Even if losing to someone an entire Grade lower was an impossibility, he wouldn't take the slightest risk. This involved the future of all his descendants.

As the old man retreated, a group of winged warriors stepped forward to take his place. They were twelve, each emanating the power of an early B-Grade—phantoms he'd conjured through the Art of Divine Providence. Unlike those conjured by weaker versions of this skill, these phantoms were absolutely real. Each possessed the soul of a high-level cultivator Travelus had slain in his youth, and so they possessed intelligence.

The twelve surrounded Jack, trapping him in a diamond-shaped formation. Twelve variations of divine power rained down on him. Jack was forced to defend. His body was blasted from all directions—his Dao shields cracked and splintered, the spatial barriers shattered, and finally, a small portion of the attacking energy smashed squarely into his body.

He growled. Each of these phantoms was far weaker than him, but not only were they twelve and perfectly coordinated, they'd also attacked the moment after his clash with Travelus, when he'd yet to regather his power. Finger-wide holes appeared in his skin—blood flowed out, then gradually stopped as he regenerated.

Jack's eyes sharpened. "Fuck off!" A tremendous aura erupted from his body, shattering the phantoms' formation and sending them flying away. Yet, they were uninjured—they'd distributed the force equally and easily survived.

If Jack pressed the assault now, he could eliminate a few of the phantoms. He could hold off the old man while gradually killing off all twelve until he could face Travelus alone. However, that battle plan required time he did not have.

He ignored the phantoms to charge Travelus Lonihor.

The old man drew back again, bringing his spear in a horizontal position, absorbing the momentum of Jack's punch and using it to fly away unharmed.

"Fight me if you dare!" Jack roared, but the old man only smirked.

"Fight me if you can," he taunted.

The phantoms converged again. Jack withstood another assault, then broke out of their encirclement and confronted the old man, who only defended. This was getting nowhere. Jack was making no progress.

Anger rose inside him. He had not come this far, he had not sacrificed everything just to be toyed with by a living fossil. His aura emanated in waves, shaking the surrounding space and bending it to his will. He roared, "When I tell you to fight, you fucking fight!"

Space warped around them. Colors emerged from the vastness of space, the endless starlight warping into the vision of a busy colosseum. It was dozens of miles wide; its stands were full of roaring, cheering people of all species, shouting at the top of their lungs.

"JACK RUST! JACK RUST! JACK RUST!"

The air itself shook by their cheers. The sand was dirty, the wind was dry, and the entire atmosphere reeked of slaughter.

The old man looked around in befuddlement. "What domain is this? An illusion? No... Spatial encapsulation!"

Jack didn't have time to respond. The twelve phantoms had

been dragged into the arena alongside the old man. They were already attacking.

Ripples crossed Jack's eyes. His body seemed to grow ethereal, an odd existence merging into his surroundings. His hands flashed with a thousand seals representing his understandings. He reached into spacetime and directly twisted it, forming twelve prisons where time and space stagnated. The phantoms of divine warriors froze midair—as if they existed in a separate, timeless dimension.

The old man looked on with incredulity. "How can you have such understandings? You are so young, so weak! This is ridiculous!"

Jack forced himself to smile. "Just because you can't do it, doesn't mean I can't."

"Hah! Trying to taunt me? You're a million years too young, boy!"

"I'm not trying," Jack replied. His smile turned into a single, hard line. "This is my battlefield. This is what I have been living through ever since your Animal Kingdom invaded my planet. In here, there is no third choice—you either fight me or die on your knees!"

The old man's eyes narrowed. "Good. Then bring it on."

Jack clenched his teeth and threw himself forward. He was nowhere near his strongest state. Battling inside this arena enhanced him while he held the momentum, but forming twelve spatial prisons to trap the phantoms was already skirting the limits of what his Dao of Spacetime could achieve. Maintaining them while fighting a high-intensity battle would be a challenge.

He simply had no other choice. If he wanted to win this quickly, this was the only path he could take.

And the old man knew it.

He did not fall back this time. He charged with his spear

extended, capitalizing on Jack's weakened state. They clashed in the center of the arena—powerful shockwaves washed over the stands, heightening the spectators' thrill. Cheers echoed, overshadowed only by the sounds of collision.

Fist met spear a dozen times. Jack galvanized everything he had but still fell short—too much of his energy and attention was diverted toward the twelve warriors. He smashed into the walls of his own arena. The audience roared, and Travelus Lonihor flew high, raising his spear to the sky. The audience changed its tune.

"TRAVELUS! TRAVELUS!"

He grinned. "What's the matter, boy? Getting bested in your own arena?"

Jack spat out a mouthful of blood, then rose from the sand. He dusted himself off. "I have faced things that make you seem like a kitty. The only thing scary about you is your age."

As Jack spoke calmly, he was calculating on the inside. This old man lived up to his age. He hadn't been intimidated by the colosseum—instead, he'd seen right through it and realized it didn't favor Jack, but the strongest warrior. That was why he'd invested heavily in a show-offish strike and then spent his momentum to earn the crowd's favor. He'd snagged that little advantage for himself, making Jack's uphill challenge even more difficult.

Unlike other opponents Jack had faced, this was a calm and methodical one. He never overextended, opting for consistent, small advantages which would eventually win him the fight. Moreover, despite Jack's repeated taunting, he remained of a mind to stall.

Reaching this point, there was no meaning in thinking further. Jack had already set the conditions as best as he could. All he could do was his best. He had ten seconds remaining—he had to make them count.

Which made things simpler. He didn't need to calculate too far—he would spend all his remaining energy in these next ten seconds, and he'd either win or lose.

Power streamed into his limbs. His short hair rose like spikes—purple sparks flew over his body, cladding him in an electrified aura.

"Hmm?" Travelus Lonihor was surprised. "The Thunder Body? *Where* did you learn that?"

"Same place you did," Jack replied. He hadn't mastered this technique yet—forcefully using it placed a tremendous burden on his body. The only reason he could stand it was his extreme physicality, and he couldn't keep it up for long.

However, he got a burst of power in return. It might be enough.

"Let's go," Jack muttered, then flashed forward. He all but disappeared. Travelus Lonihor only had time to widen his eyes before a powerful force slammed into his back, throwing him forward. He turned around, but Jack was no longer there. He was everywhere. He combined his enhanced physical speed and understanding into spacetime to achieve impossible velocities and angles. For a moment, he was a force of nature.

The old man saw a dozen Jacks assault him at once. He braced himself.

Strikes landed everywhere. A fist met his chest, another his leg, a third his chin. Jack was pummeling Travelus with a flurry of blows so rapid they seemed simultaneous. His body shook inside the armor. The impacts were so many and so omnidirectional that he remained still in midair, just trying to shield his vitals.

A powerful punch landed on the old man's face, smashing him into a wall. Jack remained midair, oozing lightning and panting heavily. The crowd roared his name. The arena shook.

The twelve frozen phantoms glistened in the sky like living stars.

The old man rose to his feet. A line of blood dripped down his wrinkled lips, but he smiled. "You're running out of juice," he said. "I don't know how you got your hands on the Thunder Body technique, but you haven't mastered it yet. It's too much for you. You'll collapse before I do!"

"Let's find out," Jack replied. He shot forward again, a lightning bolt from the skies. He was noticeably slower than before —his energy was depleting at a rapid pace. He barely had five more seconds in him. The old man faced him head-on, also going all out. Divine providence emanated from his skin—he no longer resembled an old man but a bright angel, a symbol of the heavens.

They met on the sands of the arena. Blows rained from either side. Every spear was sharp, every punch devastating. Their clashes shook the world.

And blood wet the sand.

CHAPTER FORTY-TWO
SLAYING SUPREME

A FRENZY HAD OVERTAKEN JACK AND TRAVELUS BOTH. THEY NO LONGER thought, no longer calculated. They moved purely on instinct. One had developed it through a long life of strife—the other, by a short few years of continuously risking his life. They were veterans staking it all. The colosseum had never been livelier.

Jack molded spacetime like soft dough. He pierced through it, accelerated his attacks, and slowed his opponent's. Life coursed through his limbs, maintaining his rapidly waning energy, while death was infused into the opponent with every punch. Every understanding Jack possessed operated at full throttle, his body cracking out punches with every iota of strength it possessed.

Travelus did not shrink away. The depth of his Dao was less than Jack's, but he backed it up with a vastly superior cultivation. Moreover, he possessed tricks of his own. Though he'd now deteriorated to the late B-Grade realm, he'd once approached the A-Grade. His spacetime hindered Jack's, using raw power to make it harder to manipulate. His Supremacy seeped through with every spear strike, trying to cut down the confidence in Jack's heart.

This was the final, desperate battle on both sides.

Jack was not gaining an advantage. His cultivation was just too low, and he also had to keep restraining the phantoms in the sky. The seconds passed one at a time. Eva Solvig should almost be here, and Jack was already a lamp without oil. If she arrived, he was as good as dead.

A tiny corner of Travelus's mind remained rational. He didn't have to win—he just had to not lose. As long as his energy expenditure matched the opponent's, he was good.

He saw Jack grow desperate. A massive amount of energy gathered into his fist, condensing to a terrifying degree. He thrust it out before Travelus could retreat. "Supernova!"

The old man gritted his teeth. This was the critical moment. "Spear of Divinity!"

A blinding white spear shot forth, carrying the resolve of a god. Two unstoppable forces clashed. The world was washed away. Tremendous shockwaves spread through the universe, shattering the spatial barriers that served as the walls of the arena. Even the frozen phantoms in the sky were shaken.

The void shattered around Jack and Travelus, trapping them in a spaceless vacuum. The vision of the arena around them was slowly dispersing, the cries of the spectators growing distant.

Jack's hand had shattered into bone fragments. As for the spear of Travelus, its tip had broken off. The two cultivators had been evenly matched—the difference was that Jack's electricity had worn off, his energy running completely dry. Even the Life Drop transformation had reverted.

Travelus could sense it clearly—Jack had finally run out.

As for the old man himself, though he was almost the same, he'd held back a trace amount of energy. He'd wanted to be ready for all eventualities. As it turned out, he'd been too careful. This battle was his victory. Pride entered his eyes. The two fighters were still close to each other, barely a few feet apart, but one was completely spent, and it wasn't Travelus.

He wasn't even sure if Jack remained conscious.

"You fought well," he forced out through a bloodied mouth. "To match me from a Grade lower... You are too talented. Too much of a threat. Goodbye, Jack Rust. Let me have the honor of killing the world's greatest talent."

Travelus did not have too much strength left, but it was certainly enough to finish this off. He shook his spear, casting off the broken tip, and stabbed it straight into Jack's chest, aiming for his heart. He was already relieved that this was over.

The spear penetrated Jack's skin. It split his flesh, heading ever deeper, then slammed into his ribcage... and stopped. It couldn't break the bones.

Travelus's eyes widened. "What!"

He was a late B-Grade. No matter how efficiently Jack Rust infused his Dao into his body, no matter how advanced his understandings, all of that was moot now. He only possessed the frail body of a C-Grade. Travelus should have been able to pierce him effortlessly.

Then, why...

Mid-fighting, it was hard to differentiate between the intensity of one's mortal body and the durability provided by infusing one's body with Dao. Travelus had heard that Jack was physically gifted but didn't know how much. Coupled with Jack never making it obvious throughout the fight, he'd greatly underestimated Jack's physicality.

Even now, he struggled to comprehend this. He thought Jack's Dao by itself was enough to make him a prodigy, but such a degree of body tempering was just insane!

Was I... deceived?

The old man raised his gaze. He met Jack's eyes—and he

saw that deep inside them, beneath the exhaustion and injury, beneath the impending doom, existed an inextinguishable flame. Those weren't the eyes of a dead man—they burst with resolve, more alive than ever.

Travelus had never experienced such horror. He could not explain it. He panicked. His arm drew back, pulling away the spear to instinctively defend himself, except he couldn't. Another hand had wrapped around his wrist at some point—a grip which squeezed his bones. It was like being grabbed by a planet. No matter how Travelus struggled, he could not escape. The hand holding him was completely immovable. He paled.

Jack showed a bloody smile. "Got you," he whispered. One of his hands was holding onto the wrist of Travelus—even with his Life Drop transformation undone, that still left him with one hand free. It clenched into a fist. There was nothing special about it; no Dao, no external energy. It was a pure physical fist. Yet, the moment it clenched, Travelus felt his instinct go haywire. Intense fear took him over. He suddenly felt like a mortal grabbed by a bear—only now did he realize that Jack didn't need any sort of Dao to maul him. He could do it with his bare hands.

How can he be human? Travelus thought in frozen terror. *They lied to me! This is... This is a titan!*

Jack swung. There was no Dao behind it, but there was no Dao defending Travelus either. He'd spent the last of his energy in that spear strike. This was a pure physical collision—one he was destined to lose.

Travelus's Angel battle form was still present. His body was covered in plate armor, but that did not include his face. Jack's fist slipped right in. It carried the power to obliterate mountain ranges—the face of a late B-Grade, especially an elderly one, was like soft mush.

Jack's hand met flesh, then bone, and did not halt. A skull splintered. Jack's fist dove into the helmet to the wrist, until it met metal. Only then did he stop his swing. He felt the old man's body tense, then grow limp. He slowly withdrew his fist. The plate armor dispersed, leaving only a broken body hanging in the void, and the twelve divine phantoms dissipated like they were never there.

Jack tilted his head back and drew a deep, trembling breath. He was utterly exhausted; not passing out was a struggle.

Level up! You have reached Level 343.
Level up! You have reached Level 344.

...

Level up! You have reached Level 360. Further levels locked until the development of your next Dao Fruit.

Congratulations! Titan Taunt II → Titan Taunt III

Jack was happy about the skill. More importantly, he didn't even know how many levels he'd gotten. "All into Physical..." he managed to whisper. The familiar rush of power did not flood him like it used to—it was more like a faint trickle entering his cracked body. Yet, it was enough. He gathered himself and used the trace energy he'd regained to fly through the void, barely achieving two teleportations before he ran out.

Thankfully, the *Trampling Ram* had already been flying his way. They met him halfway, already charging a warp. Brock teleported outside the ship, grabbed Jack, then teleported back inside. The energy around the ship kept building. The universe was deathly silent.

A disheveled, white-haired woman suddenly crossed the void before them. Her hands flashed as they shot out a white beam of purity. "No!" she shouted.

A golden shield appeared, slowing her attack just enough. The *Ram* tore through space and disappeared, teleporting light years away. Eva remained alone in the void, accompanied only by the nearby, headless, floating corpse which used to belong to Travelus Lonihor. Fear and rage alternated on her face.

Finally, she raised her head and screamed.

CHAPTER FORTY-THREE
THE SCARED CATS GATHER

TWO FESHKURS DISCUSSED IN PEARL BAY. THEY DIDN'T BOTHER keeping their voices down—their gossip was already the talk of the town.

"Did you hear? Hell was attacked!"

"No way, dude. It has to be fake."

"It's true! My friend has a cousin there, he told me all about it. There were explosions deep in the sky, the entire planet was shaking, shockwaves came down like rain. And, before that, the entire Prison was obliterated! Someone arrived and destroyed it instantly!"

"Psh. You idiot. Can't you tell that's fake?" The other feshkur snorted. "Just who could destroy a city instantly? Are you saying it was a B-Grade?"

The first feshkur gave a wry grin, leaning closer to whisper, "I'm saying it was Jack Rust."

"What!"

"It's true! Only he could have the strength and reason to do that. He killed a B-Grade recently, and he's at war with the Kingdom. Who else could it be? My friend's cousin said he was probably intercepted by an Ancestor on the way out, hence the cataclysmic battle."

"No way!" The other feshkur was skeptical at the start, but that was long gone now. The name of Jack Rust had an energizing effect on people, it awakened their primal excitement. They'd already learned that where that man was involved, anything was possible.

Incidentally, one of these two feshkurs had met the early E-Grade Jack in Pearl Bay eight years ago, he just hadn't gotten his name. If he knew, he'd be shocked.

It wasn't just these two. The entire Pearl Bay was abuzz with rumors of what happened in Hell, and so was the entire constellation, even the galaxy. It was too grand of an event to hide. And, since neither the Hand of God nor the Animal Kingdom came forth to dissolve the rumors, the people could only assume that whatever happened, they'd been defeated. The mysterious assailant had fled successfully.

This was tremendous news! Hell was nothing like Earthen Gemini or that Hand of God outpost. It was the second most important planet of the Animal Kingdom, a symbol of their power. Just in the annihilation of the prison city, they must have lost hundreds or thousands of D-Grades—that was a significant part of their war power!

If even Hell could be assaulted, what couldn't? The Animal Kingdom might just be destroyed tomorrow. They were dead meat!

The already wounded prestige of the Kingdom took another steep plunge. Eight years ago, they had been the undisputable overlords of the constellation, rulers of incalculable power. Now, that power had been laid bare, and it was insufficient. They'd gone from gods to clowns.

As for the Kingdom itself, they couldn't be bothered with these rumors. They had much larger problems. An emergency

Elder Council had been convened, and it wasn't just them. The two remaining Ancestors were also present—one from each leonine family—alongside the Supreme Ancestor of the Emberheart family. From the Hand of God, the ones participating were Artus Emberheart, Eva Solvig, and another late B-Grade who'd been called in by Eva.

Five B-Grades in total, with three at the late B-Grade. This was close to the peak of power in the Milky Way.

In such a gathering, the Elders of the Animal Kingdom could only sit silently on the sidelines. Even the Grand Elder was only in charge of officiating. Yet, all those exceptional personages wore grim expressions, arranged around a table displaying the image of a single man. He was young and vigorous, his eyes and fists shining purple. It was Jack Rust.

"Travelus was slain," Eva Solvig narrated grimly. "That proves Jack Rust has the power to contend with late B-Grades. Moreover, after that battle, he's probably achieved another breakthrough. The only thing saving us is numbers."

"I can't believe a C-Grade pup can reach this level," the Emberheart Supreme Ancestor said. He was similar to Travelus Lonihor in the sense that he seemed half-dead, as if he'd long surpassed the limits of his natural age. His skin was wrinkled and gnarled, while his eyes were so white he seemed blind. Unlike Travelus, however, he did not possess an elegant air, but rather one of brutality.

"He isn't just any C-Grade," Eva replied. "He's a disciple of the Black Hole Church. He's enjoyed resources that aren't found in this galaxy."

"So have you," the Supreme Ancestor said, "but I don't see you getting anywhere."

The Elders tensed, and the other late B-Grade—a scholarly-looking man with a flowing white mantle—stepped in to mediate. "Let's relax, everyone. We're on the same team."

"Jack Rust is not just a Church disciple," Eva said calmly. "Even calling him a prime genius is an understatement. He's one of the greatest talents the universe has ever seen, with the potential to easily reach the A-Grade. Being weaker than such a person is no shame for me. Everyone is."

The Supreme Ancestor gave a bitter smile.

"Let's focus on present matters," the scholarly man said. "Jack Rust is growing far too rapidly. He does not possess the power to assault us yet, not when we're all together. We should huddle up in Animal Planet and wait for reinforcements."

"You want me to hide from a C-Grade human?" the Supreme Ancestor asked. "Do I look like a turtle to you? Is this why you woke me up?"

"Do you have another suggestions?" the man shot back. The Supreme Ancestor fell silent. "In that case," the scholarly man continued, taking charge of the situation, "we're waiting."

"You mentioned reinforcements," the Supreme Ancestor said.

"Right. The Hand couldn't justify taking an Elder away from the front lines to deal with a C-Grade, but I managed to get them to send a peak B-Grade Envoy. A powerful one, too."

"How long until they arrive? And, say we wait here until then. What if Jack Rust simply hides away? You can't expect me to believe that a peak B-Grade Envoy will just wait here and waste their time."

"They are skilled in divination and spacetime," the scholarly man calmly replied. "Once they arrive, catching up to Jack Rust will only be a matter of time."

The Supreme Ancestor nodded. All the Elders present felt better as well—the heavy aura of doom slipped away, replaced by hope. Not all was lost. In times like this, the Animal Kingdom was glad it had completely devoted itself to the Hand so long ago.

"Then, I believe we are all in agreement," Eva Solvig said. "Every C-Grade and above is forbidden from leaving Animal Planet. We wait here, and there is nothing Jack Rust can do; he cannot assault us yet, nor can he level up with no one to kill. We win."

Just as everyone was about to agree, someone chuckled darkly from the side. It was Artus Emberheart. Despite his low strength, he'd been given a seat at the main table due to his relation to the matter.

Eva raised a brow. "Is something the matter, Artus?"

"Not at all, Commander," he replied. "It's just that, every time we think we have him cornered, that man always finds a way to escape. He's a cockroach."

She stared him down. "And your point is?"

"Let's make sure we don't underestimate him. When that powerful Envoy arrives, they should try their absolute best to annihilate him without giving him a single opportunity to escape."

Eva frowned slightly. "The meeting is dismissed," she said. Everyone stood and walked away, with the exception of Artus, who remained deep in thought.

Nobody was as afraid of Jack Rust as he was. He'd witnessed that man's rise to fame—been on the receiving end of it multiple times. Because of Jack Rust, he'd lost everything. A heart demon had surely formed inside him, a persistent belief that Jack would always triumph.

But Artus was more than just afraid. He didn't care about dying—he had nothing left to lose. All he wanted was to ensure Jack died with him. That he suffered.

Jack Rust and Artus Emberheart were two men who followed completely different paths in life. One had lost his son, the other his home and pride. The grudges between them were irreconcilable.

They were like two meteors about to crash head-on.

———

Jack was sprawled on a lounge chair, breathing heavily. He was resting—the battle with Travelus Lonihor had left him completely spent, and he needed some time to recover.

"Well fought, bro," Brock said from beside him. "You beat a late B-Grade."

"Barely," Jack responded. "It was a coin flip."

"But you won, and that's the important thing." A steady hand fell on Jack's shoulder. "You got levels. Next time, it won't be a coin flip."

Jack forced himself to smile. Despite his exhaustion, he could feel the tremendous power gathered inside him, the energy flooding his limbs. He had gotten much stronger, and he was ready to develop his eighth fruit.

It had been a hard battle, but the price was worth it. Jack opened his status screen, observing the stat points he'd already allocated.

Name: Jack Rust
Species: Human, Earth-387
Faction: Bare Fist Brotherhood (C)
Grade: C
Class: Gladiator Titan (King)
Level: 360

Strength: 7180 (+)
Dexterity: 7180 (+)
Constitution: 7180 (+)
Mental: 1000
Will: 1000

Free sub-points: 2

Dao Skills: Meteor Punch IV, Iron Fist Style III, Brutalizing Aura III, Neutron Star Body III, Supernova III, Space Mastery III, Fist of Mortality III, Death Mastery III, Titan Taunt III
Dao Roots: Indomitable Will, Life, Power, Weakness
Dao Fruits: Fist, Space, Life, Death, Battle, Revenge, Brotherhood
Titles: Planetary Frontrunner (10), Planetary Torchbearer (1), Ninth Ring Conqueror, Planetary Overlord (1), Grade Defier, Planet Destroyer

He'd reached Level 360. There were also more levels the System was withholding until he developed his next Dao Fruit. His Physical substats had finally surpassed seven thousand—adding on his titles' efficacy increase, he had an effective Physical close to fifteen thousand. Most cultivators at his level had around five.

He was a beast.

Moreover, that battle had finally pushed Titan Taunt into the third tier. He was finally getting used to it. He opened the description, finding an extra paragraph compared to the previous one:

Titan Taunt III: A titan's existence is so dominant it constitutes a challenge. Your extreme physicality and domineering stance not only intimidate enemies, but also provoke them. They will either fight you or cower away, losing in both cases. Your challenge manifests as a bloody colosseum walled by spatial barriers. While inside the arena, the most dominant gladiators enjoy the favor of the audience and a small increase to their power.

This was nonsensical. Ever since the Integration, this was the first skill whose System description was completely off.

At first, it had been something silly and even under-whelming—trash talking, basically. It had changed completely from the first to the second tier, as if it had become a new skill, and now the third tier's description contained an entire para-graph about things that had already been present since the second tier.

Is my System broken? Jack couldn't help wondering. *Or am I exiting its scope?*

He leaned toward the second explanation. The more he cultivated, the harder it became for the System to perfectly clas-sify his Dao and skills. Inaccuracies and malfunctions were expected. Strictly speaking, all the System did for him anymore was help him level up and detail his rate of advancement.

Which he liked, actually. There was something addictive about watching his Physical substats shoot through every ceiling in existence. Not to mention the levels ups, without which his rate of advancement would be much slower. It was the same problem Brock suffered from.

Jack released a long sigh. The rush of battle hadn't completely left him yet, but he was already feeling the urge to become stronger. "I will develop my eighth fruit. There is no time to waste."

"Sure." Brock nodded. He'd been next to Jack all along. "So will I."

"Excuse me?"

"I am ready to grow a new fruit."

"Oh. That's awesome! Good luck, Brock. Make it good."

"You too."

Jack stood with a smile and paced to his room. He'd already greeted Salin and the rest—they had left him to rest and were on the bridge playing Crazy Guy Goes to Town. He passed in front of the door, not disturbing them, just listening to their banter. His steps brought him closer to his room, and he was just about to open the door when a voice entered his ears.

"*Jack. Hi. This is Sovereign Heavenly Spoon. We're coming to pick you up and bring you to the Church forces. We'll arrive in approximately one week. Keep this absolutely secret and use the time to take care of any unfinished business in your galaxy. We won't be able to wait after we arrive—and you may not be able to return for a long time.*"

Jack paused. He instinctively tried to reply but found that his thoughts echoed only inside his own head.

"*You can't reply, obviously,*" the sovereign continued, "*unless you can perform long-range targeted telepathy. Which you can't. So, take care. Don't die before we're there!*"

We? Jack thought. He had so many questions. Why was someone that important coming all the way here to pick him up? Could it be on the orders of Elder Boatman?

That made sense. Since he'd left the Black Hole World, Elder Boatman should be able to sense the death cube again. He'd want Jack escorted over as soon as possible.

But who else was coming with the sovereign? And, most importantly, he only had one week... According to the sovereign, they couldn't wait. He had to destroy the Animal Kingdom, find a way to return to Earth, and reunite with his family within a week. Unless he disobeyed commands—but, if the Church was sending their Head Envoy to pick him up on the orders of an Elder, disobeying would be difficult. They might even drag him along.

Jack wanted to join the war against the Hand of God. That was his true stage, where he could grow and develop to his full potential. However, he didn't expect the time to go would come so soon...

Some things were not negotiable. Destroying the Kingdom

and reuniting with his family were necessary, as well as spending some time with them. If he only had one week before he was pressured to leave, he had to make it count.

Animal Planet shouldn't have more than two or three late B-Grades, Jack thought. *I will develop my eighth fruit and go there. It's gonna be tight, but I can take them. I have to.*

It's time to end this.

CHAPTER FORTY-FOUR
ATTACKING ANIMAL PLANET

JACK SAT IN MEDITATION. HIS CHEST ROSE AND FELL, HE WAS RELAXED. Deep inside his soul, he floated before a tall tree crowned with seven fruits. Now was time to develop the eighth.

Fist, Space, Life, Death, Battle, Revenge, Brotherhood... His seven fruits painted a picture of his journey through the C-Grade, the trials and lives he'd experienced. His Daos were there, as were his most signature emotions. It was like seeing his life on canvas.

Jack didn't let himself get lost in sentimentalism. He had an eighth fruit to develop. What should it be?

Resolve? he thought, tasting the name and seeing how it resonated with him. Growth? Power?

All those were concepts he embraced, but none felt suitable. Most overlapped with other Dao Fruits, and the few that didn't weren't representative enough. He didn't want to define his path through something that didn't feel perfect.

Then, what? he wondered. *I can't afford to take it slow. There is no time.*

Ah. Time. I can just go with that.

Jack cultivated space and time on the side. Of those, space

was the concept he was most familiar with, while time was more of a convenient side Dao. However, he'd reached significant understanding of both. Now that he thought about it, not having a Dao Fruit for Time felt wrong, like something was missing, and it was exactly that feeling which Jack followed to determine his Dao Fruits.

Time it is.

The energy climbed up his Dao Tree. It was slow at times and fast at others, but it wasn't the energy itself that was changing speed, it was the flow of time around it. Wherever it passed, flowers bloomed and wilted, the tree grew old then young again. All that energy focused on one branch, one flower, which blossomed into a splendid sphere.

Gradually, that sphere developed and changed shape. From round, it developed angles, growing into a shape which resembled a clock. From purple, which was the initial color of the flower, it turned yellow—Jack didn't know why yellow, but it felt suitable.

The miracle of creation was always impressive to watch. He remained there, holding his breath until the fruit was done developing, a splendid addition to his already great Dao Tree. Not just great—with all those colors on its branches, it could even be called fabulous.

"Right," Jack said, observing his newest fruit. He had the feeling that time flowed oddly around it—and also that his connection with the Dao of Time had deepened. He'd gotten sidetracked by everything that happened, and developing this fruit was long overdue.

"Eight there, one to go..." he whispered. It felt like only recently that he'd broken into the C-Grade, a hopeful young cultivator. The B-Grade felt impossibly distant back then—yet, suddenly, he was sitting right on its cusp.

How strong will I be then? he wondered. *When I establish my inner world and reach the B-Grade, will I be able to fight A-Grades?*

It didn't seem possible. A-Grades were all astoundingly talented individuals—wanting to jump an entire Grade to fight them was a bit of a stretch. Still, Jack could dream.

The important thing wasn't his strength in the future, but reaching that future. A huge tribulation still stood before him— the destruction of the Animal Kingdom, the fulfillment of his revenge, the reunion with his family, and the wrapping up of this part of his life. He needed to do that before heading over to the Second Crusade, and he needed to do it perfectly.

Eric... I swear I will avenge you.

Jack was done with his breakthrough. He opened his eyes in the real world, letting the System award him the remaining levels from his battle against the Supreme Ancestor. He invested all the points into Physical.

Level up! You have reached Level 361.
Level up! You have reached Level 362.
Level up! You have reached Level 363.

There were multiple paths he could choose to follow. Attacking the Kingdom now was risky—who knew how many late B-Grades they had and whether he'd be able to take them. If he wanted to, he could probably hide somewhere and wait for Sovereign Heavenly Spoon to arrive in a week, then ask him to help. To the Head Envoy, solving all of Jack's problems would be simple.

That just didn't feel right. Jack wouldn't be satisfied. This was his battle, his trial, his stepping-stone into the future. Unless he resolved this issue perfectly, he would always have a lingering doubt in his heart, a "what if," a thought to keep him awake at night and limit his potential.

He'd picked this fight. He wanted to end it with his own power, not by depending on the Church. It was a matter of pride—even if others might call it stubbornness. His Fist had to remain hard.

Most importantly, if he did wait for the sovereign to arrive, he wouldn't have any time to reunite with his family. He was clueless as to how to return to Earth. There had to be people looking for him with the teleporter frequency, maybe Shol or someone else, but they couldn't find him if he just hid around in the darkness. The only way would be to destroy the Kingdom and make his location public.

He could also go somewhere and declare his location, drawing the Kingdom's B-Grades away from their home ground. Except that would give the rest of the Kingdom time to scatter if he won. He didn't want that. He'd made an oath to eradicate the name Emberheart from the galaxy, and he intended to see it through.

It was time to fight. It wouldn't be easy, but after his last fruit, he liked his chances.

Jack left his room, heading for the bridge. He ran into Brock on the way. "Hey bro, All good?"

"Of course," Brock replied with a barely contained smile. "Eight fruits. And you?"

"Just the same."

"Good."

Jack's mood remained heavy. Brock followed suit. As they reached the bridge, their friends were relaxing, but they tensed up when they saw Jack's face.

"What happened?" Salin asked. "Did you develop a Dao Fruit of Constipation?"

"Are you guys ready?" Jack asked back.

"Ready for what?"

"We're going to war."

"Ohh. Sounds kinky. Is it the kind where we die or the other one?"

Jack did his best to remain grim-faced. "Both."

"Wait," Nauja said, standing up. "You don't mean we're assaulting Animal Planet, right?"

"That's exactly what I mean."

"What? Why? Are you crazy!"

Jack gave a hard smile. "Because we're running out of time." He then described what the sovereign had transmitted to him alongside his train of thought. The arrival of the sovereign was supposed to be a secret, but Jack trusted these people with his life. If they were going to risk themselves, they had to know what it was about.

"And that's about it," he concluded. "I cannot afford to wait. I have to attack the Kingdom now. Today. I won't ask you all to join me, and frankly speaking, you probably shouldn't. The only thing you would achieve in a battle of that level is to throw your lives away."

Besides Brock, the rest exchanged glances—Gan Salin, Nauja, Bomn, Vashter. They'd been through a lot these past months. They'd traveled together and watched Jack tear apart the galaxy. However, the truth was they were just travel companions. They couldn't actually participate in a battle at Jack's level.

The four of them came to a silent agreement. "We will escort you there and wait far away," Bomn said. "If you win, we will be there to celebrate. If not, we will record the battle and show your family how bravely you fought."

Jack nodded. "Thanks. That's all I could ask for."

Brock spoke up, "I will be with you, big bro. I can't fight directly, but I have ways to support you."

"Are you sure?" Jack asked worriedly. "You don't need to throw your life away."

"I won't."

Brock seemed convinced, so Jack did not insist. If Brock said something, he had the confidence to see it through.

"Thank you all," he said. "If this doesn't work out, I want you to know you are the greatest crew to ever grace this galaxy. I appreciate you sticking with me from the bottom of my heart. I wish you all great lives."

"Oh, don't be like that," Salin said, jumping up and punching Jack's shoulder—then cradling his hand. "Ow. Anyway, you got this. You've never lost before. Why now?"

"I have lost before," Jack replied, "but not this time. Not again. I will stake everything I have. Either I win or I die and my Dao shatters. This is the end."

"Always the optimist. That's what I like about you."

"It was an honor to travel by your side," Vashter said, bringing a fist to his heart. "Whatever happens, I will never forget you."

"Thank you, Vashter... and, sorry. For what happened in the past."

"It's okay. Water under the bridge—everyone deserves to make mistakes."

That phrase brought a larger smile to Jack's face than he expected. He turned his gaze toward space, piercing it to reach Animal Planet. Since they were still in the general area of Hell, it wasn't too far away—they could reach it in an hour.

"Let's go," he said.

———

Animal Planet was the capital and core of the Animal Kingdom. It was a planet similar to Earth, except larger and with more land area. Two moons circled it—the estates of the Emberheart and Lonihor families respectively.

VALERIOS

The emergency meeting on Animal Planet had just ended when every cultivator on the planet sensed a colossal aura falling from the sky. The weaker people were forced to their knees—only D-Grades and above could remain standing.

The Elders looked up with surprise. So did the Ancestors and other B-Grades. The one most surprised was Artus Emberheart. Fear and excitement merged inside his heart, flooding him.

"Animal Kingdom and Hand of God!" an imperious voice filled the sky. It reached every mountain and valley, every house and cave, every nook and cranny of the entire planet and its two moons. It carried such majesty that animals prostrated in worship.

The voice echoed still, "You have ruled as tyrants for too long. You have chased and tried to kill me, but you failed, and now you will reap what you sowed. Today is the day you die. Come out to face me."

The mere arrogance in those words was breathtaking. Jack was speaking to a planet containing dozens of C-Grades and multiple Ancestor-level characters, including three people at the late B-Grade. And he was just one man.

The low-level cultivators were all filled with awe, but the high-level ones were not. Jack Rust had shown up at their doorstep—he was just asking to die.

A swarm of cultivators rose from all over the planet. The weakest among them were Elders at the middle to peak C-Grade, people who commanded universal respect no matter where they appeared in the galaxy. Each could destroy entire continents. A crowd of such figures was awe-inspiring to say the least, more so when they were led by five B-Grades—the apex of power in this galaxy.

All those people rose into space and formed a line. Their auras blasted against the opposing side, which was composed of a single person: a young man with fire in his eyes, wearing only brown shorts and a gray cloak which left his chest exposed. His mere presence suffocated the Elders—even the B-Grades frowned at him.

It sounded ridiculous, but this man himself possessed the capital to stand against all of them. Whether he could win, however... That was a different issue.

"Good. Everyone is here," Jack said, cracking his knuckles. He was not intimidated—he smiled. "Prepare to die."

CHAPTER FORTY-FIVE
THE POWER OF BROHOOD

JACK STOOD TALL IN SPACE. HIS CLOAK FLUTTERED. HIS FISTS WERE relaxed, not yet ready to smash. His gaze crossed space, falling onto the crowd of powerhouses and piercing them all. There was only one person he cared about.

Artus Emberheart.

Jack's heart was awash with hatred. As he saw this man again, he was struck by a flood of memories. He saw himself, helpless and losing, forced to retreat. He saw Artus appear—just a clown back then—and reveal Eric. He saw the boy's unyielding expression and his body destroyed.

This was the killer of his son.

Jack thought he'd had things under control. Suddenly, a dark fire blazed inside him, one which threatened to swallow everything. Only his immense willpower managed to keep it in check—that, and the knowledge that he'd come here precisely for Artus.

Artus Emberheart was also filled with hatred. He was facing the man who ruined his life, the one who publicly humiliated him several times and had him exiled from his home faction.

Moreover, Jack had also killed Artus's son—Rufus Emberheart—during the Integration Tournament of Earth.

These two men were connected by lakes of black blood. They loathed each other with every fiber of their being. Today, there would be no peaceful resolution, only war. The difference was that, between the two of them, one had come alone, and the other had brought an army.

Eva Solvig was speaking, but Jack wasn't listening. His mouth formed a snarl. "Artus Emberheart," he said, interrupting the speaker he didn't care about. "We finally meet again."

"Jack Rust," Artus replied, the derision evident in his voice. "You finally made a mistake. Your impatience threw away your life."

"We'll see about that. I'm not as pitifully weak as you are."

"But you are also not as strong as my army."

Declaring this assembly "his" army was definitely a stretch. The only reason he'd said it was that Artus's sanity was beginning to crack. The moment those words echoed, the Supreme Ancestor of the Emberheart family snorted.

"Shut your mouth," he commanded. A wisp of his aura suffocated Artus, making him unable to speak.

Jack glanced at the Supreme Ancestor. "Who are you?"

"Perilus Emberheart. Founder of the Animal Kingdom, pioneer of the Milky Way Galaxy, and the end of my enemies." He chuckled, his dried-up skin cracking. "When they awakened me to chase after a mere C-Grade pup, I thought they were mistaken. Who would have thought this pup would soon challenge not just me, but another two late B-Grades? Truly, the world is endless. I admire your talent and resolve. However, since you are an enemy, I must kill you."

Jack shook his head. "You spout a lot of shit for someone

who's half-dead. All I heard was your last name: Emberheart. To avenge my son, you are one of those who must die."

The Supreme Ancestor's eyes darkened. "Try me, pup."

"In the name of the Hand of God," Eva Solvig said, her pure white hair fluttering, "you are condemned for treason, resistance, piracy, mass murder, genocide, and colluding with terrorists. You are hereby sentenced to death."

Jack laughed. "You're a late B-Grade, yet your words hold less weight than a fart. What does it matter? There is no justice between enemies. I also sentence you to death for all those things."

"Then I guess we must fight."

"That's why I'm here."

Jack released his aura. It blasted outward like a physical force. The fabric of reality shook, spacetime rippled. Under his might, the stars lost their luster and all life bowed to him.

The crowd of powerhouses frowned as they were struck by his aura. It was like a group of mortals facing a strong wind. Their hair and clothes billowed backward, revealing a scene like they were pressured. The B-Grades were fine, but the C-Grades had to anchor themselves onto space to avoid getting blown away.

The Grand Elder of the Animal Kingdom, a peak C-Grade, gaped as he witnessed such power. This was already almost enough to capsize him, and it was only Jack Rust's aura. Was this really the power of a C-Grade? Just how far ahead of everybody else was that man!

Of the three late B-Grades present, the white-cloaked, scholarly man who hadn't met Jack before was stunned. Hearing was one thing and seeing it was another. He'd never truly accepted in his heart that a late C-Grade existed who could face him. It was a thought as ridiculous as an ant fighting a human.

As he experienced the force of Jack's aura, as he gazed upon its unplumbed depths, sensing the spacetime, life, and death contained inside, he felt as if his entire life so far had been a lie. He was just a crook. This was what cultivators were supposed to be.

And he was facing such a man.

One thought dominated the white-cloaked man's mind. There was no mercy or holding back, no consideration for face. Since they were enemies, Jack Rust had to absolutely die.

The Supreme Ancestor was in a similar state of mind. "You do possess power," he said. "I admit that, if I was alone, you could probably defeat me. But all of us together? Impossible! You've signed your own death!"

Jack smiled. "Careful with your words, old man. Otherwise, you won't be just dead when I'm done, but also humiliated."

The Supreme Ancestor smiled. "Well spoken! Then, bring it on!" He could no longer hold back. The battle craziness which had slumbered inside him for hundreds of thousands of years was set aflame. He was the first to charge, lifting the curtain on what would become the Milky Way Galaxy's most famous battle.

The other B-Grades followed, and so did the C-Grade Elders. The only exception was Artus Emberheart. He knew he couldn't win, and also that Jack would target him. Instead of throwing his life away, he hatefully stayed back, letting others fight for him.

The B-Grades didn't care about this—one extra C-Grade would make no difference in this battle.

Facing their entire line-up, Jack puffed out his chest. His eyes widened. His fists finally clenched. Space warped around them, forming the image of a massive colosseum surrounding them for hundreds of miles. Billions of people roared from the stands. The ground was covered in blood-stained sand, the sky was clear, and the sun shone down on them all.

Jack was now a gladiator standing proudly in the sky, a single man facing an army. He was clearly the hero. The roars of the crowd shook the world with his name. His glory and majesty were clear for all to see. As for his enemies, they were relegated to a wicked mob shunned by all.

Knowing this truth hurt their pride, but there was nothing they could do. At the end of the day, they were the ones using numbers to bully one young hero. This shame was something they had to live with.

Jack's body began to grow. He became one foot taller, and two extra arms appeared below his armpits. His power climbed yet again. His body was so powerful that it appeared more solid than everything around it, as if he was the true core of existence. Waves of palpable power rolled off from inside him.

"All of you," he said, grinning, unable to help his inner battle lust, "bring it on!"

———

Animal Planet was of similar size to Earth, except with more land than water, and it also possessed two moons: one was the property of the Lonihor family, and the other of the Emberheart family.

The battle wasn't taking place too far away from the planet. On its surface and on both its moons, many people caught glimpses of what was happening. They held their breath—no matter how disproportionate this match-up seemed, it remained a battle which determined their future. Moreover, the legend of Jack Rust had long seeped into their hearts. They couldn't help feeling that, no matter what the odds, he would always prevail.

Their chests were clenched. Their hands were cupped. They stopped everything they were doing and waited for the conclusion of the battle with bated breath, only wishing they could spectate more closely.

Their wishes were heard. At some point, screens began to flare up in major cities. They depicted the battle scene from up-close, captured by a highly-specialized projection stone with extreme zooming capabilities. The angle was odd—it didn't come from Animal Planet, but from the opposite direction. There was someone broadcasting this battle from Jack Rust's side. The Animal Planet people had only detected the signal and projected it on their screens.

That someone was naturally the *Trampling Ram*. Bomn had procured a high-end projection stone which could broadcast the battle across the constellation. Brock had already spoken with the rebel leaders, who'd ensured everyone was waiting to receive it. Within the first minute of broadcasting, before the battle even began, business-minded individuals of the Merchant Union retransmitted the signal for a price, making sure it spread around the whole galaxy.

The entire Milky Way was caught off-guard. The projection appeared in most major cities. It was similar to Jack's previous battle against the planetary overseer but on a much grander scale. Everyone saw him, a single late C-Grade man, facing down an army where the weakest people wore the clothing of Animal Kingdom Elders.

"Jack Rust is assaulting Animal Planet by himself?" Some knowledgeable people connected the dots. "How! What the hell is happening?"

A tragically old-looking man in the projection spoke up. "You do possess power," he said. "I admit that, if I was alone, you could probably defeat me. But all of us together? Impossible! You've signed your own death!"

The Elders of the various major factions recognized him as a Supreme Ancestor and were tongue-tied. Their eyes widened—they were watching a once-in-a-lifetime, unprecedented, world-changing battle!

However, facing that old man, Jack Rust's reply was even more exaggerated.

"Careful with your words, old man. Otherwise, you won't be just dead when I'm done, but also humiliated."

What heroism! What bravado! Let alone everyone else, even the cultivators of the Animal Kingdom felt a deep respect for Jack Rust. To dare assault a major faction by himself and still have the mind to say such words—what couldn't he do?

This man wasn't just a hero. He was a sensation!

Every eye in the Milky Way was glued onto the battle that would decide the fate of the galaxy.

———

Jack's colosseum was a projection visible only to the people participating in the battle. The spectators across the galaxy couldn't see it, but to those inside, it was indistinguishable from reality. In a sense, it was reality.

This arena was precisely the reason why Jack dared to challenge everyone—not only because it greatly enhanced his power in such a scenario, but also because it isolated everyone inside. It hid the fact that, in reality, he wasn't alone.

A brorilla flashed into existence outside the arena. The reason Jack had released his aura so powerfully before was to prevent the enemies from detecting Brock. Now that they were trapped in Jack's arena, even if they realized he was there, exiting to attack him would be difficult. Only like this could Brock do his thing.

He was also outside the scope of the projection stone. Nobody knew he was there.

Brock brought his hands together. A large book appeared between them, dark with golden letters. It radiated a certain majesty, a completeness, as if whoever mastered it had mastered the world. The book flipped to a page somewhere in the middle. Golden images appeared—endless creatures raising their hands, warriors of all species and appearances, of all levels of power. Only one thing united them all—the fervor with which their eyes desired freedom.

Brock let go of the book, which hovered before him in space, radiating an increasingly powerful golden energy. He raised his hands. "Bros of the world," he said, letting his voice echo across the universe, "lend us your power!"

A wave of brohood spread everywhere instantly. Every bro was called to action. A pack of stray dogs on Earth howled to the sky. The blue crabs and various beasts of Trial Planet followed. Every member of the bro army of the Exploding Sun, which was now scattered around the galaxy, felt a desire to raise their hands and lend their power to whoever was calling.

All across the universe, inside and outside System space, many Church cultivators raised their hands to the sky—they were the bros Brock had made on the Cathedral. The cultivators of Earth did the same, including Vivi and the professor, and so did every single warrior in the rebel armies of the Animal Kingdom constellation.

Millions of people responded to Brock's call. Billions. A tremendous amount of power converged from all over the universe, gathering into a massive ball of energy hovering over Brock's hands. He pushed his own energy into it, as much as he could muster. The Bro Code shone like the sun, illuminating the dark space and being clearly visible from Animal Planet. So bright was its light that many weaker cultivators had to look away, wondering what it was.

All that energy was so great that the Bro Code could barely handle it. Brock roared and grabbed it again, ignoring the heat which burned his hands and eyes. "BIG BRO!" he roared. "WIN FOR US!"

A massive beam of golden light speared out, piercing space and landing onto the body of Jack. He lost his breath. The power that filled him was overwhelming; he had to let it out.

Jack couldn't win this battle alone. He'd barely defeated the previous Supreme Ancestors—one extra fruit wouldn't let him face three opponents of that level and their army. However, he wasn't alone this time. He had his bros. He had the world on his side. His greatest weakness had been the relatively small amount of energy he controlled—now, while the bro energy he received wasn't anything world-shattering to him, it was enough to push his strength another step forward.

Like this, he could fight.

This was still the start of the battle. The enemies had almost reached him, but only now did Jack react. He laughed out loud, smashing his fists together. "Let's go!" he shouted, then jumped into the fray.

CHAPTER FORTY-SIX

DESTROYING THE ANIMAL KINGDOM

JACK BROKE INTO THE MASS OF ENEMIES. HIS DAO SPREAD OUT, forming the shape of a large fist around him which came crashing down like a meteor. The colosseum spectators cried out. The enemies groaned.

But they were not defenseless. Every Elder of the Kingdom activated their powers. So did the two remaining Ancestors. The Emberheart Supreme Ancestor roared, his body flickering with crimson lightning—his wrinkled skin tensed, muscles stuck out of his scrawny arms, and his white mane stood up like rods. Though nowhere near his peak, he remained a supremely powerful individual.

The Supreme Ancestor, already using the Thunder Body battle transformation, clashed head-on with Jack's attack. The white-cloaked man assisted him, using time and space to dissolve some of Jack's momentum.

A tremendous shockwave spread from the point of impact. The two late B-Grades managed to stop Jack's assault, but the remaining force tossed the Elders behind them away like ragdolls.

Jack roared. He smashed another fist at the Supreme Ancestor, but the man was no slouch—he crossed his arms to defend, then exchanged a few strikes with Jack. His speed and strength belied his age. This was a martial arts master.

"AGAIN!" the Supreme Ancestor roared, but it was a fake. Eva Solvig appeared behind Jack, slamming down a white palm. The space behind him turned barren. He sensed lifelessness heading for his back. He barely managed to teleport away, watching the area an entire mile around his previous location turn... not dead, but something even worse. Something beyond the scope of his many Daos.

Pure—in a terrible, terrible way.

A shiver ran down his back, accompanied by excitement. Three late B-Grades besieged him, flanked by two early B-Grades and over a dozen C-Grades. What a line-up...

The Supreme Ancestor led the charge. Eva Solvig followed, ready to attack Jack a beat later and disorient him, while the white-cloaked man floated far away, constricting spacetime around Jack from a distance. None of them were simple opponents. At the same time, the early B-Grade Ancestors led the Elders to barrage him with attacks from afar.

The audience cheered. Jack laughed. "Bring it on!"

His form flickered. He used a thought to shatter the white-cloaked man's grip on spacetime, then he warped it until it seemed like there were twelve Jacks, not just one. All twelve charged up a Supernova.

Eva snorted. A white field spread around her, annihilating everything—even spacetime and the fake Jacks. Twelve disappeared—none were left.

"What!" was all she had time to cry out before a thirteenth Jack appeared behind her, smashing a punch into her lower back and sending her flying. The Supreme Ancestor flashed over, planting a knee in his chest. Jack's breath was cut short. He was sent flying, his regeneration already working to fix his ribcage, but found everything accelerating around him.

No, they weren't accelerating—he was the slow one. Time stagnated around him.

Jack tried to break the hold, but he was more proficient in space than time. He needed a moment—but that wasn't time he'd be allowed. The Supreme Ancestor flashed before him, suddenly much faster than before. His limbs turned into blurs. Fists and feet and elbows and knees rained on Jack.

The Emberheart family used a full-body martial style, but this Supreme Ancestor took it a step further. In his movements, Jack could see a shadow of the sharkens' unpredictability, the canines' ferocity, the eagler's speed. He was a force of nature barraging Jack with dozens of strikes every instant, and though he tried to defend, there was only so much he could do when slowed down.

A few strikes made it through. His knee bent backward, a chop bruised his neck. Each of the Supreme Ancestor's strikes were aimed at a vital spot, and each could fell a mountain range. Jack spat out blood, rapidly retreating, only to be met with a terrible heat at his back.

The Elders, who had been throwing attacks all this time, finally got him. A green fireball exploded behind him, searing his back and destroying half his cloak. Just as the shockwave pushed him forward, the Supreme Ancestor was there again, his limbs flowing in a bloody dance.

Jack didn't even consider defending. He let a palm land on his chest to forcefully teleport away, barely dodging a white beam released by Eva Solvig. The moment he appeared, mouth bloodied, he saw that the white-cloaked man had read his movement and teleported at the same spot before him, meeting his arrival with a spatial blade aimed at his heart. Jack twisted out of the way, letting it slice through his ribs, then threw a punch in the same movement. The white-cloaked man flew away with minor wounds.

This is impossible, Jack thought as he kept getting mobbed. *I can't take them all at once! Not like this!*

He'd expected things to go this way. He knew it would be a hard battle, but this was just too much! How could he fight when besieged from every direction?

Activating the Thunder Body would certainly help, but he wanted to save that as his last resort. He hadn't mastered it yet, so it consumed way too much energy. Wasting it here would be unwise.

Then, what?

Jack gritted his teeth. Brutalizing Aura spread around him, snaring his opponents and clipping their wings, slowing them down just a bit. Jack used that time to break the spacetime shackles around him and teleport a dozen miles to the side, directly into the middle of the gathered Elders.

"Stop!" the early B-Grade Ancestors shouted. An army of divine soldiers attacked Jack from all sides while the Elders retreated. He only snorted. Spacetime rippled around him—the fluctuations surrounded the body of each Elder, slowing them down before freezing them completely.

In his last battle, Jack had used this technique to imprison twelve phantoms with the strength of an early B-Grade each. Now that he was even stronger, trapping all these C-Grade Elders was child's play.

"Not on my watch!" the white-cloaked man shouted. Ripples spread from him, countering Jack's and breaking the Elders out of their time prison, but Jack didn't mind. He never planned to hold them anyway. All he needed was to delay them a bit so they couldn't run away.

The early B-Grade's divine soldiers stabbed him with their spears, but Jack didn't bother defending. They could only inflict flesh wounds. Power flowed into his limbs. He shot forward like a cannonball, arriving before a sharken Elder who'd just escaped the time prison. The Elder's eyes widened—he tried to run away, but in the face of Jack, he might as well be standing still.

Jack's Meteor Punch smashed into the Elder's body, shattering all his internal organs. The fist carried on, pushing the dead Elder into two more and killing them as well. Only the fourth Elder managed to escape death, though with heavy injuries.

Only now did the Supreme Ancestor manage to catch up. Seeing the Elders of his Kingdom massacred, he trembled with rage. "How dare you!" he shouted. He fell on Jack like a wild animal, his aged body exhibiting unmatched ferocity. Jack defended calmly, laughing.

"You dare laugh?" the Supreme Ancestor roared. "You dare bully the weak? Is that the honor of a great warrior!"

"You aren't only doomed, but also a fool!" Jack shouted. Mentally, however, he commanded: System, allocate all points into Physical!

The many Elders of the Animal Kingdom had arrived en masse to demonstrate the might of their faction. They hadn't been afraid that Jack would kill them—even though he could, it just wasn't worth it. The impact they had on the battle was minimal. He wouldn't risk turning his back to the real enemies just to deal with them out of spite.

However, there was something they'd failed to account for —the fact that they could give Jack levels.

In most situations, background characters weren't enough to level anyone up. Simply put, easy battles were never worth fighting. It was this eternal rule which made all the Elders miscalculate here, and even the B-Grades had missed this fact.

Jack was so strong that it was easy to forget he was still a late C-Grade. The Elders had joined the battle to show unity and bravado, but all they achieved was to deliver themselves to Jack on a silver platter. To him, they were juicy bags of levels.

Everyone understood this at the same time. "Scatter!" the Lonihor Ancestor shouted. All Elders ran off in random directions, but they were standing on sand, enclosed by colosseum walls. "It's an illusion!" someone shouted. "Break through!"

They smashed into the walls head-first. They may have been illusions, but they hid real spatial barriers underneath. Breaking through wasn't easy. Even if the late B-Grades were the ones to try, it would still take some time.

Jack broke off from the Supreme Ancestor and teleported to the middle of the colosseum. "Where do you think you're going?" he asked, his smile tainted by blood. "From the moment you decided to fight me, you lost your right to escape. It's victory or death."

"VICTORY OR DEATH!" the audience chanted after him, and Jack laughed.

"Get him!" Eva shouted, an intense sense of crisis flooding her, but her attacks landed on nothing. Jack had already teleported away. His form flickered across the colosseum like a specter of death.

Back before he entered the Black Hole World, Jack had already been able to match Eva's speed. Now, he was easily twice as fast. Even in the enclosed space of his colosseum which not even he could escape, even with the white-cloaked man working hard to limit his movements, Jack was the fastest cultivator present. Maybe he couldn't harm the late B-Grades like this, but they also couldn't catch him.

Suddenly, Jack was everywhere. The late B-Grades ran after, missing time and again. Wild attacks filled the arena as everyone tried to stop him. The Elders panicked and ran around like headless chickens.

Jack was a Gladiator Titan. Placed in this group of weaklings, he was like a wolf amongst sheep. The rushing Elders might as well be sitting still. He flashed to their sides, casually severed their lives, then teleported away again. Between teleportations, he flew at speeds untraceable by the naked eye.

Five Elders died within two seconds.

"To me!" the Supreme Ancestor shouted, incensed. The Elders rushed over—the smart ones were already there—but it was useless. Jack intercepted them midway and flitted around like a deadly butterfly, easily killing them all. Of course, the more the Elders gathered, the easier it was for the late B-Grades to catch Jack. Some attacks connected, making him spit blood, but he ignored them. His body was ridiculously sturdy, and his regeneration was godly. He could take it.

Notifications rang continuously in Jack's ears. He usually ignored them until the battle was over, but he paid attention now, telling the System to keep investing everything into Physical. His power grew. He became stronger and faster with every passing second, terrifying the late B-Grades. For someone to advance like this mid-battle was unthinkable.

When he arrived at Animal Planet, Jack had been Level 363. Over the course of killing these Elders, he'd reached 378, a difference of fifteen levels and three hundred stat points. That wasn't a minor increase.

The Animal Kingdom possessed thirty-two Elders, all at the middle C-Grade or above. Two had been killed by Jack before this battle, so thirty remained. That was their main force, the core of their faction. Every single Elder was of paramount importance.

In normal times, even the worst faction-destroying disasters couldn't get too many of those Elders because they were spread across the constellation. Now, the Hand of God had ordered them all to gather at Animal Planet, and they'd all rushed out together to face Jack, foolishly emboldened by their numbers.

That was their doom.

The cornerstones of the Animal Kingdom fell like flies. Within a single minute, all thirty of their lifeforces were extinguished. The Grand Elder had also fallen. The Kingdom lost every single one of its Elders. Even one of the two Ancestors, the one from the Emberheart family, had been caught off guard and slain—his strength had been lacking to begin with.

Even if Jack died right now, the Kingdom couldn't continue existing as a major faction in this galaxy. They only had a single Ancestor remaining, alongside the Supreme Ancestor who was just too old. Everyone else was at the early C-Grade or below.

It could be said that, right now, Jack had already destroyed the Animal Kingdom—and he wasn't done yet.

All around the galaxy, every spectator drew cold breaths. They were witnessing the fall of a giant. The million year-long reign of the Animal Kingdom... ended today!

CHAPTER FORTY-SEVEN

END OF THE LINE

THE ARENA WAS STREWN WITH THE LIFELESS BODIES OF ONCE ALMIGHTY Elders. Dozens of rulers of the galaxy painted the sand with their blood. The people watching all over the galaxy were frozen, unable to believe such a thing could really happen, while the B-Grades in the arena—the only ones remaining— were speechless.

The Supreme Ancestor had laid in cryogenic sleep for hundreds of thousands of years to protect his faction in the case of such an emergency. Yet, even after he'd awakened, he'd been unable to help. He had to bear witness his descendants, the faction he'd spent his entire life building, be demolished before his very eyes.

What was helplessness? This was helplessness!

"I will fucking kill you, Jack Rust!"

More sparks erupted all over his body. He was an old god clad in lightning, a thunderstorm taken physical form. He threw himself at Jack, uncaring about anything else. Jack charged back, then abruptly disappeared.

He reappeared before the last remaining Ancestor. This was a leonine of the Lonihor family, clad in their tell-tale plate armor and surrounded by divine warriors. He knew this was coming—he braced himself. Half the warriors raised their shields, while the rest charged at Jack to delay him.

Jack pulled back his fist. Reality itself was sucked inside. The energy compacted continuously, becoming so dense it almost collapsed the fabric of spacetime around it, and then exploded right as Jack let loose his fist.

Eva Solvig flashed behind him and smashed a palm of Purity into his back. Jack endured it. His fist exploded on the divine warriors, obliterating them all. Shiny spears and shields flew everywhere. The energy of the Supernova broke through their defenses and fell onto the early B-Grade Ancestor, shattering his armor and Dao both. He flew away—dead.

A rush of power fled into Jack's body, then abruptly stopped. He'd reached Level 380, where the System would withhold any extra energy until he developed his ninth Dao Fruit. He couldn't get any stronger during this battle, but that was fine. He was enough.

However, Eva Solvig's attack had ravaged his back. The life inside him had diminished, like he'd swallowed molten iron. A terrible emptiness filled his being. He lost his breath, sent flying away, his heart struggling to keep beating. It was only afterward that the Life Drop's energy flooded him again, refilling the gap.

Jack breathed heavily. Just a single attack from Eva almost reaped his life. Instinctively, he felt she was a cut above the white-cloaked man and Supreme Ancestor. Which was natural —she wasn't a native cultivator of the barren Milky Way Galaxy, but a high-level Envoy of the Hand of God. She was also the daughter of the late A-Grade Elder Purity. The resources she'd enjoyed were incalculable. Moreover, she probably hadn't reached the end of her potential—of course her strength would be greater than others at the same level.

Jack turned around, finally slowing down a bit. Only the three late B-Grade cultivators were left—everyone else was dead, their bodies littering the sands of Jack's Gladiator Titan arena. All three enemies stared at him with hatred. Jack smiled.

"Round two," he said, then charged.

The Supreme Ancestor roared and rushed to meet him. Eva flew beside him, while the white-cloaked man remained far away. Jack exchanged strikes with them. He was on the losing end; not only was he one against two, but the spacetime around him was heavily constricted, limiting his movements. He gradually retreated, keeping his safety.

Even after seventeen levels, this still wasn't easy. But it was manageable. And, since he could survive, Jack could formulate a plan.

Lightning flickered on his skin. In the next moment, it burst out, an armor of purple sparks swimming over his skin. The Supreme Ancestor's eyes widened. "The Thunder Body! How can you... How can you have it!"

Jack smiled, not responding. He exploded with speed. He was stronger and faster than before—so much faster, in fact, that the world warped around him, and he could barely control his own body. His punches flashed like thunderbolts. He was still in the Life Drop battle transformation, so he possessed four fists, each roaring at the limit of speed.

The Supreme Ancestor roared but was pushed back. Eva unleashed waves of Purity which Jack broke through like a stone on the shore. He kept them both at bay, so stormy and fierce was his assault. The white-cloaked man finally decided to intervene. He rushed closer, then directly formed a spatial storm and tossed it onto Jack's head.

Such a storm, if he wished it, could easily cleave through a planet. It was made of innumerable, invisible tiny blades formed of pure space which tried to tear Jack into pieces.

Thankfully, he wasn't unfamiliar with space himself. Though the blades were invisible, he could perceive their locations, dodging or dispersing them all. Of course, that slowed him down, allowing the other two enemies to regain their footing and renew their assault.

Jack turned his gaze to the white-cloaked man. From the very start of the battle, he'd been a pest. He would be the first to go.

Jack's form blurred again. Enhanced by Thunder Body, he reached previously unthought-of levels of speed. Even these late B-Grades could barely keep up. He circled them rapidly, like a typhoon, and their strikes only met empty space. Jack became a phantom, creating afterimages not through space manipulation but sheer speed.

His three opponents huddled together while the crowd in the arena stands roared, shouted, and generally caused a ruckus. They rose from their seats to cheer harder.

Supernovas exploded. The three enemies worked together to resist, releasing shockwaves which bounced off the arena walls. The void shattered. Space shook. Reality was distorted, and the infinite particles of the Dao vibrated to the same tune.

"Freeze!" the white-cloaked man shouted, using up a large amount of energy to constrict space all around them—only like that could he catch Jack. Unfortunately for him, this was exactly what Jack had been waiting for. At the exact moment when the white-cloaked man gathered his power, Jack appeared above him, smashing a Supernova down on his head.

Spacetime indeed froze—but the white-cloaked man's head was pushed down, breaking his neck and bending his spine. The ensuing explosion burned his body entirely, and the frozen spacetime returned to motion just in time to let his body flop to the sands, dying them red as many others had done before him.

"Sylvan!" Eva shouted, her voice filled with increasing panic —not at his death, but at hers. "No!"

"Caught you!" the Supreme Ancestor shouted. To release such a powerful strike, Jack had stood still, and that instant was more than enough for a master to capitalize on. The Supreme Ancestor and Eva Solvig besieged Jack from both sides, alternating their strikes to not let him teleport away.

Jack had achieved a lot of things in this battle, and they'd all come at a cost. He was currently exhausted. His Thunder Body ability was barely holding on, and the only thing keeping him afloat was the constant stream of energy coming from Brock. Now surrounded, defending was all he could do, and the occasional strike that seeped through rocked his world.

His vision grew blurry. The world lost its sharpness. Defending became an instinct, and his arms slowed as the lightning ran out around him. He was beginning to lose.

No, he thought. *Not now. Not after coming this far!*

Nobody was coming to save him. No one ever would. From start to finish, the only people Jack could depend on were himself and his bro. Brock had already done everything he could—Jack had to end this himself.

Pushed to the edge, he took a risk. He completely turned his back to the Supreme Ancestor, facing Eva Solvig entirely. He leaned into the attack even as a series of strikes landed on his back, piercing his body, breaking his skin and bones. He roared as he hurtled himself forward, through a burning wave of Purity, into Eva Solvig. All four of his fists crashed down together. The world was split in four—then erupted as one.

"QUADRUPLE SUPERNOVA!"

The impact was so massive that Jack went blind. His chest was seared by heat even as his back was devastated by the Supreme Ancestor. He flew backward, into the leonine, then both crashed into the far wall together. The arena flickered as if about to disappear. Jack felt half-dead. All his bones were broken.

Thankfully, he still had the Life Drop's regeneration. When his eyes were restored, he gazed at a massive crater in the sand. Eva's barely recognizable body lay in its midst, completely charred and broken.

So were Jack's fists. They were now slowly regenerating thanks to the Life Drop—even he couldn't endure four Supernovas at once. Moreover, he was mostly spent.

But the Supreme Ancestor was in even worse condition. He possessed neither Jack's robustness nor his regeneration—though the impact he'd received was smaller, his aged body could barely stand, and his wrinkled skin had ruptured all over. Black blood flowed from his mouth and limbs—only one arm and one leg remained intact, while the rest were broken.

This legend of the galaxy, the founder of a B-Grade faction who'd once reached the peak B-Grade, was finally at the end of his rope.

Jack stood, shaking and ready for a final battle, but it didn't seem like the Supreme Ancestor was up for it. His gaze was cloudy—Jack could feel the old man's weakness, as if he'd already half-slipped into death. Perhaps it was unavoidable. The whole point of being eternally suspended was to return for one battle.

The Supreme Ancestor gazed at the broken fields of sand. The bodies of his descendants littered it—the ruins of everything he'd worked to build. He was old, too old—and now, he was alone.

The leonine raised his head and barked an ugly laugh. More blood flowed from the ends of his lips. "Who would have thought! My life was a joke. Everything I built ruined—everything I was... lost. Hahaha! Oh, Heavenly Dao! I never thought that at my final moments, even I would be forsaken!"

Jack was in no mood to argue. "Are you done?"

"Done? Yes, I am... I'm done forever." The Supreme Ancestor gave Jack a deep, inscrutable glance. "I hate you more than I have ever hated anyone, but I acknowledge my defeat. I cannot kill you even if we keep fighting. In that case, I may as well die standing."

Jack nodded. A hint of appreciation entered his eyes. "You fought bravely."

The Supreme Ancestor sighed. He relaxed his Dao and withdrew his aura. He could always reactivate them, but it would take a tiny amount of time, and that was more than enough for Jack to kill him. He'd basically dropped his weapons.

"I surrender, Jack Rust. You may do with my old body as you like. However, there is something I may ask of you... Don't blame my descendants. They were wrong to antagonize you, but most of them are innocent. Please, don't massacre them. Let a bit of my lineage carry on. Show mercy."

Jack did not reply immediately. His hand grabbed the leonine's throat—who didn't resist—then he carried his surrendered opponent to the center of the arena. The audience shouted for blood.

"I admire your resolve," Jack finally said. "Unfortunately, the grudge between me and your descendants is far too deep."

The Supreme Ancestor's lip trembled. Suddenly, he wasn't the legend of a generation, but a sad old man. "Must I beg?" he asked in a trembling voice.

Jack shook his head. "I once swore to my dead son that the name Emberheart would cease to exist. I cannot go back on that, nor do I want to. You were a brave man, Perilus Emberheart, both in life and in death—it's just a pity that your descendants didn't inherit your honor. I will not force you to watch them die. Go on first, and I will make sure they all follow you soon."

The Supreme Ancestor's eyes had never been deeper. "I understand," he said in a weak voice.

Jack clenched his hand and snapped the other man's throat, then pulled the body into his space ring. To him, at least, he would give a proper burial. He deserved it.

Dark emotions welled up inside Jack. A war was taking place in his heart—he could sense that moment of choosing between light and darkness was approaching, but he didn't feel there was a choice, only an inevitability.

He sighed. He let the arena disappear, since the battle was over, and he quickly pocketed the space rings of Eva Solvig and the white-cloaked man—being Envoys of the Hand of God, they were the only ones who carried such things. He would inspect them later.

Finally, he turned to Animal Planet. There was only a single high-Grade individual remaining—Artus Emberheart, who had not participated in the battle. Jack's true enemy, the man he hated most in the cosmos.

He flew back slowly, not worried that Artus would escape. Indeed—as he approached, he saw the leonine wrapped in golden chains. Brock was beside him, standing with arms crossed and a stare Jack couldn't quite place.

"Hey, bro," said the brorilla. "Nice battle."

Jack nodded. His gaze landed on Artus Emberheart.

CHAPTER FORTY-EIGHT

PUNISHMENT

THE UNIVERSE HAD FALLEN QUIET.

Dozens of bodies littered the space behind Jack. They used to be overlords, emperors of the galaxy, C-Grade Elders and B-Grade Ancestors or Envoys. Now, they were all dead—slain because they made an enemy of Jack Rust. Because they pushed their enmity far past the point of reconciliation.

What goes around comes around. The Animal Kingdom had oppressed its constellation for a million years. Their widespread tyranny was bound to backfire eventually, and now they were destroyed. Without Elders and Ancestors to guide the faction, the Kingdom was left with only early C-Grade Enforcers. They were reduced to a C-Grade faction, and not even a particularly strong one. Moreover, the revolution against them was still ongoing—it was unknown how many Enforcers would survive.

It was even possible that, after everything was said and done, the Animal Kingdom would disband entirely.

This was a deciding day in the history of the Milky Way— the first time a major faction was taken down from the inside. It was also the day a new overlord appeared. Jack Rust had solidified his place as the galaxy's strongest cultivator. Even if some

Supreme Ancestor of an apex B-Grade faction could face him, no one doubted that in just a year or two, Jack's strength would have taken another leap forward.

Jack Rust, Galactic Emperor.

After the battle broadcast was over, the world remained stunned. Large cities had fallen into inactivity. Elder Councils were convened in all major factions, and even Ancestors were called to participate. They needed to discuss how to handle this —figure out their place in the new world order.

The Milky Way had changed forever.

As the person in the center of all those changes, Jack didn't care. He did not revel in his victory against the Animal Kingdom, nor was he relieved at temporarily being safe. The only thing he felt was hatred—a blazing dark bonfire which took his heart as fuel. His eyes carried death as he stared down his most hated enemy: Artus Emberheart.

Golden chains bound him, borne of the Dao of Brohood. Brock stood silent to the side, letting Jack approach, while Artus himself revealed a mixture of disbelief and bitterness.

He laughed. "Congratulations, Jack Rust! You finally win! You always win everything!"

"It's not about winning," Jack replied. He only stopped when he towered over Artus, a titan staring him down. Coupled with his fierce air, it was like he would reach down and snap Artus's neck in the next instant.

Yet, he didn't do that. He didn't just want to kill Artus; he wanted to make him suffer.

"Go ahead and try!" Artus laughed as if reading Jack's thoughts. "You have already taken everything from me. My son, my honor, my faction... Even after I managed to restart my life, you only destroyed everything again. You are a menace, Jack Rust! I wish you'd never been born! At this point, there is nothing else you can do to me, no more pain you can inflict."

Jack smiled, not responding. Artus kept going.

"You want to torture me? Try! There is no pain worse than what I've already been through. You want to utterly destroy the Animal Kingdom and kill my family? Go ahead! What do I care about them? Why should I care? They are the ones who exiled me. They never helped me deal with you. Let them die alongside their Kingdom like the ungrateful shits they are!"

The more he spoke, the more his ramblings turned from coherent speech to crazed ranting. It wasn't just his Dao—his mind was broken as well.

But that didn't mean Jack would show mercy.

"I do plan to destroy your lineage," he replied calmly. "As for torturing you... I will not dirty my hands. Someone like you is not worth polluting my Dao."

"Then what can you do?" Artus replied, laughing again. "You are powerless to hurt me! Useless, just like the day I killed your son! End my life, if you dare. Let's bring this giant farce to a close!"

Intense hatred arose within Jack, but held himself. "I will not hurt you, Artus Emberheart... However, if you think I'll end your life, you are mistaken."

"Hmm?" Only now did Artus sober up a bit. "What do you mean?"

"How long will these chains last, Brock?" Jack asked.

The brorilla raised a brow. "Indefinitely. They're powered by ambient Dao."

"Good. Can you bind him completely?"

"With pleasure."

Before Artus could react, more golden chains materialized around him. His entire body was paralyzed—he could feel everything, but he couldn't move a muscle. The golden color even seeped into him, imprisoning his soul and sealing his Dao. To his horror, Artus realized that he couldn't move his energy at all—besides his tempered body, he was like a mortal.

"What did you do to me?" he asked, roaring. "What did you do!"

"We sealed you," Jack replied calmly. "Now you cannot escape, you cannot move, you cannot contact others, and you cannot even take your own life."

Artus felt a hint of panic. To cultivators, who had extreme control over their bodies, taking their own life was simple. It served as a mental guarantee—no matter what, they would never experience anything worse than death because they could kill themselves whenever they wished. Even when Artus spoke about torture before, it was only to mock Jack— he planned to end himself as soon as this conversation was over.

To his horror, Artus realized he no longer had that option. His Dao had shattered completely, rendering him incapable of communing with the world, and the little energy which remained inside his soul had been sealed by Brock, as had his body. The only part he could still move was his face, but it was useless. Even if he bit off his tongue, that would be a laughable injury to his C-Grade body.

Artus didn't fear death or torture. However, this sense of losing control... This, he feared. It terrified him.

"Let me go!" he screamed. "Kill me if you dare! Kill me like I killed your son!"

Jack gave a dark smile. "You do not deserve the same fate as Eric. The two of you are not on the same level. My son was avenged, he was loved, and he will be remembered. As for you... Nobody will care about you, nor will there be anyone left to remember you."

Artus screamed, struggling to escape, but how could he? Though he'd once reached the late C-Grade realm, his current strength barely qualified him as a C-Grade. There was nothing he could do against Brock's restraints.

Jack waved a hand, wrapping Artus in a spatial distortion and hiding him from sight. Living beings could not enter space rings, but Jack had reached the level where he could easily simulate a similar effect.

"Will you come with me, Brock?" he asked.

Brock raised his gaze. "To the end of the world."

"Good. That's exactly where we're headed."

The *Trampling Ram* arrived beside them. Nobody spoke to congratulate Jack—they could all sense the palpable darkness in the air. Jack and Brock boarded the starship. Before that, however, they spread their perception over Animal Planet and destroyed every single teleporter on it. Nobody could escape until they returned.

Then, they teleported.

The *Trampling Ram* pierced through space in silence. The void turned heavier wherever they appeared, then almost sighed as they left.

"Jack," Nauja spoke hesitantly. "Do you maybe want to—"

"No."

She fell silent. A couple hours later, the infinite stars around them began to abate, replaced with endless darkness. Bright shapes lingered in the far distance—some were shaped as spirals, others as eggs. They were galaxies.

Animal Planet was close to the edge of the galaxy to begin with. After a few hours of teleporting, they'd reached it. Behind them lay stars—ahead, darkness.

Jack stepped outside the starship alone. He waved his hand, and space distorted beside him to reveal Artus Emberheart, completely immobile. He could neither speak nor move. Only his eyes, which remained perfectly still, emanated hatred.

"This is the edge of the galaxy," Jack explained. "Billions of light years of emptiness. Nothing exists here. No life... and no death."

Artus's eyes remained still, but a hint of horror was beginning to grow in them.

"You are not too old, Artus," Jack continued. "C-Grades can live for ten thousand years. You look in your fifties—you have maybe five thousand years left? Four? That's a decent amount of time. Cultivators pursue immortality, you know. They yearn to spend more time in this world, enjoying everything it has to offer. You, on the other hand, are about to experience a very different fate.

"In your current state, you cannot move or act in any way. You cannot struggle. You cannot try to escape. All you can do is perceive and think. I hope your mind is an interesting place, Artus, because it is all you will know for the rest of your long, long life. I will push you into the endless darkness—in there, you will be nothing but a speck of sand. Nobody will ever find you. If you are extremely lucky, you might chance by a space monster in a century or two and be eaten. If not, you will spend your remaining years alone, immobile, and helpless, floating through empty darkness."

Jack smiled to Artus's increasing horror. "Aren't you glad you cultivated to the C-Grade, Artus? You get to survive without food, water, or breathing... How fortunate of you. Enjoy your new life. This"—his eyes darkened—"is for my son."

Jack reached for Artus's back and pushed him forward. He watched as Artus floated toward the darkness, unable to scream or cry.

Jack stayed there for a few minutes, observing the ever more distant leonine. He felt empty inside. This was just punishment for Artus's crimes—the man definitely deserved it. However, acting like this also polluted Jack.

The heart shaped one's actions, and one's actions shaped the heart in turn.

Jack gave Artus a final glance as he steered deeper and deeper into the darkness. He then turned around and approached the starship. "I want to spend some time alone," he said. "Don't follow me." Jack teleported away, following the periphery of the galaxy.

A few moments later, when he was certain they could no longer perceive him, he changed course. His body angled toward the galaxy, heading deeper. He could sense exactly where he was and where he wanted to go.

There was something he needed to do, but it was something which brought him fear. He wasn't sure if he was doing the right thing. All he knew was that his hatred was too great, and that he'd once taken an oath he could not bear to violate.

He did not want this to be seen by the others—especially Brock.

Reaching into his space ring, Jack removed the starship he'd been given by the Black Hole People. It hadn't seen much use, since they had the *Trampling Ram*, but it was perfect for just himself. He flew into it and teleported away.

Stars passed by. The starship teleported over and over, heading deeper into the galaxy. A few hours later, it approached a familiar area—the one he'd just been in. Animal Planet appeared in the distance. Jack performed a final teleportation, appearing over it and stashing away the ship. His aura erupted —a tremendous wave which submerged the planet.

Jack had once vowed that the name Emberheart would cease to exist in the galaxy. He could sense that fulfilling such an oath would scar him permanently, but he saw no other way. He couldn't go forward, and he couldn't go backward. He hated himself—but he would still do this. For Eric. His son needed to be avenged, and this was the only way Jack knew.

The only way to quench his hatred.

In fact, Jack would have liked to do this in front of Artus Emberheart. The only reason he hadn't was that he needed to lure Brock and the others away so they wouldn't see this side of him. Though the *Trampling Ram* could travel faster than his little starship, they had no reason to return so quickly—they probably remained at the edge of the galaxy for a while, discussing various things. That relieved him greatly.

As for why he didn't want them to see this... He didn't dare consider it. Even he had a limit—he wasn't strong enough. The pain was agony. The hatred, endless. He needed to complete this task. To end this, once and for all.

I can allow myself one misstep, he thought. *I've earned this.*

Animal Planet was not a war camp like Hell or Earthen Gemini. It contained regular cities, with merchants, children, old people, animals... All sorts of innocent creatures who'd never seen the harsh side of the Animal Kingdom. It also possessed two moons—one was the home of the Lonihor family, and the other the home of the Emberheart family.

Jack didn't plan to destroy the entire planet. However, starting today, it would only have one moon. The name Emberheart would cease to exist.

He appeared over the Emberheart Moon. His aura fell down, laced with killing intent. He readied his fist.

A few hurried figures flew up from the moon—some elderly Enforcers of the Emberheart family. "Wait, Overlord! There are children here! *Innocent* people! Take our lives, but please, show mercy for them!"

They were panicking. To them, Jack was a god of destruction about to kill everyone. They were even willing to give up their lives to protect their children.

Jack found that admirable, though he shook his head. "An eye for an eye. This is for my son."

They shouted many things, but Jack wasn't listening—he no longer knew what he felt. The world was hazy and dark.

His fist came down. A hundred mile-wide meteor appeared, easily able to shatter the entire moon, and it radiated a Dao so intense it was unstoppable. The elderly Enforcers cried out and banded together in a futile attempt to stop it. There was nothing that could be done—millions of innocent leonines would be slaughtered.

A golden light appeared out of nowhere—the phantom of a massive staff, smashing into the falling meteor and shattering both. The elderly leonines were pushed away by the shockwave. A storm blew over the moon below.

"That's enough!" a voice bellowed.

Brock stood in the ruins of Jack's attack, his staff extended, staring him down. Though separated by hundreds of miles, they felt as if standing face-to-face—and Brock's expression was dark with rage. He shouted, "Shut the fuck up!"

CHAPTER FORTY-NINE
OVER MY DEAD BODY

JACK WAS DAZED. THIS HAD OCCURRED TOO SUDDENLY—BROCK, WHO was supposed to be far away, had appeared and blocked his attack. He'd shielded the Emberheart Moon.

"What did you say?" Jack replied, half-angry and half-surprised. It was the first time Brock spoke against him—and with such ferocity, too. This was similar to challenging him.

"I said, that's enough," Brock repeated. His fur was risen, his eyes narrowed. He was breathing heavily out of anger. "What the hell do you think you're doing? Were you really going to murder all these people, Jack?"

Jack opened his mouth to reply but was shaken. Jack?

He and Brock had been together almost since the Integration. He'd basically watched the brorilla grow up. In all that time, Brock had never called Jack by name.

For some reason, hearing his name be uttered by the brorilla's lips shook his world. Jack was wreathed in hatred, anger, despair, grief. He was trapped in darkness, and the only way out was to destroy the moon below him.

"I am getting revenge for my son," he replied heavily. "What do you think you're doing, Brock?"

"My duty." The brorilla puffed out his chest. "You are making a mistake. As your bro, I cannot allow that."

"Oh yeah? Do you really think you can stop me?"

"I don't think. I know I can."

An intense golden aura erupted from Brock's body. It washed away the stars and flooded the moon below. The elderly Enforcers were once again flung backward, and they retreated as far as they could.

Brock's aura shone like the sun, then gathered around him to form the outline of a massive, transparent, golden brorilla. It adopted a battle stance with its staff extended. Brock was in its chest, where its heart should be, in the exact same stance. His anger melted into calm resolve.

"You have protected me many times before," he said with resolve. "Now, it is my turn to protect you."

Jack was frozen. Brock wanted to fight him? He had to fight Brock? This was too much, too quickly, too sudden. His entire being protested—but the darkness in his heart rose up, engulfing his mind, reminding him that this was a challenge he had to accept. He needed to destroy this place—and whoever stood in his way would be destroyed as well.

Jack clenched his fist. A purple aura erupted, so dense it was almost physical, clashing against the brorilla's. Gold and purple split the sky—two brothers fighting.

"Why are you doing this, Brock?" Jack shouted. "Why do you have to make me do this!"

"If you kill these innocent people," Brock replied calmly, "you will never be able to return. You will have become what you hate—no better than Artus Emberheart. I will die before letting that happen."

Jack clenched his teeth. His aura fluctuated. "Don't push me, Brock! I must do this. I must avenge my son!"

"This is not avenging anyone," Brock replied. "Eric is gone.

He has already been avenged. All you are doing now is indulging in your darkness."

"How can you think you know better than me!"

"Because you are blinded, and I am not."

Brock's stance remained hard. He would not take a single step backward. As for Jack, he felt trapped. He didn't want to fight, but he couldn't bear to go back now. He couldn't abandon Eric. He couldn't let him down again. He'd taken an oath in his son's name to wipe the name Emberheart off this galaxy.

"I really will attack, Brock!" he warned again.

"Good. Come," the brorilla replied. "Let me see if your darkness can overcome the light of brohood."

More golden light erupted. It didn't only blind Jack, but it also reached deep into his soul and seared something inside it. His Dao Fruit of Brotherhood shook as if wanting to rip itself off the tree. Jack felt himself grow weaker.

What's happening? he thought. *Is the Dao of Brotherhood against me? Does it disapprove of my actions?*

At the same time Jack grew weaker, streams of power converged to Brock from all across the galaxy. The golden brorilla grew more solid, more real, until it resembled a larger and shinier version of Brock.

Jack grew incensed. "Do you think this is enough?" he shouted. "That a few tricks can close the gap between us? Do you really intend to challenge me!"

"I don't want to fight you, Jack, but I will not let you pass."

How strong is Brock? Jack tried to calculate. They were both at eight fruits—however, Jack himself had benefited from many more opportunities. His strength should be much higher than Brock's. Hell, it should be incomparable to any other C-Grade's.

So why did he feel a vague sense of threat?

Come to think of it, Jack's greatest breakthrough had come when he suffered in grief for a year. Hadn't Brock endured the same? While Jack was in the Black Hole World, Brock had thought him dead. Who knows how many insights he'd gained during that time. How much stronger he'd gotten.

Jack realized he actually didn't have a gauge on Brock's strength. By all reasoning, it shouldn't be comparable to his, or Brock would have joined him in the final battle against the Animal Kingdom.

Would he really have to attack his little brother?

Jack was trapped. Deadlocked. He roared and released his power, buffeting Brock's golden brorilla. He felt it give way. Brock was standing his ground, but only barely. Even if he could fight Jack for a bit, he couldn't win. He was strong, stronger than any C-Grade Jack had ever seen, but less so than Jack himself. His chances of victory were tiny.

So why? *Why* was he doing this? Why was he putting Jack in such a dilemma? Did he not care?

An intense anger suffocated Jack. All his other emotions had been transmuted into it. The only thing holding him back was a tiny suspicion at the back of his mind—could he be wrong?

For Brock to stand up like this, he had to be completely confident, and Jack himself had always doubted this course of action. Could it be that Jack was wrong, and Brock really was trying to protect him?

Did that even matter? The pain Jack felt at meeting his bro's full-force resistance was inconsequential. He needed to avenge his son. He needed to complete his oath. How could he abandon his child once again?

A colosseum faintly shimmered into existence around them. The spectators weren't shouting like usual—they were deathly silent. An aura of tragedy hung over the world. Jack stood in the sky, a dark gladiator facing his own brother.

"This is my third and final warning, Brock," he growled. "Step aside."

The brorilla snorted. "Make me."

That's it, Jack thought, seeing red. That's enough. He clenched his fist. His aura erupted, filled with brutality. He'd already been driven to the limit—now was the time to smash his brother unconscious, and damned be the consequences.

Jack charged.

More flashes appeared around Brock. The *Trampling Ram* came into view. Gan Salin, Nauja, Bomn, Vashter... All the people he'd traveled with for months, all his companions, stood side by side against him. They rallied around Brock.

Even if their power was completely negligible, they still banded together, readying themselves to fight him.

Jack skidded to a stop. The solidarity of his friends against him hurt him deeply.

"I may be insane, but right now, so are you," Gan Salin said, stretching out his fingernails. "If you want to pass, Jack, you'll need to do it over our dead bodies. This is us protecting you!"

"See the light!" Nauja shouted.

"Be strong!" Bomn added in anger. "You are better than this, Jack!"

Jack laughed. "All of you would stand against me? You would all abandon me? I guess I really am alone! *This is the only way!*"

"What bullshit are you spouting?" Brock shouted back. "You're losing it, Jack. Pull yourself together!"

"I'm the one losing it? Look around you, Brock. I must avenge my son, you know I need to! I must complete the oath I made in his name! I don't want to do this, but I have to!"

"Are you even listening to yourself?" Brock shouted, completely losing his composure. "How can you be so blind? My son this and my son that. That's all you refer to him as! Your son! You don't call him Eric anymore, and do you know why?

Because this isn't about him, but about you. You aren't avenging anyone. This is not grief—*it's pride!*"

Jack felt like a bomb exploded inside his head. He momentarily lost contact with the world. His heart was shaken. Pride?

Was he really avenging Eric? Or was he only lashing out about the fact that, by killing his son, someone had wounded his pride? Even worse, was this all just an attempt to excuse himself for his past failures?

His mind screamed no, but a tiny voice inside him whispered maybe.

Who am I? Jack thought, the only question he could come up with.

His aura fell into disarray. His Dao shook. Sensing that, Brock sighed in relief, then let his aura soften as well.

"It's okay, bro," he said. "It's not too late. You still haven't done anything bad. You remain whole—just see the light."

Jack looked inside himself. He saw the phantom of Eric demanding justice—but as he took a closer look, the phantom warped, turning into a vision of Jack himself. The real Eric was standing behind him, crying in silence.

"Eric?" Jack whispered.

"Dad..." Eric muttered, his voice covered with sobs.

"I-I'm doing this for you!" Jack tried to justify himself. "You deserve it. You are worth more to me than all those leonines. This is the only way I can balance out your death!"

"There is nothing to balance, Dad..." Eric whispered. "I don't want this. I just want people to stop dying. I just want... peace. Don't make more people cry. Please."

Jack's lip trembled. He, a hardened cultivator of the Fist, the overlord of a galaxy, almost lost control of his emotions. The phantom of Eric disappeared, and Jack felt pressed against a mental wall which caused him extreme pain. All his instincts screamed to back away and forget about this.

He could sense this was a trial. With a deep breath, he dared to look into himself in earnest, to step through the wall. It was the hardest step he'd taken in his entire life.

And the wall shattered. There were no more ghosts. Only Jack, the world, and the future. His pain existed only because he refused to let it go. Because he feared that, if he stopped feeling grief and fighting for revenge, it would mean abandoning Eric again.

But that was not the case. Eric wouldn't want it. He never liked conflict. All he wanted, all he ever desired, was peace.

Jack let go.

Eric appeared again, a ghost that was smiling this time. "Goodbye, Dad. Live a happy life for me, okay? Protect Mom and Ebele."

Jack teared up. "I will. I promise you, Eric... I will."

Eric smiled and vanished forever. Jack was empty. Warm fur pressed against his skin as a brorilla embraced him, hiding his tears from the world, supporting him through thick and thin, being there like only a true bro could.

"I'm sorry..." Jack managed to say.

"It's okay, bro," Brock said softly. "Nobody is perfect. We all make mistakes. As long as we have our bros... Everything is okay."

Jack couldn't reply. More people fell around them—Gan Salin, Nauja... They embraced Jack and smothered him with brotherly love, filling his empty insides with warmth. Jack was so exhausted, but also reborn. He'd seen through the mysteries of life and death today—not as a cultivator, but as a person.

"Thank you..." he whispered. "Without you, I'm nothing."

"We all are," Brock replied with a smile. "Alone, we are nothing. Only together are we real."

CHAPTER FIFTY

RETURNING TO EARTH

JACK DECIDED NOT TO KILL EVERY EMBERHEART. HOWEVER, HE HAD promised to erase that name off the galaxy, so he forced them to change their last names. The Emberheart family renamed itself to Openchest, completely humiliating themselves in the process. It was a choice for survival—those who refused to accept the change, almost a quarter of the adult population, were honorably executed by the family themselves.

It was not an easy period for the former Emberheart family. Those proud leonines had never had to bow their heads before. But for their children to survive, they steeled their hearts and did it.

On that day, the name Emberheart finally disappeared from the Milky Way Galaxy. Jack also instated an order that anyone found using that last name was to be captured, leonine or otherwise. And so, his oath to Eric was fulfilled, through not in the way anyone expected.

Jack had basically conquered the Animal Kingdom. He fell onto the surface of Animal Planet, spreading his aura with no one daring to match him. Children gazed at him with awe—adults felt terror through their closed shutters. He didn't plan to mistreat the Kingdom—didn't plan to become like them. He would simply distance himself from the matters of the Milky Way, letting things progress as they would.

After conquering the Kingdom and destroying his pursuers in the Hand of God, Jack still had six days remaining before the Heavenly Spoon Sovereign was set to arrive. He planned to publicize his location and wait for someone with the teleporter frequency of Earth to come to him. Thankfully, that wasn't necessary. He found Shol in the dungeons of Animal Planet. The monk was safe, if a bit famished. He'd been here all along, captured by the Kingdom a little before Jack's return to the galaxy.

"It's been a while, brother," Jack said with a smile, walking through a jail door. A skinny man awaited him, rubbing his wrists. His poor health did nothing to affect his good mood.

"Jack!" he exclaimed, rushing forward to hug his savior. "Is it true? Did you really defeat the Animal Kingdom?"

"Every Elder, Ancestor, and Supreme Ancestor," Jack replied. "Along with some Envoys from the Hand of God."

"But that's... That's amazing!" Shol shook his head, still stuck in disbelief. "I can't believe that my little F-Grade disciple made it this far."

"Yeah... Neither can I. Sorry for being late, brother."

"It's okay. They didn't mistreat me too much. I'm fine."

The last thing Jack did before leaving Animal Planet was release every war criminal they kept. The vast majority were just captured rebels—people who deserved to be free. He also inspected the Kingdom's vast treasuries, taking everything that caught his eye. Some treasures were more interesting than others, but he put them aside for later, just as he had with the space rings of Eva Solvig and the other Envoy.

The Kingdom was once again humiliated, but there was nothing they could do about it. Rumors about disbanding their faction were already in circulation. Jack and his bros finally took off, leaving behind a broken empire overrun with rebels.

In the near future, the Animal Kingdom would formally dissolve, breaking into numerous smaller factions which escaped to other constellations. The former Animal Kingdom constellation would be renamed the Bare Fist constellation, in honor of Jack, and would be led by a coalition of forces—at least for a while.

Jack neither knew about these nor did he care. His job was done. Instead, he traveled to the nearest teleporter hub—Derion, the poison planet.

Earth had changed its teleporter frequency after Artus Emberheart's raid. Shol hadn't visited since then, but thankfully, the professor had thought ahead. She'd had him memorize a set of frequencies, saying that if they had to change for any reason, they'd use some of the other frequencies in the set. Therefore, Shol only needed a little experimenting to find the right frequency and connect to Earth.

Jack took a deep breath, staring at the spinning purple vortex. So many feelings warred inside him—anxiety, excitement, worry, guilt... He hadn't seen his family in five years. He had no idea how they would react. How he would react.

However, he knew it would all be fine. After that knot in his heart had been resolved, he felt reborn. At peace. The happiness and sadness of life washed over him, but he remained tranquil. The worst was behind him. Whatever happened next, he could deal with it.

A hand fell on his shoulders. "You got this, bro."

Jack turned, smiling. "Thanks, Brock."

The two of them stepped into the teleporter, followed by Gan Salin, Nauja, and Shol. As for Bomn and Vashter, they'd decided to stay, taking the *Trampling Ram* and assisting the constellation however they could.

Stars spun around them. The galaxy became a speeding blur, and before long, Jack's feet rested solidly on grass. He breathed in that so familiar air. Tall trees lay strewn ahead of him, crowded by brorilla guards ready to fight.

The moment they saw him, they paused mid-assault. Then, they let out a joyful cry which spread over the trees, scaring away the birds. They rushed to hug them all.

Jack laughed. "We're back!"

A new cry responded to the brorillas. Harambe fell from the sky and slammed against the ground. His fur had developed gray tufts, and his eyes were darker than they used to be—but he'd reached the D-Grade, so he would live for many, many years.

Brock stepped out to meet him. He'd grown. At only a couple feet shorter, he seemed like a copy of his father when standing face to face. He smiled. "Hello, Father. Your son is back."

Harambe tried really hard to keep a straight face. He couldn't. Tears marred his manly face, and he lunged toward his son, wrapping him in a tight embrace. The relief he exuded was otherworldly. Even Brock was touched—he froze, then his hands wrapped around his father's back and held him tightly.

Everyone else stayed silent for this reunion when a third cry cut through the air as a black form hurtled toward them at supersonic speed. It came to a stop ahead of Jack, the force of its extinguished momentum blowing everyone's clothes backward.

Jack laid his eyes on a tall, dark-skinned woman. Her hair reached her shoulders, fluttering in the wind, while a red and blue robe covered her body. She remained opposite Jack, staring at him. She said no words—but her eyes spoke more than her mouth ever could. In those eyes, Jack could see relief, anger, hesitation. She didn't know how to react, how to greet him, what she felt. The time they'd spent apart had been so much that even their current relationship was unclear. She'd looked forward to this moment so much, but now that it unexpectedly arrived, she was afraid.

Facing her alternating feelings, Jack smiled and stepped forward. He stood right in front of her—and she did not push him away. He ran a hand over her cheek. "I'm sorry for making you worry, my love," he said. "I'm back."

She lost her breath. "Welcome home..." she finally managed to say before Jack drew her into a warm kiss containing all his loneliness, his despair, his need for her, how much he'd missed her. She melted in his arms, and he on her lips. They hugged, completely forgetting about everyone else that was present.

It was only a bit later that they simultaneously realized what they were doing. Vivi tried to pull back.

"It's okay," he said. "I'm really happy to see you. Have you been well?"

"Kind of. Have you?"

"Kind of."

They smiled, sharing each other's pain, and only then did they withdraw. Jack looked around, finding many familiar faces staring at them. Even Edgar had arrived—a scholarly man with a sharp beard and an air of confidence. His eyes hadn't lost their spark. If anything, they shone even brighter.

As Jack was about to go over and greet him, he noticed someone else. A little girl, barely six or seven years old, staring at him from behind a tree. Straight black hair fell over her dark skin, while her wide olive eyes were glued on Jack. He could see so many things in those eyes—and it pained him that beneath everything else hid hardness. This girl was growing fine, as well as she could without him.

Jack smiled warmly. "Hi, Ebele." He spread his arms.

Her hesitation melted. The hardness in her eyes receded,

and she bolted into his arms, almost throwing him backward. Her little arms wrapped tightly around his chest. "Dad!" she squealed, bursting into tears. Jack placed a hand on the back of his daughter's head, holding her tenderly.

"I'm sorry," he said with tears in his eyes. "I'm back."

She buried her face in his chest, crying her heart out, releasing five long years of worries. Her father was here. It was like a heavy weight had been lifted off her small chest, letting her breathe normally for the first time in a long while.

Jack sensed that his daughter had endured more things than a child was supposed to... But, he was here now. At least for a while. He would do his best to make up for his years of absence.

"Jack," Vivi whispered by his side. "There is something you should know. About Eric..."

"I know," Jack replied calmly. "He's gone. I'm sorry."

He watched her eyes fall into grief. It wasn't that she didn't expect this—ever since Eric had been kidnapped a year and a half ago, she knew this was by far the likeliest scenario. She and everyone else had prepared themselves. It was just that she'd always held out a little bit of hope. Now, hearing the decisive truth, that final strand of hope disappeared and left her wallowing in darkness.

Her eyes turned red. Jack felt Ebele clench his chest even tighter, her muffled sobs turning sadder. He closed his eyes. There was nothing he could do. Death was a part of life—it wasn't something he could punch away, no matter how hard he tried.

"Let's go," he said softly. He wrapped both his wife and daughter in a spatial distortion and teleported directly into their living room. Vivi stumbled in surprise. Ebele hadn't even realized they'd moved. When she raised her head to look around, she released a small yelp.

"Let me tell you everything," Jack said, sitting them both down. He detailed his experiences since he'd last left them. The Green Dragon hidden realm, his three years of cultivation there, then his return to the Milky Way and his attempts to reach Earth. He spoke about Eric's passing, not going into detail, then narrated his experience in the Black Hole World. Finally, he told them how he'd destroyed the Animal Kingdom and Hand of God branch in the Milky Way.

The two women listened, not commenting much.

"What about you?" Jack finally asked.

Vivi told him about the years they'd spent on Earth. How the professor—Jack's mother—had stepped down from running the planet and retired to a small cottage nearby. How Vivi had taken over, working herself to the bone to enhance the power of Earthen cultivators.

"We even discovered the C-Grade Dungeon of this planet," she said. "A huge ocean deep underground. It circles almost the entire planet—its volume is many times greater than all the surface oceans combined."

"Really?" Jack asked. "Are there many new species there?"

"Well, there are some."

A C-Grade Dungeon wouldn't do much for him anymore. He still had to develop his ninth fruit and receive the rest of the levels from the battle, but... Those could wait. He didn't have too much time here. He would spend it all with his family.

"And you, Ebele?" he asked.

"I practiced," she said. "I learned languages, martial arts, I tempered my body. I want to become strong."

Jack couldn't help his sad smile. He was proud, but also deeply distraught. The life of a cultivator was not easy. It saddened him to imagine his daughter going through the same things he had. The life and death battles, the danger, the pain, the tribulations, the loneliness... Her simple words, "I want to become strong," contained more depth than her mind was currently able to fit.

However, it was pointless to dictate another person's path, even if it was his daughter. Everyone had their own destiny. All he could do was help her traverse it as best as possible.

"Okay," he replied, not showing any of his feelings. "Daddy will train with you a bit, okay?"

Her face brightened up.

"Will you stay for long, Jack?" Vivi asked.

"No..." he replied. "I must go soon. They will come to pick me up, and I can't say no."

Her disappointment was evident. "How long?"

"Six days."

"Six days! You've been gone for *five years* and you're only staying for *six days*?"

It was understandable that she was upset. Even Ebele was surprised. This really was too little time.

"It's not as bad as it sounds," Jack said. "I can alter the flow of time now. It's useless for cultivating, but when it comes to spending time together, I can make it last three times as long."

Vivi pouted. "It's still not enough..."

"It never could be," he replied, then sighed. "I missed you too, Vivi. Both of you. I hate that I will have to leave again soon, but it's what I must do. Let's just spend this time together, okay? Please..."

Both looked into his eyes. Ebele nodded with understanding. "Okay!"

CHAPTER FIFTY-ONE

SPENDING TIME WITH FAMILY

TWO PEOPLE FACED EACH OTHER IN A SPACIOUS BACKYARD. THE WIND caressed the grass under their feet, while the blue sky was framed by distant mountains. The breeze blew gently.

Ebele stood with her legs spread apart and her arms raised —the combat stance she was most familiar with. Opposite her, Jack stood with his arms behind his back, looking completely relaxed. Only the faint smirk on his face betrayed his happiness.

"Begin," he said.

Ebele shouted and charged forth. Her feet took her across the grass to reach him quickly. A jab flew out, which Jack calmly leaned back to avoid. The first jab was followed by three more, which Jack effortlessly floated around. Ebele feinted a kick to his thigh, then swept in to smash him in the face. Jack raised a hand to tap hers, sending it slightly off course. He then grabbed her wrist and tossed her away.

"Again," he said.

This was a form of sparring. Of course, Jack and Ebele were at completely different levels of power, but Jack had used the Concept of Time to slow himself down a thousandfold, bringing their speed and awareness to similar levels. He couldn't do anything about his overwhelming advantage in power or durability, but that was fine. This was about technique.

Of course, even in just technique, there could be no real comparison between them. It didn't matter how slow Jack made himself. He'd been fighting for his life bare-fisted since before Ebele was born. He had battled a wide array of opponents across the universe, studied in various factions with various teachers, and had even been kickstarted in combat skills by the System.

Most importantly, his Dao of the Fist had reached such an advanced level that he no longer needed martial arts—his understanding of the Fist was deep enough that all the right movements flowed instinctively out of him. Even excluding the difference in cultivation, there was no martial artist on Earth that could face him on equal grounds. Jack was qualified to teach Ebele's teachers, let alone her.

However, this wasn't just about teaching.

Jack bent his body, letting Ebele roll over his back and awkwardly land behind him. When she tried to catch him with a roundhouse kick, he just grabbed her ankle and pushed her back. "Again!"

There was a certain excitement to sparring with your child. Her moves weren't bad. Every time she demonstrated her skills or tried a novel approach, Jack was filled with pride. This was his daughter, following the same path as him.

Ebele steadied herself and pouted. She was competitive and didn't like to lose. For years she'd fantasized about sparring against her father and showing him how good she'd become, but she never imagined the difference would be this large.

She flew in again, her moves fiercer. Her punches were like thunderbolts, her kicks like swords. Jack calmly defended against everything, demonstrating faults in her technique she didn't even know were there. She was panting, while he wasn't even breaking a sweat.

Ebele grew irritated. She leaned heavier into offense, giving him openings to counterattack because she knew he wouldn't. Her teachers would have frowned at this, but she didn't care, she just wanted to land one hit. She dove into his guard, shooting a straight punch at his abdomen.

Surprisingly, he didn't dodge. Her little fist landed against his stomach, but it felt like she'd punched a wall. Before she could retreat, his arm came around, pulling her into a hug. "Mff," she said. Jack laughed out loud.

"That's enough," he said, letting her go with a smile. "You win."

"Hmph!" She crossed her arms. "That doesn't count! You let me!"

"Maybe I did, maybe I didn't."

"You weren't supposed to let me. I want to earn it!"

Jack lowered himself to be at eye level. "It's not about earning anything. It's about getting better. And, you're pretty good! I'm proud of you."

He tussled her hair. If it was anyone else or any other time, she would have bitten their hand off. Now? She didn't even notice. She was busy being stunned. Dad... is proud of me?

He's proud of me!

Against her will, a large smile formed. "Thanks," was all she managed to say, but Jack only laughed, straightening up again.

"Martial arts lose their significance the more you cultivate, but they are the foundation on which Physical Daos are built. They help you find the way through the lower Grades. The better you understand them, the smoother your road will be."

"I know that!" Ebele hurried to exclaim. "Master Meredith says the same! Just... in more words."

Jack smiled. "I wouldn't expect any less. All your teachers

are qualified people. However, Ebele, Vivi tells me you've been pushing yourself a lot lately."

"Mm." She looked down. "I just wanted to become strong, like you. To protect Mom. Is it that bad?"

Jack sighed. "I am the last person who should advise you against pushing yourself. However, you got it wrong. Cultivation is all about the Dao, and the Dao is all about understanding the world. If you really want to reach far in the future, overworking yourself right now is counterproductive. You're only six—"

"Six and a half!"

"Right. Six and a half. This is the time for you to be a child. Martial arts and preparing yourself for cultivation are good, but you shouldn't focus too much on them yet. Otherwise, when the time comes to really cultivate, you will discover that your foundation has gaps. You should embrace all parts of life, not deny them—even the ones which seem useless."

She pouted. "But I don't want to be a child. I want to be strong!"

"Every strong person was a child once. Don't be in a rush. You'll get there when you get there."

"But—"

"Unless you think you know better than me, of course. In that case, feel free to ruin your future by pushing yourself too hard too early."

Ebele looked up to find her father's strict gaze. "Sorry," she said, not quite knowing what she was apologizing for. "I... I'll try."

Jack remained silent for a moment, not acknowledging her response. Finally, he sighed. "You know I love you, right?"

"Yeah!"

"Good. Then, you listen to me, okay? No more overworking. There'll be plenty of time for that once you grow older. For now, just be a good girl and follow the schedule your teachers give you. Okay?"

"Okay," she said, and Jack pulled her into an embrace again. With all her eloquence and maturity, it was hard to remember he was speaking to a six-year-old child.

Six and a half, he corrected himself. "Oh. Lunch is almost ready," he said. "Let's go find your mother."

She cheered. "Okay!

———

Vivi and Ebele weren't the only people Jack wanted to see.

As night was falling, he pushed open the door of a little cottage in the woods. "Mom?" he called out. "I'm here!"

A white-haired head poked out of a corridor. "Jack!" the professor exclaimed, rushing over to hug him. She seemed older than Jack remembered. Her hair had turned completely white, her eyes were tired, and many more wrinkles filled her face. Even for someone as experienced as her, running an entire planet was stressful.

It wasn't the first time Jack saw her, of course. He made sure to visit at least every two days.

"I'm glad you're still safe," she said, drawing back to take a better look at him.

He laughed. "I'm fine, Mom. Even if every gang on the planet teamed up, I could beat them with a single finger."

"I know that, but a mother can't help but worry."

Jack's heart warmed. He used to call her Professor in the past—a habit he'd picked up since joining university, a joke which stuck around. After everything that happened with Eric and reuniting with his family, Jack felt a new attachment to familial bonds. Calling her anything other than Mom was stupid; he'd only done so in the past to create some distance between them, as young people unconsciously liked to do.

But Jack, while young for a cultivator, was now thirty-five years old and a planetarch. The antiques of youth no longer suited him.

"How is my grand-daughter?" Margaret asked—that was her name, Margaret Rust.

"She's good," Jack replied as he followed her deeper into the house.

"Did you tell her to stop being hard on herself?"

"I tried."

"And?"

"I think she got it."

Margaret smiled. "You were the same way, you know. Once you got an idea inside your head, you wouldn't listen to anyone. Only your father could somehow persuade you."

"Yeah... I can see the similarity."

"Did you know I built a memorial for him? A big statue on a small uninhabited island nearby. It's called Rust Island now. I even moved over his grave—I figure it's more special than just another tablet at the Valville Cemetery."

"Oh? Do I hear a little illusion of grandeur?"

She playfully rolled her eyes. "Oh, grow up, Jack. I used to rule the planet—honoring my late husband and your father is natural. He would have loved the change—always liked to be a little extra."

"I remember." He laughed. "How are you?"

"I'm fine. The System gave us many resources, and so did you. Though I'll never reach the D-Grade, extending my life by a few decades is possible."

"I'm glad, but that's not what I meant."

She glanced at him, falling into an armchair she'd had brought over from their house in Valville. Jack sat on an equally familiar couch. "I'm coping," Margaret finally admitted. "I miss working, sometimes, but I have to admit that running a planet in wartime almost broke me. That, and also..." She shook her head. "In any case, I am no longer fit to lead. I'm old. It's much better for Vivi to take over, let her shape the planet as she wants and get the people familiar with it. After all, I'll be dead soon, but she'll stick around for centuries in the least."

Jack shook his head. "It's a pity the System didn't arrive a few decades earlier. With your talent, you might have reached the D-Grade."

"If the System arrived earlier, you wouldn't be there, and we'd all be either dead or slaves."

"Who knows? Maybe someone else would have taken my place."

"Maybe... Well, enough with those subjects. Tea?"

"Yes, please."

He didn't need to sleep, and she could go without it for a day. Jack stayed with his mother deep into the night. He also inwardly pledged to visit as often as possible.

After he left Earth this time, who knew how long it would be before he could return. Vivi and Ebele would still be here, but his mother... No one could tell.

What cruel irony. He had just looted the vaults of the Animal Kingdom and gotten many high-level treasures, yet none of them could push his mother into the D-Grade. These might be their final days together. He wanted to cherish them.

Such was the life of a cultivator: lonely and isolated. Losing track of time. Even if he used the Concept of Time to encapsulate the entire Forest of the Strong in a time distortion and stretch out the remaining few days until he had to leave, he could at most make them into a couple weeks.

It was cruelly short.

———

The Spoon Squad was crossing the sea between galaxies, approaching the Milky Way at a speed vastly surpassing that of light.

"We're making good pace!" Sovereign Heavenly Spoon exclaimed, observing the star map projection. "I thought it would take us a week, but it looks like we'll have arrived in just five days! Good job, Bottomless."

"Thank you," the cloaked form replied.

Another person approached—a homeless-looking man with tattered clothes and crooked yellow teeth. The Sage. "I had a sudden premonition," he said.

"Oh?" the sovereign replied. "Did someone find us?"

"I'm not sure... But, I think it will be safer if we take a small detour."

He pointed at the astral map, using his Dao to draw a new trajectory for their ship.

The sovereign raised a brow. "Are you sure? That seems like we're just flying in circles. It will extend our trip by three days."

"That's my suggestion. I can't really explain it—if you would rather continue in a straight line, we can."

The sovereign shook his head. "It's fine. You're our diviner—trusting your intuition is only proper. Besides, three days is a cheap price to pay for our increased safety. Take the new route, Bottomless."

The cloaked form did not reply, but the ship subtly changed directions, adopting a new trajectory toward the Milky Way which seemed needlessly long.

The Sage smiled as he returned to his seat. You're welcome, Jack.

CHAPTER FIFTY-TWO

LEAVING AGAIN

JACK HAD DECIDED TO PRIORITIZE SPENDING TIME WITH HIS FAMILY while on Earth, but there were still many people he wanted to meet. Therefore, he invited them all together.

A bottle of wine rested at the center of a table, while five people sat around it. They were Jack, Edgar, Dordok, Dorman, and Huali. Five people whose paths all led them to Earth.

"I cannot believe you destroyed the Animal Kingdom," Huali said, raising her cup. "It's like a dream."

"And I can't believe I'm sitting with the Grand Elder of the Exploding Sun," Dordok joked. He was much larger than humans, being an ogre, so the cup in his hand looked comically small.

"There is nothing grand about me," Huali replied, shaking her head. "The Sun fell during my watch. I have shamed my ancestors."

"Speaking of that," Jack said. "I've wondered about something for a while. Didn't your faction have Supreme Ancestors like the Animal Kingdom? How did Eva Solvig manage to destroy you?"

Huali sighed. "She didn't come alone. The peak B-Grade

Envoy responsible for the Milky Way Galaxy was alongside her. Before that man, our Supreme Ancestors collapsed like mortals... It was only afterward that he left for the Crusade."

"I see. Sorry for the painful memories."

"It's fine. I've made my peace with what happened. With the Kingdom and the most powerful Envoys dead, I plan to leave this planet soon and try to re-establish the Exploding Sun. I know the hiding place of one of our Ancestors—she might be able to help."

"Are you sure?" Jack asked. "There are many B-Grades left in the galaxy. You could come under fire."

"I am duty-bound to try. If fate wants my faction to die, then so be it. Thank you for letting me hide in your planet until now."

Jack nodded, not insisting further.

Beside him, Edgar chuckled. "And here I thought I could convince you to stay as a professor at my academy. A peak C-Grade would have skyrocketed our prestige."

"Sorry to disappoint," Huali said with a small smile. Edgar had been approaching her about this subject for months now. Though she'd always maintained her neutral position, they'd become friends by now.

"What about you, Dordok, Dorman?" Edgar asked. "Anyone willing to teach the new generations?"

"I might as well," Dordok replied. "I've spent my entire life traveling the galaxy on the *Trampling Ram*. Now that I've retired, I think a more stable life would do me good."

"I won't stay," Dorman said. "I'm a cultivator of the Church. Now that Earth is safe, I want to join the war."

"I'll ask the sovereign, but I don't think there's going to be a problem," Jack replied. "I'm sure Edgar has many great professors already lined up."

The wizard pouted. "Well, they're great, but not galaxy-level great, you know? I wanted to have every professor be a D-Grade or above, as well as a couple of C-Grades. Only then can my Academy stand at the highest level."

"No it can't," everyone else replied at the same time, then laughed about it.

"Yeah, laugh all you want. I gotta start from somewhere!" Edgar protested, laughing himself. "Oh, yeah. Jack, Dorman, remember that old, Asian martial arts master from the Integration Tournament? The one who fell during the final battle?"

"Li Xiang?" Jack asked. "Of course I remember. What about him?"

"His head disciple will come to the academy as a professor. You should see him—he has a fourth tier Skill."

"Really?" Dorman raised a brow. "That's more than me."

"I only have one of those," Jack said.

Huali scoffed. "Youngsters," she commented, then shrunk back as everyone glared at her.

"Oh yeah?" Jack asked. "How many do you have?"

"Well, one... but I've had it for millennia!"

They laughed again. "Hey," Jack asked Huali, "how hard is it to develop tier four or five skills?"

"Very," she replied. "Tier three is generally the limit. Only a few C-Grades manage to get a single skill at the fourth tier. B-Grades generally have one or two... But I've never heard of anyone getting a fifth tier skill. I just know it's the limit."

"Hmm." Jack frowned. "Does that mean that me having a single fourth tier skill is behind the curve? I already have the combat strength of a late B-Grade."

Huali shook her head. "The curve on skill tiers isn't about power, but about time and talent. The only reason most B-Grades have fourth tier skills is because they've spent tens of thousands of years practicing them. If anything, achieving one at less than ten years of cultivation is a wonder. The same goes for that professor Edgar mentioned. It is absolutely not a common occurrence. Even if it was, what do you care? You can jump an entire Grade to fight. If that isn't special, I don't know what is."

"Just curious," Jack replied, shrugging.

Huali narrowed her eyes. "You're already itching to cultivate, aren't you?"

"Of course I am, but I'm am no fool to waste these days cultivating. My family takes precedence."

She nodded. "An admirable sentiment. If only more cultivators were like you."

"They aren't?"

"Of course not. Having a long timespan can alter one's sense of purpose. Many people treat their families as one treats garden plants—ephemeral, unimportant, and replenishable."

"That's terrible."

"It's a defense mechanism. You can't stand the endless loss otherwise." Her eyes fell. "Time has a way to turn people into statues... But don't let me get you down. Your family is talented—I'm sure they'll live for a really long time. Enjoy it, Jack."

He scratched his head. "You did bring me down a little, not gonna lie."

"I have the solution," Edgar said, raising the bottle. "More wine."

Everyone nodded. "More wine!"

———

Jack remained on Earth for six days. In his bubble of accelerated time, that was eighteen days—a full two and a half weeks.

The sovereign was supposed to arrive somewhere around that time, but he didn't. Jack assumed they'd met some trouble on the way but didn't think anything more of it. He was thankful about the extra time.

Another three days passed outside. In Jack's time bubble, that was a week and a half. Before he knew it, he'd already spent a month with his family.

During that month, he did not cultivate for even a second. He did not spare a thought toward his ninth Dao Fruit, which he was ready to develop. Even the space rings of Eva Solvig and the other Envoy were left almost untouched—Jack only did a rough scan, taking out all low-level treasures and donating them to Earth, where they could find some use. As for the interesting, high-level stuff he found in there... He ignored them completely. There would be time for them later—now was family time.

Every day was spent with his wife and daughter. His mother was there sometimes, as were other friends. Brock visited rarely, choosing to spend most of the time with his father and the other brorillas. Harambe only appeared once—he was too overwhelmed with joy at the return of his son. Jack also visited the brorillas once, bonding with the family of his little brother.

At other times, their small family of three enjoyed time together in their house which overlooked the Forest of the Strong. The view was great. So was the weather. The days passed simply, easily, full of love. Jack and Vivi reignited their relationship. Jack and Ebele finally got to know each other—last time he was here, she could barely speak.

He gave Vivi and Ebele the gifts he'd gotten them from the Black Hole World—the statuette of a warrior mother for Vivi, and a bronze heart of interlinked pieces for Ebele. They loved them. Both women hugged Jack, and he felt there was no greater reward in the world than their smiles.

Warm, fuzzy feelings filled Jack's heart. He completely forgot about the pain of war, the cruelty, the darkness, the loneliness. This was home. His hardened soul, which had been hammered in adversity, took this time to soften and complete his transformation into a new level—his mental and emotional ascent.

Jack felt like a new man. His heart was full of love. His mind was serene. These were some of the happiest moments of his life.

Of course, not all was perfect. Eric's loss was something they'd all had time to come to terms with, but it still hung over their heads sometimes, a thought nobody spoke about. Ebele was too young to truly feel the loss, but Vivi still cried at night sometimes. In those moments, Jack would hug her and keep her in his arms until she felt better again.

Ebele split the bronze heart Jack had given her into four pieces and gave one each to Vivi and Jack. She kept the other two—one was her piece, the other Eric's.

One day, the three of them held a small funeral for Eric. Jack placed the fourth piece of the bronze heart into the empty casket, then stepped away. Though gone now, Eric would forever remain part of this family. They buried him next to Jack's father, on the newly named Rust Island. The two Erics lay side by side. It was a necessary moment for closure, but also something Jack preferred not to think about—he focused on the bright times instead.

Losing a child was something that never truly went away. All they could do was strive to keep grief from ruining their lives —learn to handle it, and learn to be happy again. So far, they were succeeding. The sun still hung in the sky—their days remained bright.

The month passed easily. Jack enjoyed time with his family, and though he wasn't full, he knew he never could be. He also saw everyone he wanted to see during this time. Even Gan Salin and Nauja visited every once in a while, though they spent most of their time touring Earth. Neither was particularly good at handling their emotions.

Finally, nine days in real time after Jack returned to Earth, the sky trembled. A sleek starship slipped out of the void, coming to rest over the Forest of the Strong. Jack had been playing with Ebele at that moment. He released a long sigh.

"Daddy needs to take a moment," he said, teleporting before the ship. Five figures appeared before him—three familiar, two strangers.

"Oh," Jack said. "I didn't expect you two."

Min Ling smiled. "How could I miss the chance to visit the home planet of the famous Jack Rust?"

"This is my home as well." The Sage shrugged. "Hello, Jack. I see you've built a wonderful life for yourself."

Jack smiled back. "I have."

"What a peaceful little place," the Heavenly Spoon Sovereign said, looking around. "This is how things should be. No war, no strife, no killing each other. Only living happily and cultivating to deepen one's connection to the world. Anyway. This is the Jack Rust you've heard so much about. Jack, these are Envoys Bottomless and Starhair."

"Nice to meet you," Jack said. The two strangers nodded back. One was a hooded figure wearing a rippling cloak—just from looking at it, Jack could sense mighty fluctuations of spacetime.

"Good time bubble," the figure said, gazing at the time distortion around the Forest of the Strong.

"Thanks," Jack replied.

As for the last person present, that was a man with long hair which seemed like the starry branches of a galaxy—the so-called Envoy Starhair. He only replied with a tight nod to Jack's greeting, as if dissatisfied with something or maybe constipated. Jack could already tell he wouldn't like this person.

"Are you ready to go?" the sovereign said. "I'm sorry to rush you like this, but we've already delayed too much. We are needed at the front lines."

Jack hesitated. The Sage spoke up, saying, "I'm sure we can afford an hour for Jack to say his goodbyes."

Starhair stared at him, but the sovereign shrugged. "Of course. Is an hour okay with you, Jack?"

Jack nodded. "Yes. I've already concluded my business in the Milky Way. I just need to speak with my family."

"Perfect. Then, we'll wait."

Jack flashed away. He hastily bid his goodbyes to the people he cared about, then spent most of the hour with Vivi and Ebele. They were heartbroken to see him leave again. As a matter of fact, so was he—but there was no choice. His place wasn't here, but in the Crusade. There was no way around it. That was his life.

"Be good until I return, okay?" he said, planting a kiss on Ebele's forehead. "Practice hard, but not too hard. Don't forget to enjoy your childhood."

"Okay," she said, struggling not to cry. Jack then turned to Vivi, who fell into his arms.

"I'll miss you," she whispered with a hot breath.

"Me too..." Jack replied, hugging and kissing her tightly. Ebele made a sound and looked away—both her parents laughed.

"I'll try to return as soon as possible, but I don't know when that will be," Jack promised. "I love you both."

"Stay safe," Vivi said. "Don't do anything stupid."

Jack smiled. "You know me."

"That's exactly why I'm saying it."

He laughed. "I promise I'll be careful. I'll make you proud of me."

"We are already proud of you," Vivi said, grasping his hand. "Just come home safe. Okay?"

He felt his heart relax. "Okay." A final kiss later, he took a step back and said, "I love you."

"We love you too!" the two women responded. Jack gave them a final glance. He buried their image in his memory. While he cultivated bitterly and alone, fighting in the far reaches of the universe, this very image would be what gave him the strength to endure.

"See you," he said, then flew away. He didn't look back—not sure he could hold his tears if he did.

Soon, he reached the sleek starship again, where the Spoon Squad awaited. Brock and Dorman were also present.

"All ready?" the sovereign asked, and Jack nodded. "Good. Then, let's board. Next stop, the Second Crusade!"

"Okay, bro," Brock replied, following the rest into the starship. The last ones remaining outside were Jack and the Heavenly Spoon Sovereign.

"Your strength is growing rapidly," said the sovereign, scanning Jack with his eyes. He then smiled. "It's time to break into the B-Grade, isn't it?"

Jack nodded. "I guess it is."

CHAPTER FIFTY-THREE

LOOT

BEING IN A SHIP FULL OF B-GRADES, CROSSING THE VAST COSMOS AT unimaginable speeds, returning to action after a month of relaxing with his family... Jack would be lying if he said this wasn't a little bit off putting. Yet, he was used to it. This was his life. Some instinct kicked in, making him ready to face everything despite his hesitation.

"How long is this going to take, Sovereign?" he asked.

Heavenly Spoon looked up from his space ring. "Hmm, about five days. The Systemless galaxy we're fighting in is not that far from your Milky Way."

"And you said this was an order of Elder Boatman?"

"Right."

Jack nodded. It made sense—their master-disciple relationship aside, Jack carried the death cube, an object which Elder Boatman deeply treasured. Yet, Jack couldn't help wondering—how much of saving him was due to the cube, and how much was due to Jack himself?

"By the way," he asked again, "will we pass close by the Heaven Egg Galaxy?"

"Not really," the sovereign replied. "Why?"

"I left something there, but... It's okay. I'll pick it up later."

The Green Dragon Realm still waited in the Heaven Egg Galaxy. By now, Jack could easily defeat Spacewind and release the rest of the Church cultivators, but he couldn't yet absorb the realm into his inner world. He'd need to reach the B-Grade for that.

Well, whatever, he thought. *I'll go back there eventually. Shi Mo and the others can wait a little.*

Which left him with only one thing to do right now. One he'd looked forward to for a long time. His eyes fell on his own space ring. After looking around and making sure nobody was trying to talk with him, he settled into a corner.

Some things were long overdue. He had to investigate the space rings of Eva Solvig and the other B-Grade he'd killed, as well as the loot he acquired from the Animal Kingdom's vaults. Not many treasures would be valuable to the current him, but there was always hope.

Though he hadn't really bothered with all these so far, he had done an initial screening. All the mundane, low-level stuff had been left with the Bare Fist Brotherhood back on Earth. He'd also recovered some artifacts of the Exploding Sun from the Kingdom's vaults, which he'd returned to Huali while on Earth.

Of all his spoils of war, only the true treasures remained in his space ring. Jack dove inside it, finding himself before an assembly of objects.

The first was a crystal ball seemingly filled with snow. He shook it gently, watching the particles—which turned out to be tiny letters—swirling and forming an endless march of gibberish. Jack channeled what he knew about the Thunder Body technique, the explosiveness it preached. He focused his gaze on the crystal ball, which was actually the technique's cultivation manual.

As he shook it, the letters moved independently of his hands, following predetermined Dao patterns. Not all letters swirled the same. Some followed the specific Dao circulation required to activate the Thunder Body technique, others copied the distinct patterns of Lightning Dao. Using his understanding of Thunder Body as the medium, Jack could extract information from both the words formed and the letters' moving patterns. The complete manual of the Thunder Body revealed itself before his eyes, allowing him to practice far more than the elementary forms he'd learned in the Black Hole World.

A small smile formed on Jack's lips. He'd been worried about comprehending such a complex manual, but as it turned out, it was created with enough expertise to make it doable. As he skimmed its initial stages, he realized that the hand-written copies he'd perused in the Black Hole World weren't completely faithful to the original. They were simplified versions meant to allow the Black Hole People to recreate part of the technique's power. That was partly the reason why Jack had learned this technique so fast—he'd unknowingly practiced the initial steps through a shortcut, neglecting to set the foundation for higher tiers.

He wasn't satisfied with that, obviously. He would re-learn Thunder Body from the beginning, the right way this time, so it could follow him into the B and A-Grades.

The more he read about Thunder Body, the more impressed he became. This was a masterful technique. It explained why the leonines were so far ahead of the other Animal Kingdom families. If the Hand of God and the Immortals knew what they were letting be wasted in the hands of a tiny B-Grade faction, they'd pull their hairs out. Or wires.

Such supplementary techniques were powerful, but the more powerful something was, the harder it was to learn. And not just because of its complexity—there were very strict compatibility requirements. Jack's Dao of the Fist required exactly the explosiveness and extreme physicality preached by the Thunder Body, hence why he could study it so smoothly. The other technique taken by the leonines, the Art of Divine Providence, was not suitable for him at all—he'd left it back on Earth to help them advance faster.

Back in the Black Hole World, he'd learned that of the twelve cultivation manuals they'd inherited, the Black Hole People had given away three—the Thunder Body, the Art of Divine Providence, and something called the Three Body Principle. This third technique was something Jack had never encountered or heard about in the Animal Kingdom—he could only assume it had been lost or stolen somewhere.

Besides these techniques, the Kingdom's wealth consisted of what Jack could only call low level treasures. Rather, it wasn't them that were low level, but that his viewpoint was far too high. He possessed many treasures which could make even A-Grades green with envy. The belongings of a B-Grade faction—and not even a particularly strong one—just failed to enter his eyes. He left them all back on Earth, where they could be useful.

What he did keep, however, were the mountains of Dao Stones the Kingdom had amassed over the years. There were over ten thousand of them—an extreme collection of wealth, even by the standards of the Black Hole Church. Jack was sure he would find some use for them.

After the Kingdom's loot came the space rings of Eva Solvig and the other Envoy. Both were late B-Grades of the Hand of God—the wealth they possessed could not be trivial. As Jack emptied both space rings into his own, he found even more Dao Stones, over a thousand in each ring. Tallying them up completely, he came to a total of around thirteen thousand stones. He was rich.

The stones weren't even the best part. Late B-Grade Envoys

enjoyed much richer resources than Jack ever had at the Church, especially when they were responsible for entire galaxies. Only the most select of items would qualify to be placed in their personal space rings. Jack had high hopes, which his generous enemies didn't fail to match.

He found a finger-sized chunk of white rock with a violet hue to it, making it seem otherworldly. Jack took it out of the space ring to check it out, then immediately felt like he was holding a mountain range. His hand dropped. He barely managed to channel his Dao and stop it before it reached the floor of the starship, otherwise it would have pierced right through.

Everyone turned to gaze at Jack, who was gritting his teeth and holding up a tiny piece of stone.

"Somebody forgot to have breakfast," the sovereign commented with a thin smile. "Put that back quickly or you'll sprain your wrist."

Jack nodded tightly, then forced the little thing back into the space ring. The immense weight disappeared immediately. He breathed out in relief. It was a good thing space rings contained no gravity.

"What the hell was that?" he asked.

"A piece of a neutron star," the Sage explained. "Heavily diluted. Otherwise, you wouldn't be able to hold it. A regular piece of neutron star that large would weigh several billions of tons."

"Billions? With a B?"

The Sage laughed. "The universe is a big place, Jack."

"I know," Jack replied, shaking his head. He knew about neutron stars. Hell, he even had the Neutron Star Body skill. It was just that he'd vastly underestimated the density of a real one. "What am I supposed to do with this?"

"You can forge it into a weapon," the Sage replied. "Or use it as a stabilizer during your breakthrough, melt it into energy, or exchange it for something more useful."

Jack had no need for weapons, nor did he lack energy with the Life Drop. He'd either exchange it for something useful, if the opportunity arose, or use it to enhance his breakthrough. No matter how confident he felt, more assurances were always better.

Putting the neutron star fragment out of his mind for now, went to his room. Sitting here with everyone was nice, but he'd like more privacy.

When he arrived and closed the door, he looked toward the next item—a pair of shorts?

He took them out of the ring and raised them high. They were a pair of unadorned pants giving off a primal, wild feeling. He felt the desire to try them on—then, remembered he wasn't an idiot, he didn't just wear unidentified clothing.

Scanning them was useless, since he was outside System space. However, he could use his own perception to get a rudimentary feel for an object's properties.

These pants seemed to be a sort of armor. Not in the sense that they shielded the body from attacks, but rather that they exuded a special life force field which amplified the body's innate defensive properties. More a protective treasure than armor. Jack whistled—he didn't even know this was possible. Whoever made these pants was a master. He could only wonder why Eva hadn't worn them during their battle.

The answer came quickly. As he inspected the item further, he realized this amplifying force field had no penetrating power. It could reach his entire body, since it was made of life force, but it couldn't penetrate any clothing. Essentially, whoever wore these shorts would need to wear nothing else.

That explained Eva's decision. She wouldn't look particularly noble half-naked. Jack, on the other hand...

He changed out of his previous pair of shorts and into the new one. As they clamped around his waist, he sensed a soothing power course through his body as if his cells were inspired. His already impressive defense shot up—and it wasn't a minor increase, either.

These shorts alone were worth their weight in gold. They were perfect for Jack, who didn't wear armor anyway. Plus, they were fashionable. They were snug, wrapping around his powerful legs, and their ends were sliced up around his thighs, letting sharp flaps dance to the wind of his attacks. He felt confident—good-looking like only a barbarian could.

His enemies would have a heart attack.

"I will call them... Naked Defense Shorts," Jack muttered. He laughed to himself, then moved on to the next item. It was... a stone?

It was white, similar to the neutron star fragment, but at a normal weight. In fact, just by scanning it, Jack could not discern its use—until it opened its mouth and spoke.

"Hi," it said in a childlike voice. "I'm The Stone. How are you doing?"

Jack blinked. "Excuse me?"

"You are excused."

"No, I—What are you?"

"I am a stone, but you can call me The Stone."

Jack felt irritation welling up inside him. He expected something more... treasure-y. "And what do you do?"

"Fine, you?"

"I mean, what is your function?"

The Stone, if possible, looked offended. "What is your function?" it shot back. "You objectivist freak."

Jack sighed. "Listen. I have all the good will to cooperate. Can you please explain what you are, besides The Stone, so we can get on with our lives?"

"Hmph! Well, if I have to," The Stone replied. "I am a sentient piece of stone. A woman with a harsh voice found me on the asteroid where I'd lived for a long time—pretty boring, if you ask me. It's where I learned to talk with myself. Not much else to do, you see. The other rocks weren't the best conversationalists—all they did was scratch the ground as they rolled."

"Okay... And what did that woman do with you?"

"Asked me bizarre questions, mostly. Like, how I can speak. What a silly concept. How am I supposed to know? How can you speak, do you know?"

"I do, actually. I'm a biologist. I can describe the exact process."

"Really? That sounds interesting. Go ahead, I'm keeping notes."

"Where?"

"In my mind."

Jack could already feel the approaching headache. "So you don't know why you can speak, where you learned the language, or how you found yourself on that asteroid where you spent a ton of time," he said. "You don't remember anything before that. Right?"

"...Well, yeah, but I would have used more words. Why are you in such a rush? Talk to me, I'm lonely!"

"You know what? I sympathize, but I'm kind of in the middle of something right now. How about I put you in my space ring for a bit, and we can discuss again later."

"Okay. Can you put someone else in there as well to keep me company?"

"Not really. Sentient beings can't go inside space rings."

"But I can."

"Yeah, and I have no idea why. I promise I'll get you out later, okay?"

"Okay!"

Jack stuffed The Stone back into the space ring, then sighed. This was so much trouble. How was he duped into adopting a talking stone?

The problem was, he was a busy man. He had more things to do than chat with The Stone—but it seemed so lonely. He couldn't just forget about it, could he?

As soon as that turtle wakes up, I'm throwing The Stone in there, he decided. *Until then, I guess I'll keep it company a bit...*

It wasn't exactly uninteresting. The inner workings of The Stone eluded him completely, which meant it was a highly intricate obj—person. It had to be something important. Maybe the old experiment of an A-Grade, or a transfused soul, or something else interesting. Either that, or just a talking stone.

Sniffing a little more into the ring, he did find an accompanying piece of paper with The Stone roughly drawn on it. It contained some of Eva's research notes.

"I can't figure it out... This stone shouldn't be able to produce sound, let alone words. It possesses no suitable inner workings. Can the Dao assume life by itself? Or is there some way to infuse stable life into objects? It's a breakthrough either way.

"I don't know how this stone came to be, but I sense that seeing through its secrets will earn me the Immortals' favor! This is world-shaking knowledge!"

That was all she'd written. Either her research had been fruitless, or she'd only acquired The Stone recently. In any case, it made Jack excited. Now, he had an excuse to keep the lonely stone—maybe he'd get something out of it. After all, he too cultivated the Dao of Life.

Come to think of it, wasn't there a ticklish pebble back on Trial Planet? he remembered. *I should get those two together. They'll have the time of their lives.*

In any case, he decided to leave the mystery of The Stone for later. Maybe the Sage would know.

I should also ask him about that mural in the Black Hole World. There was a person who looked suspiciously similar to him... Maybe later. When there aren't as many people around.

Thinking up to there, Jack reached into his space ring and took out the next and almost final item—a half-eaten apple.

This wasn't what he expected to find in an Envoy's space ring. Then, as he stared at it, he was soon shocked. The life energy inside it was tremendous, blasting his face in waves—it was like a tiny version of the Life Drop.

Good stuff! A body tempering treasure! he realized, eyes shining. *Finally, something useful! Eva Solvig had this... She must have taken tiny bites every once in a while to gradually temper her body. To someone like her, who only partly cultivated Physical, digesting such a treasure should take a long, long time. Maybe centuries.*

Jack shrugged, then tossed the half apple into his mouth and chewed it to bits. It had a burning taste, as if it made his taste glands come alive and rush to escape his body, so he swallowed it quickly.

A moment later, a wave of tremendous heat erupted from his stomach. Oceans of energy forcefully pushed their way into his body. A regular cultivator would have exploded—Jack simply burped.

His body was already a temple of physicality. His capacity for absorbing energy was much higher than a regular cultivator's. This apple couldn't harm him.

In fact, it wasn't even painful like body tempering was supposed to be. It certainly carried some special properties, probably to make it easier on Eva. Jack scoffed. To think that a late B-Grade would bother to avoid the pain... No wonder she lost to him.

As the pain subsided, Jack checked his status screen, finding that his Physical substats had increased by an entire three hundred points each!

Strength: 7880
Dexterity: 7880
Constitution: 7880

At this stage, tempering his body was hard. Every point was crucial. This apple giving him three hundred at once was a landfall, especially for such a tame medicine. He couldn't help nodding in admiration—the children of late A-Grades sure enjoyed some great stuff.

Besides the Dao stones and those four items—the neutron star fragment, the shorts, the talking stone, and the now-fully eaten apple—there wasn't much else in the two Envoys' space rings. Jack wasn't complaining—just the three hundred Physical brought a noticeable increase in his combat strength.

The only other items he'd found were two badges, one representing Elder Purity and the other a faction Jack had never of. He'd disintegrated both long ago in case they were trackable.

"Alright," he said, opening his eyes. "On to the fun stuff."

He still had a Dao Fruit to develop—his last one. And, since he was there, he might as well apply a little change to his Dao Tree.

CHAPTER FIFTY-FOUR

PEAK C-GRADE

JACK'S DAO TREE REMAINED TALL AND SOLID. EIGHT FRUITS LITTERED its branches—Fist, Space, Life, Death, Battle, Revenge, Brotherhood, and Time—all fully grown. Now was time to develop the ninth and final fruit. And before that, Jack wanted to do one more thing.

His gaze fell on his sixth Dao Fruit—Revenge. This was something he'd created back when his heart was filled with darkness, when he single-mindedly pursued revenge in a vain attempt to escape the grief of the loss of his son. It had worked well enough, but now it was purposeless.

Jack no longer believed in revenge. He believed in righteousness, and justice, but not revenge for the sake of it. Such was an empty pursuit, simply an outlet for one's inner darkness. This fruit was an imperfection of his Dao—if he broke through like this, the foundation of his inner world would be shaky, which would affect his battle power and future achievements.

Changing one's fruit wasn't easy, but it could be done. The greatest hurdle was enduring the process—something which Jack was quite confident in. He was so far ahead of the curve in

everything that even developing a new Dao Fruit was trivial. He
could handle a little transformation.

He flew close to the fruit and grabbed it with both hands. In
one swift thought, he cut off the Dao circulation to the fruit,
enduring the sense of wrongness which filled his being. Then,
he poured his will into the fruit. Its dark red skull shape was
perfectly in line with its inner darkness—this was a fruit built
on weakness and hatred.

Jack poured more and more energy into it. The fruit burned
between his hands, but he endured. His soul was shaky, and his
body suffered from the volatility of the sixth fruit's energy he no
longer controlled, but both were solid enough to persist for a
little while. Ignoring all the changes around him, Jack kept his
full attention on the fruit, which was now boiling hot.

Its skin slowly melted. The dark red rose in columns of
smoke, and its shape turned unclear as the fruit's flesh began to
melt as well. It had reached its most malleable state.

Jack stopped pouring energy into it—he didn't want to
destroy it, just change it a little—and used his willpower to
shape it. He infused it with his beliefs of justice and fair punishment, the concept of enforcing discipline as necessary. The fruit
began to wobble, slowly changing into a rounder shape.

Jack intended to make it into a Fruit of Justice, shaped as a
shield. At some point, however, his Dao of the Fist kicked in. He
watched with surprise as the fruit's round shape changed
again, elongating, turning slimmer. His thoughts and Dao
moved in tandem, and he let the transformation happen, eager
to see what would occur.

He regretted that decision as the fruit's new shape began to
stabilize. He could try to reshape it again, but this had already
taken too long, and the rampant energy in his body was beginning to create problems. With a muffled curse, he cut off his
intense pouring of energy into the fruit, letting it cool and

calmly solidify its new shape. Meanwhile, he flew a bit backward and gazed at it with an odd expression.

"Damn," he said. "How did this even happen?"

The fruit's new shape was a purple flip-flop—the Dao Fruit of Spanking.

"This is all my fault," Jack said again, sighing. "I used the spanking too many times... I should have known this would happen!"

Yet, it fit. Spanking embodied elements of justice and discipline, just as he'd wanted, and it was also similar to his Dao of the Fist in style. Moreover, it was a Dao he felt close to—though he'd always used it as a joke, never realizing it was an actual Dao.

Then again, all Daos were real. It was just about belief and consistency.

Jack sighed for a third time. He did feel a bit ridiculous, but...

Oh, what the hell. Let's spank.

He left his soul world and checked his status screen, making sure everything was okay.

Dao Fruits: Fist, Space, Life, Death, Battle, Spanking, Brotherhood, Time

Revenge had been swapped for Spanking, with no weird error messages. The operation had been successful.

"Everything alright?" the Sage asked from the side—Jack had returned to the main room so he could get assistance if this fruit transformation backfired. They couldn't see inside his soul, anyway, so he wasn't giving away anything.

"Hmm?" Jack responded. "Yeah, why?"

"You were bleeding a bit back there. And convulsing. And I'm pretty sure some of your blood vessels exploded."

"Oh, that. I'm fine. Just doing a bit of remodeling."

The Sage gave Jack a blank stare, then closed his eyes and returned to meditation. So did Jack. He was in his soul world again, facing the majestic tree from which hung a flip-flop, amidst everything else. Jack scratched his head and did his best to ignore it.

"Alright," he said, pumping himself up. "Ninth fruit time. Let's try to avoid footwear."

Changing a fruit hadn't used up much energy, so he dove directly into developing his final one. Purple currents flowed into the tree roots, then crawled up the trunk and lit up a singular branch like Christmas lights. A lone flower began to grow—it went from purple leaves to forming a small fruit, which gradually developed into something more recognizable.

During his free time on Earth, Jack had sometimes considered what his ninth fruit should be. He already had one for each of his Daos—Fist, Life, Death, Space, and Time—as well as fruits for Battle, Brotherhood, and now Spanking. All major aspects of his Dao and personality were there. Then, what should the ninth fruit be?

The answer came to him one night when he was resting in bed. Vivi was curled up against him, and he wasn't asleep yet, just basking in that feeling of bliss. If not for everything else, he'd have wanted nothing more than to stay with his family, enjoying and protecting them, making sure they were happy.

It was exactly this feeling of protecting that resonated with Jack.

He was a powerful man. Billions of people depended on him. His every casual decision shaped innumerable lives. He was a leader, a paragon, and a role model all at once. Moreover, everyone relied on him—that wasn't a duty he took lightly. He wanted to use his power to change the world for the better—ensure the safety and prosperity of those who followed him.

The Fist struck where it had to. And Jack stood with his back to his people, facing all enemies and the unknown. For his family, his people, and his brothers, he would always be there. He would never let anything happen to them.

Not again.

Jack opened his eyes, realizing that while he was lost in thought, his inner sentiments had already shaped his ninth fruit. It was a white shield in the shape of a man's back—a promise, and a commitment.

It was the Dao Fruit of Protection.

The moment his ninth fruit finished forming, Jack felt something click in his soul world. Like he was ready. The ever present streams of energy flowed together, achieving harmony, and his entire being became aligned. His Dao felt complete, in a sense—like he'd reached the apex.

Jack breathed in this feeling, enjoying the perfection it promised. He could imagine how the first cultivator to reach this point must have felt. They must have thought they'd reached the peak—the end of the road. Who knows how long it had taken for someone to think of collapsing their tree and forming an inner world, opening a whole new avenue of cultivation.

The road of cultivation was split into three major parts—using the energy of the body, using the energy of the world, and creating one's inner world. At this point, Jack had reached the limit of what was possible as a cultivator in the universe. The only step forward would be to create his own universe inside him, using its energy to truly step into the realm of gods.

Jack opened his eyes in the real world, drunk in this feeling of ecstasy. He was bathed in power—as if, at this very moment, he was reborn.

Everyone stared at him—some with pride, some with disinterest. Brock smiled widely. "Congratulations, big bro," he said, and Jack shot him a grateful glance.

"Thanks, Brock. I couldn't have done it without you."

"The nine fruits are a major threshold," Sovereign Heavenly Spoon intoned. "You are now at the dividing line between living in a world and a world living inside yourself. Many cultivators remain stranded there for their entire lives... But, with your potential, I suspect you will just breeze through."

"Thank you, Sovereign," Jack replied modestly. Though his power had spiked, he still felt an instinctive sense of dread as he faced this late B-Grade man—as if he was nowhere close to being his match. It was a good reminder that he wasn't the only talent in the universe.

"I have some Dao stones if you want to mature your ninth fruit quickly," the Sage said, but Jack only gave a wry smile.

"About that..."

System notifications rang in his ears. The remaining levels from his final battle against the Kingdom streamed in.

Level up! You have reached Level 381.
Level up! You have reached Level 382.

...

Level up! You have reached Level 399. Form your inner world to ascend to the next Grade.

Jack's smirk widened. "Thanks for the offer, Sage," he said, "but I'm already at the peak C-Grade. I had a few levels left over from my last battle."

He quickly allocated all his points into Physical, finally pushing it over eight thousand.

Name: Jack Rust
Species: Human, Earth-387

Faction: Bare Fist Brotherhood (C)
Grade: C
Class: Gladiator Titan (King)
Level: 399

Strength: 8260 (+)
Dexterity: 8260 (+)
Constitution: 8260 (+)
Mental: 1000
Will: 1000
Free sub-points: 2

Dao Skills: Meteor Punch IV, Iron Fist Style III, Brutalizing Aura III, Neutron Star Body III, Supernova III, Space Mastery III, Fist of Mortality III, Death Mastery III, Titan Taunt III
Dao Roots: Indomitable Will, Life, Power, Weakness
Dao Fruits: Fist, Space, Life, Death, Battle, Spanking, Brotherhood, Time, Protection
Titles: Planetary Frontrunner (10), Planetary Torchbearer (1), Ninth Ring Conqueror, Planetary Overlord (1), Grade Defier, Planet Destroyer

That was one hell of a status screen.

Everyone glanced at each other, then scanned him. The sovereign laughed. "There's something I haven't seen before. How about you keep going and break into the B-Grade right now? See how far you can sprint."

"That's not a good idea," the Sage quickly intervened. "Forming one's inner world is a critical juncture, and the better it goes, the stronger the resulting inner world. Jack should prepare as much as possible and amass all sorts of treasures before attempting the breakthrough. Not to mention that Elder Boatman will probably want a word with him first…"

"I was just kidding," the sovereign replied with an aloof smile, then whispered, "but it would be cool, wouldn't it?"

"Yes, Sovereign…" the Sage replied in defeat.

"Thank you for your concern," Jack said. "I'll wait. I must see Master Boatman first, and there is no rush anyway."

"There is some rush," the Sage corrected him. "We're still in wartime. Advance quickly but not hastily."

"Sure thing."

Jack leaned back, catching an odd glance from Starhair and ignoring it. Bottomless remained as passive as ever, simply muttering a quick congratulations and returning to the helm. As for Min Ling, she rushed forward and punched Jack in the shoulder. "Well done!" she exclaimed. "I can't wait for you to reach the B-Grade. We should spar then!"

"Really?" Jack said, raising a brow. "I could take you right now."

"No you couldn't."

"I sure could. I can probably face a peak B-Grade right now."

She chuckled. "What, those weaklings who weren't even invited to the Crusade? It's not that I'm doubting your strength, Jack, but that you don't comprehend mine. There are many degrees of success when forming your inner world. I'm proud to say that mine is overwhelmingly wide and solid… So, I'm looking forward to meeting you on the same level."

She winked at him, then walked away. Jack only smiled—however well she'd done during her breakthrough, he was confident he could do better. He was looking forward to it more and more. If there really were multiple levels of success, if there was no ceiling, wasn't this an opportunity to compare himself to every B-Grade from the start of time to now? Just how would he do?

He could hardly wait.

CHAPTER FIFTY-FIVE
ARRIVING

BRILLIANT GALAXIES WERE SUSPENDED IN THE UNIVERSE LIKE FISH IN AN endless sea. Their colors varied, as did their sizes, but flying between them really made one understand how inconsequentially tiny they were in the grand scheme of things.

Galaxies, however, were not as far apart as Jack expected. They were clustered together. Unlike stars, which were tiny dots compared to the massive distances separating them, galaxies were more like neighboring islands. Sure, there were gaps in between, but sometimes the gaps were smaller than the galaxies themselves.

Their starship was but a tiny fish crossing a dense archipelago.

"Enjoying the view?" a voice came behind Jack, startling him. He looked away from the large window and toward the new arrival—Starhair, the peak B-Grade Envoy whose hair resembled rivers of stars. The man stood beside Jack and gazed out the window.

This starship wasn't too small. There were various rooms and compartments. Right now, Jack and Starhair were alone.

"It's nice," Jack replied. "Better than looking at the other wall, which is just metal."

Starhair didn't laugh. Jack frowned.

"Is something the matter?" he asked.

"Nothing much. I just don't understand why we had to waste a month to escort a C-Grade."

This time, it was Jack who didn't reply. What could he say? '*I have great potential and might be able to affect the war situation?*' That would sound extremely arrogant coming from a C-Grade, even one with Jack's accomplishments. He also couldn't reveal the existence of the death cube which Elder Boatman wanted, as it was a secret.

"Yeah, I guess it's hard to understand," was all he replied.

Starhair raised an angry brow at him. "Are you mocking me?"

"What else do you want me to say?"

"Give me a reason to believe this is not a waste of time."

"Can I?" Jack smiled without meaning it. "If you believed in my talent, you wouldn't need me to say anything."

"You sound pretty sure of yourself. Me, believing in your talent? What do you think you can accomplish? I know you're strong, but you're just another cog in the machine until you reach the A-Grade. This whole mission is just an Elder abusing their authority to protect their disciple at the expense of everyone else."

"I would advise you to speak about Elders with a little more respect," Jack replied calmly. "Especially when said Elder is my master and I'm honor-bound to protect his reputation."

Starhair snorted. He turned to walk away. "I'm looking forward to your future achievements." On his way, he bumped into Jack's shoulder, probably expecting to push him aside. Instead, Jack easily remained immobile, while it was Starhair who had to turn his body. He paused, then didn't look back, leaving the room.

Jack shook his head. Another clown... he thought. In his experience, these people were divided into two types—those who hopped around asking for a punch in the face, and those who hid their intentions in the dark and struck quickly, efficiently, and unexpectedly. He hoped Starhair was the former kind.

———

The journey from Milky Way to the wild galaxy which served as the Crusade's current battlefield was neither short nor long. Bottomless steered the ship, using their extreme understanding of spacetime to constantly wormhole forward. They covered almost a hundred thousand light years a day. They passed by many galaxies, some spiral, others egg-shaped, as they speared deeper and deeper into the unexplored parts of the universe.

Jack spent most of the time meditating. He would soon attempt to break into the B-Grade—the clearer his Daos were, the better. However, without life and death battles propelling him forward, progress was slow. He focused his time on the death cube, deepening his understandings of Death.

Meanwhile, the many Dao stones he'd gotten as spoils of battle were useless to him. He couldn't level up anymore without breaking through. Therefore, he gave a lot of them to Brock, who used them to rapidly increase his cultivation base. Maybe he couldn't level up without the System, but he sure could use Dao stones.

In the five days they spent traveling, Brock successfully reached the peak C-Grade. He had grown all nine of his fruits to maturity and was ready to take the next step. Both brothers were at the same spot.

Eventually, the journey came to an end. Jack watched from the windows as their starship angled toward a new galaxy, one similar in size and shape to the Milky Way but slightly redder overall—the stars here were older and larger.

"I present to you, the Spiral Stair galaxy," Sovereign Heavenly Spoon said, materializing next to Jack. "The Church's new home."

"How far away from System space are we now?" Jack asked.

"Three hundred thousand light years away from the closest System galaxy," the sovereign replied. "And half a million from your Milky Way."

"That's a lot."

"Don't think about it in terms of distance. It's one week of traveling. I'd say that's pretty sensible."

Jack considered it, then nodded. "Where exactly are we headed now?" he asked.

"The Church forces are scattered across this galaxy. Not even I know the precise location, but I do know where Elder Boatman said he'd pick us up. See that slightly denser patch of stars? Up there, to the right. That's pretty much the area."

"He'll find us in all that?"

"Oh no, Bottomless has the exact coordinates. I just couldn't bother to remember." The sovereign gave Jack a lazy smile. "Anyway, we still have a few hours. Tea?"

"I guess."

The starship dove into the galaxy, and soon they were lost in a three-dimensional sea of stars. The scenery looked similar to the Milky Way—it was hard to imagine they were inside a completely different galaxy. Bottomless led them through a winding track, following unknown directions and reference points, until they finally came to rest near a red giant—a star which ballooned and reddened greatly as it approached the end of its life.

"What now?" Jack asked. All of them were gathered at the starship's bridge, including Dorman, who'd spent most of the time in his room. The Sage was the first to bow—immediately afterward, space rippled before them, and a hooded figure appeared directly inside their starship. The entire Spoon Squad and Dorman bent their backs.

"We greet Elder Boatman," they said as one.

"Greetings, Master," Jack said, while Brock nodded.

"Grandpa Dead, hello."

Elder Boatman scanned them with his gaze. His face was hidden, but red eyes shone under his dark hood. Covered entirely in the black robe and with a scythe hanging on his back, he directly resembled the Charon of Earth's mythology—maybe the two were related somehow, or this was a universal image in line with the Dao of Death.

"Rise," he said in a raspy voice. Everyone stood straight again. "Thank you for bringing my disciple."

"We are happy to be of service, Elder," the sovereign replied. "By the way, I heard you acquired a certain delicacy recently. Do you think I could—"

"Jack," Boatman turned to his disciple, ignoring the sovereign. "I am glad to see you well. You've grown much stronger, too—what's your current battle power?"

"I should be able to match ordinary peak B-Grades," Jack replied.

"Really?" The red eyes shone brighter. "Excellent. Come. We have things to discuss."

He waved a hand. Instantly, the entire starship was wrapped in darkness. This wasn't really teleporting—more like the surrounding spacetime died, reducing the distance between them and their destination. Jack spread his perception, but before he could understand how exactly this was happening, they had already arrived.

A starship floated before them. Calling it huge was an understatement—it stretched for at least a dozen miles and contained multiple floors. It was more like a city. Swarms of cultivators circled it like flies—either guards or people traveling from one place to another.

"My starship," Elder Boatman said with a hint of pride. "Thank you, Head Envoy. I will make sure you and your squad are rewarded appropriately. Feel free to rest here for a few days before heading to your next mission."

"Thank you, Elder," the sovereign replied. "Our navigator is exhausted from the trip, so we'd be glad to rest here for a day or two. About that item you—"

Elder Boatman waved his hand again, teleporting just himself, Jack, and Brock away. They reappeared in a grand throne room, complete with piles of bones and skeletal guards. White columns speared a hundred feet into the ceiling, giving the room a heavy, somber feel, while the ground was gray marble.

Boatman gave a tired sigh. He threw back his hood, revealing a pale vampiric face. He looked a billion years old. "Don't mind the decorations. I agree they're in bad taste, but excess is necessary at times. Please, sit."

A round table occupied the middle of the room. It was surrounded by thirteen seats, one of which was clearly more elaborate than the others, carved with skulls and velvet. That was the chair Boatman had sat in. Jack found another chair, while Brock pulled his back and sat on the ground. This way, he wasn't towering over them.

"No throne?" Jack asked.

"Don't get me started. The throne is for official hearings. When strategizing, this is where I sit—it's far more comfortable."

Jack nodded. "Thank you for your guidance, Master. Both

the death cube and the Dao Visions you gave me helped a lot. My Dao of Death has grown tremendously."

Elder Boatman gave his disciple a long stare. "But that's not all, is it? I can sense you're dabbling in more Daos. Life is there, obviously, but so are Space and Time."

There was clear doubt in his voice. Generally speaking, people avoided spreading their attention between many Daos.

"The opportunities came up and I took them," Jack replied. "I believe it was a wise choice. It's worked out so far."

"Mm. I can sense so, yes." Boatman's gaze pierced into Jack as if observing his soul. "You know best. I support your decisions regardless. If this goes well, your potential will be limitless—if hard to realize."

"Thank you, Master!"

"About your Dao of Death..." Boatman trailed off. Jack could sense the unspoken question.

"My son passed away recently," he replied. "It hurt me deeply, and I almost lost myself in grief. I believe it also gave my Dao of Death a perspective more suited to myself."

Boatman nodded slowly. "I am sorry for your loss. Death is a natural occurrence—even that of your descendants. I am glad you managed to not only overcome your grief, but also understand it. It was a pivotal experience for you. On the road of cultivation, everyone must form their own path, or they will forever be limited to a fraction of what their predecessor achieved."

Jack had already figured this out—after his experience in the Black Hole World, where his Dao of Death had undergone a subtle transformation, he'd realized that the insights Elder Boatman left him had become far less useful. They referenced Boatman's path, not Jack's. Even the death cube had shown decreased efficiency. As a result, Jack's progress in the Dao of

Death had slowed, but he could feel this was the right path regardless.

It didn't matter how quickly he followed the path of another—at the end of the day, only his own unique path had the potential to reach the top.

"I am on the cusp of reaching the B-Grade, Master," Jack said. "Is there any advice you would like to give me?"

"No. Trying to gleam insights from the experiences of others will not help you, only further your insecurity. You will naturally understand everything when you go into it. However, I will oversee your breakthrough in its entirety. With me there, nothing will go wrong—but, as for how far you can get, that will depend entirely on you."

Jack nodded. "Thank you, Master. If you don't mind, I had another thing to ask. Brock and I are brothers sharing a spiritual connection. He is also at the cusp of the same breakthrough, and he is as talented as myself. Could you accept him as a disciple as well?"

"No problem," Boatman replied, turning to the brorilla. "That was my intention as well. Brock, would you like to become my disciple? You may not cultivate the Dao of Death, but you do follow an offshoot of the Dao of Life, which is my other area of expertise."

"Thanks, Grandpa Dead," Brock replied.

Elder Boatman gave a strained smile. "You can call me master now."

"Okay, Master Grandpa Dead."

The Elder looked like he wanted to say something, but in the end he just sighed. "It is customary for a master to provide his disciples with treasures for the breakthrough," he said. "However, it's not about the quantity of treasures, but their quality. Jack, am I correct to assume you already have enough?"

Jack grinned. "Absolutely."

"And you, Brock." Elder Boatman gave him an inquisitive stare. "Your Dao is one which makes most treasures ineffective. Correct?"

"Right, Master Grandpa Dead. I have everything I need in my bros."

"Good. Then get ready, both of you. I will have people fill you in on the current status of the war and assign you positions, but that is meaningless before you break through. You must reach the B-Grade as soon as possible."

Jack looked up. "How soon, Master?"

"Tomorrow."

CHAPTER FIFTY-SIX

THE DEATH BOAT

TOMORROW... HUH?

JACK HAD SPENT EIGHT YEARS CULTIVATING. HE'D REACHED THE E-Grade in a month, the D-Grade in three, then the C-Grade in a year and a half. Since then, the other six and a half years had been spent inside the C-Grade. It had been a tremendous amount of time—but it didn't feel that long. Things had been slower.

Three years in the Green Dragon Realm, one in the Black Hole World, one and a half at the Black Hole Church, and finally one spent running around the Milky Way... Over all that time, he'd gotten used to being a C-Grade. The Dao Tree in his soul world felt intimate, while its every fruit was a sight he'd seen a thousand times.

Breaking into the B-Grade tomorrow—or, at least, attempting it—felt like a dream.

Tomorrow...

Jack didn't know how he reached his room that night. All he knew was that, when he awoke, he was on a hard military bed in a high-tech room in a massive starship in a galaxy far, far away. A tinted window showcased the starry cosmos outside, while the room itself was illuminated by fluorescent wires running through the ceiling. Besides the bed itself, a bathroom occupied part of the space, outfitted with a shower and a toilet.

Jack shook his head to clear it, then pulled away the covers. He quickly got dressed—an action which involved a mere putting on his pants and boots. It felt weird to dress like a barbarian in a starship, but who were they to judge? This was his war attire!

Today is the day I'm breaking through.

It still felt like a dream. He left his room regardless, finding Brock leaned against a wall. "Morning, bro," said the brorilla. "Slept well?"

"I think so."

"Good. So did I."

"Had any dreams?"

"Me, you, and Grandpa Dead eating bananarms."

Jack laughed. "That's a dream alright."

Brock smiled. "Are you ready?"

"I was born ready."

"Good. Let's go."

They followed the corridor, only to run into a beautiful D-Grade woman at the next corner. Her blonde hair was long and thrown back, while her blue eyes exuded a feeling of professionalism. Light blue robes covered her shapely body, and her features were sharp in a resolved way. "Good morning. My name is Literia, an assistant of *Death Boat*. I will be guiding you today. Pleased to make your acquaintance."

"Uh... Likewise," Jack responded. "Who's *Death Boat*?"

"That's the name of this starship, sir. Coined by the great Elder Boatman himself."

Jack remembered seeing the ship from afar—it had looked like a dark, ominous boat. He could picture Charon ferrying souls on it.

"Where are you guiding us?" he asked.

"Around," she replied. "I have been instructed to take you to your assigned breakthrough location, if that's fine with you."

"Oh." Jack wasn't just breaking through today—he was doing it, like, now. "Sure."

"Great!" She smiled, lighting up the walls. "Follow me, please."

Literia sailed down the corridor on her long legs, only halfway covered by her robes. Jack only had to glance at her once to suspect they'd sent their most beautiful assistant on purpose.

"Who exactly ordered you to guide us?" he asked as they followed.

"Envoy Min Ling," Literia replied with reverence. "She's an honorary manager of *Death Boat*. I presume you're acquainted?"

"Hmm." Jack narrowed his eyes. "A bit."

He did not press the issue. Brock chuckled quietly. They followed Literia down a set of winding corridors, emerging on a wider one whose right side was covered entirely in glass. Behind it, Jack had a terrific view of one level of the *Death Boat*. He was stunned. There were tens of thousands of houses—just this level was like a small city.

"*Death Boat* hosts more than just Crusade combatants," Literia explained, not hurrying along. "Elder Boatman's entire faction lives in this starship. When we escaped System space, we also brought along many survivors of Hand attacks to keep them safe. As a result, we're currently a little overpopulated... but that shouldn't affect you."

"I didn't know Elder Boatman had his own faction," Jack replied.

"Most Elders do. Don't imagine anything too grand—they just like to keep their friends, family, and disciples safe. Over an A-Grade's long life, that small community can expand to millions or billions of people. It's normal."

"I see," Jack said. "Then, all those people below are cultivators?"

"Not at all!" She laughed, a pleasant, chirping sound. "Most are mortal civilians. There are schools, shops, cafes, restaurants... Some layers even have forests and lakes. It's a whole world in here—all courtesy of Elder Boatman."

Jack nodded along. He was beginning to see a pattern. Archons Green Dragon and Black Hole had created a hidden realm in which they kept their people. Elder Boatman either couldn't or didn't want to do that, using a giant starship instead. So did most other Elders, according to Literia. It appeared there was no place in the universe where high-ranking people felt safe leaving their people.

Jack would have assumed the Black Hole Church headquarters to be such a place. Now, he knew better. While he didn't understand quite everything, he didn't need to—he would just copy those who knew what they were doing. His family and friends would remain on Earth, which he'd make sure to keep out of reach of the rest of the universe.

That was the only way to be safe.

"Are there other A-Grades onboard?" Jack asked.

Literia smiled—needlessly? "There is Elder Heavenstar. His own abode was destroyed in the process of escaping System space. Elder Boatman graciously accepted him and the survivors into his starship."

Jack had a decent impression of Heavenstar—he was the master of Sovereign Heavenly Spoon and Min Ling, a scholarly Elder known to assist the younger generation. At the banquet before they entered the Green Dragon Realm, Heavenstar had stood by Boatman when he almost fought Purity. He seemed, at the very least, to be a man of integrity.

That also explained why Min Ling was an honorary

manager of *Death Boat*, and also why Sovereign Heavenly Spoon would spare a month to ensure Jack's safety.

They continued through the corridors, circling the city and finally losing it from sight. Throughout their walk, Literia maintained a cheerful conversation with Jack and Brock, often asking about their experiences or offering hers. She was a well-spoken woman.

Of course, if they really were in a hurry, they could just teleport wherever they wanted.

Shortly afterward, the left wall of their corridor was made of glass, revealing an expanse of dust and rocks. "This is the Bone Belt," Literia explained. "Our hiding place. It extends for millions of miles, and thanks to the dense clouds of dust, it's difficult for the enemy to scout us out with their perception. They have to manually search through the entire belt, where our Envoys lie in ambush to make their job even harder."

"Hmm," Jack hummed. "Since we're hiding, I assume we're losing the war?"

Literia turned defensive. "I wouldn't say that," she replied, sounding a little hurt. "This is just the current state of things. The Hand of God is presently much stronger than us, but it won't be like that forever. We aren't the only parties of this war. When the Old Gods join, things will be much more balanced."

"The Old Gods are joining the war?"

"Of course! We're fighting on their side—how could they not help us?"

Jack had his doubts. From what he knew, the only Old God to care about cultivators was currently trapped in a black hole somewhere in the universe. Even if the other eleven knew there was a Second Crusade brewing against them, and also that there were cultivators fighting on their behalf, why would they rush over here and join? They were Old Gods. They could just retreat to the far end of the universe and remain there for billions or trillions of years. The cultivation world couldn't reach that far.

Of course, Jack also recognized there were many things he wasn't privy to, so he chose not to speak on that.

"When you say we're currently weaker," he asked, "how much weaker do you mean?"

Literia hesitated. "I'm not aware of everything, but I would say our forces are half of theirs. It's not a difference we cannot overcome with good planning, bravery, and a little bit of luck."

Jack nodded. Brock placed a hand on Literia's shoulder, startling her. "Don't worry, Pretty Bro," he said with a calm smile. "We are here now. It's going to be okay."

She struggled to form words, then her lips broke into a bright smile—one that seemed more genuine than before. "Thank you," she replied. Brock removed his hand, and she kept walking.

Jack shot his bro a questioning gaze—Brock shrugged.

Finally, they reached the end of the corridor: a decompression chamber connecting to the universe outside. It was obviously meant to shield E-Grades and below from the vacuum, but to Jack, Brock, and Literia, that was completely unnecessary. Jack teleported the three of them outside. Literia blinked in surprise.

"This is faster," he explained, to which she nodded.

"I guess you're right," she said. "Then, follow me!"

She turned into a ray of cyan light that flew into the distance. Of course, to Jack and Brock, she was beyond slow. They would have offered to lead the way, but thankfully, they could see that their destination was near.

A large asteroid hung in the distance, so large it resembled a planet. Crowds of cultivators hovered around it, and looking back, Jack could also see a large window of the *Death Boat* overlooking this spot, crowded with the faces of thousands of people.

"Is this the breakthrough location?" he asked.

"Yes," Literia replied, sounding a little embarrassed. "We know privacy is usually best, but in this case, we need a show to increase morale. We hope you can understand."

"It's fine either way," Jack said. "But won't morale drop if I fail my breakthrough?"

She looked at him like he'd made a joke. "If even your breakthrough fails, sir, then the rest of us might as well abandon cultivation and become farmers."

"That 'sir' feels weird. Just call me Jack."

She beamed. "Okay... Jack." She said the name slowly, as if enjoying it. Jack couldn't tell if she was a fangirl or an expert hostess. Her voice turned warmer. "In any case, Jack, there is no need to worry. I'm sure you'll do just fine. Both of you. We aren't just waiting to see if you succeed, but to how many miles you can grow your inner world!"

"Thanks. That's—Wait. Both of us?"

"Yes?" she replied. "The two of you are breaking through, correct?"

Jack looked at Brock, who winked. "We're bros," he said. "We walk together."

"I guess we do." Jack laughed. "There is no one else I would rather share my breakthrough, bro."

"I know."

"This is as far as I can go," Literia said as they approached the asteroid. "I wish you luck, Jack... and Brock." She'd used the brorilla's name as well—he smiled and winked at her.

"Thanks, Pretty Bro. We're bringing it home."

Literia didn't recognize the phrase, while Jack wondered where Brock had picked it up. Earth, probably. Gan Salin?

The girl flew to the side, joining the crowd which was

staring at them. Jack saw many familiar faces—Sovereign Heavenly Spoon, the Sage, Min Ling... Even Elder Heavenstar was present, sitting on a starry throne at the very front of the crowd, his scholarly aura putting everyone at ease. He smiled politely at Jack and Brock.

"Show us the power of your generation," he told them telepathically, to which both smiled.

"*Thank you, Elder.*"

They flew toward the nearby asteroid. Elder Boatman hovered alone right over it. An aura of death surrounded him, not menacingly, but like it was the most natural thing in the world.

"I have taken very few disciples in my life," he said as they approached. Though it felt like a whisper, his voice somehow spread across space, even reaching the *Death Boat*. "I believe in the two of you. Your potential is great. Do not disappoint me."

Short and to the point. Classic Elder Boatman. Yet, though he sounded strict, Jack could hear the love behind those words. Elder Boatman was maintaining absolute vigilance, ensuring that nobody would arrive to disturb them, and he also used his Dao to keep the asteroid below them completely still. This last job could have been delegated to a B-Grade, but he chose to do it personally. That showed he cared.

"Thank you, Master," both said as one. "We will make you proud."

Boatman nodded. "Then, you may begin when you are ready."

He flew away, coming to float beside Elder Heavenstar. The two of them were the only ones sitting—one had a throne seemingly made of stars, while the other of dark bone. Everyone else stood.

Nobody was within a hundred miles of the asteroid's

surface. Jack and Brock exchanged a glance. They clasped hands. "Good luck, bro," said Brock.

"You too," Jack replied with barely contained excitement. "Let's become strong."

Brock flew away, circling the asteroid to land at the exact opposite side. The breakthrough to the B-Grade was a very delicate process—even soul companions like them couldn't be too close to each other.

Jack stood alone on an asteroid in space, overlooked by A-Grades, in a galaxy far from home. The pressure was one he was used to—and it was made easier by the fact that his bro was undergoing the same thing on the other side of the asteroid.

He sat down and closed his eyes. It was time to reach the B-Grade.

CHAPTER FIFTY-SEVEN

THE BREAKTHROUGH BEGINS

BREAKING INTO THE B-GRADE WAS ONE OF THE MOST IMPORTANT junctures in the entire cultivation journey. Only an extremely small number of people reached it, and even fewer could overcome it.

Only one in ten cultivators succeeded—the rest paid the ultimate price. As a result, breaking into the B-Grade was the eternal nightmare of most C-Grades—would they spend their life in mediocrity, or would they gamble everything on a small chance to reach the stars?

This breakthrough was demonized in the eyes of the masses —they viewed it as the greatest trial every cultivator had to face. Naturally, Jack's attempt garnered a lot of attention. Every eye in and around the *Death Boat* was watching. If not for needing to keep their location a secret, they would have broadcasted it across the entire Black Hole Church.

"Do you think he can succeed?" a cultivator whispered in the crowd around the asteroid—as a C-Grade, he barely had the qualifications to stand here.

"Of course he will!" another replied. "So what if nine out of ten people die? This is Jack Rust! If even he fails, we're all doomed!"

"I know he will succeed," said a third cultivator. "I just wonder how many miles he'll reach."

"Sovereign Heavenly Spoon made it to eight thousand miles. I don't know if Jack Rust can reach that point, but he shouldn't be much worse, right? Maybe seven thousand?"

"You idiot, how can you compare a mere Jack Rust to Sovereign Heavenly Spoon? That's the greatest B-Grade of the last hundred thousand years! I say Jack Rust will reach just a bit above six thousand miles."

"Well, I think it will be seven."

"Wanna bet?"

On forming one's inner world, only one out of every ten people succeeded. However, even those who succeeded were separated into various levels based on the size of the world they produced. The deeper and wider your Laws, the sturdier your foundation, the more you could expand your world without it collapsing.

Most people reached between one to three thousand miles across. That was the crushing majority. Almost every B-Grade Jack had faced so far had fallen in that bracket, excluding Eva Solvig and the two Supreme Ancestors of the Animal Kingdom who'd reached around four thousand miles. Spacewind and Monk Uruselam, who were still trapped in the Green Dragon Realm, had both reached the five thousand mile mark, establishing themselves as elites amongst their level. That was also why they were so much stronger than the other B-Grades at the Green Dragon Realm—the size of one's inner world directly affected their strength.

It also served as a reference point for their potential.

Generally speaking, only those who reached above three thousand miles had a decent chance of stepping into the late B-

Grade. Four thousand miles signified one had a tiny chance of reaching the peak B-Grade, and five thousand garnered a decent chance of doing the same thing.

As for reaching the A-Grade, the records were unclear. After all, A-Grade cultivators could live for as long as a million years. The most widespread theory was that almost all A-Grades had reached seven thousand miles when forming their inner world. That was also why Sovereign Heavenly Spoon, who had reached eight thousand miles, was given so much attention.

As for whether that theory was true or not, only a true A-Grade could verify it, and they weren't easy people to ask.

"What do you think, Sage?" the Sovereign whispered, leaning toward the homeless-looking man. "Will he reach eight thousand as well?"

"You mean, if he will surpass you?" The Sage chuckled. "I do have a prediction... But there is no fun in telling you, right? It's much better to just watch."

"Hey! I'm the one who withholds information!"

"How the tables have turned."

An odd light shone in the Sage's eyes as he gazed at Jack—one of deep hope.

"What about the brorilla?" the sovereign asked. "Surely you can tell me about him, right?"

"I would, but... I actually have no idea!" The Sage laughed. "I guess we can only wait and see."

Dorman, who was floating beside them, didn't say anything. Neither did Min Ling. Her eyes were glued on Jack. She'd recently achieved seven thousand miles on her breakthrough—an extremely impressive feat.

Will he surpass me? she thought, biting her lip. *If he does...*

Conversation about Jack's results spread wildly across the crowd. Even inside the *Death Boat*, many knowledgeable people had shared the details about how this breakthrough worked, so predictions came and went. There were even betting stands in popular shops or squares. Most bet he'd reach around seven thousand, while stragglers ranged from three to nine.

"Come one, come all!" a large-bodied merchant shouted. "The more people you bring, the higher the rewards! The winners split the entire betting pool!"

Of course, he would keep a five percent commission as the one in charge, but he didn't feel the need to mention that. People flocked to his stand, as they did to every other. Business was booming—Jack Rust might well be the merchants' patron saint!

However, all the excitement outside didn't affect Jack in the slightest. He had already withdrawn his perception completely, entrusting his safety to Elder Boatman. He was floating inside his soul world, completely cut off from everything else, facing his Dao Tree.

There was no rush. Jack gazed upon his Dao, observing its every nook and cranny, every tiny detail. This was the complete culmination of his eight years of cultivation.

A purple fist hovered at the bottom, facing downward—its five fingers were colored purple, silver, green, red, and black. Besides the purple thumb which represented the Fist, the core of his Dao, each of the other fingers represented a Dao Root he'd once developed: Indomitable Will, Life, Power, Weakness. The foundation of his Dao.

The top of the fist was an empty wrist, inside which was buried the Life Drop—an extreme treasure of Life, a processed drop of blood from Enas himself. Above the Life Drop grew Jack's Dao Tree—nine feet tall, with roots hugging the fist below, a solid trunk leading to a crown of green leaves and purple flowers.

Nine fruits were also there, each fully grown: Fist, Space, Life, Death, Battle, Spanking, Brotherhood, Time, and Protection. The cornerstones of his cultivation path. Every single one of them felt just right—perfectly suited for him and the rest of the fruits.

Finally, a transparent, heart-shaped crystal filled with Dao runes orbited the tree crown—it was the Realm Heart he'd inherited from Archon Green Dragon, the foundational block of a separate world. It hadn't helped him much so far, but it was a great treasure—this was where it would begin to show its worth.

Between it and the Life Drop, alongside many inferior treasures, Jack could be considered extremely well equipped for this breakthrough.

There wasn't much else in his soul, currently. Copy Jack was floating about, eager to watch the change, eyes filled with deep anticipation. The door on the trunk of the Dao Tree remained shut, with the turtle—or Saint Venerable Thousand Shell—sleeping behind it. Who knew how long it would remain like that. Jack worried a bit about what would happen to the turtle during his breakthrough, but he could neither contact it nor wait for it to awaken. He just hoped for the best.

His eyes snapped into focus. He drew a deep breath, summoning energy from everywhere inside his soul. Power shimmered at his fingertips, flooded every inch of his being. In the real world, the ground beneath him shattered, creating a small crater on which he sat. Space shivered. Purple winds cracked.

And the breakthrough began.

Jack reached out—his eyes brimming with resolve. He pointed a finger at the large fist at the base of his tree. With a decisive move, he beamed pure energy at it, destroying it completely. The five fingers flew in different directions before dissolving, becoming masses of energy which Jack kept hovering at his side.

Beads of sweat ran down his face. Not of exhaustion, but of worry. The process of creating one's inner world began with completely demolishing your Dao. Any mistake from here on out would cause his soul to implode and kill him instantly.

However, Jack was too hardened to cave at simple pressure.

The large fist had dissolved, leaving his Dao Tree floating alone through Jack's soul. Already, it was trembling, its stability failing. Without a base, it would soon wilt, but Jack wouldn't let that happen. He flew over and smashed a fist into his Dao Tree. Splinters flew everywhere. His hand bled.

Only a small crater had been formed on the trunk. Jack persisted. Fist after fist smashed into the tree, steadily widening the crater. Purple juice flowed out, and the pain was intense, as if Jack was ripping apart his own heart. Yet, he continued. The crater kept widening until Jack's fist penetrated the hard bark to strike something deeper inside the tree.

The moment he did, his world trembled. With a loud, earthly moan, the tree shook and began to disappear from the base up, unraveling into pure energy. Everything Jack had spent years to create, he was now destroying. It felt terrible. He could choose to stop it, use his Dao to seal the wound and try to save the tree, but that would be meaningless. He would still die if he tried. The only way out was forward.

He let the tree unravel. He watched its roots wilt and break into scraps of wood which then completely dissipated into energy. The trunk followed, starting from the base. The Life Drop was left hovering alone, a green star in the void, as the tree above it disappeared.

Inch by inch, the tree was gone. Jack watched as it went from being nine feet tall to eight, then seven, then six. The door on the trunk faded, and the lower branches began to fall. Before long, only a little bit of the trunk and the crown remained. Even the leaves were wilting, the fruits seeming weaker.

He let the slow process continue as he watched those fruits. They were nine—the number of perfection, the apex of beauty. Ten would be too much—only nine could perfectly encapsulate the totality of human existence.

A bit of a shame, he thought. *I could have continued. Though growing fruits is trivial now.*

He gazed upon his fruits again. Concepts and energy jumped from one to the other—they formed a complete whole, a system of thought and understanding. It was these nine fruits which would serve as the foundation of Jack's inner world. The more perfect they were, the better his world would be.

So why did he suddenly feel like something was off?

A persistent feeling crept though his mind. A sense that something was missing—something was gone. Imperfection.

With the large fist gone and the Dao Tree almost disappeared, the fruits were now allowed to interact freely. He could see their concepts touch and bounce off each other. The system they created was complete, sure—he could sense that using it to create a stable inner world would be easy. Coupled with everything else, he was sure to reach far.

But would he reach the apex?

Every step he'd taken so far had been perfect. What about this one? Could it be... incomplete?

Worry gnawed on Jack's mind. He kept all the gathered energy still, waiting for the last of the trunk to dissolve before beginning on the fruits, but his previous suspicion spiked in intensity. His instinct was screaming. He was making a mistake. His fruits were perfect, but the system they created was not. It was almost perfect. Something was missing. *What?*

What had he missed during his cultivation journey? Where had he gone wrong?

Intense regret welled up inside him. He'd vowed to pursue the peak of cultivation. Was he dooming himself to never reach it? Had his breakthrough been too hasty? Even if he had, there was nothing he could do about it now except regret. He couldn't stop now.

There has to be something! he thought, gnashing his teeth. *There is just one thing missing! One concept I cannot put my finger on! If I can identify it, maybe I can find a solution! I can fix it.*

Yet, no matter how much he hoped, he knew it was hopeless. The breakthrough had begun. Finding the root of the problem now would be as difficult as reaching the sky. Even if he found it, it wasn't like he could just add a new concept to his Dao. He'd already reached the limit.

Suddenly, an old memory flashed into his mind. Back when he'd absorbed the heart of the Green Dragon Realm, he'd caught a glimpse of the entire realm, including the massive tree which supported it. That tree stretched from the base to the top, rising for endless miles. It also contained nine fruits, capturing that image of perfection.

Yet, Jack remembered catching a glimpse of something else. A tenth fruit, hiding between the leaves.

Could it be... he suddenly thought. *Could it be true? Could there be... ten fruits!*

CHAPTER FIFTY-EIGHT
PURSUING PERFECTION

JACK HAD NEVER HEARD ANYTHING LIKE THAT. HE'D NEVER EVEN considered it. Everyone spoke of nine fruits, that was the whole theme of the C-Grade. Nine was as close to perfection as one could get.

But what if it wasn't? What if there could be ten fruits, it was just that no one had been able to achieve them?

Why was this breakthrough the only fatal one? Could it be that cultivators were meant to have ten fruits, and people had just found a way to force this breakthrough at nine?

Or, maybe, nine fruits really were the limit, and the tenth fruit was the step toward an unattainable perfection? The true perfect path?

Whoever said that nine signified perfection? Bullshit! It was obviously ten, ten was the number!

Jack knew this was insane. He had no guarantee it would work, that it even could work. The only hint he had at the existence of a tenth fruit, besides his own wishes, was the tenth fruit he'd glimpsed at the Green Dragon Realm, which could mean all sorts of other things.

If Jack tried to develop a tenth fruit right now and failed, that would severely affect his breakthrough. It might even fail completely and kill him. To even think of attempting it was the sign of a madman.

Good thing he was one.

Let's go! Jack thought. His attention became razor-sharp. His Dao spread out, covering the Dao Tree and slowing down its disappearance. It was too late to stop it, but he could delay it a bit. At the same time, part of his gathered energy seeped into the remaining nine fruits, invigorating them. They were alive once again, blooming with power.

Jack focused his mind on the crown of the tree. Nine fruits decorated it, evenly splitting its energy streams. It seemed complete, but Jack now suspected it wasn't. He tried to create another fruit.

The tree no longer possessed roots or a trunk, so he force-fully poured energy into the crown. The branches shivered. The leaves fluttered, and the fruits wobbled as if questioning his decision.

For every other fruit, the process had been natural. He would pour energy into his Dao Tree, then focus on a concept. If his foundation was solid enough, that energy would automatically enter a flower and form a Dao Fruit.

That didn't happen. Instead, the energy just circulated aimlessly among the branches, not knowing where to go and finding no gap to plug. Jack wasn't one to quit easily. He grabbed that energy with his willpower and forced it into one flower which looked slightly larger than the others. The energy protested. The flower shook as if about to explode. Jack kept them both intact with his strength of will, forcing them to fuse.

His brain turned wobbly. In the real world, people stared at him from afar, noticing that he'd suddenly grown paler, and his nose had begun to bleed. Worried cries emerged everywhere.

"What's going on?" Elder Heavenstar exclaimed. "Will he really fail his breakthrough?"

"He is blocking the tree's disintegration," Elder Boatman replied—his perception was shaper and his experience richer than Heavenstar's. His usually impassive voice now contained a hint of anger. "What is he doing? That boy is an idiot!"

All across the crowd, people were worried about Jack. Some took joy in his misfortune, bragging about how he was not as great as he seemed. Even the Sage grew puzzled—his eyes were closed, as if observing something with great focus.

Sovereign Heavenly Spoon had forgotten to blink. Dorman stared like his world was broken. Min Ling was shocked, her hands clasped together. You can't fail! she shouted inwardly. Not you!

Seeing that Jack didn't immediately turn better, most assumed he really had messed up his breakthrough. They couldn't bear to watch. The majority of the crowd flew to the other side of the asteroid, where Brock was seemingly doing much better. His breathing was even, and his body stable—he even appeared ready to begin the creation of his inner world.

———

Jack didn't care about anything else. His entire being was focused on developing this tenth fruit. The energy and flower were both resisting, but he used iron will to force them into unity. This was overdrawing his mental reserves—even if he abandoned the tenth fruit right now and continued with his breakthrough, the size of his inner world would be greatly affected.

Yet, he persisted. Jack wasn't driven by the fear of failure, but by the drive to succeed. He wouldn't cower.

"Grow!" he shouted, pouring even more energy into the

flower. It stubbornly resisted—then, ever so slowly, a little shape began to emerge from its midst. It was just the most fundamental form of a fruit, far from a complete one. Yet, the moment Jack saw it, his hope was rekindled. He decided to throw all caution to the wind and go all-out.

"GROW!" he commanded. Of the massive amount of energy he'd amassed by dissolving his Dao foundation and Dao Tree, a significant portion dove into this newborn fruit. It struggled to grow. It was like the world itself resisted it, but this was Jack's soul, it was his world. If he wanted a tenth fruit, he would have a tenth fruit!

He roared and pushed harder. Veins stuck out on his temples. The nine fruits protested the new arrival to their complete system, but Jack forced them to make room. A tenth concept arrived. It wasn't one Jack had identified yet, but it was exactly what was missing, a concept true to the deepest reaches of his soul. This was meant to be. He pushed even harder.

The more this new fruit grew, the greater the resistance it faced. Jack poured more and more power into it. The energy he had amassed, which was meant to expand his inner world, was now being sacrificed to grow this tenth fruit. It was a mad gamble—one which might not even be wise. It seemed insane. Even if he did grow this fruit, with what energy would he continue his breakthrough?

The only thing in favor of this development was Jack's instinct, and he intended to follow it to the end. That was the true path. That was the Jack way.

The fruit developed slowly, from a flower, into a rod, into a shape resembling a feather. It surpassed the size of a new fruit and kept going.

Jack wasn't just making it appear. He wanted to grow it directly to maturity. That was the only way it could assist his breakthrough—it would be useless otherwise.

The fruit kept growing. Over half of Jack's amassed energy went into it, a much larger amount than any other fruit had absorbed. Its size almost reached the others. Jack felt a power forcing it down, constricting the fruit, as if the world itself wouldn't permit it to exist.

"THIS IS MY WORLD! I COMMAND IT!" Jack shouted, his eyes red. "GROW!"

The opposing energy faltered. Jack's tenth fruit sprang to full size—a white feather, light and free. The moment it finished growing, it fell perfectly into place among the system of the other nine fruits. The energy circulation between them turned smoother. All the errors were eliminated.

The opposing force disappeared like it was never there. Jack lost his breath for a moment. He stopped supporting the new fruit—and nothing happened. It stayed there, proud and true.

Ten fruits. This was perfection. This was the Dao.

And finally, Jack knew exactly what his tenth fruit was about. His previous fruits formed a system containing everything but lacking direction. Even the Fist was only a tool, a way forward, not a destination. Only this final concept was the real driving force behind Jack's every decision since the Integration.

Freedom.

He laughed wildly, the sound echoing all over his soul world. "Fear me, world!" he roared. "Perfection really is unattainable. Nobody can reach it, but I can choose to try—because I am *free*!"

New power erupted from inside him. He felt like he'd just undergone a qualitative evolution—like he'd become incomparable to before. This wasn't just the tenth fruit. It was a whole new realm, a realm in which he alone could stand.

"Inner world, here I come!" he shouted.

The ten fruits hung on the crown of his tree—an image which Jack burned inside his brain, one he would never forget.

One which, perhaps, had never before been seen in the history of the universe.

Jack grabbed his first fruit, that of the Fist. He tore it off the branch and crushed it between his hands—purple juice flew out, the fruit collapsing into pure energy. An incorporeal purple mass floated beside Jack, flanked by the remaining half of his energy. He'd just destroyed his own fruit, but he couldn't be more excited. This was the way forward. This was the path to true power—true freedom.

His all-out gamble had succeeded! What would be the reward?

He tore down the fruit of Space, then Life, then Death. The various shapes disappeared, leaving only the colored concepts floating around him. Jack laughed. He destroyed the rest of the fruits as well. The tree finished disintegrating. Only his very last Dao Fruit remained, hanging alone in the void, a white feather representing Freedom. It had only existed for a few moments, yet Jack could sense that its importance surpassed everything else he'd achieved.

"Thank you," he said, then crushed it in his hands. A tenth concept rose to meet the others, and Jack pushed his hands together, forcing all those concepts to merge. Where the colors met, his soul shattered. A gap was created. The energy he'd amassed flowed inside, guided by its own instincts to create space and time, matter and energy.

It was a world inside a world, rapidly expanding inside Jack's soul. Everywhere it touched, the previous soul world collapsed, replaced by the new order. Jack was unaffected by it, as were Copy Jack, the Life Drop, and the Realm Heart. They were simply enveloped by Jack's inner world, dragged into it.

Finally, the borders of the inner world reached those of his previous soul world and converted everything. There was no soul anymore—only a world filling his very being, exactly one thousand miles across. It was an empty vastness containing only starry dust, the particles on which the world was built.

This was Jack's core now. His inner world. The break-through had succeeded, but he contained his joy, because there was still a way to go. The borders of this world didn't really exist—they weren't in the same dimension as his body, but more like a separate island in the endless sea of spacetime. As long as it remained stable, and as long as he had the energy to feed it, it could keep growing.

He sensed it clearly. Right now, this world was in its most malleable state. Now was the time to expand it as much as he could. Moreover, the system of laws directing it was perfect, with no gaps in between. It wasn't the same system as in the universe outside, but one equally real, as if Jack was cultivating his own universe to stand on par with the actual one.

With his perfect laws in place, stability wasn't an issue. Moreover, thanks to that great stability, the energy it needed to expand was minimal.

Jack had no idea how large he could make his inner world, but he couldn't wait to find out. He spread his hands, and like a god, he commanded, "Expand!"

———

The crowd remained restless in the outside world. Most had flown off to watch Brock's breakthrough, not bearing to see a genius fall. A few had remained, however, including both A-Grades. At a certain point, the Sage's eyes flew open, filled with genuine disbelief. Elder Boatman reacted a beat later, narrowing his eyes at Jack, not with shock but hesitation.

"Jack seems to have recovered…" he muttered. "Good. However, I can sense he's wasted a lot of energy. Creating a decent world will be impossible."

"It is regrettable, but he has fallen," Heavenstar agreed with a sigh. "What a shame. I really believed in this young man."

The soul was inviolable. Even these A-Grades couldn't see inside Jack's soul, so they couldn't see he had created a new fruit. Even the fluctuations of his aura were obstructed by the tremendous amounts of power surrounding him. All they could see was that he remained at seemingly the same point of his cultivation, but over half of his energy had been wasted recovering from whatever had set him back.

Most spectators, however, couldn't even see that.

"Hey, Jack Rust recovered!" a C-Grade celebrated. "Come check him out, everyone! I think he'll begin forming his inner world soon!"

"Are you kidding me!" a voice rang in his mind—one of his friends who'd flown to the other side of the asteroid. "The brorilla has already started. You come here!"

"*He started?*"

The cultivator was surprised. Generally speaking, the more talented a cultivator, the faster they could form their inner world. In the eyes of everyone, Brock succeeding first marked him as more talented than Jack, not to mention that Jack had almost failed entirely.

I guess he really was overstated... What a disappointment. The cultivator sighed, then rushed over to meet his friends on the other side of the asteroid. Whatever the case, Brock the brorilla was now expanding his inner world. If he was more talented than the famous Jack Rust, just how many miles could he reach?

Everyone rushed over, eager to watch.

CHAPTER FIFTY-NINE
BROCK'S INNER WORLD

"It's starting!" the audience cheered. Spatial fluctuations wrapped around Brock, covering his surroundings with a pale golden haze. Hymns and chants resounded. The golden space expanded rapidly, assimilating everything as it stretched for hundreds of miles outward. Soon, it reached a thousand miles across—a golden void filled with chanting brorilla phantoms, with a large golden temple dominating its center.

Brock's inner world had appeared.

The brorilla himself remained visible, sitting cross-legged on top of the temple. His eyes snapped open, and he shouted, "Expand!"

The golden space roared outward. Hundreds of miles were swallowed in the blink of an eye. His inner realm easily reached two thousand miles across, then three, then four. Thankfully, everyone had already flown away, or they might be at danger of clashing with the realm.

"What the hell?" a cultivator shouted. "Four thousand miles already!"

"It's still going!" another replied. "Run!"

They flew away at top speed. It wasn't that the expanding

realm would hurt them if they touched it, but that they might affect his breakthrough—and Elder Boatman wouldn't let that happen.

The realm kept expanding. Golden hymns overtook the universe, ringing everywhere like divine bells. The brorilla phantoms multiplied—while they kept chanting, they began performing as well. Some fist-bumped each other, others hugged and cried, a few fought. Most laughed. They were exhibiting the ten thousand facets of brohood—the process of Brock's laws coming alive and perceiving themselves.

Reaching five thousand miles across was the dream of every C-Grade cultivator. It was a tremendously difficult feat which would cement them as extreme geniuses of their generation. Brock just sailed past that threshold, not slowing down in the slightest.

Before everyone's wondrous gazes, his inner world expanded to six thousand miles before beginning to slow down.

"Six thousand..." Many people gasped, unable to believe this. "I thought this brorilla was just a sidekick! Was he the protagonist all along?"

Sovereign Heavenly Spoon clicked his tongue. A touch of interest was entering his eyes. "I don't think I was this fast at my breakthrough..." he whispered.

Next to him, Starhair only snorted. "It doesn't matter. This brorilla and Jack Rust must have only reached this level by enjoying countless resources from Elder Boatman. However, the effect of treasures is limited during this breakthrough. True talent is all that matters. Just watch—the brorilla will abruptly run out of steam, then stop expanding."

The sovereign gave Starhair an amused gaze but said nothing.

Brock's inner world kept expanding. 6200, 6500, 6800 miles... The speed was significantly reduced from before, but his power rose exponentially with every mile. The golden space now occupied a large sphere around him, the size of a small planet. Every single mile significantly increased its volume. The asteroid simply turned into dust particles as the inner world expanded without any clash or shockwave whatsoever. Thankfully, its diameter was around ten thousand miles, so Brock and Jack's inner worlds colliding was impossible. They'd need a combined world size of twenty thousand.

Brock smoothly reached seven thousand miles and kept going.

"Heavens!" a cultivator shouted. "Just how far will he expand?"

At this point, even Elders Boatman and Heavenstar were paying close attention. A seven-thousand mile inner world was no joke. It indicated Brock had the potential to reach the A-Grade in the future.

"I think you underestimated your disciple, Boatman," Heavenstar said, chuckling. "This is a pie that fell into your lap. Let me congratulate you first."

"He kept too low a profile…" Boatman muttered. In his eyes, Brock was only Jack's follower. He never expected him to be this good.

Heavenstar smiled with pride. This wasn't his disciple, but his mood remained excellent. "How far do you think he's going to go? Will he surpass Spoon?"

"At this rate…" Boatman's red eyes flickered. "He just might."

"What a great time for our Church! Haha!"

Brock's inner world had slowed down by now. He reached 7200 miles, 7300, 7400… At this point, every hundred miles was a whole new world of potential and strength, but they were also much harder to achieve. Brock's laws began to show slight imperfections—when stretched this far, they presented gaps, harming the stability of his inner world and slowing its expansion. The energy required to push it out kept increasing.

Brock was growing tired. Every breath was laborious, every mile a hurdle. Yet, he wouldn't stop easily. He reached 7800 miles before his expansion finally slowed to a crawl.

"Almost eight thousand!" Heavenstar exclaimed. "That's almost the same as Spoon! Who would have thought that two such geniuses would appear as our Church faced extinction? The heavens truly are favoring us!"

"I don't know about that," Boatman replied calmly.

"What? You don't think the heavens are showing us mercy?"

"Not that part. I don't think he's done expanding."

"Hmm?"

Heavenstar looked over. Brock was pale and exhausted—yet, his gaze was resolute, and his aura steadied by supreme belief in himself. "Brohood is not a lonesome path," he chanted, his voice easily spreading into the audience and beyond. The entire *Death Boat* vibrated to his sound. Brock continued, "It is one meant to be walked together. I am not perfect, bros. Can you help me?"

The audience was stunned. Was he talking to them? They obviously couldn't help even if they wanted to. A moment later, however, his true goal was revealed. The golden brorillas, who had been chanting and performing feats of brohood all this while, suddenly stopped. They brought a fist to their chest. Ten thousand of them roared at once.

"YES, BIG BRO!"

The universe shook. The audience clasped their ears to protect them. Before their eyes, the ten thousand brorillas flew to the many gaps and tears revealed in Brock's inner world, using teamwork and their bodies to patch them up. Brock's laws weren't perfect, but these brorillas were doing their best to alleviate the tension.

Golden energy poured into the gaps, stabilizing them. Brorillas grabbed the edges and pulled them together. Their muscles
bulged. The tears in the fabric of Brock's inner world
contracted, no longer inhibiting the expansion as much. The
golden space accelerated again. Its expansion, which had
stopped at 7800 miles, suddenly erupted outward.

8000, 8100, 8200... Before anyone could react, his inner
world had reached 8300 miles and slowed down again. Even
the golden brorillas had reached their limit—but this was 8300
miles!

The record of Sovereign Heavenly Spoon had been broken!
Brock was the new champion!

Cries and cheers of disbelief erupted from the audience.
They were only beginning to realize they were witnessing the
birth of a legend—the birth of a future A-Grade! The Sage
nodded in acknowledgement, while Sovereign Heavenly Spoon
shook his head in self-deprecation.

"I was too full of myself," he said. "I thought my rival would
be Jack Rust, but it turns out... this brorilla is him. Brock, was
it?" He smiled. "I'm looking forward to the future."

As for Starfire, he chose not to speak. His face was twisted
like he'd eaten something way too sour.

This was just too grand an event. Even the two Elders had
risen from their seats, too excited to sit down. Seven thousand
miles indicated a chance to reach the A-Grade, but at this time,
that meant little. The Church already had dozens of Elders—
one more wouldn't make a great difference, let alone a B-Grade
with the faint chance of reaching the A-Grade in the future.
Even after passing the 7500 mark, that only meant he had
decent chances.

However, eight thousand miles was different. It was a qualitative change. If nothing unfortunate happened, Brock would
most probably reach the A-Grade in the future, and he might

not even stop at the early tier. A middle A-Grade combatant was vital to the Church as a whole. He could have an effect on the entire war!

"Brock must be protected," Elder Boatman said seriously. "Starting tomorrow, I will devote my full attention to him and train him properly. If he can rise quickly enough, he might be able to fight alongside us."

"What tremendous luck," Heavenstar said, shaking his head. "For two such talents to appear in the same era... The world really is helping us."

Brock had surpassed every expectation. In fact, he'd even surpassed the expectations people had of Jack. He made this fiasco seem worth it. Even if Jack Rust failed his breakthrough, that disappointment would be overshadowed by the joy caused by Brock.

People were already celebrating, and secretive channels of communication were already transmitting the news across the entire Church. Even the Arch Priestess was notified.

Nobody imagined... that Brock was not done yet.

Sitting in the middle of that golden space, he raised his arms. The few observant members of the audience who caught that movement cared little for it. His next action, however, drew everyone's attention.

"Bros of the world, I need you now," Brock said, sending his voice far and wide, spreading it across the universe to reach the ears of those it should. "Lend me your power!"

The audience members looked at each other, not daring to hope. They were stunned. Boatman and Heavenstar, who had just taken their seats again, jumped back up.

"Could it be..." Heavenstar muttered.

Ripples appeared at the center of Brock's soul world. The gates of his large golden temple slammed open. Phantoms were vaguely seen inside—there were dogs, crabs, and other beasts, but most were human. They were featureless and ephemeral, yet clearly contained power. The ghosts all raised their hands, mirroring Brock's motion, and power erupted out of the temple, seemingly coming from nowhere.

The inner world shone with splendor. Power filled its every nook and cranny. The golden brorillas, who were still struggling to contain the gaps, let out cries of relief. "Welcome, bros!" they shouted. "Thank you!"

Brock's entire body shone golden. A massive brorilla phantom formed around him, overlapping with his presence, and his power experienced another leap forward. He pushed out his hands, and the world was forced to obey. "Once again..." he growled, "EXPAND FOR ME!"

The new golden power smashed into the walls of his inner world. The universe shook from the impact, and the walls were pushed forward. The audience hurried to retreat farther. Even the Elders were stunned.

"How is this possible?" Hevaenstar exclaimed, half-surprised and half-excited. "This is... It's a miracle!"

The inner world rumbled outward. From 8300, it pushed with tremendous force, seeming as if it would expand forever. Yet, the more it pushed, a powerful resistance appeared, forcefully slowing it down. Brock kept pushing. The universe kept suppressing him.

8500, 8600, 8700...

Nine thousand miles was the limit. Nobody in history had ever achieved it, and the reason was that the universe itself suppressed cultivators as they approached that limit. Brock roared and pushed on, veins bulging on his temples, striving to reach as far as he could. Finally, even the golden power of all his bros ran out. His inner world barely managed to reach the 8800 mark before halting, its expansion over.

Everyone was stunned. 8800 miles. This was... sensational!

Cheers and roars erupted. People cried and hugged each other. They saw hope for the future. Most didn't even know what such an inner world signified, but they knew it was important.

Boatman and Heavenstar did know. They'd each lived for several hundred thousand years; they'd read through all sorts of ancient documents and were aware of things most people didn't qualify to know.

"He passed 8500..." Heavenstar said. Boatman was too stunned to reply. Since the beginning of the cultivation world, reaching 8500 miles wasn't unprecedented, but it did have a special name: the Sign of Archon!

Those who reached this level had a chance of climbing to the very peak of cultivation, the Archon realm! The step beyond the peak of the A-Grade.

Archons were the cornerstones of the cultivation world. Their lifespans exceeded a million years, but they appeared far too rarely. Even now, the number of living Archons could be counted on one or two hands. If the Church could get another, that would be a major addition to their war forces. Brock would single-handedly change the course of the Second Crusade.

Elder Boatman, who was famously stoic and silent, laughed out loud. "Congratulations, Brock!" he shouted in his raspy voice. "You have become a legend!"

In fact, 8500 miles was exactly what Elder Boatman had achieved during his own breakthrough to the B-Grade. Being surpassed by one's student, and so unexpectedly, too... What a feeling that was.

Brock's inner world had finished expanding, setting a record that might not be surpassed for a million years. The brorillas relaxed—the golden space faded away, receding into Brock's body and settling itself. From now on, that would be his soul and core of power. He had, in the span of a few minutes, undergone a complete transformation.

After the expansion was over, the absorption of one's inner world into their body would take a few moments to complete. While Brock remained in meditation, digesting his gains, the audience couldn't stop speaking in excitement. "That was awesome!" someone said. "I can't believe we witnessed that! 8800 miles. What a concept!"

"I would be happy if I just succeeded in my breakthrough," a C-Grade muttered, scratching his head.

"By the way," a third person said, "I think Jack Rust managed to recover and is beginning his expansion as well. Wanna go see?"

"Not really. How could it compare?" the first person replied. "They began at the same time, but Brock finished his entire breakthrough before Jack Rust even formed his inner world... That's a sign he's mediocre at best. He should be happy to just succeed."

"Don't be like that. He had all that hype built up—I'm sure he's going to reach at least four thousand miles!"

"Well, whatever. We might as well go watch."

In the eyes of everyone present, watching Jack fumble his way into the B-Grade would only ruin the aftertaste of Brock's terrific success. Some were so uninterested they retreated into the *Death Boat* to celebrate. Only half the audience remained.

Inside *Death Boat*, the betting stands had grown desolate. Almost everyone regretted betting on Jack Rust reaching five or six thousand miles. They'd already resigned their money. As for the few mean ones who'd bet on him reaching three or four thousand, they couldn't stop smiling—for once, their bitterness would end up working out.

Even Elders Boatman and Heavenstar had complex looks as

they stared at Jack, whose inner world was just beginning to manifest.

"Let's not be downcast," Heavenstar said. "It is regrettable that something went wrong with his breakthrough... But the birth of a B-Grade is always a matter to celebrate."

"Hmph!" Boatman snorted, still full of excitement. "Don't underestimate my disciple. Even if he messed up, this breakthrough is not everything. Many people have defied expectations across the ages—with enough lucky chances afterward, alongside my guidance, he can still reach the late or peak B-Grade."

"With you as the teacher, I'm sure he will," Heavenstar replied, but he didn't really believe it. He was just trying to be nice.

"Look, it's starting!" a cultivator shouted, drawing everyone's attention. "Go, Jack Rust! You can succeed!"

Most people shook their head, not expecting much. What they didn't know, however, was that Jack's apparent failure was due to him forming an unprecedented tenth fruit before creating his inner world. As for the effects of that... There was only one way to find out.

Jack's breakthrough was beginning.

CHAPTER SIXTY
SHATTERING EXPECTATIONS

JACK STOOD IN A LARGE, EMPTY EXPANSE. IT RESEMBLED THE VACUUM of space, only filled with stardust—and, if one looked closely, they would find that its particles were shaped as fists. A massive purple fist also appeared below Jack, as if a large meteor hurtling through space, except it bafflingly didn't appear to move—or, rather, it did move, but the entire inner world moved with it.

Jack felt his world's boundaries reach a soft wall. He knew instinctively it was exactly a thousand miles wide—the bare minimum an inner world needed to reach to be able to maintain itself. Making it this far meant he'd succeeded. The only question was, how much more could he expand it?

Over half of his amassed energy had been used to develop his tenth fruit. In turn, that fruit stabilized his world, letting his system of laws approach perfection. He had no idea how these two facts would influence the final size of his inner world—and there was only one way to find out.

Filled with excitement, he pushed out his hands and shouted, "Expand!"

The world blasted outward. He could sense that it was

perfect—expanding was an easy process consuming minimal energy, at least for now.

He could not see the outside world, but they could see him. Inner worlds manifested themselves physically while forming, stealing a bit of the universe's essence and using it to stabilize themselves. That was how, regardless of a cultivator's specific Dao, their inner world would contain spacetime. It was also how the universe strangled those who approached nine thousand miles across—by denying them access to any more space.

The spectators saw Jack push out his hands and roar for the world to expand. They saw its walls gradually pushing outward, slowly increasing in size.

"So slow," a cultivator muttered, shaking his head. "He did succeed, so congratulations to him, but this is a bit disappointing..."

"Well, let's see," another replied. "His speed is nothing compared to Brock's, but if he can reach four thousand miles, he will still be an exceptional B-Grade."

Heavenstar sighed, trying to console Boatman. "Jack isn't doing too bad. At least he isn't expanding too slowly."

Boatman, however, had his eyes narrowed. A hint of puzzlement could be seen through his dark hood. "This is odd," he said. "No matter how fast or slow a cultivator, their speed of expansion will decrease as they go. Don't you think that Jack's is too consistent?"

"Hmm?" Heavenstar looked over, and his eyes narrowed. "Oh. You're right. That's odd indeed."

Most people in the audience weren't as perceptive, nor did they pay too much attention. They remained numbed by Brock's achievements. Watching Jack's slow expansion felt wholly unimpressive.

"Geniuses can rise and fall. Isn't this a prime example,

Sage?" Sovereign Heavenly Spoon asked. No reply arrived. He turned around in puzzlement. "Sage?"

The homeless-looking man wore a look of extreme seriousness. In fact, throughout their travels together, this was the first time the sovereign saw him so serious—as if everything else had been a play, and only this breakthrough was important.

"What's the matter?" the sovereign asked again, growing worried himself.

"Just watch and don't speak to me," the Sage replied.

The sovereign raised a brow. Such rudeness was very uncharacteristic. Still, he turned his gaze toward Jack's inner world, watching it more carefully than before.

Two thousand miles, three thousand...

Jack's inner world expanded slowly but steadily. To most people, reaching three thousand miles was already an achievement. Some, however, were beginning to notice he wasn't slowing down.

"Is that normal?" a cultivator asked.

"He's probably afraid to expand too fast," another guessed. "He's keeping his speed constant on purpose. Does he want to trick us into forgetting his failure? That's pretty lame..."

Starhair's face, which had been twisted sour before, now wore a self-satisfied smirk. "Just as I said," he told Min Ling. "A dog remains a dog no matter how many treasures they're fed."

She didn't even spare him a glance.

Jack's inner world reached four thousand miles and kept expanding. 4300, 4600, 4900... He had already surpassed the expectations of most, and his speed of expansion remained constant. People were beginning to pay attention now. Even the most critical ones had to shut up. Whatever had happened before, a five thousand mile world was no joke.

Heavenstar sighed. "Imagine how much he could expand if he hadn't messed up the destruction of his Dao Tree. In any case, there is nothing embarrassing about this result. Jack is worthy of congratulations."

"There are no tears," Boatman replied.

"What?"

"His inner world should be starting to struggle by now. There should be visible gaps caused by the imperfection of his laws. Where are they?"

Heavenstar looked over as well. Indeed, Jack's world was as pristine as before. What was going on here?

5200, 5500, 5800 miles...

The spectators contacted their friends who'd left and urged them to return. Jack Rust's breakthrough wasn't the failure everyone expected. If anything, he was doing suspiciously well. Even inside the *Death Boat*, where many people had looked away from the projection screens to discuss Brock's achievements, were gradually starting to pay attention again.

The buzz resurfaced. The excitement returned.

Six thousand miles! With another push, Jack's inner world surpassed another mark and kept going.

It was only now that Brock finished integrating his inner world and opened his eyes. Literia stood beside him. "Congratulations!" she said. "You reached 8800 miles. That's phenomenal!"

"What about big bro?" Brock asked.

"His breakthrough isn't over yet."

Brock smiled. "How great is he doing?"

"I... I actually have no idea."

The smile turned into a frown. "Take me there," Brock said, then didn't wait and directly teleported them both to the other side of the asteroid, joining the audience.

"Come here, Brock," Elder Boatman messaged him telepathically, and Brock, after waving Literia goodbye, teleported to the side of the Elders.

"Congratulations from both of us," Elder Boatman said. "Do you have any idea what's going on with your brother?"

Brock looked over, grasping the entire situation. "I do. He's the best."

The two Elders glanced at each other and shrugged, returning their focus to Jack. Brock crossed his arms and wore an expectant smile.

In the time it took for these conversations to happen, Jack's inner world had already reached seven thousand miles. It was still expanding.

"What the hell is going on?" someone asked. "Is this a joke? He clearly almost failed before, how can he be doing so well now?"

"And where are the gaps in his inner world?" another replied. "Even Brock had them!"

Starhair looked like he'd swallowed a fly. Min Ling was giggling proudly. The Sage remained fully focused, while the Heavenly Spoon Sovereign was just puzzled.

Jack was deaf to the audience. He kept expanding his world, calmly perceiving his Daos in the process. The only reason he was slow was because he wanted to familiarize himself with his new fruit as much as possible—otherwise, he could have expanded much faster.

It was only after he reached 7500 miles that he began to sense some resistance, but he just pushed with a little more power. By 8000, the resistance was becoming significant. Jack could no longer afford to meditate on his tenth fruit—he had to push with all his power. It wasn't that his laws or energy were insufficient, but that the universe was opposing his advance.

Thankfully, his perfect Dao system let him consume far less energy than other cultivators at his level.

Jack's world reached 8300 miles before it finally slowed down. By now, everybody was stunned. They expected a failure, not another triumph. Such breakthroughs should only occur once every several hundred thousand years—how come two happened at the same time?

People were beginning to believe. Jack had slowed down, but he was still pushing on. Could he also reach the 8500 mile point? Could there be two future Archons born today?

Jack knew he could probably reach the 8500 mark if he kept pushing. However, he wasn't content with going slowly. He still had much to give. A light blazed from the purple meteor below him—the World Anchor he'd absorbed a long time ago finally revealed its function, stabilizing his world even further. It fused with the large meteor fist, acting as the core of Jack's inner world.

His expansion accelerated again. From 8300, he jumped directly to 8600.

The audience cheered in surprise. He'd crossed 8500! The Sign of Archon! This was... unprecedented!

Even the Elders had stood up again, their hands shivering. "What monsters did you take in, Boatman!" Heavenstar cried out. There was no jealousy in his voice, only excitement. This war could still be won!

Boatman laughed. All his worries melted away. He hadn't felt so carefree in several millennia. "Good job, Jack!" he shouted.

Jack couldn't hear him, but even if he could, he wouldn't reply. He still wasn't done. He reached into his space ring and took out the neutron star fragment, tossing it into the world anchor. The fragment melted, increasing the density of his inner world. Elemental particles sprayed everywhere, along with a bit of green foam. His world was even further stabilized. Not only were there no gaps, but it was even more stable than at the start of his breakthrough.

Despite that stability, every bit of expansion was hard at

this point. The neutron star fragment and his willpower together could only achieve minimal progress.

8700 miles. 8750. His expansion had slowed to a crawl, but he was still advancing, rapidly approaching Brock's record. The brorilla felt no fear or jealousy, only pride. Go, big bro, he thought. Show them who you are!

Jack knew he was approaching the nine thousand mile limit, and he wasn't satisfied. In his mind, the only thing worth pursuing was the apex. The greatest obstacle to his expansion right now was the universe refusing to give him any more of its essence. It wasn't that he couldn't push, but that he would be sacrificing some of his inner world's stability. After all, his Dao of Spacetime wasn't advanced enough to support a world yet— he needed to take some from the universe, which wouldn't let him.

Thankfully, he had another way.

His thoughts flew into the Realm Heart, which still orbited him. "Go," he whispered. The Realm Heart froze in place. Then ruptured. Endless spacetime runes flew out. His inner world became covered in ripples of spacetime which focused on the edges and started pushing.

So what if the universe didn't give him any more spacetime to use? He had his own! The Realm Heart had once created a separate world—it could do it again!

The audience was stunned. Jack's inner world broke through the 8800 mark, then the 8900. It reached 8950 miles, 8970...

Nobody even cared that he'd surpassed Brock any longer. Nine thousand miles was the limit. No one had ever achieved it. The best they could do was converge to it, but never reach it.

Boatman was shaken. He'd read many ancient documents. From the start of the cultivation world until now, there was not one account where someone had reached nine thousand miles.

Even the brightest of Archons stopped somewhere around 8950. He would need to research a little more, but he suspected Jack's current inner world was the largest in history...

And was he *still* expanding?

This was insane! What was happening here surpassed the scope of the Black Hole Church and the Hand of God, it surpassed everything they knew. Would he really reach the limit? How was that possible?

Nobody knew how Jack had achieved this, but he did. He'd developed a tenth fruit. His system of Daos was perfect. Even now, there were no gaps, which meant he could devote the entirety of his energy and willpower into pushing back against the universe. Moreover, his foundation was incredibly solid, his body was extremely sturdy, and his battle power was through the roof. He'd even used the Realm Heart, the greatest creation of a spacetime Archon, to stabilize his inner world.

8980... 8990... 8995...

Everyone was beyond words. The two Elders were shivering, unable to speak. Sovereign Heavenly Spoon had forgotten to close his jaw, while the Sage's eyes were shining, his thoughts kept hidden. Starhair had grown pale.

It felt like time had slowed down. Jack's world shivered, then pushed out—and surpassed nine thousand miles!

9010 miles!

All jaws hit the floor. How was this even possible? Wasn't nine thousand the limit? Could everyone have been wrong? Just how did this happen?

"Holy shit," Heavenstar exclaimed, completely forgetting his position. "It's over nine thousand!"

Boatman was too stunned to reply. Brock, however, did. "Of course it is," he said calmly. "That's my big bro."

"Look!" someone shouted. "He's still going! The madman is *still going!*"

Everyone couldn't to believe their eyes. Jack hadn't stopped yet. He had slowly but steadily reached 9050 miles and was still expanding, if slowly. Boatman tried to form words but failed. He was in utter disbelief.

How high can it go... was all he wondered. They'd never actually confirmed that nine thousand miles was the limit. They'd just assumed so because everyone converged there.

His confidence in his own knowledge suddenly wavered.

By now, the audience was beginning to stir out of their shock. They'd waited 9500 miles away from Jack, as was customary. Did they need to move?

As for the asteroid below Jack, almost half of it had been torn away by Brock. The remainder was now swiftly disintegrating. It was like two giant space monsters had taken a bite of the asteroid each, leaving nothing but a strip of rock in the middle.

Inside his inner world, Jack was fully focused. He was aware he'd surpassed nine thousand miles, but that was something he already expected. His talent had been at the very top, and he'd developed a tenth fruit. The only question was, how far could he go?

He wouldn't stop until he fell.

The universe resisted more fiercely with every mile he claimed. The integrity of his Daos had never been an issue. After using the Realm Heart, neither was spacetime stability—now, it was just about power, about pushing back the universe.

"Life Drop, go!" Jack shouted. A green light enveloped him. Endless energy flowed into his inner world—the Life Drop's reserves, which hadn't even been depleted halfway since he started using it, erupted without limit. There was so much life. It flooded his inner world, forcing it to expand beyond its limits. Spacetime had solidified around the boundaries of his inner world, resisting with all its might, and Jack forced his way through the shackles.

The Life Drop was the most powerful treasure he'd ever possessed, probably one of the greatest in the universe, and he was spending its energy without restraint. The walls of his inner world didn't just expand—they blasted outward.

9500 miles!

That was roughly the distance the audience was watching from. They never expected anyone to reach it—they didn't even think it was possible. Many were too dazed to react fast ernough, but a tremendous wave of Death Dao smashed into them and flung them away.

"Retreat, you imbeciles!" Elder Boatman shouted. "Give him space!"

Things had already surpassed his scope of understanding. Nine thousand miles was supposed to be the unattainable limit, but Jack merely ignored it. He'd taken the combined history of the cultivation world, rolled it up, and used it to wipe his butt. He'd forced every Archon in history to eat shit.

Elder Boatman had no idea what was going on, but he knew one thing—Jack's breakthrough could not be disturbed!

He forcefully pushed everyone away, then turned to behold this historic moment.

CHAPTER SIXTY-ONE
B-GRADE

THE LIFE DROP WAS STILL RELEASING ENERGY. IT CONTAINED A highly-compressed green ocean which was now flowing out. This was much more energy than Jack had ever utilized before, but it also had more room to spread than just his body. His inner world was flooded. The only problem was that, to release this life energy, he had to use his body as the medium. If not, it wouldn't be perfectly attuned to him, and it would negatively affect his inner world.

Though Jack's body was extremely tempered, even he couldn't take this easily. It felt like molten iron flowing through his veins. The pain was excruciating, but his will was stronger. He gritted his teeth, enduring the strain to push more and more energy into his inner world. Even as his body deteriorated, not able to handle this much longer, he kept going.

9700 miles! 9800 miles!

The energy of the Life Drop was greater than any cultivator or treasure could produce, and it was all readily usable. Jack forgot about everything else except pushing more and more of it out. The little bit of energy he'd used to create his tenth fruit already seemed tiny compared to the current flood, like a teaspoon to an ocean.

The Life Drop's reserves were rapidly dwindling. Over half its remaining energy had been used up, but Jack kept pushing.

9900 miles!

By now, the resistance of the universe had reached a terrifying level. Spatial storms raged around his inner world, suppressing it. The stars in the distance faded as tremendous amounts of energy were siphoned into stopping him. The universe itself rejected this development, refused to let him expand any farther. Jack could even sense a faint threat brewing, but he ignored it.

His ten concepts—his ten fruits—roared as one. Fist, Space, Life, Death, Battle, Spanking, Brotherhood, Time, Protection, Freedom. These were his concepts. They were not borrowed from the universe but belonged to him alone. If he wanted to use them to create a world, why should the universe be able to stop him?

A terrifying force pressured him from all sides, but he roared into his own sky, "FUCK OFF!"

The concept of Freedom flared. The life energy shaped itself into a massive fist, smashing into the walls of his inner world and forcing them to expand. The universe's restrictive force reeled, unable to stop him, before clamping on even tighter.

9980 miles!

Jack hovered in the middle of his inner world like a wrathful god of creation. His cloak flapped, his hair rose. He alone stood up to a universe. He had no more treasures to use, no more tricks, but he kept pushing outward. Veins bulged over his forehead. His entire body was charred from the inside due to the massive amounts of life energy coursing through it. Only his pants' life force amplification kept him standing. He refused to yield.

"You have no right!" he shouted. "I don't care if you are the universe, or the Heavenly Dao, or the Gods... You don't get a say here! You don't control me! This is my world—if I want it to expand, it will expand!"

He smashed the energy into the walls, forcing them to expand ever more. The universe was no longer playing around. A tremendous amount of energy had amassed, even scaring the spectators. Every mile forward, every inch, was a tug of war between Jack and the rest of the universe.

He still refused to stop.

9990 miles. 9995. With another roar, he went all-out, forcefully pushing his inner world to exactly 9999 miles wide.

Elder Boatman gasped. 9999 miles—was this the true limit? Had they all been frogs in a well?

Just how had Jack achieved this!

Reaching this point was a tremendous achievement. It felt perfect, but Jack knew it wasn't. 9999 was the maximum limit the universe was willing to allow—he could feel that clearly. Going any farther was simply forbidden.

However, that only served to enrage him more. He may have run out of energy, but if he stopped now, he would have capitulated. He would have lost. That was unacceptable. He alone controlled his fate—if someone tried to suppress him, even if it was the universe itself, he would fight back!

Jack roared. His blood vessels cracked like twigs. Blood rained all around. His limbs broke, and all of his blood boiled. Every single bit of energy left in the Life Drop exploded outward at once, erupting in a huge explosion. Jack's entire inner world shuddered as if about to collapse. Yet, even with that, the universe's complete suppression barely budged.

But it did budge. No matter how little, the suppressive force the universe had mustered with all its power had momentarily faltered. An angry, disembodied roar echoed across the world. Jack pushed outward just a tiny bit before collapsing.

Ten thousand miles. Accurate to the inch. Finally, he could sense that it was no longer the universe stopping him from expanding, but his inner world itself. It had reached its real limit. It was satisfied.

In other words... he'd fought back against the universe, ignored its taboos, and won.

Jack had won.

He couldn't smile, because he'd lost control of his facial muscles. The expansion of his inner world came to a total stop, but he was happy. He'd defied the universe. He'd taken a step into a territory he wasn't allowed to.

He was *free*.

A trickle of life energy entered his body, slowly repairing him. It was the little leftover energy from the previous explosion. At the same time, the inner world contracted inside Jack's body, integrating itself as his soul. His power began to rapidly grow. The level he'd reached was completely incomparable to before. A single finger would be enough to easily annihilate his previous self.

This was a process which happened by itself. Jack knew he had a few minutes of laying in his inner world before it was fully integrated into his body. He could have rested. However, excitement overtook him. Blue screens flashed at the corner of his vision. He took a look.

Congratulations! C-Grade → B-Grade
Congratulations! You have successfully forged your inner world, embarking on the path of godhood.
All stats +200
Free stat points per Level Up: 20 → 40

Level Up! You have reached Level 400.

Congratulations! The Bare Fist Brotherhood faction has reached the B-Grade. New functions unlocked in the faction screen.

Congratulations! For escaping the confines of the Heavenly Dao, you are awarded the Title: Challenger.
Challenger: Most people conform. You fight and struggle to carve your own path. You will either defy the heavens... or fall and be forgotten. Efficacy of all stats +10%.

Class Upgrade available. Please choose your new Class:

Jack took a moment to digest this. He'd finally reached the B-Grade. His gamble had paid off in spades—he'd even achieved an inner world ten thousand miles across. Unprecedented, as far as he knew—though the fact that Archon Green Dragon was aware of the tenth fruit raised some questions.

In any case, now was a time to celebrate.

Jack relaxed, feeling the increased stats enter his body as his inner world stabilized inside his soul. He tried to keep away the double ecstasy and focus on something else: his new title.

Challenger. That is one ominous description... But the ten percent efficacy is huge. That's almost a thousand extra points in Physical. Just how strong have I become?

I wonder what activated that title. Was it me creating a tenth fruit? Or overcoming the restraints of the universe to reach ten thousand miles? Both were things the Heavenly Dao tried to stop.

Does that mean... I angered it twice?

Jack had a suspicion of what this meant, but he didn't go down that route yet. No matter what happened next, he needed power—and his new Class was the best way to get it.

Fist of the System (King)

You have received divine providence. Devote your life to the service of the ultimate being who favored you, becoming their fist in the cultivation world.
The Immortal System offers additional benefits for the wielders of this Class, including increased attribute points and Dao Visions.
"For the Immortals!"

The first choice was one he'd already seen when he broke into the C-Grade. The System wanted to recruit him—he rejected it without a second thought.

Fist of Freedom (King)

You roam the universe, spreading laughter and liberation wherever you go. Your fist is one of justice—hard and right.
"Only when the people are free will I be as well."

Now, this... This was a Class worth considering. He did enjoy fighting for the weak. The universe was filled with oppressors, whom he was determined to eradicate.

In fact, Jack had also been offered a similar Class when he entered the C-Grade, but he hadn't chosen it then. War hadn't been his priority, so he felt it might have taken him off his route. This time, however, liberation felt just right.

This Class called to him. He almost accepted it instantly before managing to pull back and view the rest.

Fist of Death (King)

No one understands Death like you do, no one embraces it. Grief is your mantle, murder is your path, bones the ground on which you walk—Death is both the end and a beginning, a flower blooming from the grave.

"Death and Life... It all becomes one. Join the cycle."

That was a bit creepy. It did sound powerful, as well as epic. Jack could see where it came from—he'd familiarized himself a lot with death during the C-Grade, from receiving the inheritance of Elder Boatman to losing his son and almost killing an entire planet. This Class was one he should be offered.

But not one he should accept.

Death was just part of his path. Life, Space, Time... Those were all crucial to his development. As much as this Class offered a quick path to power, he'd already chosen a different one, and he would follow it to the end.

There was only one Class remaining. Jack was certain it would be enticing, but he was already convinced he'd choose the Fist of Freedom. As soon as he opened the screen of the last Class, however, he was stunned. It wasn't blue, but orange—screaming importance. There were even little frilly ends wrapped around it.

Paragon of Cultivation (Legendary)

Legendary? His eyes widened. He didn't know there was a rank above King—then again, that was to be expected. He'd done all that stuff and only been offered one Legendary Class. Their rarity had to be staggering.

He kept on reading.

Paragon of Cultivation (Legendary)
Cultivation is a journey collectively pursued by the cultivation world. By achieving an unprecedented feat, you have pushed the boundaries of cultivation forward, earning the right to be called a paragon.
Choosing this Class means you will become a cultivator the

System spares no expenses to assist. You will receive increased stat gains on every level up and the most high-end Dao Visions available, while maintaining complete freedom to innovate.
"One step per generation. That is how the cultivation world was built."

Jack had to admit it. This Class sounded awesome. It tempted him.

Yes, the Fist of Freedom was in line with his goals, but it wasn't like this Class had any restraints. It directly mentioned *complete freedom*. He could use the extra power granted by Paragon of Cultivation to more effectively fight oppressors and liberate those who suffered.

Plus, it was a higher tier Class. One based on being unprecedented. Since it wouldn't impact him negatively in any way, how could he possibly say no? Even if that complete freedom thing was a lie, he sensed that his inner world gave him the capital to suppress the System core inside his body if he wanted to. The System couldn't harm him, at least not outside System space.

This Class was extremely good.

Make me a Paragon of Cultivation, he thought, then felt intense power course through his body. Many of his wounds were healed. His spent energy was refilled. He felt so unimaginably powerful.

Congratulations! You are now a Paragon of Cultivation (Legendary).
Free stat points per Level Up: 40 → 50
Congratulations! New Skill unlocked: Immortal Commune I
Immortal Commune I: *This skill has no tiers. It allows you to seek a council with the designated Immortals through the*

System's long-range communication network. Restraint is advised as this skill consumes many System resources.

Jack whistled. The System wasn't lying when it said he'd receive its full assistance. Being able to directly communicate with the rulers of the cultivation world would be an unimaginable boon to any other cultivator. To Jack, of course, it was rubbish. The Immortals were his enemies—why would he speak with them?

There was also another notification from his new Class.

Congratulations! You have received an Archon-level Dao Vision of Inner World Perfection. You may experience it at your convenience.

Archon-level!

Dao Visions had helped Jack a lot in the past, but as his level rose, the rarity of the visions which could assist him naturally rose as well. Archons were ideal. If this Class could provide him with several such visions... How powerful would he become?

Breaking into the B-Grade with a ten thousand-mile inner world had already given him a tremendous boost in power. With such assistance from the System and undoubtedly from the Church as well, he would soar in no time!

He just had to be careful of the System thing backfiring, but he was confident he had it under control. Nothing bad would happen to him, at least until he re-entered System space.

Done with all his notifications, Jack finally took a look at his status screen. It was glorious.

Name: Jack Rust
Species: Human, Earth-387
Faction: Bare Fist Brotherhood (B)

Grade: B
Class: Paragon of Cultivation (Legendary)
Level: 400

Strength: 8480 (+)
Dexterity: 8480 (+)
Constitution: 8480 (+)
Mental: 1200
Will: 1200
Free sub-points: 2

Dao Skills: Meteor Punch IV, Iron Fist Style III, Brutalizing Aura III, Neutron Star Body III, Supernova III, Space Mastery III, Fist of Mortality III, Death Mastery III, Titan Taunt III, Immortal Commune I
Inner World size: 10,000 miles
Matter Condensation: -
Titles: Planetary Frontrunner (10), Planetary Torchbearer (1), Ninth Ring Conqueror, Planetary Overlord (1), Grade Defier, Planet Destroyer, Challenger

He shook his head. How far he'd gotten...

By now, the last steps of his breakthrough were ending. His inner world had gotten fully integrated to his body, and the remaining energy, alongside the rush of stats, had completely healed him as well. Besides the Life Drop running completely dry, he was at full power. He itched to test it out.

Which could be a double-edged knife. Jack had defied the Heavenly Dao a little too much today. He suspected the universe wouldn't just take this lying down.

He opened his eyes and stared at the stunned crowd ten

thousand miles away from him. They looked at him like he was a ghost.

"Hey," he managed to say. "Pretty good, huh?"

"Jack!" Elder Boatman roared in joy, flinging back his hood. He'd never done this in public before, but his current excitement was too much. "Good fucking job!"

Jack smiled. "Thanks!"

More people rushed to congratulate him. Before they could approach, however, they were repelled by an invisible force. "Hmm?" Heavenstar muttered. "The breakthrough should be over. Why is the suppression still present?"

It was like Jack was isolated in a large bubble enforced by the universe itself. Penetrating it required tremendous power. Boatman's face fell—he had no idea what was going on, and whatever it was, it couldn't be good.

At the same time everyone realized this, so did Jack. He looked up, his previous suspicions confirmed. A large black cloud had formed over his head—one saturated with world-ending black lightning. The rage of the universe rained over him like acid droplets. The sheer volume of power aimed at him was staggering.

He smiled.

Jack had successfully defied the Dao. The universe wasn't happy about that. It wanted to kill him right here, right now. Heavenly tribulation descended.

CHAPTER SIXTY-TWO
TRIBULATION

A TERRIBLE POWER BREWED IN THE SKY OVER JACK. A LARGE BLACK cloud, extending for tens of thousands of miles, making the cultivators present look like ants. Every storm cloud on Earth was tiny compared to this.

Jack knew what he was facing—this wasn't his first rodeo. Invigorated and recharged by his breakthrough, he felt invincible. He clenched a fist; his inner world supplied endless power, power he was eager to vent. "Come," he whispered.

"Heavenly tribulation..." Elder Heavenstar muttered in the distance. His eyes widened. "This is bad. Everyone, retreat!"

The spectating cultivators didn't need to be told twice. They flew away, and even the massive *Death Boat* was driven away a great distance.

Everyone had heard stories about heavenly tribulation. The Dao of the universe followed its own rules, almost as if it was alive—these rules had shaped the path of cultivation long before the System. However, rules meant limitations. Sometimes, a cultivator would dare to break those limitations, dare to defy the heavens, which would result in the universe itself blasting them to oblivion.

Heavenly tribulations were no joke. They weren't opportunities or trials; they were assassinations. Everyone who managed to provoke a tribulation was an extreme genius of their generation, and even then, they almost always perished.

There was even a theory that, if not for tribulations, there would be double the number of Archons in the universe.

Of course, tribulations were beyond rare. Even for Jack, whose path so far converged to perfection, this was only his second. The first had come when he broke through to the D-Grade, a combination of using treasures to greatly accelerate his breakthrough and having absorbed the Life Drop. Except back then, it hadn't been a real tribulation, just a minor one activated from afar by Axelor, the Old God of Entropy. Jack had received assistance from the spirit of Enas and managed to overcome it.

This tribulation was something far more serious. He had openly and brazenly defied the rules of cultivation—twice. He had received the gifts of the Heavenly Dao, then challenged its authority. He'd enraged it. This was a strike sent to kill him.

Jack knew all those. He could sense the power brewing in the clouds above—it was far, far superior to anything an early B-Grade should be able to defeat. He was dwarfed beneath it. He suspected that even A-Grades could fall to this tribulation, let alone him. The heavens intended to not give him a single path to survival. He might die here, on his most glorious day, just as the doors to his future opened wide.

Why did he feel so excited?

Endless energy coursed through Jack. He was more powerful than ever, so powerful that even he didn't know his limits. His battle lust awakened. He desperately yearned for a worthy opponent, an anvil on which to test his newfound strength which had never appeared before in the history of the cultivation world.

The black clouds rolled for tens of thousands of miles, roaring and covering each other as if fighting to kill him first. Thick bolts of dark lightning jumped from cloud to cloud like black dragons. The condensed power was easily enough to annihilate planets, but then again, so was Jack's.

"*Careful!*" Elder Boatman's voice reached his ears. "*This tribulation is far too powerful! You cannot take it!*"

Jack smiled. "Watch me."

He shot upward. The crowd, who had by now retreated a hundred thousand miles away, cried out in surprise. Jack was less than an ant to these black clouds; yet he courageously rushed into them, meeting them head-on.

A bolt of black lightning cracked down to meet him half-way. Jack punched it. This was no Meteor Punch or Supernova —just a regular punch infused with the might of his B-Grade power. Yet, this strike was far more powerful than anything he'd ever used in the past.

His fist met the lightning bolt and shattered it. A shockwave rolled out, disrupting space for a thousand miles, and black sparks filled the area. Jack felt a slight tingle, possessing a body far superior to anyone else at his level—mere sparks couldn't hurt him.

"Haha! Come at me, heavens. More!"

They roared and obeyed. More lighting bolts flew down. Jack smiled and rushed to meet them, smashing them in an explosion of black and purple. Just a touch of those energies made spacetime shiver; it was a level most people had never before witnessed.

Inside the *Death Boat*, people watched Jack from either screens or windows, cheering at the top of their lungs. They had no idea what was going on any longer; only that Jack Rust was attempting something impossible. He was the greatest talent they'd ever seen—how could they not cheer for him?

As for the cultivators spectating from a hundred thousand miles away, they couldn't stop gaping in awe. They had a much better grasp of the situation than the low-level cultivators in the *Death Boat*. The powers at play were terrifying; let alone C-Grades, even most B-Grades had to admit that a single one of those lightning bolts would reduce them to ash. Jack's power had already surpassed their understanding—and this was just the opening salvo.

Brock looked on proudly, but also worried. Elder Boatman's hood was dark, not revealing his face. Elder Heavenstar was glancing around. "We have to do something!" he said. "We can't let him perish like this!"

"He will not," Boatman replied. Alongside him, Brock nodded. They were on the same wavelength.

Jack kept rising. His inner world was that of a burning furnace, containing endlessly condensed power. Be it in quantity or quality, he far outstripped most B-Grades present. His Dao galloped outward, a fist aimed at the skies, demanding true freedom. Lightning bolts rained. The sounds of Jack's impacts were like drums, beating to the tune of liberation, of breaking the shackles.

The image of him rising against the heavens etched itself into the hearts of everyone watching. He inspired them. They saw paths invisible before, possibilities they hadn't even considered. If Jack could defy the heavens, then what could they do? How could they challenge their fate?

"Jack Rust!" someone shouted, soon joined by the rest of the crowd. "Jack Rust! Jack Rust!"

Their voices reached Jack's ears as he clashed against the tribulation. He grinned. This was it—this was the feeling.

So far, the part of the tribulation he'd extinguished was minimal. The clouds finally decided to up the ante. A bolt thicker than before crashed down, reaching him in the blink of an eye. Jack punched out, shattering it, but his fist went numb. His speed dropped a bit.

Another similar bolt fell, then a third. Before Jack knew it, the clouds were unleashing thick black thunder, submerging the world in low thunderclaps. Flashes occurred with every lightning bolt, coloring the scene black and white. Jack was shooting out punches, but he was beginning to be pushed down by the sheer volume of attacks.

He refused to be outdone.

"Meteor Punch!" he roared. As his next fist smashed out, a large purple meteor shot upward. It carried highly condensed power, breaking through several lightning bolts, vanquishing them before it ran out of energy. Jack roared and kept shooting. The sky poured lightning bolts on his head, while he matched their fervor in meteors, meeting it in the middle. The world shook from their clash.

The tribulation's lightning bolts turned even thicker, even more powerful, their tips now shaped as roaring black dragons.

Jack narrowed his eyes. A large colosseum appeared with him as the center. It did not contain an audience this time— instead, it was the spectating cultivators who found them- selves in the stands, supporting Jack with their cheers. His power shot up again. His Brutalizing Aura spread out, incom- parable to what it used to be, and tried to strangle the clouds above.

Jack wasn't just defending against the tribulation. He wanted to rip it apart, and that only made the universe angrier.

His storm of meteors gained ground. Even against the dragon-shaped lightning bolts, he was winning, and his energy seemed endless, his body indefatigable.

Slowly but surely, like a boulder rolling down the hill, the tribulation increased its output. Ten times as many thunder- bolts descended. They swarmed Jack's meteors, reversing his advantage and pushing him back. Jack had to fly lower, creating more space between him and the clouds.

He gritted his teeth. He didn't want to use more power, but he could sense that the clouds still weren't going all-out; if he didn't power-up, he would die. The remaining parts of the asteroid below him had long turned to dust.

"Life Drop!" he shouted. The Drop itself had run out of power during his breakthrough, but some still remained in his inner world, floating aimlessly around. Now, he channeled that energy into his body, pushing it past its limits. He grew a foot taller—two new arms appeared under his armpits, and his punching speed doubled while his power increased.

The higher realms he reached, the more energy he needed to enhance his body. Right now, he couldn't maintain this form for long. He had to make it count.

Yet, it seemed pointless. Even as he increased his power, so did the clouds. Every collision was powerful, so many teeming to tear him down that they'd overlapped. Shockwaves filled the world. The spectators had to retreat yet again, afraid of getting caught in the blast.

"Sage!" Sovereign Heavenly Spoon exclaimed. "Is there anything we can do to help?"

"Tribulations can only be faced by the individual," the Sage replied, shaking his head. "If you try to help, the universe will just summon more power to match you. It is useless. All we can do is believe."

The sovereign thought about it and nodded. "Then, I will believe. It won't be the first miracle he creates."

As for Starhair, his face seemed a bit better. "Too bad," he told Min Ling. "He had a good ride, but here's where it ends."

She was too worried to care. "If you don't shut up, I'll drive my spear up your ass."

Dorman laughed. Starhair threw her a disapproving glance, then fell quiet.

Jack was at a disadvantage. He was almost going all-out, and the tribulation matched him. He hadn't even gone through a tenth of it. He suspected it could power up even more—could he?

Everything he did from now on would deplete his energy... but what choice did he have?

Before he could think further, the tribulation's power rose again. Rather than dragon-shaped lightning bolts, actual black dragons emerged from the clouds made of electricity. They were completely lifelike, all the way to their long whiskers. Their eyes shone with intelligence. They rushed at Jack, roaring at him, and he discovered that even his Meteor Punches couldn't deal with these dragons. Each could be considered a B-Grade creature, and there were dozens of them, hundreds.

How was this a tribulation aimed at an early B-Grade!

More than ever, Jack realized this wasn't a test, but a genuine attempt against his life. This tribulation was designed to be unbeatable. He wanted to beat it even more.

A dozen dragons flew around him, their paths unpredictable, and opened their jaws to bite down. Jack's eyes flared. Purple electricity emerged from his body, his speed and power redoubling. This was the Thunder Body, which he'd studied intensely on the trip to this galaxy. He still couldn't maintain it for long, but he was running out of options.

His body disappeared from between a dragon's jaws. He flickered everywhere, teleporting all around as his punches tore their bodies apart. He massacred the dragons. Dozens of them cried out in death, dispersing into black sparks which couldn't harm him. Dozens more arrived from above—Jack faced them, killing as many as the tribulation threw at him. Within seconds, the void itself was melting, and the space around him was electrified for ten thousand miles.

The spectators were speechless. This wasn't power an early B-Grade should have, no matter how talented. It even approached the A-Grade!

Elder Heavenstar looked on silently, his eyes flashing with doubt. Jack was fighting at such a high level, yet the tribulation was nowhere near done. Heavenstar had to wonder about something so ridiculous he never could have imagined it. If he was in place of Jack... could even he survive this tribulation?

Did I really just compare myself to an early B-Grade? he wondered in disbelief. Reality often surpassed expectations. Heavenstar was one of the weakest A-Grades—he had to admit that, if Jack became just a little bit stronger, he would have the qualifications to face him. How impossible was that?

Elder Boatman's expression remained inscrutable. As for Brock, his eyes were narrowed, his body tense. The two seemed inexplicably similar where they stood side by side.

Jack smashed his fist into a dragon's face, disintegrating its entire body. He then teleported above another, ripping it apart with his bare hands, and turned to shoot a Meteor Punch behind him, obliterating a third dragon. The Life Drop transformation and Thunder Body were similar techniques—using both at once multiplied their effects. Jack's current physicality had reached extreme degrees. He surpassed planets in durability without even using his Dao.

Yet, the tribulation was just too large. Even with power almost an entire Grade above his level, he still struggled. He would run out of steam before it did. There wasn't even a contest—it was just unfair.

Despair overtook Jack's heart even as he slew the dragons. He was half-spent already, but the tribulation was mostly intact. This wasn't a trial he could hope to face. It wasn't something he had any hope against. It was just plain bullying.

"Damn you, heavens!" he roared, smashing out a fist so powerfully it tore through three dragons before dissipating. Five more flew at him, their jaws unhinged. Jack's eyes widened in anger. He shot out punches and destroyed them, but one managed to bite his leg. He lost all feeling. Even his extremely sturdy body momentarily went numb, and his leg was spasming. He regained control almost instantly, but he couldn't afford to be hit again.

This is bad, he thought. If he was already accumulating injuries, wasn't he on the road to death?

Thinking to that point, Jack changed tactics. This tribulation wasn't something he could hope to face directly—he may have overpowered the Heavenly Dao during his tribulation, but this was the equivalent of the Heavenly Dao bringing its three older cousins to beat him up.

Jack flew back, using his understandings to protect himself. He warped spacetime around the dragons, making them collide against each other. They exploded in fireworks.

The tribulation released a pulse of spacetime, directly changing the laws of the world, which completely invalidated his understandings. His Daos of Space and Time became useless.

Jack's eyes flashed with anger—he persisted. These dragons weren't just energy bodies, they were alive. He turned to his Dao of Death, spreading thin strings of Death around him to directly sever the life inside the dragons. He succeeded—dozens of them turned into mindless clouds of energy, losing their stability and imploding.

The tribulation released another burst of Dao; it directly nullified his Dao of Death, severing the strings. The laws of the world changed again, making his Dao useless. Jack roared.

Going out on a limb, he used the Dao of Life to overfill the dragons with life, making them lose themselves and their sense of purpose. Before he could even carry out his attack, the tribulation released a third pulse, completely altering the laws of Life around the dragons and making his Dao of Life useless.

"Won't you even let me fight!" Jack roared. His understandings of the Dao were nothing compared to the Heavenly Dao itself. If it purposely warped the rules to sabotage him, there was nothing he could do. Was he just supposed to stand there and die?

CHAPTER SIXTY-THREE

FUCK THE HEAVENS

MORE DRAGONS EMERGED FROM THE CLOUDS—THE TRIBULATION WAS still increasing the pace. They swarmed Jack, who dove into the fray with only his body and Fist to support him. There was nothing else he could do.

He became a devil, a killer, a perfect warrior. He danced between the B-Grade dragons and delivered swift death. They fell in droves. If they were real creatures, he might have received enough levels to survive, but they weren't, so they gave him nothing.

From afar, Jack looked more heroic than ever. He faced a flood of enemies on his own—he danced between their strikes like he could predict everything, using minimal movements to avoid and strike back. He was strong and efficient. Some called him perfect.

He was facing way too many enemies. Strikes occasionally seeped through. A dragon bit him on the arm, another at the neck, a third dove into his chest. Even enhanced as he was, the lightning contained in each of them was beyond tremendous— every dragon could easily char an entire continent. With so many striking him at once, Jack was beginning to suffer. His muscles twitched. His flesh burned. His lungs contracted. His heart would have stopped if he wasn't constantly using his Dao to keep it pumping.

Injuries accumulated on his body, but the dragons weren't running out. No matter how many he killed, more appeared to take their place. The tribulation was inexhaustible—even with everything so far, he hadn't even extinguished it halfway.

He had nothing more to give, either. With his Daos sealed, fighting like this was all he could do. The only skill he hadn't used was Supernova, but it was just too powerful—it would achieve little besides spending his energy even faster. As for running away from the tribulation, that was even more impossible. It would just warp space to follow him.

Am I really going to die here? Jack thought.

Suddenly, a golden aura surrounded him. He felt invigorated, his energy returning, his injuries healing rapidly. He glanced to the side, where Brock hovered right at the edge of the tribulation.

"You mess with my bro," said the brorilla, his arms raised high, "you mess with me."

The tribulation agreed. More power streamed into the clouds from the surrounding universe, puffing them up. They expanded to cover the sky above Brock as well, then rained black lightning.

"No!" Jack roared. The lightning Brock was facing wasn't much weaker than what he'd faced at the start. He also hadn't witnessed Brock's breakthrough—he had no idea how strong he was.

Crowds of golden brorillas appeared around Brock, wrestling the lightning into submission. The Goldenwood Staff jumped into his arms, cracking against the sky and shielding him. He could handle himself—but for how long?

The rules of a tribulation were clear. The offending cultivator had to face it alone. If anyone tried to help, more tribulation would appear, ensuring that every challenger faced the same level of difficulty.

Jack knew that. So did Brock. Yet, he still charged forth, not hesitating to risk his life alongside his brother's for a tiny chance at survival. Jack felt touched. In his entire life, having Brock as his brother was his single greatest fortune.

At that, Jack laughed. So what if he died? Falling by the side of his brother, challenging the heavens themselves, wasn't such a bad way to go!

"Face me!" he roared, attacking the dragons with more intensity. They enveloped him from all directions. Brock was still supplying him with power, but the tribulation had grown stronger to match it. No matter how fiercely Jack fought, no matter how many dragons he slew, there were always more. Over a thousand had appeared so far, with many more on the way. They were endless—and Jack, with his Daos unjustly sealed, could only fight head-on.

Or, rather, this wasn't a fight, but a slow death in battle.

Jack laughed and roared at the same time. His punches caved dragon skulls and defied the heavens. His every moment of survival was a provocation, his every strike a challenge. Lightning flowed in his veins. The Thunder Body transformation had run out, and the four-armed battle form was barely hanging on. His skin was scorched, and his organs melted. Only his regeneration kept him alive. Even his inner world, this unprecedented marvel which had just come into existence, was now a dry plane, an empty space almost devoid of energy. His mind was slow and his arms heavy, but he kept on fighting, still doing his best.

Jack wasn't a quitter. He would fight as well as he could, always looking for a chance to survive. However, the calculating part of his mind had already realized there was no way out. This tribulation was something he never had any hope against. Even a middle A-Grade might have perished.

There was nothing he could do, and nothing he could have done. His path so far had been perfect, every step immaculate. This was just his predetermined end.

Can no one defy the universe?

Perhaps he should have stayed at the 9999-mile mark. The universe wouldn't have been as enraged with him then... But, that would have been a different kind of death. Remaining at 9999 would mean conforming. He would only keep his life because he bowed to the heavens, obeyed their rules. That would mean betraying his path—the Fist, Freedom, and everything else he stood for.

Jack didn't fear death, he only feared losing himself. Even if he could go back in time, he would still do everything the same. It was all worth it.

Even if my path leads to death, I will walk it! I would rather die standing than live on my knees!

The tribulation was so full of energy it was terrifying. The surrounding space became thin and empty. In fact, the entire star area around them had been sucked dry of energy to support such an assault. The spectators had retreated thrice, opening more distance to ensure they weren't affected.

Heavenstar was clenching his fists, looking at the falling tribulation with regret. "This is unbelievable," he said. "Two unprecedented talents are going to die here? To a tribulation? I thought the heavens were finally smiling at us, but it was just a cruel joke!"

"Jack never stood a chance," Boatman replied calmly. "The tribulation was too powerful to begin with. It appears he truly did enrage the heavens this time. There is not a single path of survival left for him. All he can do is perish."

"How can you be so calm, Boatman!" Heavenstar shouted.

"Those are your disciples over there, the brightest talents we've ever seen!"

"I am calm precisely because they are my disciples," Boatman replied. A faint grin was visible through his hood. "A master should not interfere in the affairs of disciples. However, when a disciple is bullied by a higher power, is it not the job of his master to save him?"

Heavenstar's eyes widened. "You can't be serious. This is a *tribulation*! You know the rules better than anyone!"

Boatman laughed. It was a hoarse sound, yet containing deep valor. "Protect the crowd." He disappeared before Heavenstar could reply, breaking through the repelling force of the tribulation to stand directly below it, shielding Jack and Brock. A curtain of darkness spread from his body. Every dragon, every lightning bolt, every hint of electricity died immediately. The world turned black and white.

Astral winds blew, pushing back Boatman's hood and cloak to reveal a pale, thin body. He reached for his back and removed his scythe.

"Hear me, heavens," he spoke, not shouting, but his voice echoed everywhere like the degree of God. "I am Elder Boatman of the Black Hole Church! If my disciples were unworthy, I would sit to the side and watch them die. However, this is unfair. It is an assassination I will not permit. If the heavens want to bully, then I will bully them back. If you raise a hand against my disciples, then I will cut it off."

The entire world went still, then began to rumble. Space itself shook with fury. The surrounding star area for millions of miles was completely sucked dry of energy, all funneling toward these clouds. If the heavens were angry before, they were now utterly and irrevocably enraged. Since when could they be challenged like this? Since when could cultivators challenge the authority of the Heavenly Dao?

Boatman ignored the furious rumbling of the world. He stuck out his scythe, gathering a veritable ocean of black power. Jack and Brock, who were recovering below, were shaken. This was far beyond their level—far above anything they'd ever witnessed. This was a powerful late A-Grade going to war.

"If the heavens will not accept my disciples," Boatman shouted, his eyes going dark, his scythe cutting out, "then I shall kill the heavens!"

A dark curtain appeared, cutting through everything. It fell into the tribulation. The entire sea of clouds was sliced in half, thousands of black dragons dying in the cradle. Clouds disintegrated, lightning fizzled out. The fabric of reality itself moaned in fury. This was blatant challenge! This was hubris!

More energy roared in from afar, bringing with it an endless number of clouds, but Boatman hovered alone in the sky, commanding his Dao, commanding the world. The tribulation could nullify Jack's Dao of Death, but not Boatman's—his understanding already approached the level of the Heavenly Dao. Endless specters slipped into reality. They dove into the clouds, slaying anything they found. Shrill screams filled the void.

This battle had spiraled way out of proportion. The crowd was retreating at full speed, shouting and screaming.

The tribulation fought back against Boatman. Having magnified to several times its previous size, the lightning it shot down was no longer black but golden. Every Dao in existence seemed to be contained within. Boatman slashed his scythe, every slice tearing apart the world, spreading death as he shielded his disciples.

Jack and Brock stood together, slowly recovering. Their gazes were glued upward. All they could see was Boatman's back, risking his life to defend them against injustice. Jack smiled. "You know," he said, "maybe it's not that bad having a teacher."

"He is good bro," Brock replied, banging a fist against his chest. "Respect."

"Wanna help him?"

"Let's go."

They shot upward. Just the shockwaves of Boatman's battle would be enough to capsize them, but they didn't need to join directly, only shoot out their power from afar to assist. Purple and gold rained upward. Darkness embraced them, feeding on them to grow stronger, then devouring the tribulation. Reality was a mixture of black and gold—cultivator and divine.

The current battle was far superior in level to the previous one. Heavenstar was using his powers to shield the spectators from three hundred thousand miles away, yet his shield still shook, and he was finding it hard to endure. "Retreat farther," he commanded. "Go!"

Everyone rushed, and he followed, keeping up his shields. In his heart, he shouted, Go, Boatman!

Golden lightning became a maelstrom driving down in waves, already past the level of thunderbolts. Auroras filled the skies. The energy of Life clashed against Boatman's Death, sparking up the lightning to increase its power. Death and tribulation clashed repeatedly, neither giving ground. Boatman was rocked by shockwaves. He wasn't a Physical cultivator; his body shook, accumulating injuries. His organs were bruised. His robes were torn, revealing a thin body clad in darkness. Blood streamed from the corner of his mouth and eyes, while the hands which held his scythe shivered.

However, he wasn't giving ground. As he was wounded, so was the tribulation. The clouds were torn apart faster than they could form. Golden dragons perished as they were born. The universe roared in fury, but it had no more power to give.

A tribulation's difficulty shouldn't change no matter how many people appeared to challenge it. Since it was impossible for Jack, it should be impossible for Brock and Boatman as well, regardless of whether they fought together or not. However, even a tribulation had its limits. Boatman was too strong, approaching the apex of power. Tremendous amounts of power were needed to defeat him.

Even though the Heavenly Dao controlled the entire universe, that didn't mean it could collect all the power of the universe here. It had to draw from nearby areas, and after all the battles so far, the surrounding millions of miles had run completely dry. The density of Dao had reached an all-time low —drawing anymore was impossible.

Even a tribulation had its limits—and now, thanks to Jack, Brock, and Boatman giving it their all, it had approached them. Only a fragment of the previous clouds remained—and Boatman was equally exhausted. His powers of Death were running out.

"Jack!" he shouted, his voice weak. "I have weakened the tribulation as much as I can, but it remains one summoned by you! Unless you destroy your share, it will not be resolved. It will keep returning until it kills us! I will draw away the part aimed at me, and Brock will also retreat. You must use this opportunity to disperse it before it gathers more power. My life depends on you—do not fail!"

No other Elder would think of leaving their life in the hands of an early B-Grade. However, Elder Boatman... was the man!

Jack's gaze hardened. He summoned all the remaining power of his inner world. "I will succeed," he vowed.

Boatman flew away. A large part of the tribulation followed him. Brock did as well, taking away a much smaller part. Jack was left hovering alone, once again facing the clouds by himself, but this time, they were fewer and weaker. They were no longer sealing his Daos—no longer unfair.

This wasn't an easy battle, but it was one he could win—and if he could, he would.

Golden lightning blazed in the sky, crashing down as a column of pure power. Jack flew right at it. Spacetime curved around him—the column was split into many, passing around Jack like water around a stone. It missed him completely.

A golden dragon emerged from the clouds. It was vastly more powerful than the black ones he'd faced before—its strength easily reached the peak B-Grade.

Jack shot straight at it. One of his fists shone green, the other black—Life and Death. The dragon's life force ballooned under Jack's control, making it struggle to control its own body. Death came right afterward, a thin slice of darkness which cut right through that bloated power, slicing the dragon in two. Jack slipped between the two halves before the dragon even realized it was dead.

He was upon the clouds now. Just him and them. A mass of energy condensed just above, all the remaining power of the clouds forced into a blast of raw energy. It descended. Where it passed, spacetime disintegrated, reality was torn apart. It was strongest and final attack it could muster.

Jack could have tried to dodge, but he didn't. This tribulation had struck with overwhelming force to kill him, and all because he disobeyed the rules of cultivation. He didn't want to avoid it—he wanted to break it head-on.

All the remaining energy he possessed was channeled into his body. Two new arms grew, enhancing him greatly. Purple electricity covered him, further skyrocketing his power. Though Jack was wounded and exhausted, he had momentarily reached an absolute peak.

He pulled his punch back. All the pain he'd experienced

came to his mind—from despair, to fear, to body tempering, to loneliness, to Eric, to war. Everything he'd done had been of his own volition. All the pain he experienced was a result of his own actions. He alone controlled his fate, good or bad. Not the heavens. Not anyone.

The surrounding space was sucked into his punch. More and more energy flew in, all sorts of Daos, until Jack felt like he was holding a nuclear bomb. In truth, this was far more powerful. His next strike could easily disintegrate a planet.

The blast of energy shone bright in his eyes.

"Fuck your fake righteousness," Jack said, spreading his voice far and wide as his power built to a crescendo. "You call yourself heavenly, but you are just another tyrant that I refuse to obey. While I live, I will fight. I will abolish you and establish my own heavens. I am Jack Rust—I alone dictate my fate. No one else. I don't care if you are the heavens, or the Dao, or the universe..." He pushed his fist forward. "You do not control me!"

The condensed power in his fist imploded. It hesitated for just a moment, as if struggling to escape its own gravity, then erupted outward in a tremendous explosion that shook the world.

"SUPERNOVA!"

The blast of energy shattered. The sky was thrown backward. Jack's fist carried on, containing all his resolve for freedom, and smashed into the dark clouds, tearing them wide open. A new sky was revealed behind them—and the clouds broke into strips of moisture which melted against the universe. The tribulation disappeared without a sign. Even the clouds above Brock and Boatman disintegrated, as the tribulation had been defeated by the one who summoned it.

The crowd was shocked speechless. The *Death Boat* sank in silence—then cheers erupted to the high heavens, washing away the darkness, bringing new light.

A legend had been born—Jack Rust, the paragon of cultivation, a pioneer of new heights. He was unprecedented. Nobody knew how high he could reach, but they all wanted to find out.

"JACK RUST! JACK RUST! JACK RUST!"

This was the start of a new era. And Jack, having stepped into the B-Grade, was ready to spearhead it. He threw his head back and laughed. "Let's fucking go!"

EPILOGUE

A MASSIVE BALL OF DARKNESS HURTLED THROUGH SPACE. IT DWARFED planets. Galaxies appeared in its path and fell behind, the creature moving at speeds vastly eclipsing that of light. If an A-Grade cultivator stood in its aura, they would tremble. Even Archons would frown. This was an existence at the very peak of the Archon realm, one of the strongest entities in the universe.

It was followed by another ten creatures of similar power, though different in appearance. Spacetime shivered and parted before them, letting them cross incalculable distances, yet they were very, very far away. Reaching System space would take years, but they would, inevitably, arrive.

The Olds Gods were returning.

"Are the System Cannons ready?" a robotic voice called out in the darkness.

"Yes, Heaven Immortal," another replied.

A figure walked out of the darkness. It was humanoid, yet made of metal. Its face was completely featureless save for a mouth and the number 1 painted where its nose should be. A host of tubes left the back of its head, reaching back into the darkness. The creature floated as if held aloft by these tubes. They pulsed with the passing of liquid.

When it spoke, the other Immortals in the room went quiet.

"We may begin," it said. "Retrieve ninety percent of our forces from the System galaxies. I adjusted the experience gain upward and directed the System to release all monsters from their Dungeons. Perhaps the slaughter will create another few soldiers. We will regrow the population afterward."

"You are wise, Heaven Immortal," the other robots bowed and said as one.

The Heaven Immortal ignored them. It floated out of the oppressive darkness, into a balcony overlooking millions of gathered cultivators. They were in a square constructed entirely of bare metal and surrounded by high walls. The Heaven Immortal stood on the highest level of a metallic temple featuring ninety-nine statues of robots.

The cultivators cheered at the appearance of the Heaven Immortal. It knew their cheers were fake, born of fear or lust for power, but it cared little as long as they did their job.

It grinned. "We march to slaughter," it said, and the cultivators cheered again, shaking the world.

———

A woman stood on a raised platform. A colossal structure loomed behind her, a wooden temple of epic proportions. She wore embroidered white clothes which fell over her entire body, revealing only a pair of shining eyes and bare, pale feet.

An army spread before her. C-Grades were soldiers, B-Grades were commanders, and A-Grades were generals. She was the queen.

"We fight for freedom," she declared in a commanding voice. "We fight for justice. The Immortals and their System force cultivators to slay each other, rewarding power for blood. They made the universe into a giant fighting pit. They are blinded by their holy war, their joke of a crusade, but there can be no happiness in such a world, no peace. Our families bleed. Our people die. Now, we fight back. Their reign of terror will end. The world will be freed from their malevolent stain. Peace and justice will return, while blood-lusting tyranny will fall.

"Yes, we are weaker than them. We might die. But my blood burns, brothers and sisters, and I can wait no more. Even before the Gods return for us, let us not run away. Let us not live like cowards."

The army roared alongside her, fully riled up. Her voice rose with passion, and as she shouted, the cultivators below completed her declaration.

"We are heroes. We are justice. We are—"

"—*FREE!*"

Road to Mastery will continue in Book Six!

———

Make sure to join our Discord
(https://discord.gg/5RccXhNgGb)
so you never miss a release!

THANK YOU FOR READING
ROAD TO MASTERY 5

We hope you enjoyed it as much as we enjoyed bringing it to you. We just wanted to take a moment to encourage you to review the book. Follow this link: Road to Mastery 5 to be directed to the book's Amazon product page to leave your review.

Every review helps further the author's reach and, ultimately, helps them continue writing fantastic books for us all to enjoy.

———

Also in series:

Road to Mastery
Road to Mastery 2
Road to Mastery 3
Road to Mastery 4
Road to Mastery 5
Road to Mastery 6

———

Want to discuss our books with other readers and even the authors?

JOIN THE AETHON DISCORD!

You can also join our non-spam mailing list by visiting www.subscribepage.com/AethonReadersGroup and never miss out on future releases. You'll also receive three full books completely Free as our thanks to you.

Don't forget to follow us on socials to never miss a new release!
Facebook | Instagram | Twitter | Website

Looking for more great books?

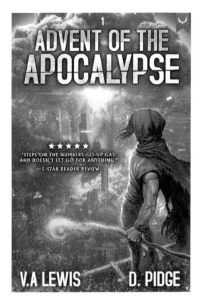

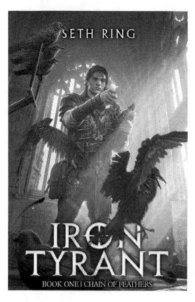

Roll over and die, or become so strong nothing can stop him. Cast into a brutal military camp by his once loving master, Mateo feels like the last six wonderful years of his life have been a lie. With the mysteries surrounding him growing, Mateo knows that his only option is becoming one of the supernaturally powerful Duelists and growing in power until he can take his fate into his own hands. That plan is thwarted from the beginning when he gets stuck with the lowest ranked Root Card against his will, ensuring that his growth as a Duelist will always be excruciatingly slow. To make matters worse, the camp he has been thrown into is completely cutthroat and survival isn't guaranteed by a long shot. Saddled with two other kids that he has never met before and a crow spirit bound to him by an ethereal chain, Mateo will need every ounce of courage, resilience, and mental acuity he can muster if he wants to make it out of the training camp alive. Don't miss the start of the next great Fantasy LitRPG Series by Seth Ring, author of the best selling Battle Mage Farmer and Nova Terra. Grab your copy today and join Mateo as he ascends through the flames of war. About the Series: Following a weak-to-strong protagonist, this series mixes epic fantasy action, mystery, cultivation, and a world with endless depth where little is as it first appears. This LitRPG/GameLit series is perfect for readers who enjoy exploring rich worlds and complex characters.

Get Chain of Feathers Now!

"Is it funny? No. It's effing hilarious!"—Matt Dinniman,
author of Dungeon Crawler Carl *Some men are born
heroes. Others have heroism thrust upon them... Sorry...
Really? Thrust? Anyway, Danny Kendrick was a down-on-his
luck performer who always struggled to find his place. He
certainly never wanted to be a hero. He just hoped to earn a
living doing what he loved. That all changes when he pisses off
the wrong guy and gets sucked into a fantasy realm straight out
of a Renaissance Fair. Getting used to a new world is tough. It's
even tougher when you're surrounded by axe-wielding
barbarians, super hot elf assassins, strange magic, and a System
AI that seems as interested in causing trouble as helping... or
maybe just wasn't interested in being assigned yet another
companion in the first place. Danny must adapt fast, turn on the
charm, and learn to emrace his given Class if he hopes to master
it and survive this dangerous new place. But he has a knack for
finding trouble. Gifted what seems like an innocent ancient lute
after making a questionable deal with a Hag, Danny becomes
the target of mysterious factions who seek to claim its power. It's
up to him, Screenie, and his new barbaric friend, Curr, to
uncover the truth and become the heroes nobody knew they
needed. And maybe, just maybe, Danny will finally find a place
where he belongs. Perhaps, even where he'll thrive.* **Jump into
this fantasy isekai LitRPG Adventure filled with**

unforgettable characters, loveable companions, unlikely heroes, slow-build power progression, and plenty of comedy. It's perfect for fans of Dungeon Crawler Carl, Scott Meyer's Off to be the Wizard, and This Trilogy is Broken! Come for the Adventure, stay for the Laughs!

Get An Unexpected Hero Now!

For all our LitRPG books, visit our website.